'*The Woman Upstairs* is perhaps less about specifics and more broadly about the sting of life's greatest disappointments, whether they be artistic, professional, personal or social. An insightful, beautifully written novel about the ways in which we fail both ourselves and others, *The Woman Upstairs* is right up there with Heller's *Notes on a Scandal.* I loved it'
Diva

'A painful account of thwarted optimism'
Vogue

'A fearless tonic for the lonely ... *The Woman Upstairs* is no dry, self-referential treatise. Rather, it's a fearless and sometimes wrenching portrait of female loneliness;
Metro

'A miracle of elegance and control'
Saga

Claire Messud was born in 1966 and was educated at Yale and at Cambridge. She is the author of three novels, including *The Emperor's Children*, a *New York Times* bestseller, and two novellas. She lives in Boston with her husband and their two children.

Praise for *The Woman Upstairs*

'Brilliantly done ... Nora is a clear-eyed and fiercely self-critical narrator ... It's beautiful, and it's moving, and it feels true'
Sunday Times

'A remarkable book'
Sunday Express

'Rage and sorrow burn so fiercely off the pages of this novel that I had to keep reminding myself I was in no respect like its heroine ... this is Nora's conversation with herself, as she spins on a "mental gerbil wheel", trying to comprehend a betrayal so foul it continues to unsettle long after the last page is turned'
Intelligent Life (The Economist)

'A faultless, suspenseful novel'
Mail on Sunday

'There's nothing small about Claire Messud's new novel, which so well realises an insidiously unhinged interior world that it constitutes a sizeable literary achievement. Call it a love story – of a warped, particular sort ... Gosh. I guess you could say I liked it'
Lionel Shriver, *Financial Times*

'Rarely has the mundane been so dazzling ... This is a world the reader so fully inhabits that it seems a helpline is all that is missing when it ends ... it roars in its own muted way, and dares to pin down things that are both excruciating and universal. To paraphrase Nora, just watch her'
Guardian

'It's exhilarating to encounter such unrestrained vehemence in a word by this controlled, intellectual author ... This is utterly different – its language urgent, its conflicts unmooring, its mood incendiary. This psychologically charged story feels like a liberation. Messud's prose grabs the reader by the collar ... In this ingenious, disquieting novel, Messud has assembled an intricate puzzle of self-belief and self-doubt, showing the peril of seeking your own image in someone else's distorted mirror – or even, sometimes, in your own'
The Scotsman

'[An] unflinching hard-hitting novel'
Daily Mail

'The writing is gorgeous, subtle, defamiliarising, catching peculiar aspects of the hyper-self-conscious twenty-first-century American life in which Nora, terrifyingly, finds herself lost. Nora's tale is universal in its longing and disenchantment'
Evening Standard

'Messud writes beautifully and wryly but the real achievement is to imbue every chapter with thought-provoking questions surrounding the place of women in literature, society and – most importantly – their own minds. Female anger has never been so readable'
Observer

THE
WOMAN
UPSTAIRS

A Novel

Claire Messud

virago

VIRAGO

First published in Great Britain in 2013 by Virago Press
This paperback edition published in 2014 by Virago Press
Reprinted 2014

Copyright © 2013 by Claire Messud

The moral right of the author has been asserted

*All characters and events in this publication, other than those
clearly in the public domain, are fictitious and any resemblance
to real persons, living or dead, is purely coincidental.*

A CIP catalogue record for this book
is available from the British Library.

ISBN 978-1-84408-733-4

Typeset in Garamond by M Rules
Printed and bound in Great Britain by
Clays Ltd, St Ives plc

Papers used by Virago are from well-managed forests
and other responsible sources.

MIX
Paper from
responsible sources
FSC
FSC® C104740
www.fsc.org

Virago Press
an imprint of
Little, Brown Book Group
100 Victoria Embankment
London EC4Y 0DY

An Hachette UK Company
www.hachette.co.uk

For Georges and Anne Borchardt
and, as ever, for J.W.

Ognuno vede quello che tu pari, pochi sentono quello che tu se'.

— MACHIAVELLI, *The Prince*

Very few people understand the purely subjective nature of the phenomenon that we call love, or how it creates, so to speak, a fresh, a third, a supplementary person, distinct from the person whom the world knows by the same name, a person most of whose constituent elements are derived from oneself, the lover.

— MARCEL PROUST, *Remembrance of Things Past*

Fuck the laudable ideologies.

— PHILIP ROTH, *Sabbath's Theater*

THE
WOMAN
UPSTAIRS

PART ONE

1

How angry am I? You don't want to know. Nobody wants to know about *that*.

I'm a good girl, I'm a nice girl, I'm a straight-A, strait-laced, good daughter, good career girl, and I never stole anybody's boyfriend and I never ran out on a girlfriend, and I put up with my parents' shit and my brother's shit, and I'm not a girl anyhow, I'm over forty fucking years old, and I'm good at my job and I'm great with kids and I held my mother's hand when she died, after four years of holding her hand while she was dying, and I speak to my father every day on the telephone – every day, mind you, and what kind of weather do you have on your side of the river, because here it's pretty gray and a bit muggy too? It was supposed to say 'Great Artist' on my tombstone, but if I died right now it would say 'such a good teacher/daughter/friend' instead; and what I really want to shout, and want in big letters on that grave, too, is FUCK YOU ALL.

Don't all women feel the same? The only difference is how much we know we feel it, how in touch we are with our fury. We're all furies, except the ones who are too damned foolish, and my worry now is that we're brainwashing them from the cradle, and in the end even the ones who are smart will be too damned foolish. What do I mean? I mean the second graders at Appleton Elementary, sometimes the first graders even, and by the time they get to my classroom, to the third grade, they're well and truly gone – they're full of Lady Gaga and Katy Perry and French manicures and cute outfits and they care how their *hair* looks! In the third grade. They care more about their hair or their shoes than about galaxies or caterpillars or hieroglyphics. How did all that revolutionary talk of the seventies land us in a place where being female means playing dumb and looking good? Even worse on your tombstone than 'dutiful daughter' is 'looked good'; everyone used to know that. But we're lost in a world of appearances now.

That's why I'm so angry, really – not because of all the chores and all the making nice and all the duty of being a woman – or rather, of being *me* – because maybe these are the burdens of being human. Really I'm angry because I've tried so hard to get out of the hall of mirrors, this sham and pretend of the world, or of my world, on the East Coast of the United States of America in the first decade of the twenty-first century. And behind every mirror is another fucking mirror, and down every corridor is another corridor, and the Fun House isn't fun anymore and it isn't even funny, but there doesn't seem to be a door marked EXIT.

At the fair each summer when I was a kid, we visited the Fun House, with its creepy grinning plaster face, two stories high. You walked in through its mouth, between its giant teeth, along its hot-pink tongue. Just from that face, you should've known. It was supposed to be a lark, but it was terrifying. The floors buckled or they lurched from side to side, and the walls were crooked, and the rooms were painted to confuse perspective. Lights flashed, horns blared, in the narrow, vibrating hallways lined with fattening mirrors and elongating mirrors and inside-out upside-down mirrors. Sometimes the ceiling fell or the floor rose, or both happened at once and I thought I'd be squashed like a bug. The Fun House was scarier by far than the Haunted House, not least because I was supposed to enjoy it. I just wanted to find the way out. But the doors marked EXIT led only to further crazy rooms, to endless moving corridors. There was one route through the Fun House, relentless to the very end.

I've finally come to understand that life itself is the Fun House. All you want is that door marked EXIT, the escape to a place where Real Life will be; and you can never find it. No: let me correct that. In recent years, there was a door, there were doors, and I took them and I believed in them, and I believed for a stretch that I'd managed to get out into Reality – and God, the bliss and terror of that, the intensity of that: it felt so *different* – until I suddenly realized I'd been stuck in the Fun House all along. I'd been tricked. The door marked EXIT hadn't been an exit at all.

I'm not crazy. Angry, yes; crazy, no. My name is Nora Marie Eldridge and I'm forty-two years old – which is a lot more like middle age than forty or even forty-one. Neither old nor young, I'm neither fat nor thin, tall nor short, blond nor brunette, neither pretty nor plain. Quite nice looking in some moments, I think is the consensus, rather like the heroines of Harlequin romances, read in quantity in my youth. I'm neither married nor divorced, but single. What they used to call a spinster, but don't anymore, because it implies that you're dried up, and none of us wants to be that. Until last summer, I taught third grade at Appleton Elementary School in Cambridge, Massachusetts, and maybe I'll go back and do it again, I just don't know. Maybe, instead, I'll set the world on fire. I just might.

Be advised that in spite of my foul mouth, I don't swear in front of the children – except once or twice when a rogue 'Shit!' has emerged, but only sotto voce, and only in extremis. If you're thinking how can such an angry person possibly teach young children, let me assure you that every one of us is capable of rage, and that some of us are prone to it, but that in order to be a good teacher, you must have a modicum of self-control, which I do. I have more than a modicum. I was brought up that way.

Second, I'm not an Underground Woman, harboring resentment for my miseries against the whole world. Or rather, it's not that I'm not *in some sense* an Underground Woman – aren't we all, who have to cede and swerve and step aside, unacknowledged and unadmired and unthanked? Numerous in our twenties and thirties, we're positively legion in our forties and fifties. But the world should understand, if the world gave a shit, that women like us are not underground. No Ralph Ellison basement full of lightbulbs for us; no Dostoyevskian metaphorical subterra. We're always upstairs. We're not the madwomen in the attic – they get lots of play, one way or another. We're the quiet woman at the end of the third-floor hallway, whose trash is always tidy, who smiles brightly in the stairwell with a cheerful greeting, and who, from behind closed doors, never makes a sound. In our lives of quiet desperation, the woman upstairs is who we are, with or without a goddamn tabby or a pesky lolloping Labrador, and not a soul registers that we are furious. We're completely invisible. I thought it wasn't true, or not true of me, but I've learned I am no different at all. The question now is how to work it, how to use that invisibility, to make it burn.

Life is about deciding what matters. It's about the fantasy that determines the reality. Have you ever asked yourself whether you'd rather fly or be invisible? I've asked people for years, always thinking their answer revealed who they were. I'm surrounded by a world of fliers. Children are almost always fliers. And the woman upstairs, she's a flier too. Some greedy people ask if they couldn't have both; and a certain number – I always thought they were the conniving bastards, the power-hungry, the control freaks – choose the vanishing act. But most of us want to fly.

Do you remember those dreams? I don't have them anymore, but they were a joy of my youth. To confront despair – the dogs at my heels, or the angry man with a raised fist or a club – and have only to flap my arms, rising slowly, directly upward, like a helicopter or an apotheosis, and then soaring, free. I skimmed the rooftops, gulping the wind, rode the air currents like waves, over fields and fences, along the shore, out over the ruffled indigo of the sea. And the light of the sky, when you fly – do you remember that? The clouds like illuminated pillows, close and moist when you ventured into them, and ah! the revelation when you came out the other side. Flying was everything, once.

But I've come to the conclusion that it's the wrong choice. Because you think the world is yours, but really you're always flying away from something; and the dogs at your heels and the man with the club – they don't go away because you can't see them anymore. They are reality.

As for being invisible, it makes things more real. You walk into a room where you are not, and you hear what people say, unguardedly; you watch how they move when they aren't with you. You see them without their masks – or in their various masks, because suddenly you can see them anywhere. It may be painful to learn what happens when you're behind the arras; but then, please God, you know.

All these years, I was wrong, you see. Most people around me, too. And especially now that I've learned that I really am invisible, I need to stop wanting to fly. I want to stop needing to fly. I want it all to do over again; but also I don't. I want to make my nothingness count. Don't think it's impossible.

2

It all started with the boy. With Reza. Even when I saw him last – for the last time ever – this summer, when he was and had been for years no longer the same, almost a young man, with the illogical proportions, the long nose, the pimples and cracking voice of incipient adulthood, I still saw in him the perfection that was. He glows in my mind's eye, eight years old and a canonical boy, a child from a fairy tale.

He walked into my classroom late, on the first day of school, grave and uncertain, his gray eyes wide, their millipedic lashes aflutter in spite of his visible effort to control them, not to blink, and above all not to cry. All the other children – most of whom I knew from the schoolyard the year before, knew by name even – had come early and prepared, with book bags and packed lunches and a parent waving from the doorway, some with their mother's lipstick still pink upon their cheeks; and they'd found their desks and we'd introduced ourselves and announced a single salient fact about our summers (the twins Chastity and Ebullience had spent two months with their grandma in Jamaica; she kept chickens – this was one fact per child; Mark T. had built a go-kart and raced it at the park; Shi-shi's family had adopted an eight-year-old beagle named Superior from the pound ['he's the same age as me,' she said proudly]; and so on), and we were beginning to establish our classroom rules ('No farting,' shouted Noah from the cluster of tables by the window, provoking universal hoots and giggles) when the door opened and Reza walked in.

I knew who he must be: everybody else on my roster was already there. He hesitated. He put his feet, in their prim closed-toed sandals, very carefully one in front of the other, as if he were walking on a balance beam. He didn't look like the other children – not because of his olive skin, his fierce little eyebrows, the set of his lip, but because his clothes were so tidy, so formal and foreign. He wore a short-sleeved dress shirt with blue and white checks, and a pair of long navy linen Bermudas, pressed by an invisible hand. He wore socks with his sandals. He carried no bag.

'Reza Shahid, yes?'

'How do you know?'

'Everybody' – I spun him by the shoulders to face the class – 'this is our last new student. Reza Shahid. Welcome.'

Everyone called 'Welcome, Reza,' loudly, and even from behind I could see him trying not to flinch: his scalp retracted up his head and the tops of his ears wiggled. Already in that moment, I loved his nape, the carefully marshaled black curls lapping their uneven shoreline along the smooth, frail promontory of his neck.

Because I knew him, you see. I hadn't known he was Reza, had never suspected he would be mine, a pupil in 3E; but the week before I'd seen him, had stared and been stared at, had even exchanged a laugh with him, in the supermarket. I'd been struggling with my bags at the checkout – the handle of one had broken, and I was trying to pick it up from beneath, while grasping the rest of my groceries in the other hand; and succeeded only in spilling my apples out across the floor. Bright red, they dispersed underfoot as far as the café area by the window. I scuttled after them, hunched to the ground, leaving my two bags and my purse sprawled in the middle of the aisle to the door. I was on my knees to retrieve the last stray from beneath a table, my left arm pressing four bruised apples clumsily to my breast, when a single, illuminating burst of laughter made me look up. Over the back of the neighboring booth hung this beautiful child, his curls dancing unkempt, his T-shirt impastoed with the filth of a day's play and the bloody-looking sauce of whatever he'd been eating.

'What exactly is so damn funny?' I couldn't help the 'damn.'

'You are,' he replied, after a moment's silence, his mouth in a serious line but his eyes mirthful. He had a strong accent. 'You are very funny, in your apples.'

Something about his face, the matte smoothness of his cheeks with their faint rosy tinge, the wildness of his black hair and eyebrows and lashes, the amused intensity of those mottled gray eyes – I smiled in spite of myself, glanced back at my piles of food near the checkout, pictured my Baba Yaga–like dance across the floor, saw myself as he must have seen me. 'I guess you're right.' I stood up. 'Want one?' I offered him the last apple, salvaged from the dust. He wrinkled his nose, barked his short laugh once more.

'Not good now.'

'No,' I said. 'I suppose not.'

As I made my way to the exit, I looked over again at his table. He was not with his mother or father. His babysitter, young, with enormous breasts, had draped a tattooed arm – the design something Celtic – across the back of the banquette. Her hair was crimson, and what looked like a safety pin glinted in the skin of her lower lip. She plucked idly at her lettuce, leaf by leaf, and watched the shop as if it were television. The boy stopped his fidgeting and stared at me, brazen and long, but without expression, and when I smiled at him, he looked away. This, then, was Reza.

It quickly became clear that his English was cripplingly poor, but I wasn't worried for him. That first night after school, I checked his file and could see that his home address was one of the fanciest university housing blocks in a cul-de-sac down near the river. That meant his parents were not even graduate students but visiting faculty, or important fellows of some kind. They, or at least one of them, would have English, would be able to help him; and they would care about it, being academics themselves, which was half the battle. Also, he himself wanted to learn. Even the first day I could see: with the other children, when he didn't know a word he'd point, say 'What is?' and repeat their answers in his funny foreign voice, slightly raspy, several times over. If it was an abstraction, he'd try to act it out, which made the others laugh, but he remained utterly sober and undeterred. Thanks to Noah, he learned the words 'fart' and 'butt' by lunchtime. I intervened only to clarify that 'bottom' and 'rear end' were considered more polite, but he had trouble enunciating 'rear end.' It came out as 'weah wend,' and to me even this seemed moving, because his efforts were so serious.

That was the third reason to know he'd succeed: his charm. I wasn't the only one felled by it: I could see the little girls gaping and whispering, could divine the boys' wariness melting as Reza proved such a sport, intrepid at games and cheerfully competitive, exactly the sort of kid you want on your team. And the teachers, even: Estelle Garcia, who teaches science, commented about him at our first teachers' meeting, 'Sometimes, you know, the grasp of English itself doesn't seem so important. If a kid is passionate enough, you can transcend that.'

I demurred, reminded her of Ilya, the Russian boy, and Duong, from Vietnam, and half a dozen kids we'd seen splutter and almost drown un-Englished in elementary school, so that you sent them only trepidatiously on to middle school, fearing they'd come back thugs, or dropouts, or worse. Sometimes, inevitably, it happened.

'You're not worrying like this in the first week? That boy picks it all up like a sponge.'

'I'm not worried about that boy at all,' I said. 'But he's an exception.'

Exceptional. Adaptable. Compassionate. Generous. So intelligent. So quick. So sweet. With such a sense of humor. What did any of our praise mean, but that we'd all fallen in love with him, a bit, and were dazzled? He was eight, just a child of eight like any other, but we all wanted to lay claim to him. We didn't say these kind things about Eric P., or Darren, or moon-faced Miles, whose dark circles beneath his eyes emanated gloom like some form of permanent mourning. Each child is strong in a different way, we always told them. We all have different gifts. We can all make good choices if we try. But Reza gave the lie to this, bound in his charm and beauty as if in a net.

When, in the first week, he knocked Françoise down on the playground, by accident, in the exuberant throes of an impromptu soccer match, he put his arm around her trembling shoulder and sat out with her on the curb until she felt ready to sally forth again. He had tears in his eyes: I saw them. When he discovered that Aristide, whose parents came from Haiti, could speak French, his face opened in delight and the pair gabbled through the lunch hour, until Mark T. and Eli complained that they felt excluded; whereupon he nodded dutifully, shut his eyes for a moment and reverted to broken English, his imperfect medium. I didn't have to tell him to do it; and from then on he and Aristide spoke French only after school was over, on their way out the door. When, also early on, the children suffered a particularly rambunctious afternoon – it was pouring; they'd been cooped up all day, the sky outside so dark that we bathed for hours in aggravating fluorescence – and in art hour – supposedly my favorite, as I am, or am supposed to be, an artist – the boys had the bright idea of squirting tempera paints from their plastic bottles, first at their papers but then, by the time I noticed, at the furniture, and the floor, and each other – when, in spite of my considerable, vaunted self-control, I raised my voice and thunderously proclaimed myself sorely disappointed – that day, at school's end, a full hour afterward, Reza stopped at my desk and placed a small hand upon my forearm, delicate as a leaf.

'I'm sorry, Miss Eldridge,' he said. 'I'm sorry we made a mess. Sorry you're angry.'

His sitter hovered in the doorway, her lip glinting. Otherwise I might have hugged him: he seemed, for a moment, so much like my own child.

~

Children. Me and children. Children and me. How did I, of all people, become the favorite teacher of the Appleton Elementary third-grade class? April Watts, who takes the other section, is like a teacher out of a Victorian novel: she has hair like brown cotton candy, whipped into a gauzy attenuated confection around her head, and bottle-bottom glasses through which she peers, vaguely, her blue eyes enlarged and distorted by the lenses like fishes in a tank. Although only in her early fifties, she wears support hose for her varicose veins and she has, poor ghastly thing, absolutely no sense of humor whatsoever. It's not on account of the hair or the glasses or the veins that I'm preferred, but on account of this last trait. I've been known – and I don't say this pridefully – to laugh so hard that I fall off my chair, which seems to make up for the thunderous outbursts. My emotions, shall we say, are in their full gamut recognizable to the children, which seems to me pedagogically sound.

It was both a great compliment and a crushing blow to have a father say to me, a couple of years back, that I perfectly fulfilled his idea of a teacher. 'You're the Gerber baby of schoolteachers' is what he actually said. 'You're the exemplar.'

'What exactly does that mean, Ross?' I asked with a big, fake smile. It was at the end-of-year picnic, and three or four parents clustered around me in the playground's fierce sunlight, clutching their miniature plastic lemonade bottles, daubing away at their chins or their children's chins with ketchup-stained napkins. The hot dogs and tofu pups had already been consumed.

'Oh, I know what he means,' said Brianna's mom, Jackie. 'He means that when we were children, everyone wanted a teacher like you. Enthusiastic, but strict. Full of ideas. A teacher who *gets* kids.'

'Is that what you meant, Ross?'

'Probably not exactly,' he said, and I was surprised to recognize that he was flirting with me. Parents at Appleton rarely flirt. 'But close enough. It was intended as a compliment.'

'Well then, thank you.'

I'm always looking for what people are really saying. When they tell me that I 'get' kids, I'm worried that they're saying I don't seem quite adult. The professor husband of a friend of mine has likened children to the insane. I often think of it. He says that children live on the edge of madness, that their behavior, apparently unmotivated, shares the same dream logic as crazy people's. I see what he means, and because I've learned to be patient with children, to tease out the logic that's always somewhere there, and irrefutable once explained, I've come to understand that grown-ups, mad or sane, ought really to be accorded the same respect. In this sense, nobody is actually crazy, just not understood. When Brianna's mom says that I *get* kids, part of me puffs up like a peacock, but another part thinks she is calling me crazy. Or that, at the very least, she's separating me from the tribe of the fully adult. And then this, in turn, will explain – if not to me then to someone who is, seer-like, in charge of explanations – why I don't have children of my own.

If you'd asked me, upon my graduation from high school, where I'd be at forty – and surely someone must have asked? There must be a feature tucked away in the long-lost yearbook laying out our plans for later life – I would have painted a blissful picture of the smocked artist at work in her airy studio, the children – several of them, aged perhaps five, seven and nine – frolicking in the sun-dappled garden, doubtless with a dog or two, large ones. I wouldn't have been able to describe for you the source of income for this vision, nor any father to account for the children: men seemed, at that juncture, incidental to the stuff of life. Nor did the children require a nanny of any kind: they played miraculously well, without bickering, without ever the desire to interrupt the artist, until she was ready; and then, the obligatory and delightful picnic beneath the trees. No money, no man, no help – but in the picture there were those necessary things: the light, the work, the garden and, crucially, the children. If you'd asked me then to winnow the fantasy, to excise all that was expendable, I would've taken out the picnic, and the dogs, and the garden, and, under duress, the studio. A kitchen table could suffice, for the art, if need be, or an attic, or a garage. But the art and the children – they were not negotiable.

I'm not exactly not an artist, and I don't exactly not have children. I've just contrived to arrange things very poorly, or very well, depending how you look at it. I leave the kids when school gets out; I make my art – I don't have to use the kitchen table, because I have a whole second bedroom, with two windows no less, for that purpose – evenings and weekends. It's not much; but it's better than nothing. And in the Sirena year, when I had my airy studio to share, when I couldn't wait to get there, my veins fizzing at the prospect, it was perfect.

I always thought I'd get farther. I'd like to blame the world for what I've failed to do, but the failure – the failure that sometimes washes over me as anger, makes me so angry I could spit – is all mine, in the end. What made my obstacles insurmountable, what consigned me to mediocrity, is me, just me. I thought for so long, forever, that I was strong enough – or I misunderstood what strength was. I thought I could get to greatness, to my greatness, by plugging on, cleaning up each mess as it came, the way you're taught to eat your greens before you have dessert. But it turns out that's a rule for girls and sissies, because the mountain of greens is of Everest proportions, and the bowl of ice cream at the far end of the table is melting a little more with each passing second. There will be ants on it soon. And then they'll come and clear it away altogether. The hubris of it, thinking I could be a decent human being and a valuable member of family and society, and still create! Absurd. How strong did I think I was?

No, obviously what strength was all along was the ability to say 'Fuck off' to the lot of it, to turn your back on all the suffering and contemplate, unmolested, your own desires above all. Men have generations of practice at this. Men have figured out how to spawn children and leave them to others to raise, how to placate their mothers with a mere phone call from afar, how to insist, as calmly as if insisting that the sun is in the sky, as if any other possibility were madness, that their work, of all things, is what must – and must first – be done. Such a strength has, in its youthful vision, no dogs or gardens or picnics, no children, no sky: it is focused only on one thing, whether it's on money, or on power, or on a paintbrush and a canvas. It's a *failure* of vision, in fact, anyone with half a brain can see that. It's myopia. But that's what it takes. You need to see everything else – everyone else – as expendable, as less than yourself.

I'm like the children: my motivations and my reasons aren't always clear. But if I can just explain, all will be elucidated; and maybe that elucidation alone will prove my greatness, however small. To tell what I know, and how it feels, if I can. You might see yourself, if I do.

3

From the beginning, then, but briefly. I was born into an ordinary family in a town an hour up the coast from Boston, called Manchester-by-the-Sea. The sixties were barely a ripple there, at the end of the Boston commuter line. It must have been our perfect beach – called Singing Beach on account of its fine, pale, musical sand, but perhaps also because it is so widely and so long lauded – that afforded me my delusions of grandeur. It makes sense that if you stand almost daily in the middle of a perfect crescent of shore, with a vista open to eternity, you'll conceive of possibility differently from someone raised in a wooded valley or among the canyons of a big city.

Or maybe, more likely, they came from my mother, fierce and strange and doomed. I had a mother and a father, a big brother – eight years bigger than me, though, so we hardly seemed of the same family: by the time I was nine, he was gone – and a tortoiseshell cat, Zipper, and a mangy, runty mutt from the shelter named Sputnik, who looked like a wig of rags on sticks: his legs were so scrawny, we marveled they didn't snap. My father worked in insurance in Boston – he took the train each morning, the 7:52 – and he proceeded very respectably but apparently not very successfully, because my parents never seemed to have money to spare.

My mother stayed at home and smoked cigarettes and hatched schemes. For a while she tested cookbook recipes for a publisher. She was paid for it, and for months she fed us elaborate three- and four-course meals that involved eggy sauces and frequently, as I recall, marsala wine. Briefly and humiliatingly for me, she fancied herself a clothes designer, and spent several months at the sewing machine in the spare room in a swoon of tobacco smoke (often she held the cigarette between her lips while running a seam; I always worried that ash would fall onto the fabric). Her output was at once unusual and not unusual enough: she made paisley jersey minidresses for girls of my size, not, at first glance, dissimilar to those off the rack ('Come here, sugarplum,' she'd call, and would hold up paper patterns against my prepubescent chest, trimming away carelessly at the paper with her enormous shears, a mere whisper from my waist, or my neck); but then you'd see she'd cut portholes around the midriff and edged them with rickrack, so that a girl's white tummy would peer through; or that she'd made the sleeves so they attached not with seams but with a flurry of ribbons, a circle of multicolored bows, that would look bedraggled after a single washing. Cheerfully impractical, she ran up at least two dozen outfits, of various designs, the summer I was nine, and then took a booth from which to flog them at the fair in a neighboring town.

I refused to sit with her there, in full view, on a brilliant Saturday in July, and went instead with my father on a tedious round of errands – the cleaners, the liquor store, the hardware store – stifling in the car but immeasurably relieved not to risk being seen by my schoolmates under my mother's hideous handmade sign. My mother was a beloved embarrassment.

She sold a few of the clothes, but clearly felt the experiment hadn't sufficiently succeeded, and the suitcase was stowed, unemptied, in the attic. Before too long, the sewing machine also migrated upward, and my mother entered one of her darker phases, until the next eureka moment struck.

Certainly my mother, unlike my father, instilled in me the sense that unpredictability was essential – 'Not to be like your neighbor: that's everything,' she would say – and because of this, because of the bright flame of her, it took me a long time to realize that she, too, was cautious and bourgeois, frightened of the unknown and so uncertain of herself that she could hardly bear to make a mark. How else could she have stayed resolutely wedded to the ordinary, to my father, to the carefully ordained and unchanging routines of Manchester-by-the-Sea?

And it explains much about me, too, about the limits of my experience, about the fact that the person I am in my head is so far from the person I am in the world. *Nobody would know me from my own description of myself,* which is why, when called upon (rarely, I grant) to provide an account, I tailor it, I adapt, I try to provide an outline that can, in some way, correlate to the outline that people understand me to have – that, I suppose, I actually have, at this point. But who I am in my head, very few people really get to see that. Almost none. It's the most precious gift I can give, to bring her out of hiding. Maybe I've learned it's a mistake to reveal her at all.

So, from our ordinary family in our ordinary house, a center-entrance colonial, with its potted geraniums on the stone porch and its charmingly untended yew hedges nibbling at the windows, I made my way out into the ordinary world, to the local elementary school, the local middle school, the local high school. I was popular enough, universally liked by the girls, even liked, when noticed, by the boys, though not in a romantic way. I was funny – ha-ha, not peculiar. It was a modest currency, like pennies: pedestrian, somewhat laborious, but a currency nonetheless. I was funny, in public, most often at my own expense.

Education was different then, and I was good at it, and so I skipped grade nine, went straight from eight to ten, which was socially a little tough at first and sealed my fate as a disastrous math student – I never learned the quadratic formula, and other important tips from ninth-grade math; just like I missed the early dating essays and the classes in how to navigate a school dance. At the time, though, I wasn't embarrassed about any of this: not embarrassed to be thrown, sink or swim, into the second year of high school, without so much as a map to the cafeteria or a primer on how cliques were lined up, or even a list of the names of my new classmates, all of whom knew one another, and some of whom knew me as their little sister's friend. No, I was proud, because I knew my parents were proud, because it was an elevation, and a revelation of the fact that I was special. I'd long suspected it, and now I knew for sure: I was destined.

When you're a girl, you never let on that you are proud, or that you know you're better at history, or biology, or French, than the girl who sits beside you and is eighteen months older. Instead you gush about how good she is at putting on nail polish or at talking to boys, and you roll your eyes at the vaunted difficulty of the history/biology/French test and say, 'Oh my God, it's going to be such a disaster! I'm so *scared*!' and you put yourself down whenever you can so that people won't feel threatened by you, so they'll like you, because you wouldn't want them to know that in your heart, you are proud, and maybe even haughty, and are riven by thoughts the revelation of which would show everyone how deeply Not Nice you are. You learn a whole other polite way of speaking to the people who mustn't see you clearly, and you know – you get told by others – that they think you're really sweet, and you feel a thrill of triumph:

'Yes, I'm good at history/biology/French, and I'm good at *this*, too.' It doesn't ever occur to you, as you fashion your mask so carefully, that it will grow into your skin and graft itself, come to seem irremovable.

When you look at the boy, Josh, who skipped the grade alongside you, and you see him wiping his nose upon his sleeve, and note his physical scrawniness, his chin's bloom of acne, next to the other tenth-grade boys with broader chests and clear, square jaws, when you observe that he still takes his lunch with his old ninth-grade friends – all of them boys in black T-shirts with glitter decals across the breast that say KISS or AC/DC, all of them with pimply chins and wet lips and hair as lank as sea-weed – you cannot see any triumph in him at all. He seems clearly to have lost, to be lost, to be a loser; because anybody knows that in the challenge you were given when you skipped a grade, social success – *modest* social success, to be sure, but still – was half the battle. When Frederica Beattie invites you to join her birthday party – a sail on her father's boat, with six other girls, two of whom are from the most popular set – you feel pity for Josh, who will never taste such nectar.

But wait: nobody ever pointed out that Josh, in his oblivi-ousness, was utterly happy. He'd already taught himself the quadratic formula; he wouldn't be stymied in any area of aca-demic advancement. In fact, he would go on to MIT and eventually become a neurobiologist with a lab largely funded by the NIH and a vast budget at his disposal. He would marry a perfectly attractive, if rather knock-kneed, woman and spawn several knock-kneed, bespectacled nerds, replicas of himself. It will all work out more than fine for him, and he will never for a second suspect that it could have been otherwise. He will not know there was a social test; he will not know that he failed it. No, a sail on Frederica Beattie's father's boat was an honor that he dreamed not of; and his yen for society, such as it was, was perfectly satisfied by his old clan, now a year behind him. He could no more have fashioned a mask than flown to the moon; and so he remained who he was forevermore. Femininity as masquerade, indeed.

It was in high school that I decided – or, as I would have had it, that I realized – that I would become an artist. Having discovered a set of sympathetic friends who reveled, precisely, in our not-grown-up-ness, a handful of girls and boys who liked to jump in puddles during downpours, or gather on the playground at dusk, as much to swing on the swings as to smoke pot behind the cupola, I found that our group loitered increasingly in the art room after school, with the head art teacher's tacit blessing. He was a stocky fellow in knee-high hunting boots and leather jerkins, with luxuriant shoulder-length locks and a pointy red goatee: he looked like a refugee from a community theater Shakespeare production, and his name, most wonderfully, was Dominic Crace.

Although the premises were officially closed, he left out supplies for us, cupboards unlocked, paints and brushes by the sink, and even, sometimes, on the worktable, the key for the darkroom. It was within its red gloom that, as an anxious junior, I suffered my first real kiss, a wet-tongued clinch with a senior named Alf, whose many-zippered leather jacket was the most splendid thing about him. I'd long thought him cool, but he proved – it was a surprise to realize this was possible – as awkward as I was, the upshot of which was that the kiss was neither repeated nor ever again mentioned. Our friendship, such as it was – something along the lines of extended family – remained unchanged; it was simply as if the kiss had never happened; and at times, afterward, I'd wonder whether it had.

Thinking ourselves subversive, pining for the decades of adventure that we had, in our belated births, so narrowly missed, we stayed in the room until nightfall and painted posters and slogans on large sheets of construction paper, and taped them up around the hallways. REVOLT, they read, in bursts of primary color, and SHUN COMPLACENCY, and DO YOU KNOW WHERE YOUR SOUL IS?, and FIGHT MONEY! KISS AN ANARCHIST!

If Dominic Crace was on our side, the janitors were, ironically, in a useful revolutionary lesson, the enemy: they roamed the halls at night charged with tearing down our unauthorized posters before the next morning's assembly. Our game was to post the best ones in corners where the janitors wouldn't find them, or not, at least, until they'd been widely appreciated. We thrilled to paint them, thrilled to hang them, thrilled, the next day, to scout for the survivors: LOVE YOUR NEIGHBOR AS YOUR-SELF, with the cerulean blue outline of a couple embracing, lasted three days on the inside of the back door to the biology lab; THEY F——— YOU UP, YOUR MUM AND DAD, which was, as a quotation, a contribution from my mother, made it a whole week inside the cupboard door in the gym where the basketballs were kept. But the frankest – SATs, SCHOOL ACTIVITIES: WHAT'S IT ALL FOR? – was held up in assembly by a frowning Mr Evers, the principal, who said that while we were all in favor of free speech, slogans of this kind were unhelpful to the fabric of our community and undermined morale. Moreover, he explained, they made a bad impression on any guests. This is not, he said, in the spirit of Manchester High School. He advised that there were many avenues for expression, and that those who needed to express confusion or discontent were welcome to submit articles to the school newspaper for publication. That, he hoped, would be an end to it.

Dominic Crace, who knew full well who we were, didn't turn us in, nor did he lock up the supplies; and we, who sniggered at

Mr Evers's pompous speech, were nevertheless like flies in a trap, lured by the delights of Crace's art room. The following year, my last, all of us who were still at the school – Alf had graduated, along with a few others, leaving six of us seniors, three juniors and a sophomore – signed up for Studio Art.

Our first homework assignment was to draw a bee inside a violin inside a pear. Everybody else took Crace literally, and drew painstaking pencil renditions of these items, ever smaller, like Chinese boxes. Nobody was very good at perspective, but for some this worked out better than for others. I didn't even try to draw. I went home and built a large hollow papier-mâché pear on a coat hanger form – in two pieces, initially, that eventually I sealed together – and I lined the inside with gold foil. I made a violin out of a matchbox and a picture of an instrument cut from a glossy magazine, and I caught a honeybee out among my mother's lavender, using the old bug-catcher from the attic. I asphyxiated him in the jar.

Having painted him with shellac, pleasingly, so he glistened, I laid the sleeping bee in the half-open violin matchbox, glued it to the floor inside the pear, and then, with my big brother's help (he must have been already living in Tucson and home for a visit with Tweety, who eventually became his wife), I rigged up a tiny bulb, like a nightlight, inside the pear before I sealed it, and ran the cord discreetly out the bottom. Crucially, I burrowed a peephole through the pear's skin, through the papier-mâché flesh, so you could peer inside it; and even now I have to say, when the cord was plugged in and the wall of gold foil illuminated the pear's hollow core, the glistening sleeping bee in his violin matchbox was oddly beautiful. I decided that it was a russet pear, and painted the outside in beautiful crimson reds, many layers of paint so it was thick and shiny. I worked very hard at it – I *loved* the pointlessness of the enterprise; it gave me such satisfaction, an answer to my earlier posters. This, Mr

Evers, I thought, this is what it's all for – and when I took it into class and set it up alongside all the pencil drawings, I had the exhilaration of seeing Mr Crace make a temple of his hands beneath his chin (a temple, mind you, that pulled discreetly at the ends of his devilish goatee) and chuckle aloud.

'This,' he announced, looking around at us one after the other with a flicker of glee that suddenly brought to mind Willy Wonka rather than Petruchio, 'now *this* is a work of art.' He paused, bent at the waist and peered in at my bee in his chamber, then straightened and whirled around. 'Whose is this? Whose is it? It's yours? I knew it. Well done, Nora Eldridge,' he said. 'Well done, you.'

4

Sirena was an artist – is an artist. A real one, whatever that means. Now she's even well known, in certain important circles. Even though she lives in Paris, Sirena isn't French; she's Italian. This isn't obvious because her last name is Shahid and her husband's first name is Skandar, and her son has the same name as the last shah of Iran – not that any of them is remotely Persian. They simply liked the name. Skandar is from Lebanon, from Beirut. Okay, someone in his family was from Palestine before that, but that's a long time ago now; and at least some part of it, on his father's side, I think, was from Beirut all along. One part of him is Christian and another part is Muslim, which surely explains a lot about all of it to someone, though not especially to me. Besides which, I wasn't talking about Skandar, who doesn't come into the story until much later, but about Sirena, to whom he was – and is – married, who is Italian and an artist.

You'd be forgiven for thinking Sirena was herself from the Middle East, on account of her skin, that fine olive skin, which on her son looked as though he'd been dusted with powder, glaucous almost, but on her elegant bones appeared at once old and young, young because her cheeks were so smooth and full, like fruit. She didn't have any wrinkles except at the corners of her eyes, and there, spectacular crow's-feet as if she'd spent her life grinning or squinting into the sun. And she had grooves from the edges of her nose to the corners of her mouth, but these weren't wrinkles, exactly, they were expression. Her nose was avian, strong, Italian, I suppose, and the fine skin was pulled tight across it, a little shiny sometimes. There, on its bridge, were dotted a few freckles, like a small spray of sand. She had the eyes, Reza's eyes, and the fierce black brows, and straight glossy black hair streaked with silver. She wasn't young – even when I met her, when Reza was eight, she must have been around forty-five; but you wouldn't have put her age so high. It was in the eyes – the life in the eyes – and the crow's-feet. Ironically, they made her seem younger.

I should have met her at the Back to School Night at the end of September – the evening on which the parents come to the classroom at dinnertime, having mysteriously disposed of their offspring, and cram themselves into their children's tiny desks and listen to the teacher expound with infectious enthusiasm on the joys of multiplication tables and the mysterious importance of learning cursive. This presentation is followed by a speech from the principal, Shauna McPhee, in the auditorium, and the requisite tepid, gelatinous pizza and warm soda afterward that we, the beleaguered and by now exhausted teachers, must stay behind to clean up.

If I'd met Sirena then, I would have made the effort to approach her, I know that; but as it was, I met her before, because Reza got beaten up. Not quite true: I've always been prone to exaggeration. But he did get attacked, and he did get hurt.

In the third week of school, on the playground after classes on Wednesday, the first truly crisp and autumnal day of the season,

three fifth-grade boys ganged up on Reza while he was playing
on the climbing structure by himself – or 'by his own,' as the
children sometimes charmingly put it. First they threw balls at
him – not small balls, big ones, basketballs, and not in fun but
hard, with vicious aim. 'I thought they were playing dodgeball,'
said another kid who'd been nearby; but unfortunately nobody
proposed the game to Reza, who wouldn't have known what it
was anyway – and then, somehow, things deteriorated further,
and one of them, Owen, a large boy and a stupid one, I have to
say, having taught him for a year and struggled mightily to be
able to promote him at the end of it, grabbed Reza by the collar,
hauled him up against a metal pillar and punched him in the ear.
He called Reza 'a terrorist' and told him the playground was for
Americans. It took a while to get the story clear, and somewhere
it involved Owen's uncle suffering from PTSD following a tour
in Iraq; but nothing, frankly, could excuse or explain the whole
appalling fiasco.

I was going over the kids' essays – well, that's a big word for
them, three paragraphs on 'What I liked most about our apple-
picking field trip'; but I was working at my desk in the
classroom – when Bethany, one of the three girls barely out of
college who are in charge of after-school free play, brought him
in to me. She'd had the wit to slap an ice pack on his red and
swelling ear, but Reza was blanched and trembling, his lashes
clumped with tears. Bethany was too young or too timid to do
what most obviously needed to be done, which was to sit him
down and put an arm around him and breathe right along with
him, to slow him down, and then without moving out of sight,
to get the cell and his file and call his mother and tell her to
come and pick him up.

I was irritated with Sirena at first, because in a slow, foreign,
small voice, she suggested that Maria, his sitter, would be
coming for him in forty-five minutes anyway. I took an audible

breath – I wanted it to be – and I said, 'Under the circumstances, Mrs Shahid, I think it would be a good idea if you came yourself and if you came as soon as possible.'

'I'll be there in ten minutes. Fifteen at most.'

'We'll be right here in the classroom,' I said. 'Come as quickly as you can.'

And I went back to sit next to Reza and I put one arm on the back of his chair so he'd feel safe, and I said, 'Do you want a lemonade? I've got one in my bag. And how about an Oreo?' And I plied him with sugar water and cookies, and I plied him for the story, and so had at least the bare and inexcusable bones of it before Sirena arrived. Reza, in spite of the tears caught in his lashes like raindrops on a spider's web, did not cry, although he hiccoughed a bit, his breathing, like his small shoulders, shuddery.

I was furious – with the three bullies, with Bethany, Margot and Sarah, who somehow had contrived not to see a thing, and somehow furious also with Reza's mother, whom I had yet to meet, for leaving him unprotected in a strange land, for having entrusted him to a system and to people she knew nothing about. If he were mine, I would never have done such a thing: I would have cherished him, surrounded him, not even as a matter of principle (although there was that, too), but because he was Reza, this luminous boy, and so precious.

When, then, she peered through the glass with a tentative knock, and cracked the door open, I leaped up ready for the sternest of encounters; but was disarmed. The agony of her eyes – they were, after all, *his* eyes – and her little run across the room to embrace him – the presence of her, in short, was enough. I can only guess what they said. They spoke in French; her arms about him, he turned his face to her breast, as if breathing the scent of her were balm. He was a big boy for such a gesture – most of my third graders wouldn't have wanted their teacher to see their emotions so exposed, and I admired them, son and mother, for their indifference to me. It took a full minute or even two before she lifted her face, disentangled an arm and extended it. 'Miss Eldridge,' she said, 'I've been look-ing forward to meeting you.'

'I'm sorry it's not in better circumstances.'

She shrugged, faintly. 'I'm glad I got your call.'

'There was an incident, on the playground.'

'So I gather.'

'I wasn't present, but from what Reza says, it wasn't at all his fault.'

She made a face as if to say, 'How could it be?'

'Our school has zero tolerance for bullying, Mrs Shahid—'

'I'm sure.'

'And we'll find out exactly what went on, and the boys will be disciplined.'

'Of course.'

'I'm particularly sorry because it seems as though the boys said – as though they used hurtful and inappropriate words. I want you to know that at Appleton, we don't have – We haven't had – This isn't at all usual. And we'll make sure that it doesn't—'

'I understand.' She stood up, and Reza with her, as if they were in fact joined at the hip. She smiled then – was it because it was *his* smile? Maybe, although in that moment that was not my thought. What went through my mind, as clearly as if I'd said it aloud, was this: 'Oh, it's *you*. Of course. I should have known.' And later, when I reflected upon it, I thought again, in words, 'I recognize you.' It was the strangest feeling, of relief and alarm at the same time. Like seeing a ghost, or having an epiphany – who is he who walks always beside you? – a feeling that you have no choice but to trust com-pletely.

' . . . so grateful,' she was saying. 'This move, so much change for Reza, it could have been . . . difficult. But he loves coming to your class.'

'We love having him.' I said this looking at Reza with a big smile, and he looked back at me with the same grave inscrutability of the first day in the supermarket. 'And I really hope that what happened today, horrible as it was, doesn't make you stop liking this school.'

He shook his head slightly: hard to know whether he meant that it would or it wouldn't.

'My little prince is very strong,' his mother said. 'He'll be okay.' She smiled again, looked at me, really looked at me – I felt she *saw* me – again. I wanted to say, 'Do you know me too, then?' to make sure it wasn't just me. But who could say such a thing?

'Good to meet you, Mrs Shahid' – and we shook hands again, at her instigation, and her hand was smallish, but strong and warm and dry – 'and I'll be sure to let you know at once how things unfold as we look into this. I'll call you. Here's my home number in case you need it. And I'll look forward to seeing you and your husband at Back to School Night next week.'

'Next week. Of course,' she said, demure and amused and reserved all at once. 'Of course. Good-bye.'

Of course. Of course. It felt inevitable, this meeting, like a chance, like a door opening. I didn't know yet that she was an artist, an installation artist, bereft without her Paris studio. After they'd left, I sat back down at my desk, my eyes not on the apple-picking paragraphs but on the branches, turning, outside the classroom window, the Norwegian maple in its crimson-tinged ball gown, ruffled against the spotless 9/11 sky. How could the leaves stand out so distinctly? Why was the sky such an impeccable blue? How could this ordinary afternoon suddenly fill me, not with the indignation I'd felt earlier, but with elation – yes, elation. Sitting at my desk, pencil in hand in the dimming light, in the long angles of the afternoon sun, I had butterflies, like a child. Nothing moved in the room but the inside of my stomach.

5

Shauna McPhee sat down with the three bullies the next morning to discuss sharing, tolerance and the importance of words. I'm sure she spoke to them about making good choices, about their own safety, and then she called in Reza and had the boys apologize one by one, and shake his hand in front of her, and only after he'd gone away again did she tell them that they wouldn't be allowed on the playground, either at recess or after school, for a week. Their parents were also informed of this, and Shauna rang Sirena to reassure her that the incident had been, as she put it, 'resolved.'

Don't get me wrong, I admire Shauna, who is five years younger than I am, also single and childless, but unlike me a star of the city's public school system. She'd already been the principal for three years then – she'd been running Appleton before she was thirty. But I do think that the only way you get on as an administrator is by understanding grown-ups better than you do children. You make a show of understanding children, but it's a show for the grown-ups. If Shauna actually *got* kids, she would have known that the three bullies weren't smart enough to appreciate the good sense of rules of tolerance and acceptance, they were smart enough only to grasp that these were, it seemed, the rules. And everybody knows that the point about rules – if you're a dull, naughty boy, with a sly glimmer of animal nous that is your greatest pride – is not to obey them but to avoid getting caught breaking them. And if Shauna understood, she'd have seen that the boys saw those ritual handshakes in her office as their humiliation, which only made them despise Reza the more. By ostensibly 'resolving' the issue, Shauna was encouraging guerilla warfare, and I knew to be on watch.

Sirena, no fool, knew too, and she called me that night at home. I had that strange high-voltage thrill when I realized who it was.

'Miss Eldridge, I'm sorry—'

'Nora, please.'

She paused on the line. A wonderful, mysterious thing, a pause on the line. Who knew what it signified? 'Nora. Yes. I'm sorry to bother you at home, but I wanted your opinion.'

'About the boys?'

'Yes, the boys.' She had a habit of repeating the last words you said to her before going on, as if a conversation were a relay race. I could never decide whether this was cultural – an Italian thing – or to do with living in translation, making sure she'd gotten it right, or just a Sirenian idiosyncrasy. 'I wanted to know if you think the boys' – she said 'boy-se,' in a lovely, slightly comical Italian way – 'will be okay now?'

'Because you don't?'

'Because I don't? I don't know. Sometimes, it looks all okay, but the children, they're angry. They don't like to get into trouble, and it makes them more angry.'

'Definitely true, Mrs Shahid.'

'Sirena, please. Or I can't call you Nora.'

'Sirena.' I tried to say it the way she did, but it didn't sound the same. 'All we can do is be vigilant, at this point. Unless there's another incident, which I very much hope there won't be . . .'

'Perhaps we can have coffee?' The voltage struck again. It was extraordinary what the body was capable of, for no reason at all. Except if she had recognized me too. And then I felt the other had been an excuse – not only an excuse, but still.

'Coffee? Sure.'

'To explain. If I can speak to you about Reza: he's coming from such a different world. It's important to me that this year in America be a good one for him. He didn't want so much to come, so . . .'

So, not an excuse. An actual reason. A chance to be a better teacher. 'Of course. When would be convenient for you?'

We fixed our date for two days after the Back to School Night. We planned to meet at Burdick's café in Harvard Square, which is strange because I don't care for it, and I don't think she suggested it. I must have proposed it as a highlight of local life; but it always feels stuffy to me, and the windows get steamed up, and it's hard to get a place to sit, and their cakes are too rich and very expensive, but it always feels wasteful, if you've gone to the trouble of going to Burdick's, not to have one. I prefer Starbucks, where the food is frankly bad and there's no awkwardness about avoiding it. It's difficult, though, to suggest Starbucks to some-one from Paris.

I've often wondered how much of the Shahids' appeal stemmed from their foreignness. I've always been attracted to foreignness. In my junior year of high school, we had an exchange student from London named Hattie, and I decided before she ever came that I'd befriend her. Ethereally pale, moon-faced with big blue eyes, she had a bleached bob that fell glamorously over half her face, and a retro black mac with a bull's-eye printed on the back. She was sturdy not in a fat way but in a strong way, and she wore black lace-up DM boots and she listened to Joy Division and the Clash. And she came from London, England. There wasn't anyone at the high school who could hold a candle to her, and I served as both her guide and her amanuensis for the year. It made me much cooler, in the eyes of my classmates. It was only halfway through her time there that she revealed that she was as young as I was, or almost, and I was both awed and dismayed, the latter because it seemed, then, that my one claim to specialness was suddenly nothing, a single arrow in her ample quiver.

But foreignness: there was nothing foreign about my father, with his unconsidered Brooks Brothers wardrobe and his upbringing in Wenham, Massachusetts. Nothing foreign about my mother but an Italian grandmother, of whom she possessed a single photograph, the ancestor having died when my mother was two; and a deeply Catholic sister who had contemplated taking orders, which seemed fairly foreign to us. As a boy, my brother Matt was so American he hated vegetables and all kinds of ethnic food – Indian, Chinese, Thai, he'd spurn it all, claiming it was horsemeat slathered in brown sauce. I'm not sure how different he is even now. No, my yearning was all my own.

'There have been Eldridges here since almost the beginning,' my father was known to say, smugly, while opening a bottle of wine or doling out mashed potatoes. 'We're old stock.' And in Manchester-by-the-Sea, a short bike ride from the grand seaside houses of the gentry, I'd think how telling was my father's 'almost,' how that 'almost' led, grimly, to our humble front door.

I always thought I'd live in Paris, Rome, Madrid – at least for a while. It strikes me now that I didn't dream of Zanzibar or Papeete or Tashkent: even my fantasy was cautious, a good girl's fantasy, a blanched almond of a fantasy. Today, even that is enough to clench my fists and curl my toes.

In the past few years, I've often thought of the Marianne

Faithfull song 'The Ballad of Lucy Jordan' – 'At the age of thirty-seven, she realized she'd never ride through Paris in a sports car, with the warm wind in her hair . . . ' – and I've felt little pricks behind my eyes. Not because I thought I wouldn't get my Parisian sports car moment – insanely, and quite erroneously, I was sure at thirty-seven, and thirty-eight, and even thirty-nine, that that moment was imminent – but because Marianne is right that the age of thirty-seven – the first of my Reza years – is a time of reckoning, the time at which you have to acknowledge once and for all that your life has a shape and a horizon, and that you'll probably never be president, or a millionaire, and that if you're a childless woman, you will quite possibly remain that way. Then there's a period of accommodation before you are formally and officially old, except that I didn't use it for that purpose. I used those years another way, or thought I did. I thought I was using them to make my life real – wasn't that what they said in the sixties? To 'realize' myself? – but it turns out I'm still in the Fun House to this day.

6

When Sirena failed to show up for Back to School Night, I wondered whether to call to remind her of our appointment at Burdick's two days later. I decided to wait and see. I was aware that this was not only unteacherly but simply not very grown up of me. I was setting a friendship test.

She passed. She came, although she was almost fifteen minutes late, and seemed to be carrying half a dozen parcels and bags with which she breathlessly and clumsily bumped the other customers: she got one of them, an old lady drinking hot chocolate, in the back of the head.

Because I'd been waiting awhile, I'd managed to snag a table. The tables and stools there are small and close together, and they're not comfortable, but we squeezed ourselves in and piled her packages underneath our feet. We kept our coats on, although it was warm, because we had nowhere to put them.

'Shopping?'

'Shopping, yes. It's my husband's birthday tomorrow.' She gave a pretty laugh. 'We always give many presents. Nothing big, but lots of small things. It's always a challenge to find the right ones. He is an – idiosyncrasy?'

'He's idiosyncratic.'

'Yes, exactly.'

'And his work is the reason that you're here?'

'Only for one year. He has a fellowship from the university, to write his book.'

'Interesting. What's it about?'

'You'll have to ask him to explain it, because I'll do a poor job. Ethics. It's about ethics and history. He's interested in how we can't tell a history truly – there's no such thing after all – but so then we must try to tell a history ethically – and what does this mean?'

'Why can't a history be true?'

'Because we always have only a part of a history. You can't make a picture three hundred sixty degrees; we can't, even in one second of a life, show everything that we experience. So how could we do such a thing for a person's history, or a people's history? A nation's history? It isn't possible.' She put her hands up in a cheerful show of despair.

'And what do you do, then? Are you a historian, or an ethics person, or whatever, also?'

'No! I could never do such things. Words are not for me.' She looked at me closely, her marbled dark eyes alight. 'I'm an artist. I make things. Installations. Sometimes videos.' She said this as calmly as if she were confessing to making cakes or collecting stamps, and I knew she was for real.

'You're kidding.'

'No. Why?'

'I'm an artist, too.'

I'd lurched inside at her admission – this! Of course! we shared – but worried, from her smile, that her first impulse was patronizing. She was thinking that making art must be a hobby for me. She was thinking that I was an elementary school teacher. But she was too polite to let on. 'Really,' she said. 'You must tell me about your work.'

'No, no. I want to hear about yours. We can talk about me another time' – I felt bold because this presumed there might be another time – 'I'm here to learn about Reza's life; which means, about yours.'

'About ours, there's not so much to say. But Reza: he's very cherished because we couldn't – I couldn't – have any more children. Do you have brothers and sisters, Nora?'

'An older brother.'

'Then you know what it's like, so important. I come from five children; Skandar from three, although one of his brothers has died. But we both wanted more children, for Reza too, you know.'

'As a teacher, I have to say that only children are often at an advantage academically—'

'Yes, because we, the parents, spoil them and spend so much time. Only children, they become like a third person in the couple, do you know? They don't get so much to be children, but little grown-ups.'

'This is your concern for Reza?'

'This is our concern. In Paris, we've made for him a world of children. He has cousins – not real ones, they're in Italy – but friends as close as cousins. In our apartment building alone he has three friends, including a girl three weeks older that he's known always. They see each other almost every day.'

'So it's a difficult transition for him, to come here.'

'For all of us, yes, of course.'

'It's helpful to know. Thank you.' I'd hoped for some more intimate revelation. I don't know quite what.

'But with the bullying, you see—'

'Yes, that was horrible, I know. I'll keep a close eye. Those were bigger kids who didn't know him, though. In our class, he's extremely popular. Very well liked. Boys and girls both. He's a very kind boy.'

'Yes, kind.'

'And he's making good progress with his English.'

'Yes. We speak only English at the dinner table now, to practice. All three of us, making mistakes. "Please pass," we say, and
then "that thing," if we don't know the word. Sometimes, we're
too tired. But Reza teaches us words now.'

'Not rude ones, I hope?'

'Those also.' She smiled.

We'd finished our coffee. The moment of recognition, the
sign – it had to have a meaning.

'But about your art,' I said. 'You were going to tell me about
your art.'

In that first conversation, she told me about her installations,
which were – as I would eventually see with my own eyes – lush
gardens and jungles made out of household items and refuse:
elaborately carved soap primroses, splayed lilies and tulips fashioned out of dyed dishrags and starch, silvery vines of painted
and varnished clothesline and foil, precisely and impeccably
made. I couldn't quite picture them when she talked about
them, but the idea made sense to me: visions of paradise, the
otherworldly, the beautiful, and then, when you're in them, up
close, you realize that the flowers are mottled by filth and the
vines crumbling and that the gleaming beetles crawling on the
waxy leaves are molded bottle tops or old leather buttons with
limbs. Her installations had names from fairy tales and myth –
The Forest of Arden; Avalon; Oz; Elsinore – but they were, in
reality, the kitchen or the laundry room, and sooner or later the
viewer would realize there was an ancient sink behind the water-
fall or that the boulders between the trees were a washer and
dryer, blow-torched black and furred with dark lint.

She told me too that latterly she'd made videos of the installations, that the story of the videos was precisely this revelation
that the beautiful world was fake, was made of garbage; but that

first she had to film it in such a way that it looked wholly beautiful and that sometimes this was hard. And also, she said, narrative was hard: when you made a video, there had to be a story, and a story unfolded over time, in a different way, and didn't always unfold as you wanted it to.

She told me all this and I could tell that on the one hand she was proud to talk about it, passionate even, but on the other, she retained a slightly world-weary air. I was a tad piqued.

'Can I see what you're working on?' I asked.

She shook her head, looked at me through the film of her hair. 'I'm supposed to build Wonderland – that's my next project. But I have none of that here with me. Maybe I can get a video for you of the earlier stuff, though it's not the same, really.'

'But why?'

'It's about the space, and my tools, and my whole world there.'

'But you can't have a year without your work!'

'No. I'd turn into a monster that neither Reza nor Skandar wanted to know. It's what keeps me from being crazy. Too much dark, otherwise.'

'I'm the same. I need to do it, or I go mad.'

She smiled, in a real way, as if she actually wanted to hear, now. And I told her about how I used to paint big messy pictures, but how when my mother was sick, and for all the years she was dying, one small capacity at a time, I stopped being able to paint, stopped being able to make any big gestures at all, and turned instead to little things, to rooms the size of shoe boxes, Joseph Cornell–scaled dioramas, as if these, at least, could not be taken from me – these are the fragments I have shored against my ruin. And I didn't explain, then, about how I stopped trying to show my work, let alone to sell it, and let go of the idea of it finding a home in the world – because somehow, in that long, slow extinguishing of life, it felt as though the one way I could try to keep my mother alive was to close in, and hold on, hold on to what I made as she had made me. I worried that this would make no sense, and this is why I didn't speak of it then. But I explained about my illuminated boxes, about making scenes and worlds in miniature, and how always, hidden somewhere, where you could barely see her or could not see her at all, there was a small gold figure that was Joy.

'It's hard for me to believe in,' I said, 'but it's also the most important thing to make myself believe. So I put her in there no matter what. Even in the death scenes, I put her in.'

'I really understand,' she said, and I could tell that she really did, and suddenly the afternoon was worth it, the sign had meant something, and we could get up and leave our awkward little table at Burdick's, separate into the now-dark afternoon.

As she gathered her parcels, fumbling again, her clumsiness charming to me, she said without glancing up, 'I'm thinking of renting a space, but the one I like is too big, too much for me. It's better to share. Would you have any interest?'

'Yes,' I said, before I really understood what she was offering. It was a very fast 'yes.'

Outside on the sidewalk, she put her hand on my arm, in the same way her son put his small hand on my arm. Now I would know where the gesture came from. 'I'll call you,' she said. 'At the weekend, you can come with me to see the studio. Maybe Saturday afternoon? Skandar and Reza can do something together then.'

'Yes,' I said, without considering that I'd promised to visit my father that day, that I'd have to call and disappoint him, a spare, gray old man alone in an apartment in Brookline, counting the hours until I came. And when I realized this mistake, I didn't waver, either; and I didn't wait for Sirena to confirm, I called him up, picturing him there in his overheated lemon-yellow sitting room with its strange, plush, old rose broadloom that my mother had chosen when they moved in from Manchester, when the cards were already on the table but she was still up to such choices – the weirdness, to me, that my mother had deliberately made it an old person's apartment, the colors and the furnishings saved from their house the ones most conducive to a powdery, grannyish atmosphere, as if, by doing so, she might will herself into old age (she wasn't then old; she wasn't old when she died), might keep herself going by simply setting the stage for keeping going – and always, when I spoke to him, I pictured him forlorn in this sea of pink and yellow, oblivious to it as he seemed to be. I told him something had come up; I intimated that it had to do with school. He tried to sound excited for me, thinking perhaps this might imply some professional advancement, while I tried to sound irritated about the obligation, as if I wanted nothing less than to go. We were both engaged in bonhomous deceit of such long standing that it was barely conscious; but surely he knew I wasn't sorry enough, and I knew that he was disappointed, and I'm ashamed to admit I was so excited that I didn't properly care.

There comes that time, that Lucy Jordan time, when your life looks small and all and always the same around you, and you don't think anything will change, you think that hope is not for you – and if you're me, then in that early period of awakening to your condition, you don't even feel angry. Dismayed, maybe; shocked; but that's just, it seems, what life is, a world in which the day's great excitement is the arrival of the Garnet Hill catalog that you will peruse in the bathroom, and where a triumph is when you take a long walk through the glorious snowbound cemetery after the first storm and somehow don't get lost among the dead, you find your mother's stone and kiss it, kiss her: that is a triumph. The stone leaves an icy taste upon your lips and your nose; and the sky, with its ridged clouds, is tinged with mauve. It's a far cry from the tony gatherings in the galleries of New York's Meatpacking District for which you once believed yourself destined; and while it is beautiful – grief, too, can be beautiful – this small triumph doesn't have about it any aspect of beginning. Let's just say that the open doors in graveyards aren't necessarily doors you want to enter.

But it looks – it is – as though that's what there is, Death or the Garnet Hill catalog, that cheery, flimsy distraction from Death; or in a pinch *Law & Order,* because on some station or other, at any time of day or night, you can find it – Detective Benson! Detective Stabler! My long lost! – and no longer be alone.

And then, suddenly, there's something else. When you least expect it. Suddenly there's an opportunity, an opening, a person or people you couldn't have imagined, and – elation! – it feels as though you've found the pot of gold, when you'd thought all the gilt was gone from this world forever. It's enough, for a time – maybe even for a long time – to make you forget that you were ever angry, that you ever knew what anger was at all.

When I went to college – to Middlebury, a small liberal arts institution known for its language studies, up in Vermont – I didn't major in Studio Art. There didn't seem much point in having gone to Middlebury for that. It was a battle, or rather, a discussion, I'd had with my parents before I chose the school. I'd applied to RISD, the art school in Providence, and to Pratt, in New York, as well as to traditional liberal arts colleges, and my parents had sat me down and told me they thought it would be a wasted opportunity if I went to study art. I wasn't surprised that this was my father's opinion; but I trusted my mother, so I listened to her.

'You'll do your art either way,' she said. 'Your art doesn't depend on a degree. To be honest, your art lives in a realm where degrees are meaningless.'

'Then why go to university at all? Why not just go and make art?'

'Look, Mouse' – my mother called me Mouse; nobody else did, not even my father, and when she lost her ability to talk I felt that she looked the word at me with her eyes – 'you're only sixteen years old. You're not old enough to vote, or to drink, or to sign a lease on an apartment. You're barely old enough to drive. You can go away to college or you can stay at home with us and make your art in the garage and scoop ice cream all day down the road. Your choice, but I know what I'd choose: get out of this stodgy little dump! See the world.'

'Why don't you, then?'

'Why don't I what?'

'Get out and see the world.'

'Oh, Mouse' – she stroked my hair, which was long then, so that stroking it meant caressing, too, the greater stretch of my back. Like a cat, rather than a mouse. I loved it. I loved being her child. I remember looking at her and thinking she was the most beautiful thing in the world. 'I've had my moment, sweetie. Maybe another will come. But for now, I'm needed right here.'

'Why?'

'Didn't you know, I make a house a home? That's what mothers do.'

'But I'll go and then—'

'I love your daddy. He needs a home, too.'

And then we were back to the college question, and it seemed that art school wasn't really a choice, because there wasn't any money – barely enough, even with loans, to get me to university at all – and it mattered to my mother that I be employable at the end.

'You're such a baby, you can go to art school afterward and still come out even. Get a master's in Painting on top of your B.A., and you'll be ready for all of it. I want you to have it all. It's not like when I was a girl, the MRS degree and all that. You won't live off pin money, off any man, no matter how much you love him. You won't depend on anyone but yourself. We agreed, right?' And there was that edge to her voice, which I thought of then as darkness, and recognize now as rage, the tone that came in her intermittent phases of despair. And so I went to Middlebury.

I always understood that the great dilemma of my mother's life had been to glimpse freedom too late, at too high a price. She was of the generation for which the rules changed halfway, born into a world of pressed linens and three-course dinners and hairsprayed updos, in which women were educated and then deployed for domestic purposes – rather like using an elaborately embroidered tablecloth on which to serve messy children their breakfast. Her University of Michigan degree was all but ornamental, and it always seemed significant that it stood in its frame under the eaves in the attic, festooned with dust bunnies, among a dozen disavowed minor artworks, behind boxes of discarded toys. The first woman in her family to go to college, she'd cared enough to frame her diploma, only then to be embarrassed about having cared, embarrassed because she felt she hadn't done anything with it, had squandered her opportunity.

The transition from pride to shame took place sometime soon after my birth, I think: I appeared in '67, and by 1970, her two closest friends in Manchester had divorced and moved away, reborn into the messy and not necessarily happier lives of the liberated. My brother was born in '59, when Bella Eldridge was but a tender twenty-three-year-old: he was what she did with her precious education.

As far as I could tell, she didn't burn over the consuming demands of motherhood the first time. In those days, all the young women around her were doing the same thing, discussing Jane Austen over coffee while their cloth-diapered brats wriggled around on the floor, the women themselves still almost students, glad to be absolved of worry about money and still blithe in their belief that life was long, would bring more to them than wall-to-wall carpet and a new Crock-Pot, with the occasional dinner at Locke-Ober or the Copley Plaza in Boston as an anniversary treat. She was young enough to be hopeful.

There are abundant home movies and antiquated slides of baby Matthew, with his slightly Frankensteinian square head and his bright blue eyes – he looks, somehow, like an infant of his time, has an all-American aspect that babies seem not to affect these days – and in the background, my mother grins, her face all angles, cigarette in hand. She grins at the swing set, she grins by the Christmas tree, she grins behind the picnic table, with its blue gingham cloth, on the Fourth of July.

In the later pictures, the few that remain of my own infancy, even the daylight looks darker. Maybe Kodak had changed their formula; or maybe the world had moved on. I was a smaller, more somber child, born three weeks early, weighing less than six pounds ('always impatient, that's my girl,' my father used to say), and with thick black hair that subsequently fell out and left me near bald for months. I look like a befuddled frog gussied up in pretty dresses, a fat foot peeking from beneath the hem, and my brother, a strapping eight-year-old with buckteeth, eyes me askance from the corners of the picture frames. My mother is hardly in these pictures at all, anywhere. She must have been taking them. There's one Christmas snapshot of the three of us, my father behind the camera: it was the year, she said, that Matthew and I both had the flu, and all of us have high color, cheeks like painted dolls', including my mother, whose long hair is a ratty mess, and whose dotted pinafore is falling off her shoulder. Perhaps because of the fevers, our eyes are forlorn – even Matt's eyes look black, and my mother's mouth is open in a half sneer, as though she were about to tell my father to cut it out and put the damn thing away.

I don't remember my early childhood as unhappy – to the contrary; the only thing I feared was my brother, who was pinching mean when he had the chance – but the record, such as it is, suggests that my mother was suffering. She was only thirty-one when I was born, but had done it all already once and

knew what she'd have to give, and knew, too, that like Sleeping
Beauty she'd waken from the baby dream to find that years had
elapsed, and herself pushing forty. No wonder she later threw
herself into her harebrained schemes – the cooking, the sewing,
the writing of children's books that nobody would publish, that
she didn't even really try to publish, all of them intended to cata-
pult her to something greater, to a world beyond Manchester, to
some early fantasy that lingered still at the corners of her eyes.
But when she signed up for classes – Mastering the Potter's
Wheel or Conversational French – it was hard to believe even
then that she took them seriously. The only paying job she ever
held when I was young was at the local bookstore over the holidays, when they took on extra staff – a couple of college kids and
my mom – for the Christmas rush. She did it several years running and grew adept at making pretty packages, with perfect
edges and curlicues of gilded ribbon.

She wasn't, in any practical way, ambitious. The friends she
had who were ambitious made their moves strategically, went
to law school at night, or studied for the realtor's exam, and
then they took steps away from the hearth, out into the world.
She both admired and resented them, the way plump women
both admire and resent their successfully dieting friends, trying,
all smiles, to force upon them a slab of chocolate cake. She
didn't keep close to the ones who went back to work, or who
divorced and moved into the city: she celebrated them with
lunches and sent them on their way, as if they were off on a
dangerous mission from which safe return was – as indeed it
was – impossible.

Do you remember the ladies' lunches of those days? The table
set first thing in the morning. Cold poached salmon and
Waldorf salad, pitchers of iced tea, sweating bottles of white
wine, everything served on the best china, and the ladies all still
there in a blue fog of cigarette smoke when I came home from

school, as though there were nothing, nothing to call them away. And the knowledge, which I had even then, that once they left the charmed circle, they were gone forever.

When I was about seven, in the week before Christmas – before, it must be said, the bookstore years; and it only now occurs to me that they were a direct result of this incident – my mother broke down in tears at the A&P, her face a map of blotches in the sallow supermarket light. I'd asked for something extra – a jar of chocolate Koogle, maybe, which the more indulgent mothers of the day allowed their children to take as school sandwiches, on white bread with butter: your dessert as a main course! The world gone haywire! – and her features crumpled.

'I'm so sorry,' she blathered, all moist and shamefully public, as I tried to push the cart along and her with it, and kept my eyes to the floor, 'but there's nothing for you or your brother. Nothing at all. I have nothing for you for Christmas. There's just no money left.' She let out a small wail; I cringed. 'I had to have the dishwasher fixed, and then that stone hit the windshield on the highway, and to replace the glass – it's all so expensive and you see, you see, there's nothing. And I can't ask your father. I can't ask him for more. So there's nothing for you at all. I am so sorry.' My mother, you understand, lived on an allowance from my father – or a salary, if you prefer: he had a bank account and she had a bank account, and each month he transferred a fixed sum from his account to hers, and with this sum she managed the household. She had spent the house-keeping money on housekeeping, and there was nothing left over for gifts. Even though I was still small, I understood the basics of this arrangement.

'It doesn't matter,' I said, trying to console without causing further embarrassment. 'I don't care about presents.' Although I did care, and was disappointed, not least because I was still supposed to believe in Santa Claus, and this outburst seemed like the Wizard of Oz emerging from behind his curtain, an unconscionable breach of propriety and of our necessary hypocrisies. 'Really,' I said again, 'it doesn't matter.'

And suddenly, then – inexplicably to me as I was, but in a way so obvious to me now – she turned viperish, rageful, a temper as shameful in the A&P as her earlier tears. 'Don't ever get yourself stuck like this,' she hissed. 'Promise me? Promise me now?'

'I promise.'

'You need to have your own life, earn your own money, so you're not scrounging around like a beggar, trying to put ten dollars together for your kids' Christmas presents. Leeching off your father's – or your husband's – pathetic paycheck. Never. Never. Promise me?'

'I already promised.'

'Because it's important.'

'I know.'

And that was an end to it. She'd dried up and put on her sunny smile by the time we reached the checkout, the only sign of her distress a slight smearing of her mascara. We were served by Sadie, the daughter of my old first-grade teacher, a girl who spoke very loudly and slowly as if she, or we, were deaf. She wore her brown hair in a single pigtail on one side of her head and it looked like the handle of an old-fashioned water pump.

'Mrs Eldridge,' she bawled. 'So good to see you! As always!'

'You too, Sadie, dear.'

'Looking forward to the holidays?'

'You bet! Isn't it the best time of year?'

'The best. I love it. Don't you love it, Nora?'

I was too busy watching my mother to answer. As she stacked the groceries on the conveyor belt there was an expression of such impassioned nostalgia on her face that she looked like a Norman Rockwell portrait. I could see her genuinely believing what she'd told Sadie, believing that it was the best time of year. Someone else had wept and yelled at me minutes before, and Bella Eldridge would never have recognized her.

⌒

My mother wasn't a weeper and I rarely saw her cry; but there was one other instance of impromptu tears that has stayed with me. It was just before Matt went off to college – in the summertime, because I remember we were freezing in the air-conditioning at the Hunan Gourmet. My brother was surly, wishing himself already gone. My father, typically mild, was oblivious to the tension at the table, to my mother's tight brightness and her habit, throughout the meal, of reaching for Matt's sleeve and then pulling back before she touched him, a ghostly sort of tic. It seemed as though I was the only one watching, the only one who could see the four of us in our leatherette armchairs, leaning over the soy-spattered synthetic tablecloth (it rucked with every human movement, then slid oilily back into place), father and son chatting in a desultory way about the upcoming football season and how my brother would have to throw his heart behind the Notre Dame team, now that he was going there, all the way to Indiana. My mother, who loathed sports, kept trying to change the subject, picking at possible threads (the campus? The journey? Matt's friend Busby's choice of Bowdoin?) like a glassy-eyed magpie: thwarted, persistent, quick. It was an evening in which I said nothing – it was like that with our family, because Matthew and I had so little relation to one another beyond his occasional insult or a quietly hostile tousling of my hair. Even when we were all four together, our parents were being either his parents or mine, in one mode or the other, able to deal adequately with only one of us, two children who merely happened to share the same accursèd progenitors. And that Hunan Gourmet outing was a Matthew Eldridge night.

It was the fortune cookie that felled my mother. Mine said simply 'Hallelujah!,' and Matt's promised, 'A short vacation is in order for you.' My father's told us, 'It isn't our position, but our disposition, that makes us happy' – and if my mother had gotten that one, things probably would have been fine. But my mother's fortune read: 'It is what you haven't done that will torment you' – which I knew only because I picked it up off the floor on the way out. When she read it, she gave a little cry, as if wounded, and crumpled and chucked it, and then became very silent, and for the last ten minutes of the meal I watched the tears trickle unacknowledged out of the corners of her eyes and down her cheeks, and I watched the tremor of her lower lip, and I watched my brother and my father throw themselves the more valiantly into the football conversation (Matt even dropped his surliness, animated in his effort) so as to pretend, altogether, that everything was fine. Nobody said anything to my mother; nobody even asked what her fortune had been. Only on the way out of the restaurant my father put his hand on Matt's shoulder and murmured, in the bluff, confidential tone of manhood at that time, 'Be good to your mother these last few days. It's hard for her that you're going.' And I, all of eight, wondered briefly whether Notre Dame involved danger, like going to Vietnam (my friend Sheila's cousin had been killed there a couple of years before, and the older brother of a boy in my class had come back not right in the head), but didn't ask.

Over the years I've tried to understand my mother's emotion at that moment – regret about an unconsummated love affair? Her own Lucy Jordan moment? Simple sadness at my brother's departure, and thoughts of all the things that now would be forever unsaid? – but all I know is that I'll never know. I decided, for a long time, that it had to do with the ending of a maternal

role, with the painful knowledge of all she'd sacrificed to raise
him, when now she was handing off her son to the world. But
more recently, I've thought that maybe it was about an unconsummated love affair after all, maybe about a flirtatious exchange
with a stranger in a train station, or an unanswered letter from
a college sweetheart, one of those secret moments when you
think that now your life will have to change, only it doesn't.
Something small but big that she regretted and that tormented
her each day. With my children, I've discovered over the years
that the simplest explanation is almost always the right one; and
that hunger of one kind or another – desire, by another name –
is the source of almost every sorrow.

While I could have, I never asked her. She might not even
have remembered crying in the Hunan Gourmet, as I'm sure she
wouldn't have remembered crying in the A&P. When she got her
diagnosis – and with it the promise of infinite torment, of so
many things she would never, never again do – she didn't shed
a tear. It was a sorrow without expression. For months she'd had
a twitch in her left hand, and thought it was nerves. She'd shown
it to me at the kitchen table when I was over for supper – the
house so quiet by then, almost vast in its quiet, no Matthew, no
me, no Ziggy or Sputnik, the hallways dark outside the kitchen's
pool of light, broken only by the distant glimmer of my father's
reading lamp in the gloom of the living room – how could a
body spend so much time reading *The New York Times*? – and
had said, with her sharp laugh, 'Just look at that! It comes and
goes. My hand with a mind of its own. It thinks it's smarter than
I am. Getting older stinks.'

'You should ask Dr. Selby about that,' I said, but in an offhand
way, because although I saw the twitch, the ripple of the muscles
of her fingers, it seemed that because it was part of her body, my
mother's body, and because we could see it, that it had to be some
version of normal. Besides which, I was busy pouring myself a

second preprandial glass of pinot grigio, because by that time I
found that if I didn't, the darkness of the house seeped into my
bones like damp, and chilled me for days afterward. I was about
thirty, then, and my mother was sixty-one, my father just past
sixty-five, a few months into his retirement, and now that their
ages don't seem so very far away, I marvel at all they seemed
already to have renounced. But it was the isolation, the crippling
boredom of it, that got me. Pinot grigio helped, and pinot noir
too. Even a beer, if that was all they offered. So I wasn't paying
the proper attention. She must have shown my father too, and
presumably he looked up from his newspaper and said much the
same thing as I did in the same distracted way, and because of this
she did nothing about it, didn't visit or speak to Dr. Selby for the
better part of a year after that, by which time the fasciculation,
as it's properly known, had spread to her feet as well, though not,
still, to her right – her writing – hand, because that would've sent
her doctorward pronto. And by the time they started the tests –
the electrodiagnostics and the spinal tap and the muscle biopsy
and the whole nine yards – she was scared, not least because she
could see that Dr. Selby was scared. For all her smiling
hypocrisies, she was very honest, my mother, and she said to me,
'I wanted him to reassure me, and when I saw he wasn't going to,
I thought, This is when the shit hits the fan.'

When they finally made the diagnosis – it took a while, a lot
of eliminating of other possibilities – maybe she already knew.
And the diagnosis – ALS, aka Lou Gehrig's, aka Stephen
Hawking's disease – was really simply the confirmation that she
was dying, which of course we all are, only that henceforth she'd
be dying more swiftly and efficiently, more horribly than most,
although mercifully without pain, her body no longer a temple
but a prison, one closing door after another, until she was con-
fined inside her mind – a room, it is true, with no walls, but
ultimately with no doors, either.

What was fascinating to me, and instructive, because I was still learning, as I am still learning, how to live, was that she did not, upon her diagnosis, jump up and cry, 'Let's visit Burma! The Taj Mahal! The pyramids! The pampas!' – all the places she'd always longed to go. Nor did she proceed upon a sayonara tour to bid good-bye to the lakes in Maine, the winter beach at Wellfleet where my parents liked to mark their anniversary by walking in the white and fog, the room at the Pierre in New York where they'd spent the weekend of her fiftieth birthday and had – sin of luxury! – breakfast in bed. Nor did she turn her back on all of it, leave the dishes unwashed in the sink, the clothes piling up in the basket, the lawn unmowed. No, she kept living as though nothing had changed. No: she simply kept living. She knew everything had changed: she oversaw the cleaning and the packing and the sale of the Manchester house, a task for which my father (he could never have been any good at business, could he?) proved useless; and she pushed him until they found the place in Brookline, and she decorated it, as I've said, as though she would see her ninety-sixth birthday there. She kept reading mystery stories, and she kept buying the same Danish pastries from the Swiss bakery, for as long as she was able, and she took each blow – the cane, the wheelchair, the obscene rounds of medication, the Darth Vader breathing machine – as though they were so many gnats to be swatted at, and then ignored.

By all of this, I could only surmise that she loved her life. She loved it as it was. Like a Zen master, she reduced to the essences: I do not need to walk around the Museum of Fine Arts; I do not need to be pushed around the MFA in a chair; I do not need the MFA at all, because its treasures, as I love them, are imprinted in my memory; and if they are wrongly memorized – a lily where there are tulips, the boy's torn hat rakish at the wrong angle – then this only makes the pictures the more mine. They may offer the ancient Egyptian portrait of a young woman, her black almondine eyes a marvel, on extended loan, but to me she hangs always in the gallery behind the mummies, surrounded by shards of pottery and antique jewels, a secret for my own heart.

But can I say, now that she is dead, long dead, that I only half believed in her? I wanted – I needed – her to revolt. I know, revolutions take vast energy, like volcanic eruptions, I know. And the sick must husband their resources (even as they are resourceful for their husbands). But I couldn't help wanting for her, couldn't help the feeling that she'd given in, that she had measured out (with coffee spoons?) what it was that she might ask of life, and having found it lacking – tragically, gapingly lacking – had decided nevertheless to accept her modest share. I wanted her ignoble, irresponsible, unreasonable, petty, grasping, fucking greedy for the lot of it, jostling and spitting and clawing for every grain of life. And I never loved her more than the day I came to see her, bedridden, sallow, grandiose only in her wheezes, I with the whiff of autumn on me and the glow – I could feel it – of having run the miles from my apartment to theirs on a crisp late October afternoon – and she glared at me and set her jaw and said, 'Get out. I can't. Get out. But never for a second think I don't remember what it's like. Don't think, either, that I can help hating you for it. Just right now.'

And I did get out – the overheating on top of the run had the sweat almost coursing down my back – and I ran all the way home again in the dusk, too cold, too tired, my feet aching on the pavement, my eyes and nose streaming from the wind and her meanness – how could she be so mean to me, of all people? – but by the time I got home I was, even in my self-pity, rejoicing: because for once she threatened not to go gently. For once, she threatened.

She called to apologize the same evening. My father must

have dialed; she couldn't anymore, then. I was going to punish her, and let the machine take it, but her voice was so small that I picked up halfway through.

'Never let the sun go down on an argument,' she said.

'Because one of us might die in the night,' I said, as I'd replied since I was small. But this time, she laughed, a dry, sad laugh. 'One of us just might, Mouse.'

8

It took my mother years to die. It's a hard art to master. During the time that she was dying, I was trying to figure out how to live. How to live my own life, that is. I knew it wasn't right that when asked how I was, I invariably spoke about my mother. Or my father. I had to try, and I did try, to overcome this, to get a life, or two, or three. I'd already come back to Boston from New York for the course at the Museum School; I'd already tried and almost given up the notion of being a self-supporting artist. There was something about turning thirty that made the apartment-share in Jamaica Plain, the sweaty bike messenger housemate, friend of a friend's ex-boyfriend, with his equipment always blocking the hallway, the intermittent babysitting gigs, slightly too close to unbearable. I'd started the Education degree before my mother got her diagnosis. I was already – mercifully to my parents, I could tell – on my way back to gainful employment.

Even as I was taking care of my parents, I got very good at practical things over those few years, like the most competent secretaries. I lived multiple lives: in the first, I had every appearance of a modestly accomplished young woman in her early thirties, capable if not interesting, easy to get on with, prompt, efficient, with unnoticeable clothes and a serviceable hairstyle, and a voice a bit higher, perhaps a bit breathier, I was told, than one was led to expect by my frame. A woman without notable surprises.

But my first life was a masquerade, my Clark Kent life, though in my second I was not a heroine at all. I sometimes hoped that someone out there imagined for me a second life of glamour and drama, as a rock star's mistress, or an FBI agent. But I wasn't the sort of person for whom anyone would bother imagining a secret life; and in that second life I was no lover or huntress or martyr, but a daughter, just a dutiful daughter.

Then there was my third life, small and secret: the life of my dioramas, the vestiges of my artist self.

You could say that my mother and father, grateful as they manifestly were, didn't ask me to give up my life. And if I chose to, though I can't see the logic of my own choice, I'd like to believe it was a purposeful choice and not simply a show of poor time management. A good number of my children are bad at time management. You see it a lot. But you can't succeed in life unless you get good at it: there's no point writing the world's best answer to the first question on the test, if you don't then leave yourself enough time to write any answers at all to the other questions. You still fail the test. And I worry, in my bleaker hours, that this is what I've done. I answered the dutiful daughter question really well; I was aware of doing only a so-so job on the grown-up career front, but I didn't really care, because there were two big exam questions I wanted to be sure I answered fully: the question of art, and the question of love.

This was the miracle of my first Shahid year. Never, in all my life, had I thought, as I did then, *This is the answer.* Not once, but over and over in different configurations, the answer to not one but to every question seemed to come in the course of that year, like music. 'On me your voice falls, as they say love should – like an enormous "yes."' Philip Larkin on Sidney Bechet: a love poem that is not a love poem. And my love life that was not a love life, but something as consuming, as formidable, as whole.

My mother was only two years dead, that fall. It felt like an immense distance then, but now, in time's accordion folds, the two events – my mother, unable even to move her head, wheezing in her elephantine breathing machine, sliding her eyes to the light, then closing them a final time; Reza at the supermarket, leaning over the bench to laugh at my spilled apples (who has upset the apple cart? I have, I have!) – seem almost contiguous. As my wise friend Didi has more than once observed about life's passages, every departure entails an arrival elsewhere, every arrival implies a departure from afar. My mother left here for an unknown there; and then Reza and Sirena and Skandar came to me.

9

The studio Sirena had found was deep inside Somerville, in a former warehouse, all brick and windows, abutting a largely disused railroad track and separated from it by a black stretch of garbage-strewn tarmac and a high chicken-wire fence, in which fluttered the tattered remnants of plastic bags, like flags of the apocalypse. Next door stood a functioning factory that produced millions of tiny Styrofoam beads, a particularly noxious undertaking that seemed destined to cause horrible cancers in those who worked there. Its chimneys blew clouds of chemical fumes into the neighborhood air, on account of which the insides of the studios harbored a lingering tang of melted plastic.

The building was a sprawling four-floor warren of such studios, some tiny, carved up by plywood and nails, and some vast, unspoiled. At the stairwell of each floor hung a huge mottled door, on rollers, like a giant's door, sealable with a great metal bolt. These doors gave me the creeps: they, the creaking floors, the padlocked cubicles, enclosures hiding who knew what – possibly paints or jigsaws or sewing machines, but just as possibly acid baths or ax murderers. Who knew what violence could take place down the alley by the train tracks on a Sunday night? Even by day, the building looked abandoned.

Following Sirena and the toothless real estate agent to the third floor – I'd never seen a realtor so battered by life as Eddie Roy, a lanky, greasy-haired man in his late sixties, only two steps from the homeless shelter – I felt nothing but misgivings: the whiff of burning plastic with an undertone of mouse, or rat; the trippable hollows in the steps from decades of trudging feet; the dim, high bulbs shedding light like dust in the corridors; the spatter and rattle of the rain upon the windows and the windows in their ancient sockets, surely like the rattling of the agent's teeth before they fell – it was all of a bleakness unimagined. I marveled that Sirena didn't seem to notice, and more than that, she seemed actually excited, her crinkled eyes glittering.

'I hope you'll like it too,' she confided, her hand again lightly on my arm, apparently unaware of my discomfort. 'It is perfect.'

And once Eddie Roy fumbled the padlock at the end of the dank hall, I could see straight away that she was right. It was – even for two; especially for two – perfect. The space, L-shaped, was vast, the ceilings easily fourteen feet high. It had windows, huge, paned, smeared, wet windows, along both sides, windows with deep ledges and loose sashes – but somehow, in this room filled with white light even on that dark fall Saturday, unlike in the scary stairwell, the rattling sounds seemed alive, exciting, like the building breathing. The wood floors, scored and beaten, were beautiful, big enough to skate on. A filthy utility sink hung in the corner of the L, a long paint-spattered metal table beside it. Aside from this, the room, like an enormous, perfect incubator, was empty.

'Yes' was all I could say, and Eddie Roy grinned, revealing his dark gums.

The rent was a stretch, but I didn't pause to worry about it then. I didn't stop to question why Sirena wanted me there – that hers was quite possibly a mercenary invitation, a matter merely of halving the cost; that she may even have imagined our paths would barely cross. I saw the light and the space and felt the auguries gathered for me, to bring me back to life, back to my art. I didn't ask myself if I needed the studio, if I would use it; I blocked from my mind the filthy alley, the echoing stairwell, the smell. All I could think was 'Yes, yes, yes.'

We signed the lease by five o'clock, at Eddie Roy's cinder-block office next to the chicken shop on Highland Avenue. It was again dark, and drizzling still, but we stood hatless on the pavement for a bit, each holding our new keys, and Sirena gave me a sudden hug, in the course of which I took in a mouthful of her hair, and had awkwardly to disentangle myself.

'For me,' she said, 'I know this will change everything. Who knows? Maybe I'll even make Wonderland here.'

'Why not?'

'It's my next project. Before we knew we would come here. I was planning it for months. Alice through the looking-glass, you know?'

'Through the looking-glass – like being in the Fun House. I know,' I said.

'What will you do?'

'I don't know yet. But I'll be doing.'

That night I went to dinner at Didi and Esther's place in Jamaica Plain. Didi and I had been in art classes together in college, but we really became friends years later when I moved back to Boston. She was – she is – almost six feet tall, Amazonian, but soft. Her skin has no lumps or pores and her hair is like an amber cloud. She wears crimson lipstick. When

I was at the Museum School, we'd walk around the pond together and play pool until late at the Milky Way and complain about our lives. Recently divorced from her college boyfriend, she was working at the BU radio station, but she chucked it in when she turned thirty-one to open a vintage clothing store on Centre Street, not far from the animal hospital. She met Esther – who is very small and high-strung, with curly dark hair and eyes like a pug – when Esther was trying on fifties party frocks to wear to her brother's wedding in Colorado. When Didi first spoke of her, she said Esther looked like Betty Boop. Esther is an oncologist at MGH, a breast cancer specialist, and it always surprises me how happy they are together because they are so different. Didi is more comfortable in her skin than anybody else I've ever known, and I've always felt that being friends with her makes me closer to the person I imagine myself to be: someone who doesn't care about all the wrong things, like money or fashion or status, but who ferrets out the genuinely interesting. And while I've grown to be very fond of Esther, who is spiky and crossish in a bracing way, I do think she cares about that stuff, even cares a lot, whereas I wonder whether Didi is even really aware of it.

When she lived on her own, Didi's apartment was decorated with posters from Godard films and chili pepper Christmas lights around the mantelpiece, and all the furniture had been salvaged and restored by her own hand. Her coffee table was a giant wooden bobbin for telephone cables that she'd picked out of the dump and painted bright orange. But once she and Esther set up house, all of that was gone. It was all Saarinen this and Eames that, stainless steel and granite, and their condo was beautiful but it looked like a boutique hotel, like nobody really lived there.

At least once they had Lili, she made it messy. Lili is their daughter, adopted from China. She's tiny, like Esther, and round-faced, with skinny brown limbs; and quiet, but naughty, in a good way. Lili was about four then, and still young enough to love her mothers' friends as if they were her own, and when I came in the door she grabbed me by the hand and said, 'Come see my world, Nora! I've made a world!'

I spent the evening's first twenty minutes cross-legged underneath a table on their enclosed summer porch, helping Lili feed gingerbread and cold tea, served in perfect tiny china cups, to an array of stuffed animals: an elephant in a Batman costume, a rabbit, a duck, even an iridescent armadillo. With Didi's help, she'd hung a paisley blanket over the table to make a tent, and the light filtered through purple and speckled. She'd denuded sofas and beds of cushions and pillows to pad it out, and had propped up a couple of framed photographs – Didi and Esther at a party; Esther pushing Lili on a swing in winter – against the table legs. She'd dressed her animals in colorful scarves and positioned her dolls so they looked in animated conversation.

It occurred to me, not for the first time, that Lili's world was not so different from my dioramas, or even from Sirena's installations: you took a tiny portion of the earth and made it yours, but really what you wanted was for someone else – ideally, a grown-up, because a grown-up matters, has authority, but is also not the same as you – to come and see, to get it, and thereby, somehow, to get *you;* and all of this, surely, so that you might ultimately feel less alone on the planet. And what was also true was that I was happy to be in Lili's hidden lair – more than happy, I was honored – but after a few minutes I wanted to get out of it. I wanted to lift the blanket and climb back into the room and stretch my limbs and leave the dollies and their crumbs and their thimble-cups of cold tea (with milk, if you please) behind, and go back to my grown-up friends and their conversation. For fifteen of the twenty minutes I stayed in there, I was humoring her.

And this was why, I told myself, I didn't want to show my art to anyone, even though showing it had always, from the beginning, been a large part of the point: I didn't want to show it because I didn't want to be humored. I didn't want anybody to feel they had to say nice things, or say anything at all, because I could tell when they were fake, I could always tell, and I hated it. I didn't want anybody to tell me it wasn't any good – just as Lili would have been shocked if I'd said such a thing to her: these were not the terms of her world at all – and I didn't particularly want anyone to tell me it *was* good, either. I just wanted to be *got*, and I didn't trust that I would be.

Only now – and I felt for my new key in the pocket of my pants – now I'd set myself up to be got or not got regardless. Sometimes Sirena would be in the studio when I wasn't there. She'd be able to look at, to touch, my dioramas, to snoop and pry. And would it be better if she chose not to? It seemed like leaving my body – or maybe my spirit? – on a table in a room for anyone's scrutiny, as if it were just a thing.

'Come out now, Nora.' Esther lifted the fringed blanket, and all I could see of her against the light was her pug eyes. 'Time to join the land of the living. Supper's ready.'

Lili protested.

'Yours too, little miss. Time to come out. You have till the count of three to wash your hands.'

Lili scrambled. Since she was small, it was easy for her. Esther gave me a hand getting up, and patted me on the back when I stood, as though I'd accomplished something.

'You seem very jolly.' Didi ladled the fish stew into bowls. There was macaroni and cheese and carrot sticks for Lili, who swung her legs against the chair and chewed with her mouth open before the grown-ups had even been served. I quelled my teacherly impulse to offer correction.

'I am jolly,' I said. 'I've rented a studio.'

'Wow.' Didi put down her ladle, sat back in her chair. 'That's news.'

'But what do you need it for?' Esther realized as soon as she said this that I might take it the wrong way, which I did. 'I mean, don't you have a studio at home?'

'I have a second bedroom,' I said. 'This is a studio.'

'That's fantastic.' Didi leaned forward again and passed the bowls around. 'I think that's fantastic.' She looked at me properly. 'So tell us how this came about. It seems . . . quick? Maybe that's why E is surprised.'

So I told them about Sirena – first about Reza, and then about Sirena. I didn't say anything about how she gave me butterflies, how our meeting had seemed full of import, how exhilarating it had been to discover that she, too, made art – I didn't say any of it, but I had the strange experience while telling the story of hearing my own voice talking, and I was aware that I couldn't modulate it properly, that my volume and my intonation were awry – too loud, too eager, too much information. It was like the moment after a few glasses of wine when you hear yourself slur your words and you wonder whether anyone else is paying sufficient attention to have noticed.

This time, though, I didn't have to wonder. When Esther took Lili to bed, Didi summoned me out onto the balcony and lit a joint. The rain had finally stopped, but all the downspouts were dripping. The trees in the yard glistened in the dark.

'Tell me,' she said, holding the smoke in her lungs and passing the joint over. 'What is this actually about, for you?'

'What do you mean?'

She exhaled. 'This whole thing, it's not only about the studio. I mean, it's fabulous, it's delicious about the studio. It's the best decision you've made in years. But you'd made up your mind before you went there, hadn't you?'

I thought for a moment. 'I guess I had.'

'So it's not about the actual studio.'

'Then what's it about?'

'That's what I'm asking you.'

I shrugged, and laughed. I couldn't say. There were not words to describe it; and no way, had there been the words, of not revealing too much. Even with Didi, I didn't want to reveal too much. 'I'm excited. Does it matter?'

She took another toke, narrowed her eyes. 'We'll have to wait and see, I guess.'

10

Remember this season. This dinner, this day, the signing of the lease, took place on the Saturday before the presidential election: John Kerry versus Dubya, in Dubya's Round Two. This was the fall of 2004. The wider world was deeply fucked, and home also. Two American wars raging – bloodbaths each, bloodbath major and bloodbath minor, ugly, squirrelly hateful clandestine wars marked by betrayal, incompetence and corruption. Don't get me started.

We'd had a young woman, a girl really, only twenty-five, come to the school the year before to speak about her NGO – she'd set it up herself, this frilly slip of a thing with her denim mini-skirt and her silver-blue eye shadow, she'd lobbied Congress and gotten millions to do it, God knows how, barely out of college, and its purpose, to count the civilian casualties, seemed such a sane and good thing to do. She spoke about it for the kids in a very gentle way, in her high and breathy voice, about how she wanted to help everybody who got hurt, Iraqis the same as Americans, and that if you didn't keep track, some folks might get forgotten. We had only the fifth and sixth graders go hear her, even so, because her job was counting bodies, basically, and however bright a gloss you put on that, you can't go frightening the tinies and giving them nightmares. I thought it was pretty brave of Shauna to have her at all, but I guess she was the niece of someone on the school board, and she actually visited three schools that fall before she went away.

I couldn't see how this kid could count for much, and then a couple of months later she was on the evening news, on CNN, in a headscarf with a clipboard and no eye shadow at all, and she was for real, and sober and impressive and she didn't even say 'like' once, and she was telling terrible stories about the numbers of Iraqis – children, families, old women – whose injuries and deaths were not being officially reported, but she was going door to door with her clipboard and with a dozen others she'd recruited, and they were doing damn good work.

And it was only about four months later that she was in the news again, *The New York Times* this time, a headline, small, right on the front and a picture on the fifth page, but with the eye shadow again, a picture taken before she went, obviously; and she was there because she and her translator had been in a car following an armored convoy on the infamous road to the airport, and some motherfucker blew them up with a rocket. And it said in the article (I will always remember this) that the last thing she said, when the soldiers came rushing to help her charred and seeping tender self splayed in the dust by the side of the road outside Baghdad, the last thing she said before she died was 'I am alive.' She was twenty-six.

But she *was* alive, of course, she'd been more alive in that short space than many are in a lifetime; and then she was dead. I took the article to show Shauna, who gets only *The Boston Globe*, but the news had been in *The Globe*, too. We didn't tell the kids, so one or two of them probably still sometimes think of her out there, counting the hurt and the dead, of whom there are still so many and whom she would be counting if she were still alive to count.

That's what that time was like. And yet, through November, I greeted each morning as though it were spring, as though instead of a daily darkening, both seasonal and societal, we were embarked upon a brilliant new adventure, finding each new day more perfectly illuminated than the last. Which I was.

It was like being eleven, and craving your best friend's company. If I woke up every morning with such zeal, every leaf or cup or child's hand meticulously outlined for me like a wonder of nature, bathed in superior light, it was because in my heart I held each day the possibility of a conversation, of adventure, with Sirena. This possibility – often a likelihood – was inextricably bound up with the excitement of the studio, of the pure, bright, drafty, shabby space where we would meet.

She spent entire days there, while I trailed in near dusk, at three thirty or so, when the angle of the sunlight was long and the air powdery, already tinged with night, a bleak and glorious winter light. We'd have coffee: along with jewel-colored lengths of Indian silk that she'd pinned to the walls in her end of the studio, a grubby rug, three small tufted poufs and a tiny Moroccan brass tray table, Sirena had installed a burner on the long table, and had provided an Italian percolator, the heavy octagonal kind that sits upon the stove, and an array of chipped teacups from the Goodwill shop. She had the gift of making things beautiful, and comfortable too, in an easy way, a gift I'd thought of as my mother's, growing up. I loved that the studio, while still Spartan, gestured in its few furnishings toward an Oriental souk. I even loved, when I went to find it empty, that she'd left dirty cups scattered about, ringed with tarry coffee grounds, and smearily marked by her crimson lipstick; and often a scarf or a sweater forgotten on the floor, as if she were saying to me, 'Don't worry, I'll be right back.'

I took to bringing snacks – scones from the Hi-Rise, or cup-cakes from the then-new shop in Davis Square, a quick stop on Highland Ave on my way to the studio – and she'd break from her work to boil the coffee, and we'd hang out and talk for three-quarters of an hour or so, until she'd stand, quite suddenly, and brush at a few nonexistent crumbs, and say '*au travail*' – which even with my pitiful French I could understand and came to expect. Then I'd wash the coffee cups and she'd sweep the floor, in two or three brisk strokes, and turn her back to me, retreat-ing to her corner of the L. I, too, would go to my corner, feeling slightly like a dog dismissed to its basket, and turn on my bright lights over the table I'd set up, and, fed on cakes and con-versation, I would work, as the night fell around us, until there was only my pool of light and her pool of light and the music from the CD player hovering softly in the vast dark space between us.

At around five thirty or a quarter to six, she'd pack up her gear and go home to Maria the babysitter and to Reza and, notion-ally, to Skandar, although for months he remained a cipher to me, heard only as the murmur on the cell phone when she spoke quietly and rapidly and, I always imagined, with faint irritation, in French.

I loved working with someone else nearby. It was like being in Mr Crace's art room all over again. What I hated – although never straight away – was the time after Sirena had gone.

For a while, I'd be so busy with the scene I was working on that I didn't notice. That fall I was making a tiny replica of Emily Dickinson's Amherst bedroom, about the size of a boot box, each floorboard in place, the re-creation of her furnishings exact and to scale. Once I'd made her room, and made *her*, as perfectly as I could, in a white linen nightie with ruffles, my aim was to set up circuitry so that my Emily Dickinson might be visited, sit-ting up in her bed, by floating illuminations – the angelic Muse, her beloved Death, and of course my tiny gilded mascot, Joy herself.

This was, I imagined, the first of a series: I wanted to make one of Virginia Woolf at Rodmell, putting rocks in her pockets and writing her final note: my idea was that there would be slides of the river, raging, and sound effects, too; and an actual copy of the handwritten note that would project not onto the diorama wall but out Virginia's bedroom window, onto our walls outside, so that instead of being small, the words would be huge. In my mind's eye, they would flicker: the flickering was, to me, very important.

Then there was to be one of the painter Alice Neel, in the sanatorium to which she was sent after her nervous breakdown at around the age of thirty. I wanted there to be an echo, you see, between Emily Dickinson's spare white room and Alice Neel's white room, the monastic and the asylum: both retreats, but of such different types. And both the province of women. I even thought about the title of my nonexistent series: *A Room of One's Own?* I thought the question mark was the key.

I loved the story of Alice Neel, in part because her life was so hard and bitter but turned out all right in the end, and in part because her art, like mine, was resolutely unfashionable for almost all of her life, and because of that she had to know why she was doing it and why she kept doing it to the last. She was the AFH: the Anti-Fun-House. I was bound to love her for that.

The last diorama I planned was to be the opposite of the others. It was going to be Edie Sedgwick's room in Warhol's Factory. Instead of trying to escape the world, Edie sacrificed herself to it. She existed only in the public gaze. Imagine that: a surface, so beautiful, from which all depth has been erased. But then, the photos, their intensity, her vitality – it certainly looks as though a soul was trapped behind those eyes.

Edie was essential. I'd spent a chunk of my adolescence in

thrall to Edie Sedgwick, in love with the insect limbs in their black tights, and the giant eyes, and the stares, even though she was already long dead in my day. She was the cool people's Marilyn Monroe – smaller, faster, brighter, more immediately alive, and more efficiently dead, an anorexic slip of a life, with no more known interiority than a dachshund. Yet if, when I was sixteen and on my way to college, you'd asked me whether I wanted to be Georgia O'Keeffe or Edie Sedgwick, I would definitely have hesitated. And I might have said Sedgwick. She'd defined something, we said back then.

But the point is that I was consumed – in a digressive, obliterating way – by my hypothetical series, and by my Emily Dickinson diorama in the first instance, by its practical minutiae. I had paintbrushes comprised of a single hair, and a loupe like a watchmaker's that I could attach to my forehead, and I'd spend three days on a miniature replica of the woodcut landscape that hung between the windows in Emily's bedroom, only to decide, once it was done, that the likeness was poor, and that I needed to begin again.

Hours and hours and hours of dollhouse labor, and I loved it, was lost in it like one of my children. But when Sirena left me, sooner or later I'd look up from my table and realize that I was alone in a tiny pool of light in a great dark room, as if I were myself the figure in someone else's diorama, manipulated in my own stage set by a giant I could not see. Once aware of my isolation, I was afraid not of it but of its interruption: I'd walk to the windows and peer into the night, trying to make sure I wasn't being watched; I'd stand at the studio door, listening for movement in the hallways, or in the neighboring rooms. If there were footsteps or clamor, I was reassured if they were loud, as though the faceless were announcing themselves; happier still when there were voices or, as sometimes, a distant radio; but if the sounds were muffled, muted, intermittent, my heart seized, and I feared that the hooded villain of my nightmares was lurking in the stairwell awaiting my departure.

Sometimes I could get over it, force myself back to my table, my Lilliputian world, and lose myself again; but on other evenings – particularly if the weather was silent, no rattling, no rain, no sounds at all but those around me – I'd succumb to my terrors, packing up in haste and banging at top volume through the building, down the hallway, down the stairs and out, always surprised by the softness of the streetlights, the bland calm of the road outside the warehouse.

11

I discovered that I wanted to work, much more than I'd ever realized, but I didn't want to work alone. The paradox was perfect: I didn't want to work alone and yet could only do my work alone. What possible answer could there be to my dilemma? Sirena. Sirena was my answer.

I tried, then, on Tuesdays, when the children had science with Estelle at the end of the day, and on Thursdays, when they had PE last thing, to escape to the studio forty minutes earlier. Once I forgot a staff meeting, and got a puzzled rebuke from Shauna: 'Is everything okay?' she asked. 'Because this isn't like you.'

'Isn't it?' I said. 'I'm beginning to wonder.'

'Don't make me worry about you, Nora,' Shauna said, and while she acted concerned I could tell from her tone she meant it. People don't want to worry about the Woman Upstairs. She's reliable, and organized, and she doesn't cause any trouble.

'Never been better,' I said, and meant it also. On those Tuesdays and Thursdays I had almost an extra hour of company while I worked; and Sirena was glad of my presence too, I could tell by the way she gathered her scarves around her and drifted toward me, even if I did no more than say hello. She'd ask about Reza, or about the other children, whose characters she came to know from my stories, or about finding a good local shoemaker, or whatever it was – and we'd be talking then, and also working or preparing to, and we'd have our coffee with the afternoon before us – it was only two thirty, on those days – and I could barely keep from grinning. Who cared about Shauna McPhee?

Occasionally, Sirena would come to my end of the studio and lean over Emily Dickinson's room. She always behaved as though it were new to her, as though this was something she never did when I wasn't there.

'It's really coming along,' she'd say, with an intake of breath, running a tentative finger along a wall's top edge. Or she'd point to the photos and postcards of the actual room spread out on my table and say, 'Wow, you've got it exactly' or 'How are you going to do that piece, then?'

I'd worried about her judging me, but it never felt that way. It felt as though she was curious, plain and simple, because she was curious about me. Because she liked me. One afternoon when she was passing me my coffee, she put her hand not on my arm but on my hand. 'My God, you know, it's great that you're here,' she said. 'I might go crazy without you.'

'To friendship.' I raised my chipped cup.

'Yes, to friendship.'

'We're both lucky, you know,' I told her. 'This is such a gift for me. Even if I'm getting into trouble.'

'How do you mean?'

I told her about missing the staff meeting, and Shauna's annoyance. 'But it doesn't matter,' I said, 'because I'm here with you.'

And then I felt I'd sounded too eager, too needy. I could feel myself blushing.

'Ah, but it's different, you see, for you. This is nice for you, but it's just an extra in your real life, which goes on every day,' Sirena said, looking not at me but out the window, holding her cup beneath her chin as if she were cold. 'But for me, I have here in Boston no real life, so this is it. This is everything. Besides Reza and Skandar, of course. Which is why I'm so glad you're here.'

I could have said a lot of things. I wanted to say that my real life had fewer furnishings than her temporary pretend life, that the mystery of my life was how it could be so much like a highway through the Great Plains, miles and miles of straight and flat with barely even a tree. And now, not merely a tree, but an oasis. I didn't say this, obviously.

Instead I nodded, looking at her profile silhouetted against the light, and the glimmer of her dark, sad eyes, and I wanted to step forward and touch her the way she touched me, but I couldn't see a way to do it that wouldn't be awkward. I guess I'm repressed, or uptight, but I was worried in part because I didn't know quite what it was that I felt – some intensity of emotion I couldn't articulate – and I had no idea what it was that she might herself feel, and I didn't want to be misconstrued or embarrassed. So although I wanted to touch her arm, I did no such thing: I nodded, I smiled, I downed the dregs of my coffee, and as I placed my cup noisily in the sink, I said, 'Well, *au travail!*' using her words, if not her gestures, for the first time.

~~

I know what you're thinking. You're thinking that I was in love with her – which I was – but in a romantic way – which I was not. You're thinking, how would I know whether I was romantically in love, I whose apparently nonexistent love life would suggest a prudish vacancy, uterus shriveled like a corn husk and withered dugs for breasts? You're thinking that whatever else she does, the Woman Upstairs with her cats and her pots of tea and her *Sex and the City* reruns and her goddamn Garnet Hill catalog, the woman with her class of third graders and her carefully pearly smile – whatever else she manages, she doesn't have a love life to speak of.

Just because something is invisible doesn't mean it isn't there. At any given time, there are a host of invisibles floating among us. There are clairvoyants to see ghosts; but who sees the invisible emotions, the unrecorded events? Who is it that sees love, more evanescent than any ghost, let alone can catch it? Who are you to tell me that I don't know what love is?

My indifference to Alf's slobbering first clinch in the Manchester High School darkroom, and my inability to see the point of a husband when I was sixteen, were not, perhaps, an auspicious beginning. But, reader, in my time, I almost married. I can't quite believe it myself, looking back.

In college, I had boyfriends, yes, in the way that girls who are chiefly popular with girls have boyfriends. For long stretches, I would pine, religiously, monastically even, for someone unrealistic and inappropriate. Then, in between the ranks of the unloving and the ranks of the unloved slipped the stragglers and wanderers against whom I had no defenses. These were my early lovers, the there-and-gone: the Englishman visiting for a semester with his talk of Wittgenstein and his crazed quiff of black hair; my roommate's brother's friend Nate up from Harvard for a long weekend, blinking behind his glasses and swigging in the cold from his hip flask of bourbon; or Avi, Joanne Goldstein's boyfriend from Israel, fresh out of the army, dark-skinned, hairy and muscled, who kicked around Middlebury for the better part of a season, smoking lots of dope and having sex with whomever he felt like, while Joanne was in class or at the gym or wherever she was and apparently not noticing.

In the summer after senior year, by which time I thought I'd never know love, I met Ben. It was August, and hot. We met on Martha's Vineyard, where I was staying with my friend Susie at her parents' house, at a picnic on Aquinnah beach, playing volleyball, the sand frying our soles, and he stood out not only because he was tall and lean but because he had about him from the first an air of patient sweetness that he never lost, something almost childlike. He asked me to dinner in Edgartown and picked me up on a borrowed moped, and winding back to Susie's along South Road after supper, with the high moon and the gnarled fairy-tale trees overhanging the road, I felt with him both safe and capable of adventure. When we came to the open field beyond which you see the sea for the first time, and it was lit by the pewter moonlight and by hundreds of fireflies, like dotted fairy lanterns, he stopped the bike and we perched on the knobbly stone wall, just looking for a while in silence – it was, actually, breathtaking – and then we kissed. I remember sighing, with both pleasure and a sort of resignation, and thinking, 'Well, that's that then.'

Ben was fresh out of college also, from Northern California originally, but moving to New York, so I hopped on the bandwagon and moved to New York too, where I rented an apartment with Susie and another girl from college named Lola, in a greasy tenement at 102nd and Amsterdam, which was not then a particularly pleasant place to live.

Ben lived in Alphabet City, and in the evenings he played in a band. He worked, days, the first year, as a mover, and he got very strong, and I worked as a waitress, and for a while it was all fun, in the way life is fun when it's provisional. But what seems fun at first can get old quickly, and soon my head hurt and my feet were tired and I found my customers demanding and rude, so I bought a suit with money sent by my parents, and I started interviewing for business jobs, and to my surprise got an offer from this management consultancy, and once something like that was offered, how could I say no?

And then I must have changed. I certainly wasn't painting any pictures. In those days, the early nineties, art seemed pointless, and it was exhilarating to have money for the first time ... I can't explain it entirely – it's as if it happened to a different person, and I look back and see who I was then and she looks like nobody I would ever have known. But because I became this person, and because Ben was deeply accommodating and because he loved me, he felt he needed to change, too. I'd say things like, 'We're not kids anymore – it's time to get serious,' and in time, he signed up for law school at NYU, which is exactly the sort of thing you do when you feel it's time to get serious but have no clue what that might entail. Needless to say, he also packed in the band, which in some way he didn't need anymore, because he had me in his free time. We were living together by then, in a tiny, dully respectable low-ceilinged postwar box east of Gramercy Park, a no-man's-land, vibe-wise, a few blocks from the Arts Club but a million miles from any art. I barely looked at art; I thought my plan to become an artist had been a fantasy of the powerless, and that with money of my own – with power! – I had no need of it.

My office was on the thirty-fourth floor; I went everywhere by taxi; I flew on planes and sat in airports and stayed up tapping at my computer late nights in hotels. I was only twenty-five, and owned four pairs of Christian Louboutin shoes. I possessed a fancy oversized white sofa and the most expensive comforter money could buy, from Sweden (an item I still enjoy). And when Ben asked me to marry him – over a dinner so rich in a restaurant so elaborate that we were the youngest patrons by twenty years and probably the only ones without gout – I realized – not straight away, but in the weeks that followed, with the diamond bright and heavy on my finger (what use had I for a diamond?) – that Ben the white-collar criminal defense lawyer bored me, sweet though he was, and that I didn't care about the sofa or the shoes or even the comforter, and that I didn't even *like* fancy food, which either made me constipated or gave me diarrhea.

You didn't expect this of the Woman Upstairs. I had a love, and a love affair with a worldly life, and I left it. If I'd married Ben and moved to Westchester (you know, don't you, that we would have moved to Westchester?), then, years later when my mother got ill, I wouldn't have given myself over to her as I did, because there would already have been children (you know, don't you, that there would have been children? Just as you know that eventually, inevitably, there would have been a divorce), and at least one of my life's exam questions would have been properly answered. But there would have been no art, no oxygen; and there would have been those jobs, and all the things that went with them, and there would have been Ben, who, guileless as he was till the last, I came to despise for his very malleability, his likeness to myself, almost, and to look upon – quite wrongly, I now see – with contempt.

I don't know where he is now, more than a decade later, Ben Souter ('My suitor Souter,' I joked in the beginning), but I hope for his sake that he married happily and has bonny children and a big house, and I hope he's raked in his millions while remaining ever sweet.

Nor was he by any means my last, all those years ago. I don't need to enumerate them to you – briefly the married man; for much longer, the weary graduate student; the boy ten years my junior who told me – the only person in my life I think actually to say this to me – that I was sexy. This perhaps makes me sound defensive. Which I suppose I am. Because before the Shahids I thought I understood love and what it was and how I felt about it; and they turned it all upside down. The very fact that I can tell you without blinking that I could kill them – that above all I could kill her – says all that needs to be said. Oh, don't worry, I won't. I'm harmless. We Women Upstairs are that, too. But I could.

12

In the two weeks before Christmas, two things happened. The first was what I'd feared, in my studio solitude in the dark. I'd been trying to fight my terror, to sit tight through its spasms, and keep working into the evenings at Emily's diorama. I was working on Emily's bed, and there was no sound but the knocking of the radiators and the intermittent distant shipboard roar of the furnace igniting, blowing, juddering into sleep again. I'd let the CD player lapse into silence, because I wanted to be sure I could hear any human sounds, and feared that music would muffle them.

And then, as I sanded and whittled in my pool of light, I *did* hear sounds. The distant tramp on the stairwell, faint and almost hollow, and then footsteps, starting, stopping, ginger footsteps, growing louder, pausing along the corridor – would I catch the rattle of a padlock, the squeak of an unoiled hinge? – and no, the walker came on again, advanced ever closer. The steps, as my nightmare dictated, came to my door. The end of the hallway: nowhere else to go.

I put down my paper, my sanded sticks. My hands hovered over the table, and I was aware from the bowl of silence in the room that I held my breath. I didn't want to scrape my chair along the floor. I could hear my heart. Did light show under the lintel? Perhaps – but wait: a knock. Not a random knock, a quiet, rhythmic knock, like a secret, or a message. *Dum-da-da-dum-dum.* And again.

Should I open? Did he know I was there? Did he know who I was? Was the rhythm a sign, or a meaningless fact? Was it someone knocking on the wrong door, or something far darker?

In my flurry, I moved. The chair let out a furious, maiming shriek.

The knock again, louder this time. Again the same rhythm; again twice. An announcement. And then, a rattling of the handle.

What now? What now? So important, my authoritative teacherly voice told me, not to cower like a child; but I picked up my X-Acto knife and checked that the blade was extended.

'Who is it?' I scraped my chair now as loudly as I could, a reversal of strategy, and stomped, in what I hoped was a manly way, toward the intruder. 'Who is it?'

The voice on the other side – a man's – said something I couldn't grasp. I came up so close to the door that I imagined I could hear him breathing on the other side. He emitted a cough, a smoker's cough, into which I tried to read an entire personality.

'Who is it? Speak clearly please?' The schoolteacher at last triumphant.

And then I heard her name, pronounced not as I pronounced it, but as she herself did. See-rreh-na. As if by an Italian.

I put the X-Acto knife in my rear pocket – with a mental note to remove it before sitting down – and fiddled with the bolt and swung the door wide, almost angrily, to try to take the visitor by surprise.

Indeed, for an instant, he looked surprised, like a silent film actor miming surprise, eyebrows aloft and mouth involuntarily agape; and then he recomposed his features into a pleasant, almost ingratiating, smile and extended a hand. 'And you must be Nora Eldridge?'

I hesitated.

'Not only my wife's friend and colleague.' He put the emphasis heavily on the second syllable – col-*league* – which made him sound both foreign and important. 'But also my son's *institutrice*. How do you do?'

This was Reza's father and Sirena's husband. 'You must be—'

'Skandar. Skandar Shahid. How do you do?' He extended a strong, square, hairy hand, even as he stepped forward and I backward into the studio. 'Sirena is not here?'

'She left over an hour ago.'

He peered skeptically into the tidied gloom at her end of the room (so he'd been here before), and then back at my circle of eggy light. 'And you have the elves' workshop,' he said, smiling.

'I'm sorry?'

'You are – I just meant you're like the shoemaker's elves, hard at work in the night to make something perfect.' He smiled, but did not show his teeth: a gentleman. 'And also, what you are making is very small.' Which meant he had also looked at my diorama, and possibly at my sketches too. Which meant that they'd leaned over my table together, or at the least that he'd perused my belongings, my work, in some idle, prurient way, while Sirena put on her coat, or boiled the kettle. Somehow it had never occurred to me that he could have been there.

'Yes,' I said. 'It's small. I concede that.'

'You can see that?' He laughed, and here a glimmer of tooth was visible. 'I'm so glad.' He paused. Like his wife, he spoke with an accent, but unlike Sirena's, his was clipped, tidy. 'Shall I make some tea?' He stepped toward the sink, still with his coat buttoned up. His leather shoes, wet and ruined, left dark marks on the floor. I found his proprietary gesture quite surreal.

'Tea?'

'Would you prefer coffee? Sirena is always for coffee, and I, I am for tea.'

'But Sirena isn't here – she's gone home.' I must have sounded rude, because he stopped and turned to look at me as though I'd surprised him again.

Have I said that for all I found his behavior unreadable, Skandar Shahid also proved, superficially, to be pretty much my ideal man. He was the sort of man I would have eyed, on the subway or in an airport, and wondered about; the sort of man before whom, had I been seated next to him at a dinner party, I would have felt tongue-tied and bashful; the sort of man – a grown-up – I would always have thought I could never know.

Neither tall nor short, neither fat nor thin, he had luxuriant dark wavy hair, worn slightly long and now graying, as though he'd stood for a while in a snowstorm. His eyes – but I'd thought Reza's eyes were his mother's? – were Byzantine, ovoid, heavily lashed and dark as wells. They were magnified by glasses, but the glasses were somehow discreet, so that what you saw were enormous eyes only. He had pleasingly rounded cheeks, a nose neither bony nor bulbous, a drawing lesson of a nose, and dark lips, slightly pouting. I wanted at once to touch his chin and feel the evening sandpaper of it. I smiled and said, 'Sorry. Tea would be great.'

He filled the pot at the sink, turned on the burner, all comfortably with his back to me. 'Do you know if there are biscuits?' he asked, rummaging among the coffee tin and tea boxes. 'Wouldn't you like a biscuit?'

'We're fresh out, I'm afraid.'

'Fresh out?' He turned, amused. 'I like that. Fresh in, fresh out. If I'd come earlier, you would have had them.'

'I guess so.'

'So this is what you and Sirena do, eat "cookies"' – he said the word as if it were foreign, in quotation marks – 'and chatter like schoolgirls?'

'I suppose that's it. This whole studio thing, it's an excuse to gossip.'

He swiveled his head on his neck like a bird, looking at me from the corner of his eye, and he smirked. 'That's very good. That's very good.' He seemed to have found a remnant of biscuit of some kind, and nibbled on it. 'You are serious, though.'

'Serious?'

'Sirena says you're serious. This is what matters. Not whether you sell for thousands or know the fancy people. That you are serious is important.'

'Of course.'

'You look serious.' He peered at me, amused, as he handed me my tea. 'Milk?'

'No thanks.' I thought for a moment. 'Does *she* sell for thousands, then? Does she know the fancy people?'

'Fancy? What does it mean? Something different to someone different. But yes, she is, she does, whatever it means. She's started to.' He gave another big, cryptic smile. 'In Paris, of course.'

I felt some internal elevator drop in its shaft; what is commonly called a sinking feeling. Somehow, I had contrived not to think about Sirena's artistic life outside our private world, about its before and its after.

'This is one reason it was hard for her to come this year – for her career, things in the past year or two really started to, to "take off"? at home. Exhibits, the best gallery, reviews, you know. There aren't here the same opportunities . . . but I told her, find a studio, work, like a retreat, with no distractions. It will be good.'

'And is it?'

He finished his tea, deposited the cup with a flourish in the sink. 'It *is* good. She has found a place, and she has you.'

'She has me?'

'For cookies and chat, a col-*league,* who is serious too.'

'Right.'

'Like many artists, Sirena, when she is sad, can get very sad indeed.' He looked wistful, but strangely as though this had nothing to do with him. 'So we are always happy for her to be happy.' He looked at his watch. 'She's late. For once I'm on time, and she's late.'

'She didn't mention that she'd be coming back.'

'We're going to a film, just together, and we agreed—' He interrupted himself, made a great mime of slapping his forehead. 'But we changed. We changed the plan.' Again, the watch; then guttural rumblings of exasperation. 'She will already be at the cinema. Can you tell me the fastest way to Kendall Square?'

I tried to give him the simplest possible directions, but had the impression he wasn't taking them in. His distress seemed genuine enough; but I didn't trust, as he hurried off down the corridor, uttering politesses as he went, that he'd make it to the cinema on time, or possibly even at all.

As I put away my things for the evening and washed out the cups, I constructed a story whereby he'd come, on purpose, in the hope of meeting me. Not because he wanted to know me for himself, but because he wanted to see who his wife spent so much time with, to get the measure of me. Maybe – wasn't it remotely possible? – she spoke of me with the same barely contained excitement, the slight breathlessness, with which I spoke of her.

It's the strangest thing about being human: to know so much, to communicate so much, and yet always to fall so drastically short of clarity, to be, in the end, so isolate and inadequate. Even when people try to say things, they say them poorly, or obliquely, or they outright lie, sometimes because they're lying to you, but as often because they're lying to themselves.

Sirena, after all, rarely spoke to me about Skandar. I imagined that because she didn't speak of him, he didn't preoccupy her thoughts. I understood him to be a given, possibly even an ambivalent given. She talked so openly about her work, and her anxieties and fantasies about it, and about the malleability of different materials, and about her complicated feelings about video. She worried that the fashion for video was affecting her interest in it, both her attraction and her repulsion, which I understood. She said that it was one of the things she admired about me, that I had no truck with fashion, that I followed my instincts with such calm. I didn't tell her that I couldn't do otherwise; but I was thrillingly gratified by her praise.

Or she talked about Reza – she loved to talk about him, his escapades, his funny comments, his malapropisms in English ('*Maman,* what is a doggy dog world?'), stories of his early childhood. She even talked about her own girlhood, the large family of siblings and her tyrannical mother, deaf in one ear since childhood and correspondingly voluble, as if making up for the sounds that didn't reach her by putting out a great din into the world; and her father, as soft, as she put it, as a Camembert in summer. She talked about how close she was to her youngest brother – so much like Reza in temperament, she said – and how tempestuous her relations were with her older sister, eighteen months from her in age, who had longed for family but never married, and who doted oppressively on her nephew whenever given the chance. She told stories of her youth, of backpacking through Southeast Asia, and being so stoned in northern Thailand that she spent almost a week in a stupor in a hut in a village near Chiang Mai, with her then-boyfriend forcing her, every so often, to eat or to drink so as to keep body and soul together.

She talked about all these things, but almost never about her husband. What was I supposed to think?

When she spoke of him, it was in connection with Reza, about the three of them doing things together, like speaking English at the supper table or ogling stingrays at the aquarium; or about logistics, at which he was clearly very bad. Skandar showed up two hours late; Skandar forgot altogether; Skandar never paid the bill; Skandar lost the receipts/car keys/telephone number. She had a weariness, half indulgent, half despairing, when she mentioned these foibles, a particular sardonic set to her lovely mouth.

'You must like it, really,' I once said when she explained that the reason no Shahid had attended Back to School Night was that he'd been assigned the job and, forgetting or claiming to, had gone instead to hear a lecture at the Kennedy School. 'Isn't it partly why you married him?'

'I loved it *then*,' she said. 'He seemed so free. But you get tired of it, you know.' You, too, might have thought him an ambivalent given.

When I got home that Friday evening, I Googled the pair of them. It seems strange in retrospect that I hadn't done it sooner, but I realize now that I hadn't wanted to know what the world thought of them, of her. I'd wanted her to be mine, the way my Emily Dickinson diorama was mine, without a world before or after or outside. It was how we all want life to be, no hubbub or white noise, no distorting mirrors. And so no doubt looking them up on the computer was a mistake.

There they were together, photographed at a cocktail party next to a beaky, long-haired fellow in a rusty velvet jacket; there was Skandar on a panel about Raymond Aron and the philosophy of history, caught behind a long table with his name on a sign in front of him, mid-speech with his eyes shut and his hands raised like birds in flight, a blur. There was a shadowy photograph of Sirena at the opening of her installation of Elsinore, holding a champagne flute and glaring at the photographer, grave and moody and wearing skinny trousers and high heels, her hair piled up on her head with chopsticks. There were links to his essays, in French, unintelligible to me; and his listing as a professor at the École Normale Supérieure; and clips from the papers about Sirena's exhibitions – two of them, mostly, the Elsinore one and another two years before it, again all in French. When I clicked on 'translate this page' I got a comical soup of errors syntactic and grammatical, along with some obvious howlers on the diction front – a lesson, surely, in the fundamental impossibility of cross-cultural exchange – but I could see that the terms in which Sirena's work was praised were extravagant, almost uncomfortable. One review in particular raved not so much about the extraordinary constructions of Elsinore but about the video series that accompanied them. This, they said, was Sirena's true genius, her ability to thrill and amuse and shock and surprise us with her set of six three-minute shorts, each describing the relationship of a creature – including a human observer, filmed unawares from behind; a live snail; and a plasticine Hamlet, which the reviewer liked best – to the spaces.

~

Not long after, I had a dream about Skandar, that kind of bright, real dream that stays with you into the day and changes you, as if something – what? – has really happened. It's so visceral that it can't then be expunged from your memory, as though it were written on the body. It was a sexual dream. We were naked together in bed in an apartment that wasn't mine, but I knew it wasn't his, either, and I somehow knew from the high, white, opaque light in the windows that it was in Europe – Amsterdam, maybe, is what I thought, where I've never been. I got out of bed to put the kettle on, and I said, 'She'll be here soon, you know,' and he said, 'She doesn't mind. She likes it.' Likes what? I wondered, and got back into bed with him, and then he had his fingers in me and I came. Then there was the kettle boiling and the doorbell ringing (my alarm clock, obviously: time to get up) and I got up to deal with these things but I wasn't frightened, he'd said she liked it, and when I turned back to look at him, my whole body still tingling, he was leaning against the headboard and sniffing, like a perfumer, at his cunty fingers, with a sly faraway smile and just a glint of tooth.

13

The second thing happened only three days after the first, at the beginning of the last week of school before vacation. I'd been anticipating it for so long by then that I'd forgotten to keep worrying, so was duly shocked, even frightened. It shows how long-lived anger is, the desire for vengeance: it has a nuclear half-life, and it teaches people patience in the most sinister way.

Reza was attacked again. This time more surreptitiously, more brutally. Under the lackadaisical eye of the after-school girls, Bethany, Margot and Sarah – feckless texters, busy planning dates on their cell phones – a massive snowball fight had been allowed to erupt among the children. There were two dozen kids or so in after-school, and all but the most timid were involved: they'd formed teams, and built a fort, and I, kept from my studio by an appointment with Chastity and Ebullience's mother and Lisa, the reading specialist, to discuss strategies for dealing with Ebullience's gloating about Chastity's dyslexia, or rather, about her own ebullient lack thereof – anyway, I conducted my meeting with the shouts and laughter a joyful tympani through the windows, and it sounded like childhood should sound.

But in among them like an evil spore lurked Owen, the angry

fifth grader who'd attacked Reza before, just smart enough and just dumb enough to think of packing his snowball with rocks; and the misfortune that he chose a sharp one, and the greater shame that his aim was good (hard for it not to be: he was, it was later established, only a few feet from his target), and the greatest shame that Reza didn't see it coming.

Reza, one girl said, fell at once to his knees, and she could see blood through his fingers – his fists over his eyes – before she knew what it was. And she said she heard the fat boy mutter 'Oh, shit,' before he turned and ran away.

Inside, we registered the blow as silence falling, as if outside the world in chorus took a breath, as if a curtain fell upon the scene. Then Bethany started to blow the whistle, three sharp toots, the emergency kids-line-up-NOW whistle, and I had to say 'Excuse me' to the twins' mother and step to the window. I remember the sky glowed that dull illuminated gray of incipient snow, and when I placed my fingertips upon the glass, it was cold. And looking down I could see first Bethany's panic, her flailing pseudomilitary gestures as she herded everyone toward the big double doors. Only then did I glimpse Margot bundling someone to the side entrance, someone hunched, who'd dripped blood in a magic trail upon the battered snow – even in the gray light, or perhaps the more because of it, the blood gleamed scarlet – and I had only to look and not to think to know I knew that coat. I knew that hat – black and white with a pom-pom on the top – I knew it.

'Excuse me,' I shouted, 'an accident!' – more loudly than was necessary, and was out of the classroom to the bafflement of the mother and my colleague Lisa.

I reached Shauna's office at the same time as Margot and Reza. Velma Snively, Shauna's secretary (and a veteran of thirty-seven years at Appleton – some people called her Shauna's boss), had emerged from behind her desk and called for compresses:

'Don't stand there,' she snapped at Margot, who was crying, even as she drew Reza to her significant bosom. 'Get the gauze from the first-aid cupboard. Get the sterile water. Over there! Over *there*!'

'It's Miss Eldridge, Reza,' I announced, in case he couldn't see me. 'You're going to be fine.' I tried to reach him, but Velma's arm interceded. 'Was it *in* the eye? Is it in the *eye*?' I tried to wiggle around her, but there was no 'around.' Her flowery top emitted a snakey sound when touched.

'Don't you think we'd better have a look at it, Velma?'

'I'm *going* to, Nora, if you'll stop crowding the poor boy.' She reached out for the wad of gauze that Margot had found, and waved it in the air. 'Cold sterile water! Cold water here! We need to clean this boy *up*!'

The gauze was removed, moistened, returned to her palm; she gave no quarter in the meantime and held him to her with her other arm. He was very still, but for the shudder of his sobs, like a stunned animal.

When Velma had daubed the blood away – and there was a goodly flow of it, although it had begun blackly to coagulate around the edges of the wound – it was clear that Reza's eyeball itself had been spared, but that the gash, an inch long, was so close to the corner of his eye that it looked as though, like a late fruit, it might split the skin there and open the socket.

'A Band-Aid's not going to patch this up,' Velma observed grimly. 'The boy needs stitches.'

At this point, Reza whimpered slightly, his first sound, and looked at me in terror.

'Don't be afraid, sweetie. I'll take you.'

'*Maman*,' he said.

'I know. I'll call her straight away. She can meet us at the hospital.' I could picture her, content in our studio in her not-knowing, carefully carving aspirin flowers with her hair falling in a net over her work; and I could picture her fumbling for the cell phone in her coat pocket with that faint click in her throat that she used, or I imagined she used, when she thought it might be Skandar.

'Have you got your stuff?' I asked, stupidly. 'Margot, get his backpack for me? We'll go in my car, right now.'

Velma stood back, releasing him, and cleared her throat. 'I'm going to check the medical form, Nora. You can't just take him anywhere.'

'Children's. I'll take him to Children's: it's the best, if they have to sew it up again. Let's put a compress on for the trip. Do you think you can hold it, sweetie? Hold it there with your hand?'

Velma sighed, shook her head. 'We should have the mother come here,' she said. 'That's the rule except in an emergency.'

'You don't think this is an emergency? His mother is a friend of mine,' I said (and do you know, even in that crazy moment I was proud to say this, like turning a trump card, and proud to think that it was actually true). 'And I know she wouldn't want us wasting any time. I'll call her on the way and she'll meet us in the emergency room. Come on, Velma, you know it's the right thing.'

Velma shook her head again, just slightly. 'I know it's what's going to happen, Nora; but I need you to call this boy's mother right here before you go. I can't have you take him without her say-so.'

So I called Sirena from Velma's office. I cannot convey the strangeness of that. I was self-conscious so many times over: to be the one to tell Sirena the news, as though Reza had been stricken on my watch (Margot was still in the room, her face fixed in a rictus of anxiety); to have them all hear me speak to her, since I didn't know how to modulate my voice when I spoke to her any more than I did when I spoke of her; afraid to sound either too intimate or too formal, too loud or too soft; and in front of Reza, too, who surely had no clear sense of the extent to which his school and home lives were, almost behind his back, intertwined. He knew that his mother and I made our art in the same studio, but he had no idea what, practically, that might mean, and surely didn't understand that when he was at after-school, or shunted into Maria's care, his mother was, more often than not, nibbling biscuits with me, chattering, as his father had said, like a schoolgirl. Or rather, like a childless artist, than which there could surely be no greater betrayal.

But I made the call, stiff and stern and fake in my voice, the teacher's voice Sirena hadn't heard since the beginning, and still I was sure that Velma looked at me oddly. I told Sirena what had happened, and that his eye was okay but would need stitches – at which point I heard a muffled sound on the line and said, my tone all wrong for Velma's office but I couldn't help it, 'Don't cry, Sirena, don't cry; it's okay,' and she said, 'I'm not crying. I'm putting on my coat' – and I told her we were going to the ER at Children's and we'd meet her there.

'I don't know the way,' she said.

'Take a cab – call one. I'll bring you home again.'

Which, eventually, I did. But not before we were seven hours in the emergency room. ('They always do that at Children's,' Esther explained later. 'It *is* the best care, but it means they've got a reputation to uphold. They can't afford to make mistakes.') He was seen by a nurse; and then by a resident; and then by the attending doctor, who summoned the ophthalmologist to be sure; and finally by the plastic surgeon, who happened by good fortune to be checking on a patient elsewhere, and who sewed him up in tiny, tidy stitches. Between visitors to our clammy curtained booth – vaguely reminiscent of a fortune-teller's at the fair, but strewn with medical posters and lit by a ghastly gray light – where we grew hungrier and more glazed by the hour, stretched vast swathes of useless waiting time. At first I offered to read to Reza and then I suggested that I fetch everyone something to eat, but I could tell that Sirena, still anxious, didn't want me to go. Skandar was out of town, and she didn't want to be alone if something was really wrong, more wrong than it seemed. So I said I'd stay until the doctor pronounced; and by then it was almost the end, because the stitches themselves, four of them, so near to the edge of his eye, were a matter of minutes, a neat pull of needle and thread, rather like my mother repairing my downed skirt hem between breakfast and school, except that the sandy-haired doctor didn't bite the thread with her teeth when she was done, she snipped niftily with gleaming little scissors and ruffled Reza's hair – he was so bleary he was almost asleep – and said, 'Don't worry. Nothing's changed. You're still going to break hearts with those eyes,' and she knew and we knew that this was true; and then she said he could go home at last.

I drove them down the alley off the riverbank to their town house. Reza had fallen asleep in the car.

'Do you want some help? I can carry him in.'

Sirena's eyes were sunken hollows in the gloom. 'Nora,' she said, 'you are so very kind.'

'It's not kindness,' I said. I picked him up in my arms as she worried the front door key, and I followed her into the darkened house bearing my warm burden (his breath tickled my neck), and I climbed the stairs behind her and laid him on his bed. Shoes off, coat off, trousers unbuttoned and off, covers up, and in all this he barely stirred, so deep was his exhaustion. I stood looking at him while she went to put on the kettle, the lights. He lay on his back with his arms on top of the blanket, his head upon the pillow, his cheeks flushed pink, and when he breathed out his lips pursed, slightly, in a little 'o'. My God, he was beautiful, all perfect promise. And before I left him, I stroked his hair and bent to kiss his brow. He smelled of the hospital. He shivered a bit in his sleep.

Skandar wasn't there, but in some way he was, and I felt a vague, lingering guilt at my dream, as though I'd done something wrong, had tried to steal Sirena's child and husband both, as though she might look at me and know it.

So I found myself near midnight at Sirena's dining table, drinking mint tea and eating toast with butter and plum jam. The place was oddly soulless – renovated in the eighties, rented furnished, with ugly, solid, institutional chairs and a tinted, speckled glass globe hanging from the ceiling. The walls were stuccoed, the floors beige wall-to-wall. The kitchen cabinets – visible behind the vintage pass-through from the dining area – reminded me of an old man's Cadillac: antique but carefully preserved, at once touching and hideous. It shouldn't have surprised me that the Shahids lived in such a place – they were passing through, after all – but it did. They were so special, and this place so nondescript.

Sirena and I hardly spoke, for a long stretch. I could hear her, and myself, chewing toast. She looked exhausted.

'He's going to be fine, you know,' I offered at length. 'The surgeon wasn't kidding. Nothing's changed.'

Sirena's eyes were wet. 'Nothing's changed. You say this, but we know it isn't true. Not about his face – his face will heal. But what have we done, to bring him here to this? What has Skandar done? Nobody wanted to come but him – but who can be the wife who says "No, we cannot go"?'

It hadn't occurred to me that she disliked it here, disliked the very idea of here. 'I thought Reza was liking it – school and everything?'

'What's the point of not liking it? I tell him at bedtime stories about his friends at home. He knows we'll go back, so it was okay. But now this?'

'The boy who did it will be properly punished this time. He might even be expelled.'

'And for Reza, does this make a difference? Not at all. Now Reza knows he lives in a world where people can throw rocks at you just because of who you are, just because they don't like your name or your skin.'

'You do know it isn't normal, right? That's one unhinged kid, who's got real problems. It has nothing to do with Reza personally; I think he can understand that.'

'When you're an Arab or you have a Middle Eastern name, it's never personal, but it's always *there*. I was anxious about America, but then I thought, in Cambridge, Massachusetts, of all places . . .' She trailed off, then began again: 'Do you know what it's like?' A tear had come out of her eye and was finding its way down her cheek. 'Most of the time you don't think about it, not consciously. But sooner or later, someone will make a comment that has to be explained away. You know, Skandar had cousins in refugee camps. His brother was killed in a bombing in Beirut – at twenty-three. Vanished into dust. Skandar grew up lucky, but he knows all too well what it's like. I know it's important for Reza to take all this in, to know about it – but later. I want – I wanted – for Reza to have a childhood like I did, where all you have to know is how to be a child. No rage, no hatred, no cry for vengeance. No stone-throwing. There's time enough for all that – for history – later; and I thought with luck and enough time we could make him whole, round, not warped by this legacy. Of all my worries about coming here – not this. And now, this. You see? Everything's changed because he can no longer be free of it. Because this, now, is the beginning.' She wasn't really crying, but she put her head in her hands, and her hair fell over her face. When she looked up again, she was smiling. 'You probably don't even know what I'm talking about.'

'I think I do.'

'Never mind. It's okay. As you say, his eye will be fine – that's the most important thing.' She stood, piled the plates. 'It's late now. Not time for more melodrama. I don't think Reza will be at school tomorrow, but you must be, so you must get home to sleep.'

At the door, like my mother, she turned on a new and brilliant smile. 'Nora, my dear, I can't ever say enough thank-yous for tonight. What would we have done without you? You're a true friend.' She extended her arms, and I saw that she was offering me a hug. I'm not much of one for hugs – they make me uncomfortable – but I stepped into her embrace and hugged her back. She didn't try to kiss my cheek, but instead clasped me tightly against her, long enough for me to unstiffen and properly hug her back. I could feel the lumpy hooks of her bra through her sweater. She smelled of perfume and the sharp sweat of fear. I don't know where it came from, but I felt like crying. It had been such a long day.

'I don't know if I'll be at the studio tomorrow,' I said, pulling away at last.

'I don't think I will be,' she said.

'When does Skandar come?'

'Maybe earlier, now. We'll see. He doesn't really believe in a crisis – he's seen too many and he says they're almost never really real.'

'Easy to say from the outside.'

'Always. Good night.'

'Call me if you need my help?'

From her mysterious smiling nod I knew she wouldn't call me. And I was right.

Then there was the waiting. Reza didn't come to school the next day, or the next. Or the next, Thursday, by which time I understood that we wouldn't see him again before the holidays. On the Wednesday and again on the Thursday after school I went back to the studio and found it abandoned – the coffee cup she'd been drinking from when I called from school standing half full on the counter. On the Friday, on the Saturday, the Sunday, I couldn't bear to go back alone.

They were returning to France for two weeks, but I didn't know exactly when they were leaving. I kept waiting for Sirena to call – to tell me how Reza was faring, to report on his state of mind, for God's sake even to ask whether there was any homework he ought to be doing. By Thursday, it occurred to me to call them – think of all the things that might have happened: Reza's eye might have gotten infected, or he might have become hysterical or despondent, or Sirena and Skandar might have had an enormous argument about any of it – about Skandar being away, or about being in Cambridge in the first place, or even about the fact that *I* had taken the boy to the hospital – any of these might have happened. They might have decided to leave early for France. They might have decided to return home for good. The one thing I didn't want to believe was that they were going about their days in that dingy town house in perfect and consoling uneventfulness, and simply not thinking of me at all.

Don't think that I wasn't aware the whole time of the tenuousness of my claim: she might have called me a true friend, but wasn't I essentially just a common schoolteacher and a sometime co-tenant? There were, in my own life, people I'd treated as cavalierly: one was always aware of the hierarchy, however much one tried to pretend indifference to it.

And yes, in all this thinking, in the deafening silence, I started to be angry, a little. Who were they to ignore me? What sort of manners were these, not only in the broader, human sense but

even professionally, even if there were no more intimate connection – perhaps all the more so in that case – didn't you owe
your son's teacher a phone call, when she'd rushed him to the
hospital and stayed there with you for hours, just to say that he'd
be back and when, or wouldn't be back, but that he was fine, or
Christ, that he wasn't really fine, but even then, to say one more
time 'thank you' because you know, in life, when people put
themselves out for you it behooves you to express gratitude.

Above all, in my anger, I was sad. Isn't that always the way,
that at the heart of the fire is a frozen kernel of sorrow that the
fire is trying – valiantly, fruitlessly – to eradicate. And I was
aware, in all this emotion, that as soon as she called – if she
called – all would be forgiven. Every time my phone rang, my
heart turned in vain hope. It was a reflex; I couldn't control it.

Owen had been expelled by Shauna, efficiently, unceremoni-
ously, before noon on Tuesday morning. The school was thick
with the gossip of it, from smallest to largest, and Reza's fall to
the ground, dripping scarlet blood in the snow, became
mythic, almost Homeric. There were whispers that he was
brain-damaged, that he'd been blinded, that the Shahids were
going to sue – all kinds of garbage, from the playground to the
staffroom, and repeatedly colleagues would stop me in the hall
or in the bathroom to check the veracity of one rumor or
another. Somehow, this hubbub blew past me like a dream: I
could hear only the wind in my head.

On Friday morning we had the holiday assembly, where my
class performed *The Fir Tree* from the Hans Christian Andersen
story – God, it felt apt to me that week. Luckily, Reza's part as
a woodcutter had involved only three lines, which young Noah
cheerfully usurped and delivered with gusto. Then everybody

did a dance to 'I Have a Little Dreidel,' after which a Nigerian girl named Ethel, in the fifth grade, performed a soaring rendition of 'Silent Night': the remarkable voice emanating from her slight chest billowed vast around us all, rich and clear, like some extraordinary divine food. Then Shauna said a few upbeat and largely inane words about the season's festivals of light and the new beginning to which we all were looking forward – with no mention at all of the incident at the beginning of the week – and then, suddenly, it was lunchtime, and vacation.

The children dispersed both swiftly and slowly, their lovely disharmonious babble overtaking the air all the way to the ceilings, as they stuffed their packs and donned their gear and hugged and patted one another, depositing cards and parcels on my desk like religious offerings, some of them discreetly, so I wouldn't notice, others proudly, some of the girls clutching at me, hugging my hips, my tummy, my arm; the boys less forthcoming, almost shy in some cases, and each of them calling, on their way out the door, 'Bye, Miss E! Happy holidays, Miss E! Have a good Christmas! See you next year – get it? Bye! Bye! Bye!'

And then there I was, alone in my classroom with the fluorescent lights, the pile of bright trophies on my desk, the noise fading down the hall, the stairwell, the mid-day winter sun at the windows, my life suddenly empty, gone. I put away books, dusted the blackboards, tidied my pens into the drawers. There was a teachers' lunch in the staffroom, but I didn't want to go – the pleasantries we exchanged were always the same, only this time, surely, there would also be gossip about Reza, about Owen, about Shauna's decision not to mention them in the assembly. I put on my coat, hunted for a grocery bag in which to stow my booty. (How many cards had I accumulated, over my teaching years? But in the pile there was not one from Reza, so none that I wanted.)

It would have been the perfect day to go to the studio, where Emily D's solitary bedroom awaited my solitary attentions. Instead, I slipped out of Appleton without saying good-bye, dropped my things at home and went to the matinee of *Closer,* a movie with Jude Law and Natalie Portman and Julia Roberts and Clive Owen that made me feel a hundred years old and completely alone in the universe.

My dad was feeling under the weather, and this helped me. He's simultaneously stoical and hypochondriacal, my father: he'll be trumpeting ostentatiously into his linen handkerchief while insisting that nothing's the matter – his voice a croak, his eyes red-rimmed and filmy – and then suddenly he'll wave his fork at you and confide, alongside the jiggling speared sausage or lettuce leaf, that he's read in the Mayo Clinic newsletter about an underreported but devastating viral bronchitis, every symptom for which he seems to have; or about the warning signs for prostate cancer that have him worried about how often he urinates (he never says 'pees'); or about adult-onset diabetes that could explain why he seems so often to take an afternoon nap. He doesn't want you to feel concern about his symptoms but would like you to be aware, as he is aware, that at any and all times he is, or may be, stepping closer to death.

I went with him right after school ended to the old Isabella Stewart Gardner Museum. We were supposed to attend a concert in their cavernous music room, a string quartet on a wooden dais in front of two hundred retirees and music nerds in rustling coats in the dark in the middle of the day; but he decided at the last minute that his cold symptoms – a vigorous postnasal drip that had him constantly clearing his throat, a stream of catarrh that required much nose blowing – would spoil the experience both for him and for the rest of the audience. So instead we wandered the galleries with their familiar contents, tiptoeing among the masterpieces that seemed still to have Isabella's dominating fingerprints upon them, all the way up to the room at the top where she herself, immortalized by Sargent, proud and myopic, stood guard over her domain. Afterward, we scurried down to the tearoom to get a table ahead of the concertgoers. My father, who in age has developed a sweet tooth, ordered hot chocolate and a cake.

'Your mother loved this place,' he observed, as he always did, as though that were reason enough to come.

'The tearoom, you mean?'

'The whole thing. That courtyard. All those ferns. She loved that. Whenever we came, she'd say so.'

'Do you love it too?'

'Bit dark for me. Nice art, but it's all jumbled up. Seems like it needs a good spring cleaning.'

'We didn't have to come here, you know.'

He shook his head, even as he was blowing his nose. I could see a small crusty scab on his bald pate: another skin cancer that would have to be burned off. 'It's good for me. I know that.'

'What, culture?'

'It was your mother who loved these things. But it's important to do them sometimes, even if you don't love them. And it's nice to be with you.'

'I don't get it. Why's it important? If you don't enjoy it, then why, especially at your age . . . '

'At that point, why anything, Nora? Don't be silly. You get dressed because you get dressed. You don't ask if you *enjoy* it. You eat most meals because a body's got to eat. And it's the same with the museums: once in a while, you've got to do it.'

'Standards? You're saying it's about keeping up standards? That seems weird to me.'

'Is this interesting, Nora?'

'To me it is. You're saying that you should do things *as if* you cared about them, even when you don't?'

'Sometimes you might learn something.' He fumbled at a bit of cake that had fallen from his fork. 'Life isn't just about doing things you enjoy, you know.'

'God knows I know that. But the museum isn't like, I don't know, property taxes or anything. It's supposed to be a pleasure.'

'I didn't say it wasn't pleasurable.'

'Yes you did. You implied it. I mean, we could go to the movies, or whatever, instead.'

'Nora, why are you doing this? Can't we have our cocoa and talk about nice things? How was the Christmas assembly with the kids?'

'Holiday assembly. Nobody says "Christmas" anymore, Dad. It was fine. I'll leave it alone now, but I want to say that it seems important, you know—'

He put his hands up. 'Nora. Please. Let's say we've come here for your mother. It makes me remember how much your mother enjoyed it. Is that good enough?'

'Of course, Dad.' I sighed. I sipped my tea. 'So the third-grade play this time was *The Fir Tree*. Do you know it? From the story by Hans Christian Andersen . . . '

From my father, then, I tried to take the WASP's advice to live *as if*. As if the Fun House were real life. As if I enjoyed things I didn't enjoy. As if I were happy, and as if I hadn't been abandoned by the people I loved.

Didi wasn't buying it. Three days before Christmas, at the busiest time of year, she left the shop in the hands of Jamie, her employee, for two hours, and took me to tramp through the snow around Jamaica Pond, smoking pot and sipping hot mulled wine from a thermos.

'What's eating you, doodlebug?' Her cheeks were ruddy from

the cold, her vivid hair blowing from beneath her cap. She has big feet and took big strides, planting herself with each step.

'What are you talking about?'

'Vegas, Vegas. What happens here, stays here. I won't even spill to Esther, I promise.' She always said that and I never knew wholly whether to believe her. 'You're miserable about *something*.'

'How can you tell?'

'You're wearing makeup. Sure sign. Spill it.'

'There's nothing to spill.'

'Flirtation in the corridors? A tasty new science teacher? A fireman who waves when you pass the station each morning?'

'Ridiculous.'

'Somebody's maligned you? School politics again? That Shauna bitch?'

'She's not a bitch. She and I don't always agree, but she's not a bitch.'

'Do you think the FBI has us bugged? What's going on?'

'Nothing's going on.'

'So that's the problem.' She stopped marching and looked straight at me, straight through me. 'It's the studio, isn't it?'

'What about it?'

'It's that woman, and the studio. It's your work. It's about your art. I can tell.'

'What can you tell?'

We walked on a stretch in silence. She knew when to wait. It was like shucking oysters: a skill.

'I'm not working,' I said. 'Not at all.'

'But that's crazy – it's vacation week. You don't have the brats, you don't have to travel. What's going on?'

'I can't bring myself to go there.'

'Is it a process problem? Are you stuck?'

'No.'

'It's a personal problem. It's the Siren. Let me guess: She takes up too much space? She doesn't stop talking? She smells bad!' Didi giggled a dopey giggle, and then caught herself. 'Are you crying?'

'No,' I said, but there were tears behind my eyes and even as I blinked I saw her see them. 'It's nothing.'

And then, I tried to explain. I explained about the weeks of work and conversation, the autumn in which I'd come somehow to feel that Sirena and Reza were mine, were my family almost, my secret; and then the strangeness of meeting Skandar, and the greater strangeness of my dream, that it made me self-conscious even to recall; and I told the story of the attack, the hospital, being in their house; and then the silence afterward.

I kept thinking, as I was telling Didi, that somehow what was in my head – in my memory, in my thoughts – was not being translated fully into the world. I felt as though three-dimensional people and events were becoming two-dimensional in the telling, and as though they were smaller as well as flatter, that they were just *less* for being spoken. What was missing was the intense emotion that I felt, which, like water or youth itself, buoyed these small insignificant encounters into all that they meant to me. There they were, shrinking before my eyes; shrinking into my words. Anything that can be said, can be said clearly. Anything that cannot be said clearly, cannot be said.

By the time I finished the telling, I was desolate. The cold of the wind and the snow on the path, the rimed, graded ice of the pond, it was all inside me, and my heart, small and shrunken, was without.

'Don't you feel better for talking about it?' Didi said, her giant's hand gently on my shoulder.

'Not really,' I said. 'I think I feel worse.'

'So you're in love with Sirena, and you want to fuck her husband and steal her child. Have I got it right?'

'Not one bit.'

'You summarize, then, in twenty words or less. How would you account for it all?'

'It's like waking up, you know? At school, each year, I take out this coffee-table book about the wonders of the world, both natural and man-made, and it's full of the most incredible photographs – of Ayers Rock, the Great Wall of China, Angkor Wat, Petra, the Eiffel Tower, the Pyramids—'

'I get it.'

'And the point is that whenever I lose faith in my life, I look at those pictures and I think, "You haven't been here" and "You haven't seen that," and I'm suddenly filled with wonder, like the sky opening, you know, to think that all this exists, and hope, because I might someday experience some of it – the smells, the sounds, what the light is like.'

'So, okay?'

'So this fall, them, it's been a bit like that: the sky opening; hope. A feeling of possibility. Yes, hope. Like maybe it isn't all over yet.'

'Why would it all be over?'

'Because I'm thirty-seven and single and I teach elementary school and wear clogs every day.'

'I'm thirty-nine next month. Almost forty. I like to think of it as a whole new decade beginning. It's gonna be great. I know it – Esther is forty-two, after all, and she just gets hotter by the minute.'

'By the minute?'

'To me, yeah. But that's not the point. What's got you so downcast, then? They've given you hope, and now they've gone away for the holidays. I don't get the big downer. They wouldn't have invited you over for Christmas dinner even if they'd been here, would they? Or would you have invited them to join you and your dad at Aunt Baby's place in Rockport?'

I was laughing in spite of myself. We'd circled the pond and were almost back where we'd started, close to the Jamaicaway and the roar of the traffic. An old lady was walking her old dog along the footpath toward us, a gray-muzzled black Lab that picked through the snow as though it pained his paws; but she, the old lady, was muttering to herself, shaking her head in its woolly cap and laughing, like me.

'Come on, it's got to be hormonal. You don't have any actual reason to feel sorry for yourself.'

'I took Reza to the hospital. I stayed with them half the night. And then they don't even call to say he's okay?'

'So they're bush pigs. Raised by wolves. No big deal. That describes half of America and probably more than half of the world at large. A handwritten note on personalized stationery would've been ideal, but hey, you can't have everything.'

'But they might not even come back.'

'Why wouldn't they come back?'

'She hates it here, she told me; and now that Reza's been attacked twice . . . it seems possible they'd stay in Paris.'

'Then you'll get the whole studio all for yourself. Come on, Nora, you're being ridiculous.'

'If it seems ridiculous to you, it's because I haven't properly explained to you what it feels like.'

Didi tossed a stick out onto the ice, where it skittered and slid, and made the black Lab, now far away, bark. 'You've told me all right. I get it. But you have to stop thinking that what you're feeling isn't in your control.'

'It isn't. You can't help how you feel.'

'Says who?'

I shrugged. 'It's cold. Can we go back now?'

'Okay. But you know, you don't even have to feel the cold if you choose not to.'

'Right. Really.'

'You're making up stories in your head. There's nothing real in them. You don't have any idea what those people are doing, or thinking, or why your Siren didn't call. You're just making stuff up.'

'I'm not a fool, you know.'

Didi put her arm around my shoulder. She emanated heat, even in the frigid air. 'Nobody's calling you a fool. Just a pessimist. If all you know is that you don't know, can't you let go a bit? Or at least make up a good story?'

'My OCD gets in the way.'

'So put your OCD to work for you. Get back to that studio and sit down and finish Emily's room. So that whatever happens when they come back, or even if they don't come back – which I seriously doubt – you'll have the satisfaction of having used the time. My mother always said there's no sense worrying about things you can't do anything about.'

'A cliché for every occasion.'

'That's my mom. But she's no fool, either, you know.'

So I tried to take Didi's advice, too. Christmas itself was spent in Aunt Baby's condo by the sea in Rockport with her – my mother's sister – and my father, two lonely and mild septuagenarians not even given to sentimental reminiscence, stultifyingly locked in their present, their small ailments, the weather, the television news, which news was full of nothing – although only a day later, when the tsunami struck in Asia, it would be full of death. We labored jauntily through an enormous meal – the dry turkey I was involved in overcooking, the vast tray of candied yams, the bready stuffing and roast potatoes and the limp green beans – serenaded by the tinkling loop of Christmas carols from the Vienna Boys' Choir that Aunt Baby had loved all my life.

Heavily jowled and powdered, physically so different from her birdlike sister, my mother, Aunt Baby, arthritic, limped in such a way that every step put me in mind of her unoiled bones grinding in their sockets. Even with, or perhaps because of, her carefully outlined crimson mouth, she looked like my dead grandfather in drag, had sparse white hair voluminously flossed to mask her scalp, and a scratchy deep voice. She smelled strongly of Yardley English Lavender, difficult, in the twenty-first century, to procure on the open market.

She'd never married, was devoutly Catholic, and what I most feared becoming: doughty, self-sufficient and utterly without issue. I sat on her pristine sky-blue couch and tried not to see, on every flat surface, the rows of framed family photos of my brother and me growing up, of my parents and grandparents, of my second cousins in Atlanta, her cousin June's three kids, similarly recorded from layettes to graduations to weddings, and even the newest additions, my niece, my cousins' kids, in frames as carefully dusted and apparently antique as the rest. It had always been faintly effronting to me, the way Aunt Baby claimed our family lives as if they were her own, as if Matt and I were her offspring instead of her sister's. 'Get your own life,' I'd wanted to say, 'you can't have mine!' But how could she have gotten her own life when she'd given it over to the care of others – her parents, her relatives, fellow parishioners. She'd always been the sidekick. Even in dying, my mother got to play the starring role. Now I would want to ask her where she stowed her fury and how she managed always to appear so calm, so humbly thrilled by the smallest attentions (I gave her an espresso machine that Christmas, and although I later discovered she never used it, she grew wavery and emotional when she opened the package: that I'd thought this much of her! That she'd been so valued!), but she is a casualty of these last five years, blessed, as she would have seen it, to suffer an aneurysm in the parish office and never to regain consciousness, a sweet death in repayment for her life of devotion, and a burden, mercifully, to no one.

I can imagine, now, what it cost her, to be our Aunt Baby, an overaged infant to the last, instead of the grown-up named Cecily Mallon that she might have become. Knowing my own life and how little of what most matters in it is seen on the outside, how remotely my own outline resembles my reflection, I'm sorry to think that the real Aunt Baby is now lost forever. I, who so feared resembling her, couldn't ask, and know that nobody else thought to, so brave Aunt Baby lived 'as if' until the end. Although then again, maybe she followed my father's precepts so assiduously that her soul and her self in the world became one.

At least Christmas in Rockport was quick. We went before noon, we helped to cook, we took a drive along the shore to watch the waves bash whitely on the rocks in their eternal rhythm; we ate, cleaned, left. By nine thirty on Christmas night I was back at my apartment, having dropped my father in Brookline on the way home. I'd done all of the dishes for Baby before we left, leaving her to sit in the overheated living room with her swollen feet up on an ottoman, gossiping languidly with my father about the ailments of their generation.

'You heard about Ruby Howard? Bernie's wife? It's not Alzheimer's – it's the worse one, the Parkinson's one. Lewy Body? You know what that is? Terrible.' A long silence, during which time they might both have been napping, and then Aunt Baby again: 'And then Pete Runyon – you remember him from your church? They moved up here when he retired, and his wife, Beth, developed emphysema – she's home, mostly, now, with her oxygen tank on wheels. I've been round to see her a few times lately, cheer her up. But now Pete's got a cancer diagnosis. The bladder, I think. Or maybe the prostate – but not the easy kind, if it is. Beth's very discreet, and it's clearly something with his waterworks, something private. She didn't want to say, exactly. It looks bad, though.' She sighed. 'Don't you think it's worst when both people in a couple are sick? I always do. It's different when you're on your own – you're both more of a burden and less of a burden. I mean, you've got to get into a home, no question about it, and that's that. No gray areas. Take Alice and Robin Meynell, for example – do you see who they are? Well, she had a stroke last spring and . . . '

And on. I cleaned pots, Baby cleaned out the medical closets of all her acquaintances, and my father, phlegmatic, digested. At the door, between warm and cold, I kissed her soft, grainy cheek, I held her clawlike hand in mine, I took my father's arm, shepherded him across the residual ice – a black swoop here and there along Baby's tarmac walk – and settled him in his seat. At the other end, I pulled the car under the porte cochère – his building, concierged, had salted assiduously – and accompanied him all the way up to his apartment door, carrying for him his Trader Joe's grocery bag modestly half full of presents (a new electric razor; a biography of Hamilton; a pair of cashmere-lined gloves) with a Tupperware container of mushy yams on top.

I was, by then, burning, not sleeping. Who would do the same for me, in my dotage? Who would be my good girl? Would it be Matt and Tweety's precious Charlotte? I couldn't see it. No: I derived a certain bitter thrill in thinking that I'd manage to the end on my own, a thrill of denial and austerity, a thrill not unlike a dieter's pleasure at her gnawing stomach. I will be continent. I will continue. I will not spill into the lives of others, greedily sucking and wanting and needing. I will not. I will ask nothing, of anyone; I'll just burn, from the inside out, self-immolating like those monks doused in gasoline. Spontaneous combustion, almost. Almost. Merry Fucking Christmas to You.

In my fury, I did the strangest, most unlike-me thing: at ten o'clock on Christmas night I drove myself through the slick and empty streets, festooned with pagan lights, to Somerville, to the deathly quiet of the warehouse, where I scuttled nimbly up the sagging stairs, my keys between my fingers like a weapon (even in my fury I had room around the edges to be afraid), and I let myself into the studio and locked the door behind me.

It was freezing – the heat had obviously been turned down for days – and at that I hesitated, wondering if I'd made a mistake. But I fixed some coffee, and I turned the music on, and I rifled among Sirena's things and found a pair of fingerless gloves made of soft black wool. When I put them on I felt like a character in a *Masterpiece Theatre* production ('Please, sir, can I have some more?'), but they did the trick; I could wiggle all digits without stiffness. I sat down at my table, not in my pool of light but with every fucking overhead light and standing lamp and desk lamp in the entire studio on full blast, as much light as I could get, a Ralph Ellison ocean of light, and I got to work, at long last, with Emily D.

Every time I thought I heard a noise, I'd listen harder to the music, or sing along with it, or stomp my feet. It was Christmas night: there wasn't anyone in the building. There wasn't anyone in the street. I was all by my own, as the children say, and I would stay that way till the end. Fuck them all, and if anyone tried to break in or scare me or rape me, I'd give them a piece of my rage.

I worked without moving for four hours, and then, too chicken to go to the bathroom down the hall, I peed in a bucket in the corner of the room and washed it out in the sink and sat down again to work for another four hours, only I got very tired, a blind sort of tired, the sort where your eyes can't see anymore and go all blurry as though you were having a stroke, to the point where I couldn't trust what I was making and had to stop awhile. So I put my tools down and I wrapped myself in all her scarves and shawls – they smelled of her perfume, of lemons – and I put a couple of her cushions down on the little rug and the least dusty bit of the floor, near the chairs, and I lay down with my coat over my feet, and right there in the bright light, with the music still playing (it was a five-disc boom box, with a loop: Annie Lennox, Joan Armatrading, Joni Mitchell – old stuff, girl stuff, my reliable musical mates seeing me into slumber), and knowing that I would live with Emily into the new year, and that I would finish Emily's room – maybe even finish the electrics that would allow Emily's visions – before I had to go back to school – knowing, that is, that I was on fire and where I wanted to be and angry enough, for once, to be my own self, I closed my eyes, ran my tongue across my mossy teeth and went immediately to sleep.

PART TWO

1

By the time school started, Emily's room was ready. All it lacked were the projections, her own magic lantern illuminating her words, Death himself, the Muse, Joy. I'd spent the week from Christmas to New Year's almost entirely sealed in with Emily. I'd had dinner with my father once, and had met a group of four girlfriends for drinks – intimates for years, they seemed to me raucous and silly that night, a million miles from my world – but aside from those excursions, I'd been long days, long evenings, in my private white-lit space, sanding and gluing and whittling, eating stale cheese sandwiches wrapped in wax paper that I fixed, half asleep, in the mornings at home, and browned apple quarters and bars of expensive, almost crumbly, Italian chocolate, very dark, in gilded foil, that were my reward when things went well. I didn't sleep there again, because I'd felt my age the morning after Christmas, my bones sore, my joints stiff; but I'd conquered some demon and no longer feared the dark. No: that's not quite true. I still feared the dark – when I quit the building near midnight, I raced like Cinderella down the stairs, two at a time, before the clock might strike, and dashed to my battered VW Golf as if to my imminently vanishing gilded pumpkin coach – but I was more in love with Emily, that week, than I was afraid of anything else. I felt pure and quiet and proud; and alone with it, like Emily herself.

As for the others – the Shahids – I'd cauterized, or thought I had. If I'd said to Didi that it was a wound, she would've scoffed; but it was, and at her urging, I'd forced it to scab. Which was all very well until they came back.

On the first day of school, when I watched him stomp in his snow boots into the classroom with his backpack and his black-and-white pom-pom hat in hand, a hard look set upon his tender face that, when he saw me, saw me smile, softened, reciprocally, into a grin of such real and direct affection, a grin of the furry-lashed eyes – his dear, scarred eye! – as much as of his lips, and when I saw that smile, my smile, for me, my innards somersaulted as if I were a teenager blown a kiss by a pop star.

I hadn't known for sure, had I, that he'd return. No call, no e-mail, no note – I'd even wondered, fingering Sirena's scarves in my studio, catching their vestigial scent – not our studio, in those days, but mine – whether I'd dreamed the lot of them, whether all my talks with her had been no more real than my fantasized sexual encounter with her husband.

There is a story by Chekhov like this that had fascinated me in college. The black winter of my second year, assailed by doubt at not having gone to art school, I'd read it over and over. 'The Black Monk': about a man who imagines himself visited by a ghostly monk, with whom he has life's vital conversations, about creativity, and greatness, and the meaning of existence. The monk assures him of his importance, of his exceptional talents. Then he realizes that the monk isn't real; that he himself must be mad. But how much better to be mad in the company of the monk, than to be sane, and constrained in his aspirations, and alone. And mediocre. That, worst of all, is what he has to acknowledge, when his family forces him into clarity: that he's nothing special after all. Sirena had been my Black Monk, and perhaps she'd been only a delusion.

But there was Reza, quite suddenly, in our classroom at Appleton, holding out to me, with almost a blush, a tacky key chain of the Eiffel Tower, a belated Christmas present. So he – even they – had thought about me, too. They'd missed me. My first thought was that she'd be at the studio at that moment, and I had half a mind to skip out of school, to leave them all behind, and go to find her. Never mind that I'd accomplished as much in my ten solitary days as I had in all the weeks of talk leading up to them – she was my Muse, my alcoholic's bourbon on the rocks: irresistible.

Reza's eye didn't look too bad. He'd had the stitches out; the scar – tidy, tidy, I'd seen the surgeon at her seam, hemming his flesh – was red, still, and looked raw, but didn't cause alarm among the children. If anything, it gave Reza a rakish air, as if he were a beautiful little bandit. He deflected all questions about the incident, with knowing smiles and taps upon the shoulder: an initiate, he gave nothing away.

He did, however, expand about Paris, about the bumper cars at the Bastille and his favorite bakery, where a warty old woman named Léonie gave him a *palmier* every morning because she was so happy to see him. He told about the white plastic Christmas tree that listed wildly in the lobby of their building, and the resident dogs that lifted a leg in passing against its synthetic trunk, so that quickly the entrance grew redolent not of pine needles and snow but of stale urine. Reza was, for a child, and given the gaps in his English, a good storyteller, and he managed to make everyone laugh, which made us all feel, after the interruption of break, like a family again.

I didn't go to the studio that afternoon, because I didn't want to seem pathetic to myself. I didn't want to want so much to see her. It was my austerity choice, my show of independence. I didn't even know whether she'd be there. Instead, I went for a run and bought fresh trout from the fishmonger, and went home.

I'm not a cook. I'd bought the fish but didn't want to prepare it; I'd taken it out of the fridge and put it back again, and was eyeing the cans of soup in the cupboard when my buzzer rang, downstairs. I almost didn't go down: it was cold in the stairwell, and I expected it to be kids selling magazine subscriptions or the MASSPIRG guy shilling for handouts. As I approached the door, I switched on the outside light, my frown at the ready.

And there she was, in a long black puffy coat, carrying a big bag: shorter, one eye lazier, her hair more ragged than in my mind's eye, but smiling, arms out wide, her elegant curled lip stretched over her slightly prominent front tooth, her crow's-feet crinkled.

'*Carissima!*' she exclaimed. 'My dear, dear Nora! How have you been?' She took my upper arm with her hand, tightly, and led me inside and shut the door behind us. 'Hard at work – you've been so hard at work! I was there this afternoon, at the studio. It is perfection, this little room you've made—' She was almost herding me up the stairs, but stopped, held me at arm's length, and looked at me: 'What extraordinary work you've done, Nora. Your Emily's room is unlike anything else.'

'Oh, hardly.' I was delighted, and bashful. 'What are you doing here?'

'I've brought you something. To eat. I brought it from Paris for you, and I thought, Maybe this will please Nora for supper tonight, and it will give me a chance to say hello, and thank you.'

'Thank you?'

'Ah, Nora! You know why. I've felt terrible that we never properly said good-bye, that I never thanked you. When what would we have done without you? I hate the e-mail, and the telephone too – especially in English, I get confused – but at last here I am, with a foie gras and a bottle of Sancerre, and some very special panettone, to say "Happy new year."'

'Foie gras?'

'You don't like it? I worried you might not. Don't feel you have to eat it. I'll bring you something else – a quiche? A stew? What would be nice?'

'I love foie gras. Really. Thank you.'

She was all aflutter. She was happy to see me. She felt guilty about having left without saying good-bye. She had brought me a foie gras. Could I have been more content? I poured her a glass of her Sancerre, although it wasn't properly cold. I debated offering to put in ice cubes, but decided not to.

There she was: Sirena in my kitchen. She'd never been there before. She said nice things about my apartment. She admired the art. She threw her puffy coat on the sofa and sat at the kitchen table as if we were settling in for a long tête-à-tête. I, like the yellow fat around the foie gras as I scooped it out of the jar, was positively deliquescent.

'How was it to be home?'

'Home? Oh, Nora. I only wish it were home, the way Cambridge is home for you – this beautiful apartment, which smells of you and speaks of you, the place you know so well and that knows you. But what I always forget and then rediscover when I return is that I don't belong in Paris, not really – I'm a foreigner there, too. For whom is Paris home, really, except the concierges gossiping in their corners?'

'But you must've been pleased—'

'Yes, I know what you mean. Reza so loves his little friends. And Skandar his big ones. It was a relief, in some ways – not to feel so responsible for them.'

'But for you?'

'I have history there, and friends, and colleagues; and home is where my boys are, of course. But do you know this idea of the imaginary homeland? Once you set out from shore on your little boat, once you embark, you'll never truly be at home again. What you've left behind exists only in your memory, and your ideal place becomes some strange imaginary concoction of all you've left behind at every stop.'

'So you didn't have a good time?'

'I did, and I didn't. I missed you, and the studio, my work – I wasn't like you, you see – no creation for me, just a great many meals in restaurants and the busyness of holidays.' I didn't entirely know whether to trust her: she was seeming false, to me, as if onstage.

'When did you get back?'

'A day or two ago. Skandar had to be in New York by last night – another conference. Meetings. You know how he is.' A rueful smile. I thought of how often she was on her own – but with Reza. Not like me. Not truly alone.

'But I want to hear about you,' she said. 'A new year, a new beginning. What have you been up to while we've been gone?'

'It's been pretty quiet, really. Getting on with things.'

'Christmas?'

'With my father and my aunt.'

'Not the troublesome brother?'

'Matt? He doesn't come at this time of year. When you have your own family, you're absolved, aren't you?'

'Absolved? Not where I come from. My mother came to stay with us, and my oldest sister. It was very noisy at our house. Reza was profoundly spoiled.'

'That sounds like what Christmas should be.'

'Yes, I suppose. But you see, everyone has a part to play. In this theater, I'm a daughter and a sister and a mother – never an artist. I could be, I don't know, Luc Tuymans, and it would mean nothing to them. They allow no room for anything but my duty.'

'Tell me about it.'

'You? But you're so free! I envy you that. How many times I thought of the studio and of you in it, working. Or of you thinking, calmly, here in your lovely apartment – it's not exactly how I imagined it, but not so far off. While I was making beds and stews and presents and silly conversation ...'

'The grass is always greener ...' I thrilled to think she'd thought of me – had thought enviously of me. 'I was worried about Reza.'

'He's done so well. You've seen his eye, yes? The scar will be quite discreet ... You were so good to him, and to me, that awful evening.'

'You were worrying about the emotional stuff.'

'Emotional stuff. Ah, yes. Boys throwing rocks. But children are resilient. It's good we went away – he's had a chance to forget. He had some nightmares, but couldn't tell me what they were about. I don't know if they were related. Who can say? Shauna McPhee tells me the boy was expelled.'

'Straight away.'

'So: now a new year, a new beginning. I've vowed not to complain. I'm too good at it, and need to practice other skills. I've also vowed to work very hard – it's no time at all from now until May. The months will be gone before we know it; and I've promised my gallery that I'll come home ready for my exhibition. So: *au travail!*' She stood up as she said this: time to go. And then: 'What have you promised yourself for the new year?'

I hesitated. I hadn't made any new year's resolutions. That night I'd spent in the studio, oblivious to the time, aware only too late that the ball had dropped in Times Square, I'd wished Emily D happy new year: I'd lifted her, in her lacy nightgown, from her high, narrow bed, and had stroked her glossy head; and then had returned her, carefully, to her doll-house life. Happy new year to you. 'I've resolved to be more independent,' I said.

'You? But you're more independent than anyone!'

'More alone, maybe.' And for some reason I thought of my mother, each day more trapped, until she was buried in her aloneness. 'It's not the same thing, you know.'

2

Because I'd complained of my solitude, I worried that Sirena's invitation to dinner the following week was a pity call. I was invited for 7:30. I arrived at 7:40, afraid I was late, carrying a bottle of expensive Italian red – Barolo, I think – recommended by the girl behind the cheese counter at Formaggio. I had the feeling when he opened the door that Skandar was surprised to see me.

'Ah! You're here. Sirena, Nora is here. Come in.' The entrance was very narrow, the stairs heading straight up, and Skandar had to back up them in order for me to get in the door. It wasn't clear what physical salutation, if any, was in order, so we did nothing but bob and smile awkwardly.

'I haven't got the wrong day, have I?'

He shook his head, laughing, and reached for my coat, backing up the stairs the whole time.

'The wrong time?'

Sirena appeared at the summit, with Reza beside her, already in his checked pajamas. 'Welcome! So much better than your last visit to our house. This time, we offer you superior food to toast and tea.'

They'd set the table with flowers and candles, so the horrid tinted globe light was turned off, and by lighting strategic lamps around the space, they'd managed to make it almost attractive.

'Come, Miss E, come see my room.' Reza at once took me by the hand and pulled, while his father poured wine and his mother returned to the stove.

I followed him there to find that it, too, was transformed, by a slowly spinning magic lantern that cast upon the wall the colored shadows of jazz musicians playing – a green drummer at his kit, a rose saxophonist, a burly blue outline wielding a bass guitar. A large poster of a running soccer player – French, I assumed – took up most of the wall above his bed, and flickered in the light almost as if alive.

'That's Zidane,' Reza explained. 'He's the best. He used to play for Juventus – do you know them?'

'No.'

'Let me explain . . . ' He pulled me down to sit beside him on the bed and began to recount, with more enthusiasm perhaps than clarity, the trajectory of Zidane's career, on both the French national teams and the league teams.

'Reza' – his father was smiling in the doorway, holding a glass of red wine and a scotch with ice – 'your time with Miss Nora is in the day, at school. This evening is for grown-ups.'

'In a minute? Please?'

Skandar said something in French. He handed me the glass of wine and retreated.

Reza smiled conspiratorially. 'I have three minutes,' he whispered, 'but nobody will know if we take four.'

⌒

Reza had already eaten, and although he sat for a while with us, swinging his legs and picking idly from a bowl of grapes, he didn't volunteer much, nor even particularly appear to be listening, and before the starter of imam bayaldi and crostini had been cleared he'd asked to be excused and had gone to read *Astérix* in his room.

This was a shame, really, in spite of his odd superfluity; because in the same way that three people only barely constitute a family, a meager and Spartan sort of family, so too three people barely constitute a dinner party. This is especially true when two are intimates and the third an alien, an Upstairs Woman with manners and insufficient temerity. There is, about such a scenario, an aura of hard work – at least at first. We were all very polite, toiling through our excellent eggplant dish with its crusty toasts. We talked about school; how long had I been there, Skandar asked, and how did it compare to other schools? And then more broadly, how did American and French educations compare; and yes, please – because it really does help – another glass of red would be lovely ... And then, bit by bit, it got less stiff. Sirena talked about her schooldays in Milan, and then Skandar spoke of his education in Beirut, at a French-language college, and how his parents had sent him to boarding school in Paris for the last two years (it was, he said, like something out of an old French movie, brutal and competitive and austere, with students flipping out left and right from the pressure, and horse-meat for supper. 'Stray cats picked through garbage and howled in the alleyway outside the kitchens, and we used to joke that *they* were in the casseroles') and how this had altered forever the course of his life without him even knowing it at the time. 'Half of my friends from home – maybe more than half – went instead to the American University there, in Beirut; and then they ended up coming here, to the States, for graduate school or whatever. Which means their lives are in English, at least, or are American – all the way, in some cases.' He paused. 'A couple are in Canada. In Montreal, you can eat your cake and have it too –

speak French and English and Arabic also, because there are so many Lebanese there now.'

'And how's it different for you? You're in America now – you're at Harvard. You can't get closer to the American establishment than that.'

Behind his glasses he opened his eyes wide in an ironic gesture that made his eyebrows dart up his forehead. 'Yes, I suppose,' he said. 'But that isn't my point, really. There's a way of being in exile, for the educated of any non-European country, that can be very comfortable in its worldliness . . . '

'The land of silly accents,' I said aloud, without quite meaning to.

'What do you mean?' Sirena frowned.

'Something a friend once said. She worked in radio, but somehow she was invited to an academic dinner, all these old professors at Princeton, and she said half of them had won the Nobel Prize, and that not one spoke English without a silly accent. She said she felt like she'd taken a plane to the land of geniuses with silly accents.'

Skandar smiled vaguely.

'Not that I'm saying you guys have silly accents.'

'But it's quite so, your friend is exactly right. In this country, there are pockets like this, almost like low-lying clouds. We're in one here. They are in America, or on it, but they have very little to do with it, and we – the brown, the black, the yellow, the Jews and Arabs from all over – we congregate, each in our diaspora, and make a world of familiar conversation, a small life in our ivory towers. And we bark at one another in our silly accents, in what is to most of us a foreign tongue. I always marvel that we manage to communicate at all. But maybe we manage to say more than we think – or maybe less. I'm not sure.'

'English is the tyranny,' Sirena put in, looking cross, as if the language itself could be blamed.

'But isn't it similar in France? You were saying the other day that you don't feel really at home there, either.'

'In France,' she said dryly, 'people speak French rather than English.'

'But also now more English.' Skandar was highly amused. 'And sometimes even German. It's not uncommon to encounter colleagues with whom one might speak all three languages, in different moments. There, you are *in Europe*, not floating on top of it like an alien body.'

'I'm not sure I understand.'

He paused, drank. From his eyes I could tell he was ironic and serious at the same time. 'In Europe, for good or bad, history is always there, the context is always present. When I say I'm Lebanese of Palestinian extraction, from Beirut, that I'm predominantly a Christian by heritage, and then that I went to university in Paris, that I teach at the École Normale, a great deal is immediately known about me – of what I am and what I am not. Still more can be gauged by my clothes, my demeanor – and I will be placed by these things. Not only by my fellow professors with "silly accents," but by the greengrocer or the taxi driver also.'

'What's so great about that? Especially if they're wrong?'

'I'm not saying that it's good or bad. I'm just explaining how it's different.'

'You mustn't be defensive of your country,' Sirena chided. Her irritation had been subsumed in the business of the main course. She was ladling up bowls of lamb stew over rice, fatty and spicy and fragrant.

'In America,' Skandar went on, 'there are places like Harvard, where I walk in the door and some version of this happens and I think no more about it. Not, here, so much about my social origins; more about my philosophical ideas, my academic affiliations. I'm known, in a certain way. But mostly—' The wry smile again. In my Barolo fog, I registered that it was a sexy smile, confidential somehow. 'Mostly, in America, I'm a cipher. If, to a person on the street, I say I'm from Beirut, he might ask me where that is. If I say I have Palestinian relatives and that I was raised a Christian, he may wonder "How is this possible?" And if I explain that I went to university in Paris, he might wonder that I've done such an illogical thing. In America, Europe and the Middle East seem very far away indeed. If you're a Lebanese who comes here for university, to study, then you become immediately American. You're accepted, which is wonderful, but you're given an entirely new suit of clothes, a new outline, that has no context, and you must grow to fit it, or fit it to shape you, or whatever. You come with no baggage.'

'Bring me your tired, your hungry . . . That's what this country is *for*.'

'Of course. I'm simply saying that if I'd come to this country at eighteen, instead of going to Paris, my shape, as well as the shape of my life, would be different, in countless ways.'

'But we are who we are,' said Sirena, in a slightly warning tone, the tone of a spouse who has heard it before, or who feels that her husband verges on the garrulous. 'And now, being who we are, we must eat. Nora, eat!'

I put a forkful of her extraordinary stew in my mouth, thinking, 'This, of everything this evening, is what I ought to remember: the explosion of flavors, pine nuts, lamb, cumin, currants' – but I was only half attending to my food. I was watching Skandar trifle with his portion while he spoke, and watching him speak only to me, as if Sirena were not in the room. Three is a difficult number, I thought again.

'Don't you think it works both ways, though?' I asked, eventually. 'I mean, if I go to live in Europe, or in Beirut, don't I suddenly appear, um, denuded? Here, I have my context; but there, I'm just an American.'

Skandar's eyes were, at this, appraising. As if assessing my Americanness as an attribute. '*Just* an American? Never. A beautiful woman like you, in France, or in Lebanon, would be seen above all as a beautiful woman. Not so, Sirena?'

Sirena gave a weary nod. 'I'm going to say good night to Reza. It's time he put out his light.'

A few moments later, she reappeared and interrupted her husband: 'Nora,' she beckoned from the hallway. 'Would you come for a moment? Do you mind?'

'Of course not.'

Reza sat up in bed and reached out both arms to embrace me – again, I was hugged, as if affection were commonplace. 'Good night, Miss E,' he spoke softly in my ear. 'You're the best.' Then he pulled back and bestowed upon me a luminous and loving smile. I know it sounds silly, but as if he were my own son. As if he actually loved me. I bathed in it; but felt angry, too, at all that Sirena had and seemed to take for granted, idling placidly in the doorway with her arms crossed and a dreamy faraway look.

'*Bonne nuit, chéri*,' she said to him, and something more, in French, as well, as we withdrew, and left him to the darkness and his brilliant spinning jazz musicians dancing across the wall.

⌇

Because it wasn't far – or because . . . I could imagine reasons that flattered me, and others that had nothing to do with me – Skandar offered to walk me home. It was only about six blocks, across the slope of the most prosperous stretch of Cambridge, past the dark, still gardens with their looming snow-tipped trees, past cavernous houses in which a single upstairs window shone yolkily out, illuminating a small swath of icy lawn; or past others, shrouded entirely by the night, like sleeping ogres.

Skandar smoked as we walked, cupping his cigarette inside his
hand like a fisherman in a gale. I was made awkward by him, by
the silence, though he didn't seem to notice, and I could think
of nothing better to say than that the streets were very quiet,
which pointless observation he ignored.

'A pretty girl like you,' he said, not looking at me, 'you have
no husband, no children?'

'Not right now.'

'You had a husband, then?'

'Almost, a long time ago.'

'A boyfriend?'

'Skandar, please . . . '

'I don't mean to embarrass you. But when Sirena told me you
were single, I thought surely there's a mistake, maybe you're just
very private.'

'No, nobody special right now.' And after a moment, 'And I'm
not gay.'

'I know you're not gay.'

Did he think I'd been flirting with him? 'How are you feeling
about Reza?'

'What about Reza?'

'About what happened at school, before the vacation.'

He shrugged, blew icy breath and smoke. 'Am I asked to have
feelings about it? I don't think so, ultimately. I wish it hadn't
happened; but what good does this do? I can wish it wouldn't
happen again – but here too, if I'm wishing the impossible, it
will do no good at all.'

'You're a cynic, then.'

He, usually slow in his movements, turned very quickly to
look at me, and his glance seemed almost angry. 'Cynic?
Absolutely not. I am a realist. I am a pragmatist. But I'm also an
optimist. Otherwise, I couldn't do what I do.'

'Which is?'

'To what end does one speak about the ethics of history, about the moral questions inherent in the very history of history, if not then to look to the future and hope – no, not to hope, to work, for better?'

'I suppose—'

'No, this is serious. I'm a man who studies and reflects, but I'm committed to the conversations going on, wherever they take place, among whichever parties. And they matter.'

I imagined a gilded halo around him, but it was the pinkish fizz of a streetlight. This was the trouble with places like Cambridge, Massachusetts: these people – these men – who thought they were God's gift; and yet about whom there remained some aura, and the possibility, just faint, that they *were* God's gift – it couldn't be gainsaid.

If they were a meal, I would have eaten all the courses with equal relish: each so distinct, and so uniquely flavorful. I had no way to conceive of them all together – I have to be clear about this, because otherwise you might think that I was fond of *a family*, that their family-ness was a pleasure to me; and you might infer from that that there was trust between us (a fact really true only about Reza), a mutuality the existence of which I always doubted. I was in love with Reza. I was in love with Sirena. I was in love with Skandar. All these things were true; they were not mutually exclusive, but they also, most important, did not, as far as I could see, pertain to one another.

Didi's construction – that I was in love with Sirena but wanted to fuck her husband and steal her child – wasn't right. I wanted a full and independent engagement with each of them, unrelated to the others. I needed their family-ness – how else would each of them have been brought to me? – and yet I despised it. I didn't want to be with them together (although that was preferable to not being with any of them) and I hated to think of them all together, in the evenings and on the weekends, without me and with barely a thought for me.

As for trust, I had so little: 'Why would he want even to talk to me?' I asked Didi, the next time I saw her. 'Why would he choose to walk me home, in the freezing cold, in the dark?' I couldn't quite admit to myself what I wanted her to say, what reassurance I was after, but I was physically aware of my disingenuousness, a tightening in the center of my chest – can you clench your esophagus?

'Do you need to ask? Men will be men will be men.'

I shook my head so hard it hurt. 'It isn't. It's not so simple. It can't be.'

'He can want your approval without himself wanting more.'

'I suppose—'

'I want you to want me,' she sang, 'I need you to need me ...'

'Live at Budokan. I know. But what does he want with my approval?'

'That's his way, perhaps.'

'It doesn't feel like a "way" – it feels specific, to me. There's a way of talking – of looking – he is looking *at me*, do you know what I'm saying?'

'You're saying he has the seducer's eyes.'

'No – it's much more transparent than seduction. He's not trying to impress me; he's really trying to talk to me; he's—'

Didi put a hand on each of my shoulders and looked me straight in the eyes. 'If he's good at his job,' she said, 'you won't think he is doing a job. That's what it means to be a seducer.' She let me go. 'Everybody, for such people, is the exception. You know that. Everybody is an individual to be conquered, and you're only as good as your last conquest. Which isn't about sex, necessarily, although it can be. It's what people said about Bill

Clinton – he always made you feel you were the only person in the room.'

'So you're saying that's his thing? And all he really wants is a quick blow job under the table?'

She shrugged. 'I'm not saying any of that. I've never met the guy. I'm saying that the world contains such people. If it's shaped like a maple leaf, the color and texture of a maple leaf, and you find it underneath a maple tree ... that's all I'm saying.'

But I knew better, even as I feared worse. Both with Sirena and with Skandar, I veered between fantasies of intimacy and of bleak rejection. Doubt, that fatal butterfly, hovered always in my breast. What did I bring to them? Who was I to them, neither glamorous nor obviously brilliant nor important in the world? And yet, all three of them looked to me for something, even if none of us could tell what it was. Each of them wanted something, and their wanting made me believe that I was capable. Not that I was an extraordinary woman, exactly, but only *not exactly* that. Something quite like that. Which always since childhood I had secretly wanted to believe – no: had in my most deeply secret self believed, knowing that the believing itself was a necessary precondition to any doing at all – but had never allowed myself to let on. It's not right to say that they made me think more highly of myself; perhaps more accurately, that they allowed me to, in their wanting. My lifelong secret certainty of specialness, my precious, hidden specialness, was awakened and fed by them, grew insatiable for them, and feared them, too: feared the power they might wield over me, and simply on account of that fear, almost certainly would.

So began, ironically, my babysitting season. Not the obvious pastime for a Not Exactly Extraordinary Woman; although I see, in retrospect, that it was the perfect – the inevitable – trajectory for the Woman Upstairs. Even at the time, I was aware of how it looked. Plenty of the teachers at Appleton Elementary, the young ones especially, did some babysitting for extra cash. I'd always been disdainful of this: it seemed a sure way to undermine one's teacherly authority. So much so that when Sirena first suggested the notion, I felt a chastening frisson, as if I'd been struck.

We were lying on cushions in the studio and I'd been laughing at her account of a formal Kennedy School dinner she'd attended, at which the snowy bigwig beside her had held forth for twenty minutes about the unelectability of the Democratic Party (himself a Democrat, without which the lecture might have been considered aggressive), with a glob of red soup glistening upon his chin. She said it seemed almost to be winking at her, the way it caught the light.

'Do you think he had botched dental surgery, and can't feel anything on his chin, so food routinely gathers in that little hollow? Or do you think if you get big enough in politics, in that behind-the-scenes sort of way, it's suddenly okay to fart in public or to have bits of food on your face? Or maybe he's from outer space, or like a person with autism?'

'In English we have a word for it,' I said. 'It's "asshole."'

'Don't,' she said, 'because it makes such seeping liquid only more upsetting.'

And we laughed so hard the tepid coffee splashed out of my cup and into my lap; and then somehow even that seemed related to the soup glob, and we laughed all over again. And only when we were catching our breath from laughing, both of us exhaling those strange almost sobbing breaths that accompany crazy mirth, did she say, very serious all of a sudden, 'You know, I've been meaning to ask for your help with something. To do with Reza.'

'What's wrong? Something at school I don't know about?'

'No, no – you mustn't worry so much. It's more about home. With Skandar's commitments, especially this term, we have to go out so much, you know. When Skandar isn't traveling, then three, sometimes four times a week – it's terrible. I hate it.' She sighed. 'And Reza hates it most of all. He weeps, often. He clings to me – we have fights – can you believe it? Or worse, he sulks. He goes into his room and shuts the door and won't come out to say good night, or let me in.'

'That doesn't sound like him.' I heard my teacher voice come out of my mouth. 'Have you tried talking to him about it? He's old enough, really – he's eight.'

'And seven, as they say, is the age of reason. I know. So yes, I've talked about it with him; and so now I ask your help.'

'Mine?'

'Because he says that it's only bearable, these evenings, if *you* come.'

'If I come? Come with you to the events?'

'Come to him, of course! Not every time – that would be ridiculous ...' She laughed, and it was not the same kind of laugh as before, and I knew that she knew that what she was asking wasn't quite right. Even when it was couched as Reza's request rather than her own, it was strange. It put us on a different footing, a different trajectory. I must have looked hurt.

'It isn't a business proposal, my friend.' She had her hand on my arm and seemed even to stroke it, as if I were a cat. 'It's a family proposal ... Oh dear, is it a cultural difference we're having here?' Much eye movement. 'In Italy, it's only the closest people that you can ask in this way, as if you were his *zia*, his auntie. You can picture him, can't you? So solemn and furious, and I said, "What would make it okay for Mummy and Daddy to go out and leave you? What could possibly make it okay?" And his face lit up, with the joy of asking an impossible dream; he said, "It would be all right if Miss E would come." Then, he said, it would be much better than all right – it would be better even than having *you* at home. And I looked sad, so then he said, "Well, it would be just as good." You know his face in such a moment – who can deny him? I promised him I'd ask you, because it would be his happiness ... and you mustn't feel you have to say yes – but the idea that you're upset when I ask, this I can't bear – my friend?' And as if the reach of her arm had been but an introductory tentacle, she rose and embraced me, one of her absolute, enveloping hugs that I found so unnerving.

'Of course,' she went on as she released me, 'we will pay you. That goes without saying.'

This made things even worse. 'Don't be ridiculous,' I said. 'I love Reza. I love you. I wouldn't hear of it.'

'But Nora – I insist – think of it, the amount of time—'

'Are you joking? Either I'm family or I'm not family. You wouldn't pay his auntie!'

'Ah, Nora.' Sirena shook her head. 'You are an extraordinary woman. And yes, of course you are family. Give me another hug.'

By which time I felt a fool, an uptight fool, for my boundaries and my rules. She honestly made me feel that I was honored to be chosen; that I was, in this role, irreplaceable.

In those next couple of months, everything and nothing happened. You could say, from the outside, that Miss Eldridge, a third-grade teacher in her late thirties, broke one of her cardinal rules and babysat, not once but numerous times, for one of her pupils. So what? You could say that she made unexpected progress with her artwork, launching not one but two room-boxes at once, in a general spirit of expansion; and you could add, accurately, that she became actively involved also in the creation of her friend Sirena's installation – in all sorts of small, practical ways, from sewing to soldering assistance, to the wiring of tiny lights and the placement of video cameras. And third, you could mention that during this stretch of manic unfolding – of wanton disinhibition – this same Miss Eldridge experienced, in conversation with her friend Sirena's husband, Skandar – or perhaps, more accurately, over time, with her own friend Skandar – a sort of awakening, a type of excitement about the wider world that she hadn't thought, in midlife, still possible.

You know those moments, at school or college, when suddenly the cosmos seems like one vast plan after all, patterned in such a way that the novel you're reading at bedtime connects to your astronomy lecture, connects to what you heard on NPR, connects to what your friend discusses in the cafeteria at lunch – and then briefly it's as if the lid has come off the world, as if the world were a dollhouse, and you can glimpse what it would be like to see it whole, from above – a vertiginous magnificence.

And then the lid falls and you fall and the reign of the ordinary resumes.

And if this happens, in youth, slightly more often than the passage of a comet, then in age it seems to happen not at all, or not at all to ordinary people like me. So that if I tell you that over the months from February to May of that year, 2005, it was as if a series of little explosions were being detonated in my brain – if I tell you that I had this lid-lifting experience of the world not once but more times than I can properly count, like some extraordinary prolonged cranial multiple orgasm, an endless opening and titillation of my soul – then you will perhaps understand why, for years afterward, I thought that saying 'yes' to the babysitting had without question been the right thing to do.

It became a ritual. And again, as my time with Sirena was kept almost a secret from Reza (in that it was never spelled out to him that we were together), those afternoons when I'd slip away in double time from Appleton to Somerville, to the studio in winter, blanched and window-steamed against the darkening light outdoors, a newborn-ness in its bright light – so too were my evenings with Reza a secret, and part of their wonder was their secrecy, as of a strange sort of almost affair, if that analogy can be imagined uncorrupted by the flesh. I mean that on those days when I'd be going in the evening to their town house by the river, Reza would know it, and knew also, from his parents, that he shouldn't make public reference to it. We played a dance of glances, of surreptitious significant smiles, that might have perturbed anyone who saw them, exchanged as they were between a boy of eight and a woman who might have been, but wasn't, his mother. Probably on average twice a week, I'd go from school to the studio, and from the studio home to drop my car, and then would walk – sometimes almost run – directly to the Shahids' house; and in this way, in the course of a single day, would enjoy each of the flavors after which I pined: Sirena-time, Reza-time and then – because he always saw me home to my door – Skandar-time.

My job, which for some years had loomed so large in my life, shrank, in my mind, to a shadow of itself, as these other employments took its place. You might have thought, talking to me, that I was barely teaching at all, a morning or two a week – but the truth is that my kids somehow made room for my need to let go: they made no trouble, or almost none, that winter and spring. The remedials struggled valiantly, and didn't lapse into truancy. The families, like dormant volcanoes, shed no molten rock upon their young: no breakups, no violence, no disappearing parents, no catastrophic illnesses. The boy in the second grade – not strictly my purview, but still – who was diagnosed with a brain tumor had the infinite luck for it to be benign. The gods were smiling.

You're thinking, 'But this poor woman, this middle-aged spinster, from where could she have conjured the idea that she had *a family;* or rather, that she had any family besides her father languishing in his ointment-pink apartment, and her Aunt Baby encrusted in her Rockport condo among the memorabilia, and, like a remote galaxy, Matt and Tweety and their kid out in Arizona?' But families have always been strange and elastic entities. Didi is much more my family than Matt could ever be. And I knew it, with each of the three Shahids, intuitively. I needed them, sure, and we can all argue about the moment when the balance tipped and I needed them so much that *I*

would be hurt. But you can't pretend they didn't need me too, each in his or her way. They wouldn't necessarily have admitted it – except Reza – but you can't tell me that they didn't love me. The heart knows. The body knows. When I was with Sirena, or Reza, or Skandar, the air moved differently between us; time passed differently; words or gestures meant more than themselves. If you've never had this experience – but who has not been visited by love, laughing? – then you can't understand. And if you have, you don't need me to say another word.

4

In late January, or perhaps early February, Sirena began to build her world in earnest: Wonderland. She'd spent the fall making the smaller bits – the soap and aspirin flowers in all sizes and in a rainbow of colors, the rain-storm of slivered mirror shards that would hang from the ceiling on near-invisible wires, stored in bags and boxes in her end of the L.

Now what had looked like an artist's equivalent of doodling was revealed to be purposeful: she unfolded for me, one early evening when we both stayed late, her blueprint. Like being shown the inside of her head, it made those little currents, those jolts, tickle all down my spine. This was surely an intimacy greater than any nakedness: to see this page spread out upon the worktable, with its erasures and its smudges and, given that it was Sirena's, a coffee ring or two, and all of it overlaid by her notes to herself, tiny, tiny insect-writing possible with only the sharpest of pencils and legible only, by anyone other than herself, with a magnifying glass.

She was building a Wonderland for everyone. Each of us would be Alice. And while it was, in part, about the mysteries of the imagination, it was also about a spiritual discovery of the existing world: Sirena was mixing together Lewis Carroll and the vision of a twelfth-century Muslim named Ibn Tufail, who wrote a story about a boy growing up alone on a desert island, discovering everything – including himself, and God – for the first time.

Sirena wasn't, like me, constrained by reality, by what actually *was* or *had been*. She took on storybook worlds, plundering other people's imaginations but not their histories. Maybe it's what made her – what makes her – a real artist in the eyes of the world, whereas I count as a spinster with a hobby, the sort of person about whom appalling words like 'zany' are used. But there's nothing zany about it. My Emily Dickinson room is exactly that: Emily Dickinson's room, constructed to replicate as precisely as possible the room as historians have determined it actually was, but in miniature. Always, I have an engagement with Death – because my art isn't, after all, about what is or what might be, but about what *was*. You could call each of my boxes a shrine.

Sirena, on the other hand, is engaged with the life force. We all want that, really. It's what attracts us: someone who opens doors to possibility, to the barely imagined. Someone who embraces the colors and textures, the tastes and transformations – someone who embraces, period. We're all after what's juicy, what breathes. If you're really clever, like Sirena, then you create a persona – or maybe, more disturbingly, you become a person – who, while seeming impressively, convincingly to eschew fakery, is in fact giving people, very consciously, exactly what they want. Wouldn't you call the person who builds a Wonderland – a Wonderland that you can see and touch and smell, that both is and is not Alice's Wonderland, and is also some twelfth-century Islamic Robinson Crusoe's Wonderland, is both East and West, Then and Now, Imaginary and Real, and somehow, because of its freedom in *not* being wearingly faithful, becomes above all *your* Wonderland, or yours and Sirena's at once, as though you were intimate with her in some way, wouldn't you call such a person a Purveyor of Dreams? You would, and some Frenchie critic subsequently did, and if you're wondering what could possibly be wrong with being a Purveyor of Dreams – I mean, you could say, isn't that what Art is for? – you should keep in mind that the desire to be that, to do that – to be the fittest at artistic survival – requires ruthlessness. Maybe that, really, is as good a definition as any of an artist in the world: *a ruthless person.* Which would explain why I don't seem to make the cut.

That evening, when we stood over her blueprint and I marveled, she asked me again for help. It was only a couple of weeks after the babysitting request, because I remember that I'd been to take care of Reza only twice, then, and there was, in my heart, a particular rush of thankfulness to Sirena: this in addition to all my other complicated passion, because I thought in some way she'd finally given me a son, my son. I cooked supper for him; I read to him; I scolded him about his homework, not as a teacher but in a parental way; and after kissing his forehead and smoothing his duvet, I perched in his room on the hard chair, in the penumbra, as the jazz musicians paraded brightly around the wall, watching the gentle rise and fall of his small bundled self until he fell asleep.

It was new, then, this thing with Reza, and it made me love Sirena all the more because it seemed almost a biblical gift. It really felt as though Sirena had bestowed upon me the flesh of her flesh, and I was savoring it most richly, still new, when all of a sudden there came, unbidden, another: the blueprint, unfolded.

'What do you think?' she asked me. She put her hand on me, of course. She looked up at me with the famous almond eyes, wide. 'Does it look like – what do you think? Is it a land of reason and a land of marvels at the same time?'

How to answer, when mostly I was feeling the hand? And wondering, as I always did, what I felt about the hand.

'It's a map.'

She clicked her tongue. 'You mustn't tease me. There is a map, there are the furnishings for my world' – she gestured at the bags and boxes – 'but now there are other, bigger things to build. The island itself, if you like.' She sighed. 'It doesn't entirely make sense, because in Paris the shape of the space is different, not long and narrow but more a strangely divided rectangle. I'll make it like a pathway, a journey. But I must build it here first, to see, obviously for the scale of it, but also to get started on the video.'

This was her big idea. She wanted to build a version of her Wonderland in the studio, she said, so that the Appleton kids – *my* Appleton kids, my third-grade class – could come and discover it. She would film their discovery. This was her plan. After that she might make other videos, she hoped, but the one she cared about was the kids. 'And here's the thing, you see, Nora, my dear: I cannot build the Wonderland, and I cannot make the video, without you.' She crinkled her eyes, her mouth, in her most endearing smile. 'You know this, don't you? After all our conversations.' She sighed. 'I never worked before with the help of anybody. But you – with your help, we will make something wonderful – a wonderful Wonderland!'

'Yes, sure—' I felt so many things at once. Chief among them excited; but also, afraid. Yet again, some boundary was being broken. I would let it break, because I wanted to; but what would it mean, to bring my kids – to bring her kid, our kid – here?

She was already imagining it: 'The Jabberwocky, to go – in English?'

'Snicker snack.'

'Yes, the Jabberwocky, his eyes, eyes of light in the darkness – the suggestion of monstrosity, it's better.'

'I guess.'

'Because then it is each person's monstrosity, yes? You see? I don't tell you what is monstrous, just like I don't tell you what to love. I simply allow you to imagine.' She had taken her physical self back into herself, arms crossed over her chest, her shawl clutched round, but still, the smile. 'Because each of us has our own fantasies, our own nightmares.'

'True.'

'What is for me perfection, you don't even think twice about.'

'You never know—'

'You never know. Exactly. So we must keep the doors as open as possible, let as many fantasies come into Wonderland as we can. So that everyone can see themselves there.'

'Wonderland always seemed to me like a pretty scary place when I was a kid.'

'Yes! Scary, but we want to be scared.'

'I guess.'

'With mirrors and lights – like children, we want all the emotion, good, bad, and then poof, we want the emotion to go away again. We will do this, for the children, for Reza's classroom, when you bring them here . . .'

'It depends, surely—'

'Because in the end, we want above all to be safe, yes? Almost everybody wants this in the end.'

We stood over her map of Wonderland and she told me that she couldn't build it without my help. She wanted to bring together two different ideas of wonder, one imaginary and one spiritual. On the one hand, she had her story about a boy, then a man, raised alone on an island, and of his solitary discovery of science, and of spiritualism, culminating in his worship of a God he'd come to believe in absolutely – a worship that took the form of a spinning trance. She would mix this antique Eastern mysticism with a different kind of wonder, a modern Western wonder, that was Alice in Wonderland's: a place where reason – and the ground – didn't remain stable, where the imagination confused good and evil, friend and foe. One Wonderland was about trying to see things as they are, she said, about believing that such a thing as clarity was possible; and the other was about relativism, about seeing things from different perspectives, and also about being seen, and about how being seen differently also changes you. Both possibilities were amazing and frightening at the same time; but only one of them, she said, could lead to wisdom. She wanted her artwork, she said, to offer the possibility, at least, of wisdom. For this, she said, she needed me.

I was too dignified to gush or fawn on her. I had enough masquerade in me for that. I told her – truthfully – that I hadn't worked with anyone else on an art project since high school – those heady afternoons in Dominic Crace's lair. I mentioned that I was hoping, now that Emily was to all intents and purposes finished, to continue with the cycle, although perhaps not in chronological order – and that there was, after all, barely any time, just a few hours in the afternoons. But her eyes were smiling at me as though I were actually saying, 'Yes, yes, of course, YES!' and I knew that she knew that, and that we were both excited about it.

That was in the middle of a week, the beginning of February; and by the weekend I was canceling another visit to my poor father in Brookline, in order to drive Sirena to a vast used clothing warehouse south of town, recommended by Didi. I'd promised I'd take him to the medical supply in Belmont to look for a raised toilet seat to ease his bad hips, and I figured, guiltily, that another week or two with the old seat would surely not be too bad. Sirena and I were going to choose a mountain of light blue dresses and pinafores – Alice clothes – from which to sew the canopy of her new sky.

There was, to this, an element of the costume department back in college, a sort of 'what the hell' good cheer completely antithetical to my pious and oh-so-precise reconstructions; and it was – how could I have forgotten this? – *fun*. It was simply fun to turn up the radio and the heat in the car to full blast, to sing along, like hams, to Macy Gray – 'Try to walk away and I stumble . . .' – and then to roll into the Avril Lavigne hit of the time that the third graders loved without having the faintest idea about the emotions it expressed. 'My Happy Ending,' it was called: 'You were everything, everything that I wanted . . . All this time you were pretending / So much for my happy ending . . .' – we bawled the lyrics like teenagers, and Sirena's funny Italian lingering upon the endings of the words themselves ('my happy-e ending-e') made us laugh still more.

The actual sky was vast and blue and impeccable and American, the very canvas of possibility, the gray highway stretching out before us, salted white as sand, and the bay to our left, as we headed south, all glitter in the winter sun. I was so happy it was like a food, like I'd been stuffed with it, a foie gras goose of happiness; happy enough to know, *fully*, that I was happy, and foolishly, for one second, to dare the thought: 'Imagine – imagine if each Saturday morning could be like this,' and in the middle of the singing I blushed, not even looking at her, because even just having it I knew there was something wrong about the thought. Another boundary crossing – an acknowledgment to myself, so fleeting but so dangerous, of how hungry I was.

I have an old friend from college, long lost, who used to say that you should never let yourself think of a journey as long, because then it will feel long no matter what. By the same token, it's important, when you're the Woman Upstairs, never to think of yourself – but *never*, do you understand? – as alone or forlorn or, God help us, wanting. It will not do. It cannot be. It is the end.

At the warehouse, we rifled through racks and bins of all kinds – vast shapeless nylon granny dresses, shrunken, felted woolen dresses, polyester stretch pants, sheets and blankets, sequined netting, iridescent organza, animal print plush jersey jackets, bolts of corduroy in extraordinary shades of plum and puce and pear. Sirena fingered everything with her eyes closed, as if the garments had messages in braille upon them – 'It's to know if I can work with this,' she explained, when I teased her. 'Some fabrics, the synthetics, the fake ones, like some people, is this' – and she mimed scraping her fingernails on a blackboard.

'Are there people you don't like, then?' I asked. It hadn't occurred to me before.

'Nora!' She shook her head incredulously. 'Aren't there people *you* don't like?'

'So many of them.'

'I can't work with people I don't choose, not in this way. For me, life's too short. Yes? *Life is too short.* When they' – she mimed the fingernails – 'then they must go. Like the fabric, I don't take it home; so with the people, they're the same. Not for me!'

'There must be a word for that,' I said. 'What's the word for that in Italian?'

'*Respingere*, maybe – to reject, to return something.'

'Re-spinge? I love that: "Spinge it!" Ditch the dope and spinge the sponge! Spinge him again – re-spinge him!'

We were excitable enough to laugh even at this, and it passed then into our vocabulary, part of the lexicon between us, so that when I was annoyed with someone I'd say, 'Spinge her,' or Sirena might complain, giggling, that we should 're-spinge the sponges.' It doesn't seem very funny now, but it became one of our things, after that.

On the way home, we realized we were famished, that it was late. The afternoon sun, still bright, hung now coldly low in the sky, and the heat in the car had that prickling, parched quality that comes when it's genuinely freezing outside. We decided to get something to eat.

I don't know why I thought of the Italian bar up behind Davis Square. Mostly it was the sort of place you went for drinks, when it was too late for everything else; and it wasn't a place where you thought of eating, much. But years before, before my mother was even sick, a lifetime ago in my artist phase, when I'd thought I might yet turn out to be the person that I wanted to be – whoever that person might have been – I'd spent a long afternoon there with two friends – a hilarious and beautiful gay guy, Louis, who cut hair fantastically well, and cut mine for a while, and who was killed a couple of years later on the Mass Ave bridge riding his bike in the rain at night; and a woman named Erica I'd known in New York, who'd been at law school with my boyfriend Ben but dropped out to work with the homeless, which makes her sound worthy, but actually she was as funny as Louis was, and maybe that's why I thought of the bar, because we'd laughed so much that seven-hour afternoon, sitting in front of a superior tureen of Italian wedding soup made, I remember, by the barman's Sicilian mom, and what amounted, in the end, to four bottles of a delicious Nebbiolo, a bit more than one each, which, drunk over seven hours, was the perfect amount. The bar had no windows to speak of and operated in an eternal darkness, out of time, so we went inside in one era and came out in another, like time travelers. I'd loved that stretch – it had happened only the once, when I was at an age where I thought that was, or ought to be, what artists *did* – and maybe for that reason, or maybe for the soup, I suggested that bar and we went there.

The owner was still behind the counter, fatter now, and balder, but he'd been both fat and bald all those years before. Sirena and he, with some kind of ethnic telepathy, seemed able to tell from looking at one another that they should speak Italian, and within moments they were deep in animated conversation, and he was promising to cook for us with his own hands his mother's special pasta with broccoli and anchovies – it would seem that she had, in the intervening years, gone to meet her maker. He set us up in a corner booth, tufted oxblood leatherette up our backs higher than our heads, and on the walls the requisite photographs of Sophia Loren and Anna Magnani, and three whole candles for ourselves. Aside from an older guy having scotch at the bar, we were the only customers. When we came in, Sinatra was on the sound system, but the owner said something to Sirena and she laughed and he put on instead something older and nightclubby, a woman singing in Italian, and Sirena was loving it – she closed her eyes and swayed and hummed along, for a bit.

Sirena and I had our bowls of pasta and our red wine and our candles and our booth. We were tired from the long trek, and I had that tingling under my skin that comes after the cold, at once invigorating and strangely soporific. It was all feeling like a dream, and in the middle of this dream I had a revelation. Sirena was saying something, and I couldn't quite hear it, or follow it, because of how I was feeling, so I was just looking at her, watching her talk, her elegantly inelegant stubby hand resting on her wineglass, the crinkles in the corners of her eyes, the crazy darkness of her brows and her tickly lashes, the glimmer of the candlelight on her dark irises and on strands of her hair.

And suddenly I thought: 'I want to stay with you. Actually, for-ever. I do.'

And she saw me looking at her, in a fond and foolish way, and she cocked an eyebrow – to say what? 'I see you'? 'I understand'? 'We are here together'? – and took my hand in hers and held it as it lay on the table. 'Today we had a great day, yes? If only each day was like this one, *cara mia*!' And I barely heard her, because I felt her hand upon my hand, all through my body. I felt her skin. I really felt it.

You don't ask to have such a thought. You also can't take it away, once you've had it. I'd never had such a thought about Sirena, not in all the time I'd been in love with her. But I had the thought unbidden, just like that, in Amodeo's bar, and in the first instant of having the thought, I wanted to laugh, and I wanted to tell her. The only person I could think of who would really understand was Sirena herself. And then, at once, I had the horrifying presentiment of her recoil. What if she didn't feel the same way? And what if she did feel the same way? And how could it be that all the great welter of emotion I experienced in her company would be somehow and suddenly summarized by – reduced to – this?

With the distance I have now, I can see that it was one small thought among all the other thoughts that drift like dust motes through a cluttered mind. But it was a thought I made an object, and held on to and turned over and over in my hand, as if it were an amulet, as if it gave meaning to what had come before; and holding on to it changed everything again.

If you were me, and you had this revelation – but lo, I don't just love, I *want*! – and you wanted to but couldn't tell Sirena, what would you do? You'd tell Didi. As it happens, if you were me, you'd find yourself unwisely telling both Didi and Esther at the same time, in the sticky booth at their favorite pub in Jamaica Plain, the very next evening, even though you knew you didn't want Esther's opinion. But your revelation was burning so in your hand that you couldn't hold on to it a second longer.

If you were me, you'd be surprised by their unified reaction; and then surprised at your surprise.

They didn't quite laugh, but Didi made a sound, with beer, in the back of her nose, that was infuriatingly close to laughter.

'You're making fun of me? I tell you this huge thing – this

huge thing for me – and you're pretty much my closest friends, and you *laugh* at me? Am I going crazy here?'

'Hey, Nora Adora—'

'No. For real. I might have to—'

'Take a deep breath. I wasn't laughing. Esther wasn't laughing. Were you, sweetie? We love you. Calm down.'

'We somehow knew what you were going to say,' Esther said. 'We were laughing at our goddesslike prescience.'

'Oh, fuck you,' I said. 'You were laughing at the dumb straight girl who's finally coming to her belated awakening, sad creature that she is.'

'Come off it, you know us better than that. You do. Honestly?'

Esther was making pug eyes at me, and Didi was holding on, rather sweatily, to both of my hands, as if they both feared I would bolt.

'Because we anticipated it – which wasn't so hard – I mean, you did say you'd had a revelation yesterday and we knew you weren't out with your dad – we talked about it. We discussed it.'

Didi squeezed my left hand more tightly. She wore a lumpy ring that cut into my finger and I flinched, which I saw her register. 'We discussed it, and we decided that you're wrong.'

'What's that supposed to mean? How can I be wrong about what I felt? About what I *feel*? If I can't tell, then I'd like to know who could.'

'Trust us,' said Esther. 'We're experts. We can tell.' She was joking, but only halfway, and I hated her in that moment, a frank hot flush of hatred.

'I know it seems bizarre,' said Didi, still clutching. 'I don't mean this as some, you know, questioning of your judgment—'

'Nor as some judgment of your experience,' Esther broke in. 'I mean, your *experience* is obviously totally valid.'

'Gee, thanks. Big of you.'

'Calm down, sweetie—'

'Let go of my hand. I'm not your sweetie.'

'Listen here,' said Didi, in her sharp, no-nonsense, long-lost radio voice, letting go of my hand and drawing herself up to her full height, which, even seated, was much greater than mine. The red neon of a Bud sign lit up her hair from behind. She'd become a giant fairy-tale genie. 'Listen here, Miss Eldridge. Stop answering back. Listen to what we've got to say, and then we can talk about it. Okay?'

She made a mistake in using the word 'we,' in including Esther, but I nodded as I pulled my hands to safety in my lap.

'Nobody is denying your girl crush.'

'Crush?'

'Objectionable term, but accurate diagnosis.'

'Crush?'

'I told you to listen, quietly. Hear me out. Okay?'

I made my eyes into slits.

'So, you've known for ages how you feel about this woman – she inspires you as an artist, she makes you laugh, she makes you feel alive. All these things are true, and wonderful and rare, and it's also true that often they are linked to sexual desire. Up till now, you hadn't made that link – because—'

'Because I was afraid to.'

'That's not what I was going to say, actually. Because it availed you nothing. Because it wasn't going to get you anywhere. Because you didn't need to. Because it seemed to you as though your emotions were getting expressed well enough anyhow, your need for intimacy was being met, and that – the whole physical thing – wasn't necessary. It wasn't the point.'

'Okay, and so now that's changed.'

'Wait. What I'm saying is that everything is always changing, from one minute to the next, and that maybe this sudden urge to kiss her, it's more like a power surge than a permanent change in voltage – do you see what I mean?'

'What Didi means, I think . . .' Esther began, but Didi knew me well enough to raise a warning hand.

'What I mean is that, yes, there was a moment when your affection and delight were bubbling over and seeking a means of expression and you wanted something more. Bang. In that moment you totally did. I'm not denying that. But I'm really wondering whether that's actually some seismic Sapphic shift in you. You know that I of all people would be all for it if it were – there's nothing I love more than women loving women. But in this case, I think Esther and I are in agreement here, we're really wondering about that. It seems like this could be part of a different story, you know? A piece from a different puzzle.'

'What's in it for you, to deny me my revelation?' I said, more petulant now than angry. 'Why do you want me not to be in love with Sirena? Why?'

'The only person we care about here is you, Nora. I know you love her, but I don't give a shit about this Italian chick. And I don't want to see you throw yourself needlessly in harm's way. I'm not denying your feelings, I'm just asking a question about the story you're choosing to tell about those feelings, that's all.'

I rolled my eyes. The overlap between my theater of annoyance and my actual annoyance bordered on the awkward. 'Who made you my fucking therapist?' I said, my arm already outstretched to signal to the waitress that we needed another round. 'I'm not paying for these services.' And I managed a laugh, though it came out more like a guffaw, and then I asked them about the obscure local women's soccer team they loved and often went to watch, and how it was doing – not well, as it turned out. I closed the conversation down.

Just because someone tells you in a reasonable way that you aren't really feeling what you're feeling, it doesn't make the feeling go away. In this case, if anything, I became more convinced of the truth of what I'd felt in Amodeo's, certain that I'd had a revelation, something like a conversion. But certain now, too, because of Didi and Esther's reaction, that I had to keep my knowledge a secret, *from everyone*.

You might wonder how this was different from all that had come before, from months of being more generally, less specifically, in love. You might think it was essentially the same. But I felt I'd finally awoken, that the world was at last clear to me and that its shapes made sense. Not only did I have hope in a general way, I had something specific to hope for. I was certain that I *understood*. And certain that if I tried to explain what I understood, I would be – as I had been, with Didi and Esther – misunderstood.

When my father asked mildly if I was dating anyone – clearly, in his inarticulate way, fretting about my calcifying spinsterdom, unable to see, as my mother would have, that I had almost fulfilled her dream of independence – I snapped at him that I was too old for that kind of nonsense, which false bitterness made his voice, when he protested, small and sad.

But it was as if my revelation had opened a door in my head, into a further room where all life was suddenly potentially titillating, where everything was secretly part of my secret. Whenever I saw an article, or a book, or a film about a hidden or unrequited love, I thought it had been placed purposefully in my path, so I wouldn't feel alone. When I was driving anywhere, or ambling the supermarket aisles, or lying in bed at night boiling my toes against the fake fur hot water bottle I'd bought on sale in January, I was now always thinking about Sirena.

No, let me be precise: I wasn't actually. That would suggest real things. In a way that hadn't been true before, I was thinking about my thoughts about Sirena. I was imagining telling her about my feelings, or I was imagining her confessing, in her particular lilting way, that she found me beautiful, or thought me a great artist, or on one occasion I imagined her saying that she could not now imagine her life without me. What conversations we had, in my head! What honesty, what pure transparency, what a perfect meeting of minds.

How much did Reza feature in these visions? Well, sometimes I'd picture the three of us, installed in a farmhouse in Vermont, or in Tuscany, or in a thatched bungalow on a Caribbean island, in order that we might live cheaply enough to make art, and grow a resplendent garden from which to feed ourselves. I knew the layouts of these various houses, the unfolding of their rooms. I built them in my mind, and we inhabited each of them at different times. I knew how the morning sunbeams fell in slats upon the terra-cotta floors in Italy, and the sounds of chickens scrabbling in the yard outside, audible as soon as you opened the casement window. I knew how the snow from the field behind the house reflected white in the bathroom mirror in Vermont, where the steaming water in the clawfoot tub smelled of sage, and Sirena, stepping into the bath, dropped her slippers – Moroccan babouches – one and then the other on the pink and purple round rag rug in the middle of the white painted wooden floor. I knew the kiss of the rising Caribbean wind, warm upon my ruffled arm hairs, if I stood in the shadowy doorway and squinted at the passing schoolchildren in their navy and white uniforms, kicking up dust as they ambled by, and I scanned their knots and clutches for Reza, his laughing olive face among the chocolate and coffee faces of his peers.

In these fantasies, Reza would always call me Mommy, resting a small, hot hand upon my shoulder while I worked on an art project at a table in the sunlight, or washed lettuce at a porcelain farmhouse sink, and even as they seemed completely surreal – sturdy-skinned bubbles unconnected to the standing traffic or the rows of cereal boxes or the almost sweaty duvet which surrounded me in reality – these imaginings were more vivid and more alive to me than much that I could see and smell and touch. As with my earlier dream about Skandar, I had to remind myself, for a second, that the scenes hadn't taken place – or, as I saw it, that they had not *yet* taken place.

And what of Skandar, of whom I had also dreamed? Well, in that spell of late winter, he didn't yet feature in my fantasy life. He would have to wait, quite literally, until spring.

Let me explain that, in spite of myself, for several months – and in some less pressing way, for several years – this state of fantasy was, in the wake of 'the Fabric Weekend,' which might more aptly have been called 'the Fabrication Weekend,' the country to which I largely decamped and in which I preferred to stay.

I knew it was potential rather than actual, but I didn't understand then that it wasn't Real. I didn't see that I'd made it up. When Sirena took my hand between both of hers and said, 'What would I do without you? You are my angel, my heart's best love,' I believed her. When Reza said, 'I never want you to go away,' I believed him. I built houses, and entire lives, upon those beliefs. If you'd told me my own story about someone else, I would have assured you that this person was completely unhinged. Or a child. That's always the way.

6

I was happy. I was Happy, indeed. I was in love with love and every lucky parking spot or particularly tasty melon or unexpectedly abbreviated staff meeting seemed to me not chance but an inevitable manifestation of the beauty of my life, a beauty that I had, on account of my lack of self-knowledge, been up till now unable to see.

I was crazy. I was crazy in the way a child is crazy, in the way of someone who believes, with rash fervor, that life can be – that it will yet be, and most certainly – as you would wish it. How could I have been so foolish? My mother, of all people, had taught me by example, by the whimsical panicked procrastination of my childhood and then, more brutally, by the prolonged, involuntary shutting-up-shop of her body, that this was a preposterous dream, that fate was a jailer. But I chose, in that time, not to heed her lessons. We wouldn't be proper children if we didn't disregard our parents' most vital instruction.

My mother, toward the end, had said to me, but with a sweet smile, 'Life's funny. You have to find a way to keep going, to keep laughing, even after you realize that none of your dreams will come true. When you realize that, there's still so much of a life to get through.' And I'd been offended, because I wanted to believe, as her child, that I'd been a dream come true; but above all, I'd pitied her. I'd still somehow believed I'd be different from her. I hadn't yet had my Lucy Jordan moment, a moment from which the Shahids had granted me a long but finite reprieve.

Happy, crazy – the name for it doesn't matter. It was like the world was filled with light. This is the trouble with clichés: they describe something truly, and that's why we use them over and over again, until their substance is eroded to dust. But these things are true: I woke up earlier, more refreshed. I had more energy; my mind moved more clearly, more quickly. I caught no colds, I had no aches, I was luckier, I got on better with people, I laughed more, I worked more, I slept better. I was awake in my life in a way completely new to me, and I knew that anything – ah! my art! – anything! – was possible.

It's also true that I developed a constant, unignorable itch, the side effect of the love drug. The itch subsided only when I was with one Shahid or another, or when I was working. As soon as the last school bell rang, my itch was there, waiting. I might be walking around the reservoir with Maggie, who taught sixth grade, or driving my father to see the orthopedic surgeon about the pain in his hip, and I'd be apparently listening to and even participating lucidly in the conversation ('Yeah, it'd be great if Ling's father could do a Mandarin after-school unit next fall – I think a lot of kids, and parents, would be really into that.' Or, 'Well, I think Dr. Fuchs's take on the replacement is that the pain is totally worth it, and you're up to the rehab. He wouldn't have suggested it if he didn't think you were up to the rehab'), but really inside my head I was attending to my unmentionable itch, I was reliving and reinterpreting conversations ('You won't be here till six?' – she'd sounded disappointed. She tried to make it seem she didn't care, but I could tell she'd been disappointed!), I was wondering what she was doing at that moment, I was wondering how long till I could call and find out, I was wondering when I could next get to the studio, and how long I'd be able to stay. I was wondering, as I often did, whether she or anyone else could tell the difference in me, whether my revelation, my awakening, had any outward mark.

Did I say anything? To anyone? And risk awakening from my amazing awakedness? What do you think?

All the exhilarating advantages of my condition, and also its inconvenient effects, led me to want to be at the studio as much as possible. In February, and in March, and in April too, every Saturday, and almost every Sunday, I'd sit or stand or lean or carry all morning, building Wonderland, Sirena's Wonderland, laughing and being silly, sometimes just watching, able to ignore the unmentionable itch because it Was No More. And then we'd eat something. After the first couple of weeks, we took turns bringing lunch, and I lingered over my choices in the shops on a Friday evening: flavored breadsticks or big Swedish crackers like enormous communion hosts, wrapped in crinkly white paper; olives, cheeses, cured meats; dolmas; burek; sweet peppers stuffed with soft curd. Tubs of ratatouille, piperade, anchoïade. Endive leaves; strips of fennel. Purple broccoli stalks. Heirloom tomatoes, which cost a fortune in early spring. And sweets: I'd bring such sweets – the famous Highland Avenue cupcakes or sesame buns soaked in honey, or salted chocolate oatmeal cookies, or *loukoum*, or extravagant bars of Italian chocolate from the deli down the road from my house – always I brought enough for Reza, even for Skandar, substantial portions of sweets for the others, to assuage the guilt of my happiness.

There was, in these months, a new side of Sirena, obsessive and imperious, one I hadn't seen in the fall, and it might, I suppose, have seemed to me selfish. But I was in thrall to her passionate single-mindedness, not least because, as her virtual assistant, I was included within it. Like a madness, her

Wonderland was everything to her, and while she didn't care to talk about it generally, she did talk about it with me. As in, 'I think we need more rain sheets, more, yes? ... I'm trying to decide whether the shards should be actually dangerously sharp – what do you think, Nora? We don't want to draw blood, but shouldn't it hurt to touch it?'

February vacation week, she signed Reza up for robotics camp at the Science Museum and we spent all day every day at the studio. She started to become an organic part of it, like the sink or the chemical smell in the hallway. By mid-March she hardly changed her clothes, or washed her hair, her fingertips were cracked and discolored from the paint and glue, her jeans, like her hair, more stiff and bespattered at the end of each day. She filched her husband's cigarettes and smoked them with her coffee, one grubby hand palming a chipped cup, the other flicking ash onto the floor. The studio started to stink and was freezing – she threw two windows open wide to clear the fug, with only moderate success.

Sirena was turning, before my eyes, into my ideal of an artist – as if I'd imagined her and, by imagining her, had conjured her into being. And here's the weird thing: her existence as an ideal woman artist didn't feel as though it thwarted or controlled me, I didn't look at her and think, 'Why are you almost famous and I'm only your helper?' I don't recall having the thought even once. Instead, I looked at her and saw *myself,* saw *what suddenly seemed possible for me, too, because it was possible for her.*

And the weirdest thing is that in that time, in addition to sewing together dresses, and sowing flowers on Astroturf, and stringing broken mirrors onto fine wire, in addition to making tapes of cricket sounds and animal-in-the-undergrowth noises, and in addition to fashioning Jabberwock tusks that would ultimately be discarded and forgotten, and rigging up the piercing little bulbs that would be Jabberwock eyes, in addition to

working out for Sirena the camera settings for the kids' video –
the Appleton plan, as we called it – and in addition to my regular teaching load and the higgledy-piggledy bustle of my spring
term classroom – times tables! Tadpoles! A trip on the school bus
to the MFA! – and to my dream nights as Reza's beloved Auntie –
in addition (what had I done with my time up till now, I had to
wonder, and have to wonder now again: Does Being Happy
simply Create More Time, in the way that Being Sad, as we all
know, slows time and thickens it, like cornstarch in a sauce?),
anyway, in addition to all these things, *I made my own art.*

It seems hard to credit it, but I did.

I worked on not one but two rooms from my cycle, at one
time. Even though I ought, technically, chronologically, to have
set about building Virginia Woolf's workroom at Rodmell, with
her notebook open and her shawl draped over her chair and her
last note propped upon the mantelpiece, I somehow couldn't
bear to – it was not a season for suicide, not in my life at any
rate – and so I set about doing the rooms for Alice Neel and
Edie Sedgwick, which weren't exactly cheerful in themselves; but
I found, somehow, a joy in them.

The Alice Neel room was to be the sanatorium suicide ward in
small-town Pennsylvania where she was locked up after her breakdown. She'd lost her two little girls, one to diphtheria and the
other to her fickle Cuban husband, who'd promised to send for
her but never did, and, leaving their daughter with his parents,
went on to Paris alone. I wanted to get into the barren room the
memory of her little girls, but also I wanted to slip into the corners the ghosts of her future sons, the two devoted and adored
boys who stuck by her through thick and thin – through so much
thin; and at so great a cost to themselves – as she grew old and
fat and plain and was all the time poor, so long unrecognized,
obsessed with her work, piling up her unsold canvases in the
narrow hallway of her grimy walk-up apartment – but through

it all, she'd have those boys, both of whom would flee bohemia for the professions, solid and bourgeois and aggressively uneventful in their days, carrying in them all the pains of her life, of her lost youth and their unknown, lost siblings, but never abandoning her, not ever; and somehow it would have seemed wrong, in the new, golden light of love with which I saw the world illuminated, to make my Alice's room reflect only the nadir, her darkest isolation, when she felt forsaken by life and by art and by love.

I still wanted my rows of white-draped iron beds, the high white windows unadorned, the swabbed white linoleum floor; I wanted her white nightgown, torn at the shoulder, her hands to her ears in a Munch-like scream. But I wanted the colors of Cuba, of motherhood, of the future, in the interstices, outside the windows, high up the walls, like shoots coming up through the earth, the promise of spring.

For Edie, beautiful Edie, the strangeness was that the joy was already in the room, even as it was killing her. When, as a woman, you make *yourself* the work of art, and when you are then what everyone looks at, then whatever else, you aren't alone. Edie was never, on the outside, alone. Emily, Virginia, Alice – the woman artist so fundamentally isolated. And then Edie: never alone. Never invisible. Arguably, also, never seen; and in that sense, more than alone: annihilated.

But to imagine her room was in itself strangely pleasurable. How free I felt to do it, because hers was the only wholly *imaginary* room, the only one not based on a photograph or a painting or a description of an actual place. I could make it up: a room lined with blown-up pictures of herself, and in between the pictures, windows, and outside the windows, people crowded around, watching her, the spectacle of her. As if she were in the Christmas display at Bloomingdale's.

I reserved the making of my rooms for myself. Which isn't to say they were hidden from Sirena. I mean simply that I worked on them only when Sirena wasn't there. I waited. I held back. I knew everything about her project, you see, whereas she knew only a bit about mine, and I chose to see this as my triumph, some small upper hand. My dignity, if you will, in subservience.

And of course I wasn't afraid in the studio anymore. I had a myth of my own invincibility. You can't imagine, if you've never been fearful that way, what a liberation it is to be free of it. You can say it had been silly, that I'd tortured myself for years with an artificial anxiety, and I can't dispute that this is so; but somehow Sirena – or Reza, or maybe even Skandar – set me free from this. I stopped cowering. She gave me that gift, too.

I was free and unafraid enough to play my music loudly – Fats Waller or Chubby Jackson or Joe Marsala and His Delta Four for Alice Neel; the Velvet Underground when working on Edie – or to smoke a cigarette or even half a cigarette that Sirena had left behind. There came the week in which I was inspired – ridiculous, I know – to try to Be Edie, and I brought lots of makeup and I painted my face in front of a sliver of mirror salvaged from Sirena's stores – its very sliverness apt, like some relic from the Factory – powdering my skin white and blackening my eyes into great, dark, glimmering hollows. I didn't cut my hair off, but I slicked it back, and in a white T-shirt and black leggings, cursing myself for having boobs, for being close to forty, for not being tiny, I danced dervishly nevertheless and took Polaroids of myself doing so, with my mother's old camera. The images were blurry and partial – an eye and nose, an oiled glint of hairline, a moving arm half blocking the frame – but this somehow seemed in keeping with the spirit of it all. I took my shirt off and took pictures of that, too, impressed by the retro quality of my own out-of-focus torso, my breasts in their plain white bra high and distinct in the camera's record.

In those solitary studio nights, I wandered up and down the small pathways of Sirena's semi-assembled Wonderland. I gazed up at where the Alice-dress sky would later hang. I sniffed the aspirin flowers, I held conversations with myself, or with Sirena, in a loud, almost abrasive tone. I spoke in silly accents and pidgin Cuban Spanish, as if I were Alice Neel's mother-in-law telling her she couldn't have her daughter back. I built Alice's sanatorium beds out of fat, white-coated electrician's wire and sewed their tiny tufted mattresses from striped Irish flannel stuffed with foam, busy as the fairy-tale elves, bemoaning out loud, in curses, the first diminishings of my middle-aged eyesight, and repeatedly pricking my forefinger. I laid a carefully joined parquet of sawn Popsicle sticks for the floor of Edie's Factory room, and painted coat upon coat of stain and varnish to perfect its toasty hue. I framed the plate-glass windows of her hexagonal space – all windows, no doors – and sealed them carefully with putty, old-style. I laid the parquet boardwalk in the space around her room, the Edie-viewing-room, which I planned later to crowd with spectators. But I never got to the spectators themselves, which seems to me to make sense, now.

It was a riot. Like a third grader, I was *in my life, in life.* I was alive. I thought I'd been wakened, Sleeping Beauty–like, from a Long Sleep. In fact, I didn't seem to need much sleep, as if all the years of struggling in a slumber had at least set me up to dispense, now, with rest. I sometimes left the studio at one, or even two, and I was in the shower by six thirty on a school day, bright and neat as a pin in my classroom by five to eight, with a surreptitious wink for Reza, who was often a mite tardy and easily anxious about it. For so long I had eaten my greens and here – at last! – was my ice-cream sundae.

There was another strand in this tapestry. What does it sig-
nify that I'm loath to tell you, slow to tell you? I want to say
it was separate, that it was on another account. But that would
be a knowing lie, and not-telling becomes, in the parlance of
pious Aunt Baby, a Sin of Omission.

Almost every time I stayed with Reza, Skandar walked me
home. When it snowed, he put on a hat, an old-fashioned trilby
sort of hat, of battered elephant-gray felt, and he looked like a
gangster in spite of his glasses. The gangsters' accountant, maybe.
When it was raining, he carried a vast umbrella, of the sort they
have at hotels and golf clubs, and he gallantly held it over me as
if he were my valet. He didn't seem to own gloves, but didn't
complain of the cold, and smoked cigarettes in hoodlum fashion,
cupped in his hand, as we walked. It took less than fifteen minutes to go from their town house by the river up to my
triple-decker on the wrong side of Huron Avenue. It wasn't far.
And in the beginning, in the cold months, we went straight. In
February, when there was a lot of snow, he'd walk behind me
down the icy, narrow shoveled paths, and we didn't talk much. It
was hard to hear, single file like that, and by the time we got to

my door, I could feel that my nose was red and I could see that his nose was red, his hands deep in his pockets, and he'd smile a smile at once goofy and vague, as if he wasn't quite sure who I was, and he'd say, 'Well, thank you again, and good night to you,' with a general, whole-body gesture that seemed as though he were clicking his heels. He'd wait like a father until I had the key in the lock, and then he'd set off back again down the road, stepping gingerly because of those leather-soled dress shoes.

The day after Valentine's Day – I was relieved they hadn't asked me to babysit Reza on that day – they were going out to another fancy dinner, at the home of the dean of the Kennedy School, and at the studio beforehand Sirena told me that Skandar wanted to cancel.

'He's not feeling well?' I asked. I was sewing something, I know because I have a distinct physical memory of hunching and squinting, and when I looked up at Sirena it took a moment for my eyes to focus.

'You don't read the papers?' she asked. 'Or listen to the radio?'

'What are you talking about?'

'I'm talking about Hariri.'

I shrugged a small shrug.

'Rafic Hariri? You've not heard.'

'I didn't see the papers today.'

'The prime minister of Lebanon – assassinated yesterday, along with twenty-two other people – his bodyguards, colleagues. They blew up his motorcade outside the St. Georges hotel – it made a crater in the road the size of a small house.'

I looked at the floor and shook my head. 'Wow,' I said.

'That's the trouble with being here. It all seems so far away that nobody pays any attention to anything.'

'Who did it?'

'Who knows? Israel, Syria, Hezbollah – lots of people wanted Hariri dead.'

'Did Skandar know him?'

'He'd met him, more than once. Skandar is very upset – you can understand. His country is in mourning and in turmoil; and here, at the university, even at a private dinner, they want him to talk about this as if it were an idea, not a man, so many men.'

'He was in favor of him then?'

She clicked her teeth. 'Americans see everything too simply – a good guy, a bad guy, does he have a white hat or a black hat? But it's the wrong question. You should ask Skandar if you want an answer. He'll give you an entire course, if you let him.'

So that night, as he walked me home after the dean's supper, at which, I later learned, Skandar had spoken to the assembled company for half an hour, explaining the context and then the potential fallout from Hariri's assassination – as Skandar walked behind me still on the sidewalk in places but not all the way, I asked him about the attack. He didn't hear me the first time and I had to turn around to ask again, and he almost bumped into me and we both felt awkward.

'Ah,' he said, when he understood what I was asking. 'That's a complicated question.'

'But you're upset.'

'Violence is very upsetting, wherever it takes place, whomever it hurts. But my poor Lebanon is a special case, a very particular story. To be still recovering from our terrible war, to be trying to create our skin all over again, to make a whole body – and then, this. Sometime I'll try to explain. But where would I begin? My beginning? The war's beginning? The century's new beginning? Here, with Hariri? Depending where you begin, you'll tell a different story. We'll have time for them.' And he left it, that evening, at that.

I, in turn, went home and turned on my computer and Googled 'Lebanon war.' Not that I hadn't known about the civil war – when I was a child, everybody knew there was a war in

Lebanon, and if, for example, you'd said to me 'Sabra and Shatila' my brain would automatically have added the word 'massacre' – I'd absorbed something, after all, by osmosis. But I couldn't have explained what the massacre involved or even who was massacred, and I certainly couldn't have told you that the civil war lasted fifteen years. As I read about it, I felt I should have known – I was a schoolteacher, for God's sake, and Reza was a child in my class! Sirena had mentioned once about Skandar losing a brother in the war – hadn't she said bombings? – but then again, I didn't know all the facts about Vietnamese boat people (some of our kids were the children or grandchildren of boat people), and I couldn't have given you a proper rundown on the history of Haiti, even though we had Haitian kids at Appleton; and we'd had a boy from Oman and there was a girl now in fourth grade from Liberia, and I would've had to Google that to know the first facts beyond where it was located on the map, and in all the year she was in my classroom, I never had. I thought then that maybe Sirena was right about the cotton wool of my American life, that I'd been swaddled and protected from the world. This was a Fun House of its kind, this strange place of safety into which 9/11 could erupt as if from nowhere, as if without logic, to our utter surprise.

Already liberated into what seemed an anti–Fun House reality of the emotions – a knowledge of love – and then on the cusp of my artistic freedom also, I longed now, too, for the expansion of my intellect. I wanted already to have known about such things as Hariri's assassination, to be able to make some sense of them. It was like my World Book of Wonders, only better, and worse: the complexity, the enormity of the world was suddenly briefly apparent to me, a giant looming object in the periphery of my vision. Almost too big, but not quite. It was there, and I wanted to know it.

My walks with Skandar unfurled with the spring. After the February break, we proceeded side by side and the evening return became a small social event, a natural time for conversation. The distance between their house and my house became too short for our discussions, so we expanded our walks. The first time this happened we stood for ten minutes on my doorstep, and while I felt it would be strange to invite him in, we were both cold and growing numb. Finally he said, 'Shall we walk a little more, to finish our talk but also stay warm?' And then we walked four times around the block before finally he agreed that he'd better be going. That was only the beginning. The next time we walked up to the Hi-Rise bakery and back. And each time farther and farther. Over to Harvard Square, and back in a loop that practically passed by their front door again. The walk that finally felt we were breaking an unspoken rule didn't come until the end of April – a rule-breaking time, in the same week as my solo Edie Sedgwick impersonation. Spring was in the air, that soft feeling against the cheek and the nubs of bright leaves on the branches, rustling about. We tramped all the way to Watertown and up through the edges of Belmont and back. We walked for over an hour and a half, along empty streets – it was a weeknight, near midnight – beneath the pinkish streetlights and the breathing branches, our talk punctuated by rare lone cars. In my mind, it seemed significant that we never crossed the river. He never took my arm. We never touched at all.

As far as I know, he didn't pretend to Sirena that he was walking by himself. As far as I know, she knew we were walking together. She never mentioned it. Once when I referred to something Skandar had talked about, she waved her hands as if warding him off and said, 'So much talk! I love him, but he's always talking – jabber, jabber. You're so good to listen. Sometimes I say to him, "Skandar, it's too bad there isn't a job that's just *talking*. That would be the job for you."'

'He could be a talk show host.'

'You think it's funny, but he couldn't do it. A talk show host *listens*, no? A talk show host is listening, but Skandar is just talking. No, for a job he'd need to be a talk show *guest*.' She giggled. 'But this isn't a job.'

'All talk and no action,' I said, to say something. That was the closest she and I came to discussing my evening wanderings with her husband.

She was right, though: he was the talker. I told him that having him take me home was like listening to Scheherazade, but he laughed and said I had it backward, then, that I should be telling him the stories – 'Where I come from,' he said, 'it's the woman who is the storyteller. The man is her prisoner.'

In my urge to read the runes at every moment, to find hidden import in everything, I took this to mean, in a flirtatious way, that he was offering to be my prisoner. I took it to mean he was attracted to me. Oh, come on, I took all those walks to mean that he was. Not straight away, not especially. But over time – the amount of time he gave to me, the attention – and who was I? – and that he gave it while his wife and son were at home, and his bed was calling. I took all this to have meaning.

What did we talk about? Sirena was right: he loved to talk; and he might have seemed a bore, but he was a wonderful speaker. Even when he told me a story two or three times, I was rapt.

On the first night of true walking, when we circled my block four times, he told me about his maternal grandmother's village house in the mountains, and staying there when he was small, a boy of five or six, and how he was quite sure he'd seen a jaguar or a panther in the night garden, even though she'd insisted to him over breakfast and again at lunch that there were no such animals in Lebanon.

His big brothers scoffed and said he'd either dreamed it or

seen the neighbor's tabby, inflating it in his tiny mind; but in the subsequent days there were two nocturnal sheep killings higher up the mountain, and everyone in his family changed their tune.

Skandar, like every good storyteller, allowed for the possibility of ghosts and sorcery. 'I always assumed,' he said, 'that it was someone's dark spirit, his avatar.'

And then he went on to explain about the local bey's son, a boy in his late teens at that time, handsome as a god but cursed by rage, who'd beaten an old donkey so badly it had to be shot, that same summer. It was a famous incident in the village, for which the boy received no known punishment, and Skandar said he'd always wondered if the cold black cat slinking across the yard was not this boy's black soul, or the devil who'd claimed it. And then, with a smile, and lighting another cigarette – the last of that first long walk – he said, 'Of course, that black soul would have its moment, and its comeuppance, too, over ten years later, after the war began.'

'How so?' I was like a child, panting for the next chapter.

'Ahmad Akil Abbas,' he said. 'By 1975, he was like all of us, that much older, his soul that much darker. A lot of drinking, drugs, a lot of so-called courage. And in '77, maybe '78, he organized a local militia – a band of bandits – that murdered Christian neighbors in their beds. Thank God my grandmother was already dead by then – hers was a mixed marriage, a true love match, and this sectarian warring would have destroyed her. The Khourys next door to her had their throats slit and their hands cut off. Their three children had gone to Buffalo, New York, and were too frightened to come back even to bury them; so the other Christian families in the village buried them instead. There weren't many, already then. Those who could leave, left. But for Ahmad Abbas, when you live this way you also die this way, even if you're as beautiful as a god, and not long after the Khourys, Ahmad was also murdered and left in the alley behind his father's house, next to his precious motor-cycle. He'd been fed his own testicles. And maybe that, too, was the work of a black cat. Maybe it was the spirit of Leyla Khoury herself. She was stout and placid with a gurgling laugh that came out of her like water from a pump, slowly and then faster, and she was a fantastic cook. Maybe it would have occurred to her to serve him his testicles for his last supper. Maybe she had the last laugh.'

It was impossible not to listen. I would have walked to Provincetown and back. Skandar's youthful experiences were so far from Manchester-by-the-Sea. When I was fifteen, I painted faux-anarchist slogans after school in the art room and tried to hang them up around the halls. For me, a day trip to Faneuil Hall was the acme, the ne plus ultra. When he was fifteen, he saw neighbors and classmates slip out of view, either into mili-tias or out of the country; and eventually he, too, boarded a plane for Paris and finished school as a boarder there. When he was barely more than twenty, still studying in Paris, his oldest brother was killed by a bombing: he'd been visiting a friend, had stayed overnight, and the apartment building was destroyed. It was another family friend, working with the Red Cross, who'd pulled his body from the rubble.

'When you're young – but even now – how do you under-stand this?' he said when he first spoke of it, walking the night streets. 'You can't understand it. It makes no sense. You can allow yourself to be swallowed by your anger, but this will kill you. And yet how can you look at the panther, how can you look him in the eye, when he won't stay still? When he's nowhere and everywhere, belongs to no one and to everyone? So if you're me, how you deal with this is that you say, I'll look at how we talk about the panther. I'll study the history of history, the ways that we tell the stories, and don't tell other stories, and I'll try to understand what it says about us, to tell one story rather than another, to tell it one way rather than another. I'll ask the questions about what is ethical, about who decides what is ethical, I'll ask whether it is possible, really, to have an ethics in the matter of history.'

'I don't know quite what that means,' I said. I didn't want to seem stupid, but it was more important to me to try to follow. He had very handsome square hands, and he waved them about in the cold air, displacing smoke, or breath, or both.

'Why did I start with the panther? Is it that I'm trying to make you see, and feel compassion for, the small six-year-old boy that I was? Now this will be your first thought about Lebanon because of me. Well, maybe Hariri first – I would have avoided that if I could. So, violence first, but second, the small boy full of dreams. But I could have started by telling you about PLO raids into Israel at that time, the mid-sixties, or about the war much later, or about the Israeli role in Sabra and Shatila, or I could've started by telling you how Beirut is today, all beautifully rebuilt like the city of my childhood and yet different from it. I could have told you the Hariri story, which I haven't yet done . . .

'What does it mean, you see, that the first thing every American child knows about Germany is Hitler? What if the first thing you knew was something else? And maybe some people would say that now it's important, after the Second World War, it's ethical and vital that Hitler is the first thing a child knows. But someone else can argue the opposite. And what would it do, how would it change things, if nobody were allowed to know *anything* about Hitler, about the war, about any of it, until *first* they learned about Brahms, Beethoven and Bach, about Hegel and Lessing and Fichte, about Schopenhauer, about Rilke – but all *this,* you had to know first. Or one thing only, the Brahms Piano Quintet in F Minor, or the *Goldberg Variations,* or *Laocoön* – one of those things you had to know and appreciate before you learned about the Nazis.'

'But the world doesn't work like that.'

'No, it doesn't.' He smiled in that vague way, as if amused by a joke only he had heard. 'But what does it mean that it doesn't? And what would it mean if it did?'

Skandar didn't always – or even often – tell stories about his youth, although surely, as he insisted, it was significant that he told one of them first of all. He talked about their time in America, and global politics, and Paris, a bit; but often about Lebanon, its history – bits of history over centuries, millennia: Phoenician history, Roman history, Ottoman history. He told me that Rome's capital in the Middle East, Heliopolis, could still be visited, a hundred kilometers over the mountains from Beirut, and he described its enormous scale, the columns reaching to the skies in the middle of an arable plain, and the snowy mountains at the horizon. He described fallen stone blocks taller than any man, scattered like so much gravel around the site, and the beautiful, dwarfing temple of Dionysius, almost intact, with its perfect mosaics and elaborate friezes – the result of hundreds of years of labor by the Romans in the time immediately after Christ. He made you think that Pontius Pilate might have walked there, or certainly his grandson.

He told me about the community of the fishermen of Tyre, who considered themselves the earliest Christians because they'd converted when Christ preached to them, well before he was crucified – so they claimed they were technically Christians before Christ himself was a Christian. He told me about attending the recent wedding of a young Palestinian friend of his at a beach club by the sea south of Beirut, more than four hundred people from all walks of life gathered with the soughing surf behind them, the stars overhead, dancing and singing and drinking orange Fanta (no alcohol at a Muslim wedding – I was shocked by that: four hundred sober people at a feast), while the bride in her resplendent finery arrived at her celebration gliding the length of a giant swimming pool on an inflatable raft draped in white satin, pushed from behind by invisible swimmers, as flaming Catherine wheels illuminated her path on either side and fire-eaters and sword-swallowers performed at the end of the pool in her honor.

'This is typical,' he said. 'He's a writer, my friend, he doesn't have much money. His bride is a schoolteacher. But if you're going to celebrate, in Lebanon you must do it properly. So Sirena and I, we came from Paris for the party, we sit at a table and next to us is an old couple from the camps, in traditional dress, and their daughter, very pretty, with sparkles in her hijab.

'We greet each other, but otherwise we don't speak, and the daughter sits and smokes her nargileh, and the mother sits and chain-smokes Gauloises, filling up her dinner plate with wrinkled white cigarette ends, like grubs, and the father, who has very few teeth, drinks all the bottles of Fanta on the table, sip after sip. They don't smile, or get up to dance, they eat barely at all. It's hard to know what they make of it.' He paused. 'I've been in the camps, I can picture the sort of place they live – fluorescent lightbulbs, flaking paint, mismatched chairs. The glitter in the daughter's hijab – she will have saved for months to buy that cloth. And the father with no teeth and creases in his skin like canyons, he will have been no older than I am, although I thought of him as a grandfather. And they sit next to us, and there's the question in my mind, who has had to travel farthest, them or us? In our lives, we span many worlds and many centuries, sometimes without taking a step.'

He said this while we were walking, and I laughed and gestured at the Cambridge streets around us, and replied, 'And sometimes you take many steps and stay in just one world.'

'Yes,' he said. 'That's possible, too.'

Although that was not my experience of our walks. If, in the studio, I felt free to travel to imaginary lands, and in fact to travel into someone else's imaginary land – an altogether unforeseen adventure – then as I walked the city streets by night, I was transported out into an actual world, a world of wonders the existence of which caused me to marvel, and to dream. Suddenly, at the age of thirty-seven, I was the opposite of Lucy Jordan: all I could be certain of was that I'd been wrong to be certain of anything. Who could tell me, with any plausibility, that I'd never ride through Paris in a sports car, with the warm wind in my hair? I walked to Heliopolis, I idled in Tyre, I fucking *built* Wonderland! I felt like one of my third graders, like Chastity and Ebullience with their pet chicken, or like José when he made his exploding volcano for the Science Fair. Lili with her hidden world under Esther and Didi's porch table had nothing on me. Not even Reza, in his little bedroom of dreams, with Zidane kicking the ball on the wall and the jazz musicians parading in the dark – even his imaginary worlds were mere villages next to the travels on which my soul was embarked that spring.

It's no wonder that I came to dress up as Edie, to dance around the studio half drunk in my underwear. I was suddenly aware, almost in a panic – a joyful panic – of the wealth of possibility out in the world, and also within myself. My everyday Appleton life, my phone calls to my father, my occasional beers with friends, my Saturday-morning jogs around the reservoir – what was all that, but the opiated husk of a life, the treadmill of the ordinary, a cage built of convention and consumerism and obligation and fear, in which I'd lolled for decades, oblivious, like a lotus eater, as my body aged and time advanced? I felt all this with the zeal of someone newly wakened – by God, I *felt* and *felt* and *felt*.

In those heady weeks it seemed clear that I owed it not only to myself, but also to my mother – that my fear (the fear that had kept me from pursuing my art more seriously, that had kept me in Boston, that had kept me employed, and surely had kept me single, also) was in fact just *her* fear, that I'd shouldered all her anxieties and disappointments, along with her basic good-Catholic-girl-ness, an inability, ironically, to have faith – truly to believe in the value of my own efforts, in the uniqueness of my own soul. Oh great adventure! Life there, before me, the infinite banquet lying in wait.

8

The two weeks before my mother died are branded in me, each hour of each day of her final hospitalization. I remember where her room was in the unit, how it was, and what was in it, the print on the wall, and at any time, where I was in the room and what the light was like and when my father was there and at what point Matt arrived – without Tweety and the brat, who appeared only for the funeral and seemed chiefly to have seen it as the occasion for a dark-colored shopping spree. There are times in life like that, where you know intuitively that everything hinges on this time and nothing will be the same again, when, as a consequence, your brain remembers, it notices the small things – the male orderly with splayed feet who hummed Chopin waltzes while he mopped, or the young respiratory therapist with heavy brows, who couldn't look at you when he was explaining that your mother's lungs, even with help, were now giving out – he looked about six inches to the right of you, as though you were a shadow of some other self that stood, just there, just beside you, which, in that strange time, felt almost possible. Your mind retained all these things of its own accord, as if they might be necessary to know – simply because it was Important. The mind will do this.

And sometimes – as with my mother dying – you have some idea of what it is that must unfold, and some inkling, however inadequate, of what it will entail. Whereas at other times – as in the last weeks of April and the beginning of May 2005, when it got warm and cold again, when it rained a great deal, it rained as if the gods were disconsolate, as if spring were a sorrow, although I was filled with such joy – you sense the importance, but only that. What it is and what it means you may not fully understand, not for months but for years.

I can tell you that it was on a Tuesday night that I walked with Skandar all the way to Belmont and back again, and it was a night when it had rained earlier but the rain had stopped, and the dark sky was streaked with scudding clouds. There was a smell of earth about, of soil, rich and dark, as we passed the cemetery where my mother was buried, and again when we reached a neighborhood of houses, of small, square gardens that were laid out like open chocolate boxes on the modest street. The new leaves rustled in the breeze over us, and sometimes drops of water fell upon our heads.

That evening, I remember, I'd played chess with Reza after dinner, and he'd let me win – it was one of his favorite things, magnanimous child, to see his own superiority and then to relinquish it. Afterward, at bedtime, I read him an abridged *Three Musketeers* that he enjoyed; and when it was lights-out, he'd asked whether, instead of sitting in the hard chair as I usually did, I might lie alongside him, as his mother would if she were there. I hesitated only a moment before laying myself down, the length of his narrow bed, my arm up under my head so I could better watch him; and he rested his beautiful hand upon my other arm, just to be sure of me, so like his mother, and he closed his fine eyes and went almost immediately to sleep.

So I remember that night, that Tuesday, because it was when I took new steps in my closeness to both son and father: the same night, although they didn't know it, one and the other.

And on my long walk with Skandar, after he and Sirena came home from their supper, it was new, because I also talked. We were passing the cemetery and I asked if he'd ever walked there, because it was so beautiful, but he hadn't, and I told him about going to see my mother's grave, and then I told him about her, Bella Eldridge, and her years of illness, and her admirable, grown-up combination of competence and resignation, and how furious it made me, how looking at her life I felt like a ravenous wolf, I wanted her to have had the chance to devour the world, to be greedy, to be sated. He laughed and said, 'Why don't you want these things for yourself, instead, who are here on earth to enjoy them? Don't you think she'd want you to want them for yourself?'

'But I do,' I said, so emphatically that I almost reached to touch him. 'I *do* want for myself. Enormously.'

'I would never have known that,' he said. 'If you hadn't told me. You seem wonderfully calm in your life, as though it's in enviable order. As though there's nothing extra that you would require. You don't have messes, or make them. You're so generous to everyone – to your school, to Reza, to Sirena – even to me. You don't look like a ravenous wolf.'

'Well I am,' I said. 'I'm starving.'

We were passing an ice-cream shop at that point, and he made a joke about how, if it were open, I could be satisfied.

'I could eat every last spoonful in that place and it wouldn't fill a corner of my hunger,' I said.

'Then you must find a way to feed yourself.' He was quite earnest now. 'You must ask for what you need.'

'Need?' I laughed. 'That's a complicated word, isn't it? Who needs anything, really, besides some food and water? I've already got much more than I *need*.'

'But if you're a ravenous wolf . . . ' He looked off into the distance, smiling as ever. 'I can't think of you this way, you see. It doesn't make sense to me. What is it that you want?'

'Life,' I said. 'All of it. Everything. I don't want to miss it. I don't want the prison doors to close.'

'Prison doors? But really—'

'I know. It doesn't make sense to you, who grew up with war and misery all around you, and I know terrible things have happened in your family – your brother – I know. But trust me.'

And I told him – which is odd to think, even now, because of course I hadn't ever properly told Sirena; bits and pieces, maybe, but not the whole story – about how I'd grown up with my mother's longing and had never found a way to fulfill it, how I'd always thought there were rules about what was possible and allowable, even though I hadn't known, really, who'd made those rules. How in high school, art had seemed the way to break the rules, to get around them; but how it hadn't, then, seemed properly grown up, afterward.

'Who says you have to be grown up?' he asked.

'Tell that to an elementary school teacher! I don't know. It seemed like, who did I think I was, to think I could be an artist, you know? And it didn't seem like I could make a living—'

'Did you try?'

'I couldn't bear to be a failure. It seemed worse to try and fail than not to try. And then my mother, you see—'

'Yes,' he said, 'I do see.'

And we walked along in silence for a while.

'Service,' he said, 'is one of life's great joys. It's a privilege to be in service.'

'You're joking, right? What does that even mean?' I'd always thought of my service as my enslavement.

'It's a great relief, a gift, to be faced with a job that you know absolutely you must do for the benefit of someone else. For whatever reason: out of love, or duty, or something else. As long as you give yourself to it. You don't need to worry about anything but doing that job well, and the satisfaction, when you do, is very beautiful.'

'That isn't what I meant at all.'

'I know,' he said, 'but that doesn't make it less true.'

Then, you see, I had in my head a certainty that I had to say something to Sirena. It was a time when everything was significant and related to every other thing, and when Skandar said this about the joys of service, and when he said I must find a way to feed the wolf, I understood these things to pertain to Sirena, or rather, to Sirena and me.

All that Wednesday at school, my hands trembled when they were at rest, as if I'd drunk too much coffee. It was a freakishly warm day, a summer's day like a hot flash, and I sweated, too. My innards flipped and twisted the way they did before I took a plane. I couldn't eat the salad I'd brought for my lunch. I couldn't sit still. I thought about saying something to her, and I couldn't imagine how she might react.

All my life, I'd shied away from things I couldn't imagine. My basic feeling had been that if I couldn't imagine it, it wasn't a good idea. It was the same with my mother's illness: imagine the worst and you can protect against it. If you can't imagine it, then there's no protection. Not good, not good.

This conviction was behind my renunciation of the artist's life before I'd begun to live it. I couldn't imagine how to be an artist *in this world.* Looking around at my fellow art school students, at the ones we all knew were going to make it, I couldn't imagine pleasing the bigwigs from the galleries and museums, the fashion-makers who organized biennials. I couldn't see myself schmoozing the way the class stars did, flattering older artists and seedy has-been critics to try to wangle an opening for their own advancement. I saw them at it and I couldn't picture myself doing it. I could have rattled off the bullshit about fragmentation and identity and the tropes of gender, whatever the fuck they are, and Roland Barthes and Judith Butler and Mieke Bal – I could do that, they taught us how to do it, that's what art school seemed mostly to be *for,* but I couldn't do it with a straight face and I couldn't even *imagine* doing it with a straight face, and that's why I went to get my master's in Education and appeared to myself and to the world to have forsaken my one dream.

But you see, my dream in my head of being an artist, and my dream in the world of being an artist, I couldn't – until Sirena, I couldn't – connect them. And I forsook the world for the dream in my head, because there, and in my second bedroom off Huron Avenue, and then finally, in that blissful year in Somerville, I could have the dream that I was an artist, it could be real, without any of the bullshit that passes, in the first part of the twenty-first century in the Western world, for being an artist. I could be an Emily Dickinson of an artist.

And here's another thing I was fretting over, as I covered the small distance between the cake shop and the studio, the sidewalk and the studio door – did I think that Sirena was a wonderful artist because I was in love with her, or was I in love with her because she was a wonderful artist, or was I in love with some idea of her that was far from the truth, in which case should I actually be asking myself what, really, in my heart I thought of her art – what *did* I think of her art? Maybe I didn't know. But the moment I became aware of the question, I knew it mattered very much *to me.* It mattered more than almost anything: my answer to that question would surely determine whether I was at last living in reality; or whether I was still dreaming, trapped in my endless hall of mirrors.

After all that obsessive spinning on my mental gerbil wheel, after all my worrying and reconfiguring – you know, don't you, that when I got to the studio and opened the door and called out her name in a cheery singsong, there was no reply. No sound at all. Lights off, everything still. I put down my almost cold coffee and the bag with the cake in it and my handbag and my tote bag containing the folder of high-resolution shrunk-down photographs of Edie Sedgwick, and I walked from one end of the L to the other, moving more and more slowly, because I couldn't get my head around the fact that she wasn't there. In those few minutes, scoping the joint (and the spring afternoon light was flooding in, I remember it exactly, great dust-dancing beams of it, and the studio smelled slightly of glue and old apples, as well as of Sirena's cigarettes), I wondered whether actually I was going nuts, losing my grip. Because I'd been so *certain* that she'd be there, bent over some finicky detail, or smoking by the open window, or even lying on the cushions wrapped up, like a papoose, in her scarves – I'd been so certain of my reality that the facts were at first impossible for me to accept.

The next day, I didn't know at first whether I'd go there or not. I broke one of my rules, and asked Reza if his mother was okay.

'How do you mean?' I was struck by how good his English had gotten: his intonation was native now.

'She wasn't in the studio yesterday, and I thought maybe . . .'

He laughed, a little bark. I remembered him all those months before, in the Whole Foods, with the apples. 'My mother never gets sick,' he said. 'Papa says she's like a superhero. No, she went away.'

'Away?'

He was keen to get out the door. I could hear his friends agitating in the hall. 'But she's back now. She came back in the night.' He threw this over his shoulder, and was gone.

When I made my way to the studio that afternoon, it was humbly: the story in my head, my desire for some confession, my wish to activate a drama between us, to lay claim to her attention, was up against some stronger reality of hers. Whatever had taken her away like that, so suddenly, would take precedence over me. As was so often the case – we Women Upstairs! – her life would be shown to be more important than my life.

She was there, her hair in a messy bun, a streak of blue ink across her forehead. She was leaning over a large picture book when I came in, clasping one of her shawls at her breast, and when she turned she threw her hands wide, dropping her shawl, and her face opened into an enormous, natural, crooked-toothed grin, against which I had no defenses.

'Nora!' She stepped swiftly across the room, light-footed. 'I have such news!'

'Everything's all right then?'

'Everything is all right? Everything is *great*' – only she said 'great-e,' in her particular way. She fiddled with her hair, making it fall around her face. 'Let me make us some coffee – I'll tell you—'

She eyed my bag. 'I didn't bring anything today,' I said, not telling her that I'd eaten an entire cupcake the day before because she wasn't there, and that I'd felt so sick I had to go home.

'It's better,' she said, fussing with the coffee, the pot, the water. 'I rely too much on your sweet things.'

I flopped down on the cushions. 'So what's up?'

'You know, yesterday I was in New York.'

'You didn't tell me.'

'Ah, in my busyness – I must have forgotten. Or maybe because of being nervous, I didn't want to spoil my luck.'

I waited a moment, then asked, 'So did you get lucky?'

She shrugged, smiling again. 'We'll see,' she said. 'But it looks good. This week, one thing, the week after next another thing; we'll see.'

'Come on, Sirena. Just tell me. What's the news?'

She sat beside me, leaned in conspiratorially: 'Yesterday, I had lunch with a friend of mine who is an artist, a seriously good artist, a man in his sixties – he makes sculptures – sexy also, with a deep voice – and he wanted me to meet an important art critic. A woman from the university. She's older, very famous, and she is curating, for two years from now, an important exhibition of art by women, feminist art. It will be unlike anything before – the museum in Brooklyn is opening a new wing, a feminist wing, and this will be the first exhibition, to open the building ... Exciting, no?'

'So she wanted to meet you?'

Sirena gave a laugh, a 'modest' laugh. 'To meet me? Ah, no, she didn't even know that I exist-e. Frank – he's my friend – he makes it seem a coincidence, or friendly, that we're meeting for lunch this way. He tells her I'm looking for a gallery in New York – which is true, of course, and not next week but the one after I go two days to meet with two galleries that may be interested to represent me. So this is the official question, if there is one, for the lunch, which one of these is best, and why, or whether I should be with a different gallery, another one, so. But really, secretly, Frank wants her to think of me for her big exhibition. There will be something like forty artists, and she wants it to be international, and I?' – Sirena made a film-star face, her hands held wide on either side of her cheeks – 'I am *very* international!'

'That's amazing. I mean, it'd be—'

'It would be a whole new level, yes? Of exposure, recognition, standing – can you imagine?'

'Yes.' I could imagine. How far from my world she would be catapulted, and how fast. 'That's completely amazing.'

'It hasn't happened – it may never happen, I know – but I think she liked me, we laughed a lot, we got on very well – but what a dream, no? What a dream come true if it does.'

By which I felt it was asserted, or confirmed, that the dreams that were, for each of us, to the fore, were very different; and that the imaginary conversations that had so energetically circled my mind were not, at least, for today. Today was about Sirena. Of course it was. 'I wish I'd brought a cake after all,' I said brightly. 'We should be celebrating.'

'Celebrating? Not yet! No! We're waiting – not till this critic decides – that could take ages – but until the meetings in two weeks, these gallery owners – this could change everything.'

'You didn't tell me any of this before.'

'I'm superstitious. I'm not logical – I worry about spoiling my chances, about making bad luck.'

'But you'll tell me now.' I didn't say it as a question. If I sounded weary, she didn't notice.

'So I shouldn't – I hope it's okay with the Fates – but I'll tell you, yes, because otherwise I might explode.' She went on to describe the two gallerists she was going to meet. One was a young woman in her early thirties who'd only recently struck out on her own, after working for ten years at an established SoHo gallery, the name of which meant something even to me; and the other, Elias, was a guy in his forties, Middle Eastern, edgier, who'd had his gallery for a while and had attracted some attention in the art world for his bold choices. He, she explained, was a friend of a friend of Skandar's, which was good in the sense that he was somehow a known quantity, his outline made sense and his track record was good, and he'd approached her when he heard she was in the States for a year. But the young woman had written to her in Paris, at her home address, not even knowing she was in the United States, and had said that the Elsinore installation had moved her to tears and that she'd never been able to forget it, and that if Sirena didn't yet have any American representation, then she, Anna Z, would be happy to fly to Paris to talk it over with her – 'and *that*,' Sirena observed, 'is a commitment. That's passion.'

Sirena was full of the pros and the cons of each of these possibilities, stumbling over her words in her enthusiasm, now that she'd allowed herself to talk about it. I wasn't jealous – how could I be, when I, with my dioramas, had turned my back so deliberately upon the Eliases and Annas of this world? – but I wished I could more clearly see that it had occurred to her – that it might however slightly have worried her – that I might be.

'What does Skandar say?' I asked eventually, and noted the familiar flicker of exasperation.

'Skandar? What do you think? He can see it this way, he can see it that way; but, he says, it's not a matter of how he sees it at all. For all he talks, my husband sometimes doesn't say very much. In this case, officially he has no opinion. But I know he'd like me to choose Elias. His family is Lebanese. Has Skandar given you his special talk about the fishermen of Tyre? Yes, so: from Tyre to Princeton, via the long road – this is Elias. This is what Skandar, in his heart, would want.'

'You don't *know* that,' I said, mildly resentful that my thrilling conversation with Skandar had been revealed as 'his special talk.'

'Believe me, I know him. I know it. And have to be careful that I don't choose to please him, or else to displease him. I must make my choice alone.' She sighed. 'I wish you could come with me. I'd like to know your opinion of these people. You see so clearly.'

'Well, maybe – depending – when do you go?'

'Thursday and Friday, the week after next. I'm afraid it's impossible.'

'If it were in a few weeks—'

'I can't change the meetings. It's too bad. I'll tell you all about it when I come back. It's in the future. But enough: How are you, Nora my friend, in *your* work?'

Did she care? What I wanted was a sense of her spontaneous engagement, the feeling you have with your closest – that I have with Didi, for example, but not with Esther – that they don't have to be careful, that their reactions are kind and genuine at the same time. Even as I say it, I realize it's a lot to want. Maybe I'm registering an intractable discontent, born of my doubt about whether and how much she loved me, and whether, or how, I might ever know.

You'd think it would be an easy question to ask – do you love me? – but you'd think that only if you've never wanted to ask it yourself. That afternoon, instead of openly confessing as I'd dreamed of doing, I raised the question of departure.

'Isn't it wild how fast the time is going?' I said. 'I can't believe you guys will be leaving before too long.'

'Wild. I know,' she said.

'When do you go? I should know, but ...'

'My show opens the sixteenth.'

'July sixteenth?'

'July sixteenth?' she laughed. 'In Paris? That would be like not having a show at all!'

'June sixteenth? In Paris? How did I not know that?'

'I think I haven't been saying so out loud, to try not to be too much afraid. I've been pretending there is more time.'

'The sixteenth? But Appleton doesn't get out until the twenty-third. You can't go before then. And what about the kids? What about the kids coming here? I thought we said the end of the month.' We had already largely set up the space – the flowers, the mirror-shard strands of rain, the beginnings of the Jabberwock eyes – and we'd spent two rainy afternoons a couple of weeks before installing the video cameras for the shoot: we were, in some practical way, ready to go at the studio end. But to bring my kids there required time-consuming paperwork at Appleton: the approval of a field trip from Shauna's office; the permission slips signed by the parents. It couldn't be done overnight.

'Don't be such a schoolteacher, Nora. We'll work it all out. I can't possibly be here when there is my opening in Paris. We haven't yet discussed things at home. Skandar also, his plans are complicated – conferences here, in Montreal, in Washington – eh, *basta*. We'll figure it out.' And with a sweep of her arms at the studio around us: 'And we must bring the children, while there's still time. That isn't dispensable! Let's fix the date today. So much to do before we get there – mountains to climb!'

'Wonderlands to build.'

'So, *au travail!*' And she was up on her light feet, her back to me, into her universe, gone.

⌒

She was so flippant about it – only two months before her Paris opening, and I'd just heard the date for the first time. When I got home that evening I took out the calendar, looked at it, all laid out on paper, the little boxes of days. Much would depend on how much she could finish in Cambridge; but she'd certainly have to leave by the beginning of June. I needed to steel myself for that. They wouldn't pull Reza out of school, would they? Skandar would stay. Or maybe they'd ask me to look after him, if Skandar had to go for his conferences. I could feel along my arm the heat that Reza had emanated as he drifted off to sleep – I could do that, I could take care of him.

That was Thursday. Friday I knew she wasn't coming. If I was alerted ahead of time, this wasn't any problem. Not only kids are like this. As a teacher, I know from long experience that if you warn people beforehand, things go better. I knew I'd be alone at the studio, I planned to be there late, I took my brown cardboard salad box from the Alewife supermarket and a cheap bottle of red wine from the liquor store next door, and I gathered my mother's Polaroid camera – this was before the film was like gold dust, so I took along plenty of it – and all my Edie paraphernalia – more of it than you might imagine your average middle-aged third-grade teacher to possess – and I went to Somerville.

I've told you about this. I got a bit drunk. I played the music pretty loud. I danced, and posed, and I took pictures. I was being free, and I suppose in some way it was an exorcism – surely that's not the right word? By allowing Edie's ghost to inhabit me, I was banishing the meek and accommodating Miss Eldridge, the calm and responsive Miss Eldridge, the good friend, good daughter, good teacher, doormat Miss Eldridge, the Miss Nobody Nothing that everyone smiles at so cheerfully and immediately forgets. I was getting rid of her.

I danced and drank and smoked and took cartridges of blurry Polaroids of myself, as if I were Robert Mapplethorpe and Patti Smith at one and the same time. And this went on until the whole bottle was empty – I drank most of it, but somehow a goodly bloody dollop ended up on the front of my Edie white T-shirt. It was a splotch on my left boob that then dribbled downward, so it looked like a bleeding heart. And then I took it off, so I was dancing in my white bra, stained in one spot by the wine.

And do you know what I did, in that dizzied state? I tiptoed into Sirena's Wonderland forest and I lay down on the Astroturf grass with the flowers waving around and above me and casting shadows on the walls in the half-light, like dancers; and I closed my eyes and I slipped my flat hand under my waistband, and I tickled my own stomach, following with my blind fingers its declivity between my hip bones; and with my fingers seemingly independent explorers, I traced a blood-ringing, singing line down either side of me, over my hips and into the fur of my groin, and from there into the wetness between my legs; and I wasn't, for a while, Edie or Alice or Emily or anybody but *a body,* or I was another Nora altogether, and with the grass prickly beneath me, and both my hands now against myself, inside myself and on my reverberating skin, all there was, was *yes, yes, yes,* and I was in Wonderland, and for that brief unashamed, unhidden time, I was free.

9

I got up the next morning a new person. At least, I thought so. Replete, I looked at the self I'd been all week – all month – for months – with mild dismay, the way an ex-smoker looks at his former, needy self, and marvels. I got up, I called my father, I drove to Brookline, I took him to brunch at Zaftigs, and then I drove him to the arboretum and we walked for a long time among the trees in their young maiden green and their bursting Disney blossoms. He limped because of his bad hip, but every time I asked he said he wanted to keep going, so we did. It was cold, but we didn't overly notice, and I could see the color of health spreading in his saggy cheeks, my dear, gray father, so nobly struggling on. I was sad to have neglected him.

He talked about the Red Sox game he was going to watch later that day – against Tampa, I think it was – and we talked about my mother's love of flowers and blossoms, the zeal of her gardening, but we laughed at how bad-tempered she'd get when her plants died on her, when they didn't make it through the winter. As if it were a personal insult. I said I'd always thought it was because she didn't control anything in her life and she felt at least the plants ought to listen to her, and that her confidence was devastated when they didn't.

My father looked at me like I was nuts. He said, 'What are you talking about? Your mother controlled everything in her life, in *our* lives. She chose where we lived and how we lived and what we ate and when and what we wore and who we knew and how and when we saw them. She chose how many kids we had – your brother and you, she chose; I wanted six of you – and also when we had you. She controlled everything always, and that's why gardening made her so damned mad, because she found one thing on this earth she couldn't fully be in charge of. She was a piece of work, your mother. She was fantastic. I never knew anybody people loved so much, but my God she was a bossy so-and-so.'

I was partly shocked when my father said all this – as much by his vehemence, too, the sight of him in love, his eyes alight in their pouches, a fleck of glistening spittle on his lips – and partly also full of wonder, because I thought for the first time that it was natural, and clear, that each of us would have a different story of who Bella Eldridge was and of how it had been. It stood to reason. Sirena and I, too, would have different accounts of our shared year, and that hers wouldn't match mine – well, that wouldn't invalidate mine, just as my father's picture of my mother didn't invalidate my picture. Somehow, briefly, on that day after Being Edie, this all seemed just about believable.

I got my dad home in good time and picked him up a six-pack and a jumbo bag of extra-cheese Doritos on the way. My mother would never have allowed him those things, it was true, and my dad in his resumed bachelorhood took freedoms that I could tell excited him, as if he were a small boy getting away with something.

I'd decided not to go to the studio all weekend, which made

me realize how much a reflex it had become. After I dropped off my father, I headed home over the BU bridge as if to Somerville, and realized only at Central Square what I'd done. I was almost sure Sirena would be working that afternoon, but I didn't go to find out. If she wanted my help, she could ask for it. I went home, I went for a run, I had a shower. I'd told myself I'd read a book, but I didn't feel like it. It seemed depressing to turn on the TV. I e-mailed a few people but tired of that, too. I called Didi but they were out and her cell was off.

Finally, in the early evening, I called Sirena: I left her a message, as professional as I could make it, confirming the date and time for the Appleton third-grade field trip. There were permission slips to get signed, I reminded her. We had to plan ahead. I made scrambled eggs on toast and went to bed at eight thirty, terribly hungry but not for food. So much for my state of repletion.

Sirena didn't return my call. I didn't know why, but I wasn't going to humiliate myself by asking. I held out almost a week, with every kind of crazy story in my head to explain her silence. On Thursday night, I caved. I waited till late, well after nine, before I went over to the studio. I told myself this had nothing to do with her at all, that this was about Edie and Alice and my need to get back to work on them. I'd left the Polaroids on my table, and I'd only really remembered them that day. I knew it was too late – I knew Sirena well enough to know that even if they were facedown, especially if they were facedown, she would have looked at them, scrutinized them, had opinions. I was ashamed to think of it. Maybe her silence was caused by her contempt for the photos – me, blurry in my bra; me, wild-eyed, taking pictures of myself in something like fancy dress; me, *preposterous,* and preposterously, inappropriately, unhumble ...

Fun House Nora, the Woman Upstairs, we like her because she's so thoughtful of others. Because she isn't stuck up.

Which one is Nora? I can't quite picture her ...

You know, that nice third-grade teacher – not the one with the cotton-candy hair, the other one.

That's who I'm supposed to be, the other one: 'No, not the really great artist in that studio – the other one.'

'Not the beautiful woman in the knockout dress – the other one.'

'The funny one?'

'Oh yeah, I guess she's that. The funny one.'

Sirena might think the Edie Polaroids were funny. She might think they were some sort of joke. That would be okay, if they were a joke.

So on Thursday night, I went over to see about my rooms, about my artists, to look over the photographs I'd made. I went to retrieve them, a salvage operation if you will. Unavowedly, I went to see what she'd done during the week, what progress she'd made without me. I went partly hoping that the studio would be exactly as I'd left it, that whatever had been going on – something had been going on – it would have been big enough to keep her away.

Already in the stairwell there were sounds. Wafty Eastern music, not her usual thing, chatter, banging. There was the movement of life, of lives. As I walked down the corridor, I thought maybe she was having a party; but the sounds weren't party sounds.

They didn't hear me come in. They were too busy. That's not quite true: one young woman, in her mid-twenties, in a skimpy black tunic with huge eyes, a very white face and curly ringlets of that rare auburn that looks dyed even when it's not, broke away from the huddle and came toward me.

'I'm so sorry. Is the noise bothering you?'

'This is my studio,' I said. Not nicely. I couldn't help it. My eyes turned on my own end of the L, to my table and my things. Someone had dropped her jacket carelessly over my work chair, and had slung shopping bags and a handbag on the floor beside it; but otherwise my stuff, from a distance, looked okay. I could see the jagged pile of Polaroids on my side table: I couldn't tell whether that was where I'd left them, or whether they'd been moved. 'Who are you?' I asked, trying with only minimal success to sound less annoyed. 'And what are you doing here?'

'I'll tell Sirena you're here – you must be Nora?' I could see from her glance – down, up, down, resting on my dowdy clogs, that I wasn't as she'd expected. 'I'm Becca,' she said. 'I'm the makeup artist.'

Upon entering the studio, here's what I saw: Sirena, at the center of a small clutch of dark-clad people, in dim light, huddled around a film camera. Sirena was the director, I guess. The camera person was a lanky guy with a shaven head and a silver bullet in his dark eyebrow. He had a dotting of stubble, like smut, across his chin, and a black T-shirt from which his long arms stuck out white in the gloom. Later, when he stood up, I'd see that he was enormously tall, at least six and a half feet. He was the only man.

Aside from Sirena and Becca, there were three or four other women. One of them seemed to be responsible for the lighting, and darted down into the Wonderland area to fuss with spotlights and two big silver reflecting screens. They were all young except for a tall, long-nosed woman in her late forties or early fifties, with big dark hair and stylish red rectangular glasses. She was a friend of Sirena's, Marlene, a Hungarian photographer from LA, in town on a Radcliffe fellowship.

They were all focused on a woman in white, head to toe in pure white, with a funny tall white cap covering her hair, like a Smurf's cap without the fold – it stood straight up. All you could see of her body was her face, including her ears, which stuck out, and her hands and feet, which were a lovely even light brown. She wore a long-sleeved plain white dress with an enormous skirt and white leggings. She seemed to grow out of the Astroturf like the carved flowers around her.

Becca scurried over and whispered to Sirena, who swiveled on her high stool (where, too, had that come from?) and blew me kisses with both hands. But she didn't get up: she indicated that she couldn't, right now; and so I put my things down and made my way over to the camera as they turned on some Eastern music, a mesmerizing sort of whiny wavering, and started filming again.

At once, the woman in white began to spin, first slowly and then at greater speed, and the vast circle of her skirt billowed out, rippling gorgeously up and down. The wind it made shook the aspirin flowers on their stalks, and they, too, danced. I could see her actually dancing, down at the end of the studio, and then, in the camera's screen, a miniature version of her dancing also, and the two sights were the same but different. When I looked at her in real life, she seemed to me almost to create a haze around her, a visible air; but in its tiny-fying precision, the camera recorded her spinning like a science.

I stayed for more than an hour, but they were still working when I left. In fact, I left during a break in their filming before what was, Sirena told me later, the final take. She wanted – and ultimately she got – seven perfect minutes of unbroken spinning, her dervish – on hire, or a volunteer, from the local Sufi temple – twirling without cease, without stumbling, in her meditative trance, seven magical minutes. She got these minutes – Sirena never doubted that she would, even though it took almost seven hours for her to be satisfied.

When they broke for Thai food, Sirena, jolly, and public –
masked! – in a way I'd never before seen, introduced me around.
The cameraman was called Langley. He had a goofy manner,
and was older than I'd thought, though not as old as me.
Marlene seemed at first curious, at least curious enough to paste
on a big smile; and then when she found out I taught elementary school, her eyes, like a lizard's, hooded over, and she
retreated into her pad thai. Sana, meanwhile, the Sufi – originally named Carolina and the rebellious daughter of Puerto
Rican Catholics – stood to one side, daintily eating slices of
papaya dipped in lime juice, miraculously without spilling even
a drop upon her pristine garments. She produced, from within
her folds, a linen handkerchief, and carefully wiped her lips and
her fingers when she was done. Radiant, she barely spoke: it was,
for her, a spiritual event.

This was not obviously so for Sirena: 'Where've you been, you
crazy girl, these past days?' she asked, without waiting for a reply.
'You've missed all the excitements! It's too bad – we've had such
adventures. And this is the last.' She clapped her hands. 'This is
the centerpiece.' She turned to the beatific woman in white:
'And Sana is our star!' Sirena crunched on a tiny spring roll. 'But
all of them have been fantastic. The little girl, the older woman –
wasn't she extraordinary, Marlene? Marlene's been my right
hand, the person to steady me – because photography, still pictures, up to now, is not so much my thing – video, but not so
much the photographs.' She chewed, and even that seemed to
me theatrical. 'But the pictures, they've come out well, no?
Marlene is so brilliant a photographer, it's almost shaming to ask
for your opinion' – she put her hand on Marlene's arm in that
way that I'd thought was for me – 'but you were so kind as to
say' – she was talking to Marlene while telling me the story –
'that you thought they were good—'

'I told you, sweetie, they're phenomenal. You know that.' And

Marlene then said, as if she'd turned to look at me, but without turning at all, 'She's so full of false modesty, this one! This installation will make her name.'

'Can you come tomorrow afternoon?' Sirena asked me, fixing me properly with her gaze at last, and for the only time that evening. 'I'll show you the images – now, with the computer, it's all right here – but you'll say whether you agree. For the little girl, Marlene and I have different ideas.'

'She wants to have the head show, the chin and the mouth, for the expression,' said Marlene, still looking at Sirena rather than at me. 'But I think it's better without the mouth. Because then for the young woman you have the mouth, and for the middle-aged woman—'

'Don't call her that,' said Sirena, laughing. 'She's the same age as we are!'

'And we, my darling Sirena' – somehow she rolled the 'r' the way I'd always wanted to – 'are also middle-aged. Be proud of it!' But surely, I thought, looking at Marlene, at the impression she gave that her meager flesh pulled wearily away from the bone – surely this woman wasn't the same age as Sirena? Sirena wasn't nearly so old. 'Anyway, our contemporary, we see her mouth and nose, maybe even the bottom of her eyes, and then—'

'Yes, yes,' Sirena interrupted, 'Nora knows: then we see all of her, of our wise woman. As she sees all of herself. Finally. Nora knows this already. We've talked about it.'

'Many times,' I murmured. It seemed to me I'd suggested it. The Thai feast was winding down, and Sana the refulgent Sufi had excused herself to go to the bathroom. Even mystics needed to pee. I wondered how she'd negotiate the grimy artists' bathroom in her voluminous white skirt; but when she returned, she looked pristine as ever.

Needless to say, there was no question of my working on Edie or Alice. And there was no question that Sirena might have missed me: she'd been surrounded by disciples and helpers and colleagues, above all by Marlene – whose work, I remembered Sirena telling me, had been included in a group show at MoMA – who reminded me of what the art world was like and why I'd turned away from it. All these months had been mere housekeeping before the real guests arrived. Sirena didn't need me at all.

I managed to smile a lot. Before she drifted back into Wonderland, I told the Sufi that she was beautiful, and she looked at me as though I'd spoken to her in Aramaic. I thanked Becca for the spring rolls, even though I'd eaten only one. As I gathered up my stuff, I discreetly swiped my Polaroids into my tote bag. Even glimpsing the fuzz of my chin and shoulder – my white bra strap – in the picture on top of the pile, I was washed with such shame that I felt sick. This amateur silliness. This self-indulgence. Who was I kidding? Had they flipped through them? Becca? Marlene? Heading out, I peered one last time through the gloom toward the distant field of light where Sana was preparing to twirl: she was lost to me. I could see nothing but a shimmering white blur.

10

The next afternoon, the people had vanished, and so too had their equipment. Sirena must have taken out the garbage, even, or had Becca do it, because there was no evidence at all of their presence – except, perhaps, that all the coffee cups were clean, which wasn't normally the case.

'Nora!' she called as I came in, without looking up. 'Come see!' She sat at her computer, and as I approached she set the video of Sana to play. 'Langley sent this over just now. We can tinker, of course – but look!'

The colors were so bright – the Astroturf so green, the flowers so fully lilac, lemon, rose. And Sana, except for the lovely olivey bits of her – those hands! Those ears! – was pure, pure white. The video was completely silent, like a dream.

'What about the music?'

'No, no, you see – didn't we discuss this? Maybe with Marlene – I'm sorry. Nowadays I can't remember.'

'We didn't discuss the music.'

'I want it to be silent. Completely silent. Ibn Tufail's recluse on his desert island didn't twirl to any music – didn't *know* any music – but nature's, or what he might have imagined in his own

head. So I want it to be silent. But then my question is – and I
have to decide so fast – whether also, in addition to the silence,
we give them music to choose from.'

'I don't get it.'

'So, I want each person to find, in my Wonderland, as much
room as possible for her own Wonderland. You know this. For
his own Wonderland, even. So what if you have no imagination,
or if your dreams need help? So then, maybe, around the video
room there are sets of headphones, yes?'

'Yes?'

'Maybe four – or five – maybe even seven.'

'Seven?'

'Because there are life's seven stages, because there are seven
photographs, seven veils, seven unveilings, because there are
seven minutes of dancing, because seven is the most magical
number there is.' She threw up her hands and then took a cigarette from an open pack on the table. They weren't Skandar's
brand – she'd bought them on her own, for once.

'So there are seven sets of headphones. It seems like a lot.
Kind of cluttered, maybe.'

Sirena shrugged. We were both watching Sana dancing on the
screen. One hand was turned toward the sky, the other earth-
ward. She moved her fingers as though they were petals in the
breeze.

'So?'

'So each set is different music. Maybe not even all music. Yes,
one is what Sana is actually dancing to, Omar Faruk Tekbilek.
I must make sure I have the permission. But then one is surely
birdsong – spring birdsong, a nightingale and a blackbird,
maybe, together. Maybe one is something popular, contemporary – I'll have to ask someone young. Maybe Maria will know?
But no, she'll listen to horrible music, for sure. And then there
may be city sounds on another – New York traffic, for example.'

'That doesn't seem so contemplative. Not exactly the sounds of enlightenment.'

'Not of itself, okay. But look at the video, look' – we both looked – 'and imagine the sounds of horns and brakes and tires, the screech and racket of it. And suddenly her dancing, her prayer if you will, her *resonance* – suddenly the power of her Wonderland is even greater, do you see? Even more free. Because she can be transported there in her own mind, by her own thoughts, not only when the music, like Pavlov, tells her to be; or not only when the birds are singing, like in heaven; but even when the outside world is in total chaos' – she said 'kah-os' – 'and disarray.' She waved the cigarette at the screen and the smoke hung, for a second. 'This will be beautiful,' she said. 'And true.'

I waited a moment for her to go on. When she didn't, I said, 'That's still only four.'

'Four what?'

'Sets of headphones.'

She glared at me, then cackled. 'I didn't know you could be such a *rompicazzo*, Nora. I like this very much. Very much.'

After I made coffee, she said: 'The photographs. Before you go, you must look at the photographs. Because I've got to order the prints in France. As always, they should have had the order yesterday. They're to be on muslin, very big, almost seven feet tall – even with the computers now this isn't so easy, the size of it, on fabric, and to make seven, it takes time. There isn't much time, now.'

'Yes,' I said. 'I guess that's true. So little time.' The week before, when she'd told me the date for her show in Paris, seemed very long ago. Suddenly everything was over: the focus had changed. The Shahids were all looking away from me now. We were hurtling, or I was, toward the end of it all. The terminal patient headlong toward death. The very awareness of finitude speeding everything up, when you most wanted to slow it all. I knew that wasn't what Sirena meant. She meant that there was so little time until her show. So little time until she was lost to me.

'Show them to me then,' I said. 'Let's get on with it.'

The little girl wasn't so little as all that. I was almost shocked, but also deeply moved, to see her naked. It was a part of Sirena's purpose that the child not be five or six, because there's no shame in being naked at that age, the washboard-fronted children with their unobtrusive boy and girl genitals all but interchangeable along the beachfronts. No, the shock lay in seeing the newly awakening body of this child who must have been around eleven – who was, Sirena confirmed, eleven – the poignant, rosy puff of her breast buds, the nascent rounding of the hip below her waist, but these curves just a suggestion still upon the tight band of her torso, the long, straight perfect limbs of a still god-held child, trailing her clouds of Wordsworthian glory. And there, at the pubis, a few dark strands, the beginning of her hiddenness, but the tidy, childish split of her still frank and clear to the world. In all of them, she stood straight, leaning slightly on her left hip, her right foot slightly splayed, its angle minutely shifting from frame to frame. One hand, her left, reached toward the camera, loomed larger, its smooth square fingernails both carrying, and grasping for, the promise of adulthood. None of the photos showed her face, but the exact cropping point differed, and in some, her chin and mouth were visible. They'd pulled her hair up, so you couldn't even tell what color it might be, and she was defined, then, by the exposure of her delicate neck, like a stalk, slightly long for the rest of her, and fragile. In one picture – the one showing most of her, that Sirena wanted to use – she bit her lip slightly, and you could discern a mere hint of tooth, pressing the perfect ridged rose of her lip. It was breathtaking.

'You see, there, you understand, yes?' Sirena said. 'It is the moment of hesitation: she reaches forward, but she's uncertain. She wishes also that she might stay. She's relaxed, but also awkward. A child, but not.'

'Which is why you absolutely cannot use this one,' I said. 'Trust the photographer. Trust your friend. She knows what she's talking about.'

Sirena threw up her hands again and rolled her phlegmy irritation in her throat.

'You're just using one of the girl, right? Only one picture? Don't you see, if you use that one, it may seem clear to you what story it's telling, but precisely because of her mouth, because of that tooth, it's actually telling a story in a way the others aren't. And as soon as it's telling a story, people can interpret it however they want, they can take that picture and put their own story onto it. And even if it seems so clear to you what it says, you can't control what they think it says. I thought that was central to your Wonderland, that each experience of it should be open, unique.'

'Yes, of course, but this picture—'

'To you it says, "I hesitate on the cusp of knowledge." And to a hundred thousand people, that's also what it says. And then to a hundred pervs in the hundred thousand, it says, "That little girl wants to fuck me. I knew it."'

'But this is ridiculous—'

'Have you read *Lolita*? I rest my case.'

Sirena emitted more rumblings but she did not contest what I had said.

'This one,' I said, pointing to the headless version in which the girl's neck looked most swanlike, and in which, also, the forefinger of the reaching left hand was slightly raised, and by some cast of the light, had around it a rim of shadow, accentuating also its length. It gave the photograph a slightly religious air, some echo of the gestures of medieval Madonnas. 'This is the one you must use.'

'You really think so?'

'I know so.'

She sighed. 'Maybe,' she said. 'Maybe you're right.' Which grudging comment caused me elation, until she went on, 'I'll ask Marlene to look again. She didn't choose this one – hers is this' – she pointed at a different image – 'but I see why you take this. It's the finger, yes? You're right about the finger. I didn't remark it, but it's true.'

The pictures that followed were of a twenty-two-year-old, whose moles decorated her fair skin like erotic paint splatters and whose mouth, a pretty bow-shaped mouth with a strong cleft in the upper lip, curled upward in what seemed to be barely contained amusement. There would be two of her, two of all of them henceforth, and in one she, too, stood straight to the camera, though with her hand coyly covering her privates; and in the other, half turned, with her arm extended in embrace of the air, you could apprehend in profile the ripe heft of her breast, with its sharp dark nipple, and the exuberant, even youthful, burst of pubic hair at her groin.

For midlife, Sirena had two sets of photographs. The first was of a tallish woman, slightly heavy in that ponderous, maternal way – her breasts full and unevenly drooping, their nipples pointing in faintly disparate directions like misaligned headlights. The skin of her round belly was puckered, presumably by childbearing, and this was at odds with the otherwise trunklike firmness of her, the fullness of an inhabited body, with its tracery of purpling veins upon the thighs and its scars – an appendix scar, and a seam, too, around one knee. The woman's face was visible almost to her eyes – the strong lines from nose to mouth, the cheeks still round but less than fully plump, the incipient wattling beneath the chin. But in one of her two photographs, the one in which her strong, elegantly veined hand clasped her side, she was laughing, open-mouthed and laughing, and even without seeing her eyes you felt the strength of her, and she was beautiful.

I felt both envy and contempt for this faceless woman – forty-four years old, Sirena told me, with three children. I felt envy because my own body, for all it was younger in every aspect, for all it hewed, more closely, to some statuesque ideal – mine, I felt, was a body in waiting, a body yet unused. And while I had, at the first, an instinctive young person's revolt at the careless blowsiness of this middle-aged body, I had also a sense of alarm that in spite of my efforts to stay young, time would ravage me also, and that like an unopened flower I might wither on the vine. Whereas this, I thought, is the open flower on the cusp of its fading: this is the fullness of life.

The second set of midlife photographs astonished me. At first I couldn't think why they were there – why two models in this case? – but in an instant I recognized the silver chain around the neck, the curve of the nose, the clavicle with its single small mole, like a dark pearl.

'Why did you take yourself?'

'Well, this is the question. Marlene took these . . . ' So Marlene had stood with the camera and recorded Sirena in her nakedness: somehow, for Marlene to do this was fine. 'And really, she's a better photographer than I am.'

'I don't think so.'

'You're very loyal. But the rest of the world thinks so, for a reason. So, if there are reasons to use my body – it's the right age, I'm the artist, I'm not then asking anyone to do my nakedness for me, if you like . . . ' She sighed. 'And in such an installation, this is important, too. I want, as you say, for everyone to have their own journey in Wonderland, their own life's journey. But I'm making this art because of where I am in my own life's journey; so it's the right thing to do to put my own body here, to show myself in my travels.'

'So why the hesitation?'

'It's not about my cesarean scar, if that's what you mean! I'm not ashamed. But it's also not my photography. To me, this is peculiar, it's like a shift in perspective, do you see? Am I showing the world through my eyes, or am I showing myself to the world?'

'Well, it depends.'

'*Sì*. It depends. So I must choose. But you must have an opinion?'

My opinion was that her nakedness was beautiful to me, that her body was at once more frail, more childlike, and yet more sturdy than I might have imagined. I hadn't realized that her olive skin retained a youthful sheen all over, as if she were made of butter: the hip bones either side of her flat stomach were like polished knobs. I hadn't understood, in all this time, how much higher her left shoulder was than her right. It made me happy to see her crooked tooth peeking when she smiled. 'I think it's a decision you have to make by yourself,' I said.

'Maybe I'll have a revelation.'

'Couldn't you use both? One of each?'

'It's about the symmetry. I could have seven different women, otherwise. But this means more photographs; and I have no time.'

'You could set up one more shoot—'

'No,' she said, and here sounded almost bitter. 'This is what Skandar says, as if there were endlessly more time. The gallery wants everything by June first. Already the place that makes the big prints on fabric, for this size, wants six weeks. There aren't six weeks. Maybe they can rush for me, they say; but if there's a mistake, or a problem, there's no room for failure – *there is no room!*' She was very nearly shouting. 'And so much to do. The heart, I wanted to cast the plastic heart here, but now it seems, to put in the pump, the best place is in Paris; but it must be done to exact specifications – I'm trying, for early next week, to get a friend of a friend to help me do it here – because I go on Thursday to New York, for the galleries, did you forget? And then I'm not back until Saturday or maybe Sunday, and another week is lost. Lost, you see?'

'I see.' It was what I was supposed to say.

'It's not the same for you, you have no deadlines, no commitments, you have all your time, an ocean of time! But for me, it's always running against the clock. Someone always waiting, Sirena you're late, you're late – here, at home, Reza, Skandar, the fucking babysitter, the gallery in Paris shouting down the telephone – it's always too much. And this show – it's very important, it's my chance. I'm getting older, and yes, there are the beginnings, I've had nice attention, but each time it only matters more. If I fail, it will be the end. Each time this is only more true. Unless I can really climb over the wall. I have to, this time. This matters so much.'

'I see,' I said again. I don't need to tell you that she was flaying me alive.

'So, no more pictures. I'll choose one or the other, by tonight. Maybe I'll choose blind and see what comes back.' She gave a harsh laugh and daubed at her eyes. She'd gotten quite worked up. No, of course I wouldn't know what it was to have a chance, or a life, at all. 'So, we haven't quite finished with the photographs. There's still my wise woman, and hers are the best.'

'I'd better go in a minute.'

'No – you came to do your work. I'm sorry, to get all worked up – I'm so tired. I'm overwhelmed. My dear friend, look quickly at the photos, and then go to your work – I know you haven't been at your table for many days now. I just want you to see my prize, the best ones.'

They were indeed, in spite of the glory of the others, the best ones. Sirena explained that the woman, aged eighty-three, was in her yoga class. She was herself a painter, as it turned out, and a child therapist who, although officially retired, still consulted. She was widowed. She had no children. Her name, not that it mattered, was Rose.

In these photos, we saw all of Rose. She had bunioned feet and fingers so badly warped by arthritis that you wondered how she could hold a pen. She had, on her diminished right breast, the white scar of a lumpectomy – breast cancer at fifty-eight – but it was barely noticeable, really. Her breasts were Tiresian withered dugs, like the breasts of native women in my history classes, breasts so far from either the erotic or the maternal that they could barely be called breasts, were more like near-empty sacks appended to her rib cage. Her skeleton was everywhere visible, almost protruding: her breastbone shimmered beneath the skin's surface, like the shadow of mortality; her ribs; the odd, jaunty poke of her uneven hips; the knobbling of her knees . . . And this in spite of her amazing freckling: her skin was everywhere so mottled that you couldn't tell foreground from background. Not the gentle smattering of moles that sprayed the young woman's neck like kisses – Rose had a Jackson Pollock for a body, a human casing as marked as any canvas, so intense that she almost seemed dressed in her nudity. I loved that in all this, her fingernails and toenails were carefully painted, not garishly but deliberately, shell pink, an old lady's vanity.

But ah, to see her face! After the faceless bodies of the others, to be given the gift of her face all but brought tears to my eyes. And such a face. As freckled as, or more so than, the rest of her, her pigment a mask, her wrinkles almost folds, but here, here, the spirit shone. Her pale blue eyes glittered clear, and fierce, and resoundingly joyous. Her strong, compact nose broke the ocean of her face like a ship's prow. Her teeth, so white, reassuringly crooked. And her pure white hair, oiled and straight, impeccably parted and pulled back from her face, glowed.

In one of the two images Sirena had chosen, Rose was dancing, half a twirl, in an almost-echo of Sana's dervish spin. In the other, the most beautiful of all the photographs, she held out both her arms to the camera, as if to a child, with a smile at once welcoming and conspiratorial, as if saying, 'Come, come, and I will show you all the wonders that I know.'

You couldn't look at Rose in her nakedness with envy, or contempt, or even sorrow: I looked at her with awe, and I thought, 'Let me come with you.'

And then I thought, in spite of my fury at Sirena just then, that if she did nothing else at all for her installation, if Wonderland were only that photograph, she would have made a beautiful and inspiring thing. I thought that Marlene had been right, this would be the making of her. She hadn't needed me to sew together the canopy of Alice dresses; she didn't need the aspirin flowers or the broken mirrors – all of it, ultimately, otiose, however clever or beautiful. This was the real moment: this was her Wonderland.

'These are fantastic' is all I said. And she laid her hand on my arm, that way, and really looked at me, and said, 'Thank you.'

11

The next week, Sirena went to New York, although not before we'd confirmed our Appleton adventure for the Monday almost two weeks hence, in the afternoon. We'd bring all the kids, but she'd film only the ones whose parents agreed it was okay. For the others, I'd provide an art project, at my end of the studio. I prepared the permission forms with two sections, and sent them home to all the parents.

In the end, Sirena would choose Anna Z as her gallerist, in what seemed at the time a bold, even risky choice – would the gallery even survive? Who knew? – but over the past years, even through the difficult times, they've both thrived, and the success of each has fed the other, so that now Anna is credited with having 'found' Sirena, and Sirena, perhaps more accurately, with having 'made' Anna.

But that was for later. Sirena was gone. Obviously, I'd known she would be. I hadn't been at my boxes for over a week, although it felt much longer. I'd been so firmly put in my place during those days. I'd barely resisted the impulse to tear up my Polaroids – who had I thought I was? How could I have borne for anyone else to see? – but still I couldn't look at them. I'd stuffed them in the back of my underwear drawer, as if they were racy porn, instead of sad and tame. Not only did I feel ashamed, I felt ashamed of being ashamed. Neither Alice nor Edie would have had time or patience for my prudery, silly cow that I was.

The point was to be good at it – at art – and not to care. It wasn't clear which of these was the more important, or whether simply in caring one fell at a crucial hurdle. Would it have been better not to be good and not to care? Obviously, above all – I had Rose in her splendid nudity in my mind's eye – it was important to be good. Sirena, fuck her, was good.

But that, I told myself, was no reason to abandon my artists and their habitats. *They* were good, even if I wasn't especially – doubt! Doubt! The enemy of all life! – and I owed it to them: so when Sirena was away, I went into the studio on Thursday and again on Friday, and stayed late into the night, to select and carefully to frame under glass the perfect reduced prints of Edie that, once installed, would look down upon her in her sealed room. Even as I filed and measured and glued, I thought: What are these images, even? They aren't new. They don't, as Pound so wanted, *make it new*. A magpie cobbling, they don't owe anything to my own efforts. Or rather: given how labor-intensive my efforts were, my failure of effort was something bigger, somehow more grandiose, a failure that I could sense, like a blind person, but couldn't properly identify.

But why, I asked at the same time, why judge what wasn't yet made, not yet fully itself? The dioramas aren't in competition with anyone, with anything; they're your expression. Yours.

Yours? How can they be *yours,* when they're simply primitive homages to actual great artists of one kind or another?

But as a sequence, they have a logic—

And that logic is entirely subsidiary. It's a follower's logic.

But aren't we – most of us – followers?

But do we want to be? Surely a work of art isn't simply about what *is*? Do you leave a door open for what could be, what we want to be?

Even as I filed and measured and glued, I was thinking more about Sana twirling, or the girl-child reaching, or Rose embracing, than I was about my own work. I was thinking about the intimations of monstrosity in Sirena's world, about the Jabberwock eyes, and of the film she proposed to make of the children, and of what, exactly, it might be like.

It was around ten o'clock on Friday night that I became aware, as months before, of footsteps in the corridor, of a shuffling pause on the threshold, before the inevitable knock. It was warm, and I had all the windows open, so that the rustling of the leaves outside was like a voice, whispering, and it was so calm, and astoundingly I found that I was also calm, or almost. I didn't grab for my X-Acto knife, or bead with sweat. Besides, I recognized the knock. 'Who is it?' I called, as I walked to the door; and in response, again, the particular knock.

Skandar stood outside, a smattering of greenery on one shoulder of his messy suit jacket, as though he'd walked through a bush.

'Hey.' I smiled. I couldn't help it. I felt a surge of something so strong it was almost like being sick. 'Wow.'

'I was at a supper, not far away. Some Lebanese graduate students, talking a lot. Near Davis Square.' He wore the goofy smile, and surely had had a few drinks. He was carrying a paper bag. 'I thought you might need a break,' he said. 'I thought either a drink or a walk. So I brought a bottle of wine – it's red, I think you like red? – and I brought—' He looked down.

'Your shoes.'

'Yes. I brought my shoes. Which I will need if we go for a walk.'

'Certainly around here,' I said, taking the bottle out of the bag. 'Come on in.'

He was diffident, almost shy, his manner very different from that of his first visit, when he'd behaved as though he were my host, rather than the other way around.

'Sit down,' I said, pointing to his wife's cushions. 'I'll get a couple of glasses.' There were only coffee cups in sight, those pretty, chipped ones, so emphatically hers. I poured red wine into two of them, and felt alluringly bohemian doing so, and wondered how much I owed to her any bohemianism, and any allure, I might have. But just then it didn't matter. Even the thought was an anticipation of guilt. I hoped he wouldn't comment on the cups. He didn't.

'So,' he said, frankly sheepish. 'So. Thank you.'

'Thank *you*.' I raised my cup in salute, drank. I was touched by his awkwardness, and by my own. There was silence for a short while, because all I could think of to say was 'Who's with Reza?' or 'What news from Sirena?' and these were both things I didn't want to say. He was looking at me, in this time, very still, like a cat. I wondered briefly how much he might have had to drink.

'Did the students feed you well?'

'Falafel. Kebabs. You know.'

'I've got some pasta salad left over if you want it. Whole Foods. The rotini with pesto kind.'

He made a gesture, childlike rather than wolfish, of assent. I passed him the brown box. I made a show of washing the fork at the sink before I gave him that, too.

'Anything new?' I tried again. 'In the wider world?'

'Ay. In Lebanon, today, another bombing. North of Beirut.'

I hadn't expected this sort of an answer. I'd intended the question more lightly. It took me a minute to say anything. 'Did anyone die?'

'Five or six people wounded. You won't see much about it here. It's only worth reporting if someone dies.'

'Do they know who's responsible?'

He kept his head down, struggled with a wayward rotino. 'The elections are in three weeks. Different voices want to make themselves heard. It's a problem.'

'Were you talking about this with the students?'

'You know how students are—'

'I know how *my* students are,' I said, 'but they're eight years old.'

He smiled. 'Isn't it much the same? They have their opinions and they don't really want to hear yours, unless it coincides with theirs. It's always the same.'

'Well, in that sense, we're all the same.'

'I often think,' he said, 'that almost everyone is a child. That if you suddenly were to take off the masks of each of us, we would all be revealed as children.'

'I didn't know I had a soul mate so near at hand.'

'I'm sorry?'

'I say a version of that almost every day. Sometimes I tell myself, when I'm dealing with annoying adults, to picture the kid there. Because no matter how annoying the kid is, I can feel compassion for him or her.'

'Always?'

'Almost always.'

'What kind of child were you?'

'Fun,' I said, although even as I said it, I realized I was picturing my mother, not myself: my tanned, angular mother in a lime-green golf skirt and a white sleeveless polo, with beaded sandals and enormous shades, a cigarette in one hand, a G&T in the other. She was flirting with Horace Walker from down the block, and she was emphatically not a child. 'I was a very fun child. And you?'

'Serious.' He stood up from the cushions, not without effort.
'Do you mind if I smoke?' He didn't wait for a reply. 'I was
much too serious as a child, and as a consequence, not very
interesting.' He downed the contents of his coffee cup in a single
swallow. 'I should be going,' he said.

'You just lit a cigarette,' I said.

'True.'

She was there in the room with us, even though the lights at
her end were turned off. I didn't need to name her. 'Do you
want to see the installation so far?'

'In a minute,' he said. We both knew I was talking about her
installation, not mine. 'I'd like to see what you're working on
first.'

I didn't know that I believed him – didn't we all really want
to see her installation? I poured more wine into his coffee cup.
'Fine,' I said. 'Sounds good. Which one did you want to see?'

'All of them,' he said, 'if possible. How many are there?'

'Three. Well, two, really. One whole, and two halves.'

'Great. Show me.'

He pored over them, one after the other, squatting down and
closing one eye to peer directly in the windows, rather than looking at them from overhead. He moved very slowly and he looked
very carefully, and whenever he wanted to touch anything, he
looked at me first, questioningly, and waited for my permission.
While he was looking, he seemed very much the serious child he
claimed he'd been, and it pleased me – it excited me – how
gravely he took my rooms, my artists, and how there was no
gushing and no exclamation, just silent care. He took care. I
loved him for it, and couldn't help comparing him with his wife,
and thinking how much steadier, how much more freely his own
person he was.

When he was done at last, he stood back and he looked at me,
instead, in the same serious way. 'These are remarkable,' he said

finally. 'Quite extraordinary.' He filled his wine cup, lit another cigarette. 'They are at the same time truthful, and emotional – and so small.'

'So *small*?' It didn't sound like a compliment.

'They put so much in so small a space. It's like a Persian miniature, painted with a single bristle: tiny, precise, here is an entire world. Everything that matters, all emotion.'

'Yes.' If that was what he meant, then okay.

'But the question is why? Why so small? To speak softly, but to tell the greatest truth? Or, like the Persian miniatures, to be portable, to be able to go everywhere, and still to show, by their beauty and intricacy, their owner's vast wealth? Or in this case, is it because they don't feel they're allowed to be bigger?'

'How do you mean?'

'Why not a whole room, a life-sized room, for each of these? Why only a little box?'

I shrugged, aware of unexpected stinging behind my eyes.

'Or again: Why, when there's so much emotion in these rooms, in these artists – why is it all sad?'

'I put Joy in each room. You only have to look for her. She's there – a golden amulet.'

'Okay, fine. But why, one time, just one time, is she not the biggest element? Why does Joy not take the whole room?'

There were tears in my eyes. I could feel them pooling. I blinked repeatedly so he wouldn't see them. I suddenly understood that whatever else, Sirena's art was joyful: that it was true – even if she wasn't necessarily true – and joyful at the same time. My art was sad, because my soul was sad. Was this right?

'Do you think my soul is sad?' I asked him.

'I think your soul is lovely,' he said, and although he was still serious – as far as I could tell, he was completely serious – I was also reminded of Didi saying, 'If it looks like a maple leaf and it feels like a maple leaf and it lies under a maple tree . . .'

'I think that you don't think so, but your soul is beautiful,' he went on, and he took my left hand between his two hands, which were square and fleshy and hot and dry, like a furnace, but all these things excitingly so. 'And I think it has a great capacity for joy and for sadness both. You don't need to worry for a moment about your soul. Rather, you need only to move all of your emotions out of their little boxes, and let them take up the whole room.'

'They wouldn't just take up a room,' I said.

'I know, your insatiable ravenous wolf. But how will you know his rampaging, unless you free him from his cage?'

I was both in the moment and outside it, aware of the theater and the kitsch of it – how could I not be? – and yet wholly involved – my fingers, my skin, my heart. Inside my ear, Didi's voice was laughing – 'silly!' – and Sirena's voice I wouldn't even imagine, the cry of it, like pain, and my mother in the background, quietly whispering, 'How dare you, Mouse? How dare you? Who do you think you are, Mouse? Who do you think you are?'

But then, the pull upon me was not who I thought I was; it was who *he* thought I was: not Emily, or Virginia, or Alice, or Edie, or even Sirena. Not a Woman Upstairs. Not one thing. That I did not myself know my outline did not, at that point, matter at all. To someone, I had an outline, implausibly a worthy one. When his hands moved to rest, warm, even, like hot stones upon my back, just to be nakedly Nora Eldridge seemed, briefly, as though it could be forgiven; as though it could even be enough.

12

At first, I thought it could all be okay. Skandar and I had a conversation – oblique, weird, but a conversation – about how this was meaningful but wrong, and how it couldn't continue. I was baffled, you see: this wasn't a story I'd lived inside my head. The bead didn't fit my thread. And yes, I believed I could simply will it away, because I had to, because there was too much at stake otherwise.

How strange that to feel oneself clearly, transparently, compassionately seen by one precious person meant to risk vile distortion in the eyes of another. Always we tell the children it's best to be honest; but I knew, too, when to lie, in order to be true to something greater. It hadn't felt false, or willed, or like seduction, or like a mistake. It hadn't felt in conflict with my friendship with Sirena, or my love – my mad love – for her.

My sadnesses were many, but there was not, among them, a sadness at what we'd done, the absolute moral value of which didn't seem to me to be negative: if you could only separate that bead from its neighbors, take it out of time and hold it up to the light, how beautiful and clear a bead it would be. If you were to make a room for the artist Nora Eldridge, and depict in it that

experience, it would be joy. I don't know what to say about the
fact that for a time we lay upon the Astroturf, among the wavering aspirin flowers. I can't explain it; or I couldn't then.

On Monday morning, I almost choked at the sight of Reza at his
desk, in his pressed T-shirt with a lock of black hair curling
straight up to the sky. Now, suddenly, I saw not so much his
mother's eyes but his father's nose, his father's lips. His own
goofy smile. I must have looked oddly at him, as he forced, in
return, a stretchy, Gumby-esque grin, the grin of someone who's
done nothing wrong but is nevertheless afraid of being accused.
Even from the front of the room I could see the scar by his eye,
my scar; and with the sight of it came the memory of the doctor
at the hospital, sewing her fine seam.

I didn't choke, I didn't stop, the day was launched, the moment
passed, and in the unwavering routine of 3E, in the absolute famil-
iarity and hullabaloo of my children around me, it was the events
of Friday night, rather than this, that seemed like a dream; and as
the day went on, I forgot about them. And then, that afternoon,
we had an Appleton-wide staff meeting – Shauna in love with the
sound of her own voice, droning on about plans for the end of the
school year: our talent show, our fund-raiser, our school-wide
picnic – and I didn't even try to go to the studio. I wasn't sorry.

On Tuesday afternoon, I felt myself lacking in courage; but
aware, too, that the encounter had to take place – that as with
Reza, with Sirena, too, I had to step across the awkwardness and
proceed to the next scenes, the scenes of her finishing Wonderland,
of our excited bond over her glorious installation, over our shared
understanding that hers was the art, and the life, that mattered.

The shock was to recognize from the moment I entered the room that for Sirena there was no discontinuity at all between then and now. Her blithe greeting, her fervid hair-twiddling and shawl-adjusting, all were unchanged. She was the same Sirena who'd hopped on the morning Amtrak to New York five days before, blissfully, selfishly oblivious and full of the excitements of her trip.

'It's so hard to decide – they both are really great' – 'great-e' – 'and they both want me to go with them. I'll need your help, Nora – I trust you so much. When I showed my naked ones to Anna, she had tears in her eyes. She said they were stunning – and I said to her, "Be careful. You must imagine them in their context, in relation to the other pieces of the installation" – and she said, "Sirena, that's great, but whatever you put around them can't make them less stunning. More so, maybe, but not less."'

'And the other guy?' I couldn't help but be excited for her, even if she was a braggart. Somehow I could feel all my feelings separately – and the cloud of guilt, too, with its inadmissible tinge of triumph; I could keep it all in my head at once.

Because even I couldn't hide from myself that not only did I want Sirena and Reza and – now, most tangibly – Skandar (don't ever let anyone tell you that the imaginary is equivalent to the real: your skin, your vast, breathing skin, will insist otherwise), but I also wanted Wonderland, I coveted *her very imagination,* and wished it were mine.

I listened to Sirena talk about the two gallerists and their spaces and the promises they'd made to her, and I was with her and not with her at the same time. It wasn't like at school with Reza, where the everyday realities had simply supplanted and replaced the other. Here, Skandar hovered in the studio, a shadow across the windows' bleached light; and the fact that she couldn't see him between us didn't make him go away. Confusingly, I didn't love her less, or long for her less, although I envied her more. If she'd put her arms around me then – well, in some metaphorical way she did put her arms around me, she had done so from the beginning; and perhaps I'd even thought, all those months, that she could really *see* me; and on some level I believed it even after Skandar stopped, and looked, and actually saw – even then, so late, I believed that she could see me, and so my guilt made Skandar a shadow that I marveled that she could not see. I thought, 'This is going to be hard. Harder than I realized.' But I didn't think, 'This is going to be impossible.'

That Thursday night, I went to sit for Reza. I expected it to be my first time together with all three of them at once, but Skandar wasn't home: meetings at the university, Sirena said. Some end-of-year thing. She'd join him at the dinner party.

She was distracted, not chatty – rushing to change her clothes, almost peremptory in her list of what there was to eat, of who might call. I fought not to see her brusqueness as a sign, as ill will directed at me. You know how it is: a criminal anticipates suspicion. She reappeared in a black caftan covered with a riot of colorful embroidery, a heavy medallion at her throat. When at last she paused on her way out the door, I couldn't resist: 'Is everything okay? Have I upset you?'

'Upset me? How absurd! You could never upset me. I'm so sorry – I am – out of it. Beset by difficulties in the practical things. If I were only in Paris, I could sort these things out. I'm thinking I'll have to get on a plane and go there – but with Reza – so complicated. Now the term at Harvard is finished, Skandar is traveling so much … So: my head is full of nonsense – like a chess game. If I move this piece, and then that piece – then, so. And if you don't look far enough ahead, then bang, you are in trouble.'

Didn't I know it. 'If I can help . . . '

'You're here, aren't you? You're my greatest help.'

'Put it all out of your mind for tonight. Have fun.'

'Some hotshot economics professor and his psychoanalyst wife? And that tall man with a face like a horse who's always on the television! I've been stuck with him before – he's so boring and his breath is terrible, like a dead mouse. Who has time for this bullshit? I should get Skandar a professional wife. No, you're the lucky ones – you and my little Reza.'

And in truth, we *were* the lucky ones: that evening after we ate, Reza and I sat on the living room floor building a free-form spaceship out of Legos. Using pieces from a great bucket of abandoned creations, we spent over an hour at it, calculating its perfectly symmetrical rocketlike tower and finding the shapes necessary for its wide, ovoid base, complete with lights and windows and opening doors. We created detachable roomlets, some with wings, some with tank wheels; we found Lego people – stringy, hammer-headed Star Wars creatures, a couple of solid fellows who looked like farmers, a grass-skirted cannibal or two – and populated our space station. Each time we added a person, Reza invented a story for him, about where he came from, what he did, why he was there.

'When I grow up,' he said, out of the blue, 'I'm going to be an architect. I want to create worlds for people. And maybe,' he said with a glint that reminded me of his father, 'maybe creating worlds will create new people, too. Do you see, by changing his hat, I've turned this farmer guy into a heart doctor? Isn't that cool?'

I was waiting for him to walk me home. He'd always walked me home. But this time, soon after eleven, Sirena came alone.

'I'm exhausted,' she said, as she dropped her bag and keys on the dining table. 'I couldn't stick there a minute longer. Skandar and the mouse-breath man were involved in deep conversation. I don't know what Skandar thinks he can persuade him to do – go on CNN and insist on a two-state solution? Who is so foolish, in this country, who wishes to remain employed? So I said to him, "Skandar, maybe you're going to save the world tonight, but I must get some sleep . . . "'

'It *is* late—'

'Yes, and you're teaching in the morning. I'm terrible, to forget – I'm sorry. It's raining, a bit – do you want me to call you a taxi?'

'It's okay. I'll walk.'

'At least take the umbrella.'

So I took from Sirena the golf-sized, striped umbrella that Skandar had more than once held gallantly over my head, and I walked myself home. The distance felt longer than it had in months. Had he stayed there on purpose? He must have. Was the dark upshot of our brief numinous hour to be the loss of so close a friend? Because, as I realized only then, after all our walks and conversations, I could have counted him as a friend.

Henceforth, inevitably, Skandar was often uppermost in my thoughts. Sometimes I'd seem to forget, and my obsessive imagination would follow its old familiar trajectory – to the imaginary Vermont farmhouse, the peaceable artistic gynocracy, where a mere hand upon the arm set the veins pumping in double-time. And then, into the fantasy, as into a dream, would come the thought: it's not like this anymore; the world has changed. Just the way, even at that time fully two years after my mother's death, I'd catch myself thinking about her as alive; and would suddenly remember, an admonitory finger of grief upon my breast, that she was gone.

Sometime over that weekend, Sirena decided that she needed to fly to Paris to sort out the casting of the heart for her Wonderland. It was too complicated to try to clarify things on the computer or over the telephone, she told me on Monday morning, when I called to confirm the details for the school visit that afternoon. If the heart wasn't right – it was to be open, split in the middle, on a Lucite dais a few yards in front of the film of Sana dancing; and it was to spray out, every few minutes, a particular rosewater scent – then, as she said, the heart of her installation wasn't right. She'd leave on Tuesday, on the late Air France flight for Paris, and said she'd be back the following weekend. So I knew that, on Monday, and maybe it affected me somehow.

The kids were hugely excited. Any field trip is a hit – you could take them to a sewage treatment plant and they'd love it – but this one was weird and free, and even more fun because of it. Kids like breaking the routine, riding the school bus in the middle of the day, the feeling of possibility. We left Appleton at eleven thirty, right after their early lunch. They were unusually rowdy in the bus: Noah climbed over three rows of seats before I could get him to sit down; Ebullience had a spat with Miles over some hand-held computer game they ought not to have had in the first place; Sophia started to cry because she said Mia had pulled her hair. I had to raise my voice and threaten to turn around and go back to school. It was that kind of a beginning.

That said, I felt good about the excursion. Almost all the parents had said yes to the filming – it must have seemed cool to think their kids would be in some kind of movie – but I'd also arranged, at my end of the studio, for us to make papier-mâché masks. I'd had the kids read an abridged version of *Alice in Wonderland* the previous week, and we'd looked at old illustrations of the Cheshire Cat, and the Jabberwocky, and Tweedledum and Tweedledee and the Mad Hatter: I'd told them they could make masks of any of them, or of any other character they chose. The plan was to break the kids into two groups, to have one half start making the masks while the other was running around Wonderland, and then to switch them over. The pedagogical reasoning behind the afternoon wasn't entirely clear even to me, but none of the parents had questioned it. I figured it was pretty memorable for kids to see a real artist's atelier.

Things started out well. When we got to the studio, the kids seemed awed by the oddity of it all, and they sat quietly in a circle on the floor in the middle of the L while Sirena explained to them who she was and what she was doing. She was pretty good at talking to kids, better than I'd have imagined, and she talked about making art as a kind of magic, and also as a kind of play. Interestingly, Reza didn't come forward to hug her: he sat squeezed between Noah and Aristide, fidgeting and behaving like one of the boys. I remember thinking that he'd changed, that way, in the course of the year: he'd been so openly affectionate with his mother back in September. But maybe it was discomfiting to be her kid, in this big white studio, in front of

everyone, even embarrassing; maybe he felt funny, too, to see me
and his mom both here together, and to think that this was our
shared space. I don't know.

Sirena explained that the children were free to treat all of
Wonderland as a stage, almost as if they were in a play. 'I know
you've read about Alice,' she said, 'and I want you to pretend
that you've gone down the rabbit hole too. Here you are, in this
weird place, and anything can happen.' She pointed to the two
cameras we'd set up weeks before, high up at either end of the
Astroturf lawn. 'In Alice's Wonderland, she never knows if someone is watching her. Maybe the camera's on, but maybe it's not,
so don't even think about it. Think of this as an adventure, and
a game. You can play in groups, or you can play alone. You can
make this space what you want it to be.'

We'd hung the mirror shards on their strings from the ceiling
to create glittering partitions in the space, and we'd laid out the
Alice-dress sky along the ground in a swirling river of fabric that
meandered the length of the room. We'd sown whole clusters of
aspirin flowers, and some soap tulips, and had scattered around
candies and jelly beans for the kids to find. We'd dragged her
poufs onto the Astroturf lawn and draped them with burlap, so
they looked like boulders. In far corners, we'd hung up several
pairs of little red lights, for Jabberwock eyes, and when they
flashed, an MP3 player let out roaring noises – quite scary ones,
in fact.

All the children wanted to play in Wonderland. Inevitably,
making masks seemed like a consolation prize. But we divided
them into two groups and told them they had forty-five minutes for their first activity. Then we'd have a break for juice and
cookies, and then we'd switch. The bus would be waiting outside for us at two p.m.

Reza and Noah and Aristide were all in my group first, along
with three other boys and a gaggle of girls. Even though they

were disappointed to have to wait for Wonderland, they were psyched by the idea that they could make masks and then play with them. I pointed out that the masks would need to dry, which made the boys feel they had to work fast. I helped all the kids shape their mask forms out of coat hanger wire: we measured their heads, and then bent the wire into noses and cheeks. Then, with relatively little acting out, the kids laid on the layers of gluey newsprint, molding the flesh devotedly around and around and around their metal bones.

Noah's Jabberwocky came out looking like a cross between a bull and a horse, its long snout punctuated by gaping nostrils. Aristide made the Cheshire Cat, or said he had, although he hadn't given it any ears, only an enormous smiling mouth, which was good enough. Reza chose the dormouse, a minor character, capably executed. Its nose was pointy, and he gave his mask prominent ears, but he was particularly proud of its whiskers, six dangling bits of string glued onto the end of its nose like a straggly mustache. The boys finished before the others in the group, and asked if they might cross over early into Wonderland.

They'd been so good, and it was almost time anyway, so I let them. I should have asked Sirena if it was okay with her; I hadn't realized how involved she was with her cameras, up on ladders to adjust them so they'd track specific kids; and how little involved she was with keeping watch.

It all happened so fast. I was helping Sophia with her walrus mask – a bigger task than either of us was really fit for – when I saw, out of the corner of my eye, that the boys' play was turning rough. At first I didn't do anything, because I figured Sirena was on top of it; but then I stepped down toward the middle of the L, and realized that her back was turned and she was focused on filming Ebullience and Chastity wrapping themselves up in the Alice fabric and twirling around. Meanwhile, behind her,

Reza and Noah were scuffling, and Aristide was making breath-
less noises of alarm; and then I distinctly saw Reza punch Noah
in the jaw.

'*STOP!*' I shouted – and when rarely Miss Eldridge of
Appleton School shouts, the world knows about it. '*STOP* right
now!' I thundered down to where they were, wiping my gluey
hands on the seat of my pants. I grabbed both boys by their shirt
collars – it's something teachers used to do a lot, but aren't supposed to anymore – and I lost it. I felt personally disappointed
by Reza – I don't know how else to put it. He'd let me down.
'What in God's name is going on here? Reza Shahid, you have
some serious explaining to do. I *saw* what happened, with my
own eyes. What has gotten into you?'

Reza glowered, shrugged.

'Noah: you tell me. I can't believe Reza would hit you without being provoked.'

He, too, shrugged. Then I saw clasped in his fist several
aspirin flowers, dangling on their wire stalks.

'You picked the flowers?'

'Nobody said we couldn't.' This was true: nobody had said
they couldn't. Noah went on, 'And then Reza jumped on me.
Like some kind of crazy guy.'

'Is that what happened, Reza?'

Reza looked angrier than I'd ever seen him, but he didn't say
anything. He scuffed his feet against the Astroturf. I had the feeling that wasn't the whole story.

'Did Noah say something that upset you?'

Reza looked up: he looked for his mother, and found her, and
some wordless exchange passed between them, to which I was
not privy. He still didn't say anything.

It was only at this point that I realized everyone had gathered
round in a circle, and that Sirena was standing behind the
children, watching. It wasn't clear what she was thinking. I

hadn't considered it in the heat of the moment, but now every-thing seemed hideously weird: I'd been extra-angry because I felt betrayed by my own kid, my special boy, the boy who wanted to make the world better; but here, like a slap, was the reminder that he wasn't mine. Here was his mother, and the look on her face was the look not of *my friend* but of *his parent,* if you see what I mean: whatever she was thinking, it was a mother's reac-tion to seeing her son disciplined by a teacher. I was his teacher, an outsider; that's what I was.

It was one of those moments when life's disguises are stripped away, when you see clearly what is real, and all you can say to yourself is 'useful to get that learned.' The only thing I could think to do was fully to take on my teacher role, and play it to the hilt. I got bossy with the kids: 'Don't stand there staring,' I said to everyone else. 'This doesn't concern all of you. Go back to your games, or your masks. Noah and Reza, you're both going to sit over there against the wall and I don't want to hear any-thing more out of either of you.'

For a moment, nobody moved. I saw some of the kids, including Reza, look at Sirena. She closed her eyes and nodded slightly. And then he went, and Noah went after him, both of them hanging their heads like convicts.

I took Aristide aside and asked him what had actually occurred. He said that Noah had said mean things about Wonderland, had called it 'crappy.' He'd said, 'Your mom's idea is really dumb. Does she think we're, like, two years old?' And then he'd quoted something from television or somewhere: Noah, obsessed with flatulence, had said, 'I fart in her general direction.' He was trying to be funny, Aristide explained, but Reza couldn't see it.

Sirena didn't come over to talk to me straight away. Maybe she didn't want to seem to make a big deal of it. I never told her what Noah said to Reza. I don't imagine her son did, either. She did go over to speak to Reza for a second, as he huddled against the wall, and she looked stern, but mostly she was in a hurry to get back up her ladder and monkey with her cameras, to try to pull a decent video out of the fiasco. The kids weren't playing so freely after that, though; it didn't feel natural anymore. Even after their snack, after the groups switched over, there was a slight pall over the afternoon. It wasn't the same.

As we were lining the kids up to leave, Sirena appeared at my elbow.

'I'm sorry about that scene,' I said.

'Don't feel bad,' she said. 'You've got to run your class your way. You've got your rules.' She sighed. 'It's a shame because it wasn't the same, after. Kids are so sensitive, they absorb everything.' And then, 'Don't worry about coming back to clean up. I'll take care of it.'

'Thanks, Sirena.' I didn't usually call her by name like that. It seemed almost to echo in my ear.

'I think we're saying good-bye for the week? I go to Paris tomorrow.'

'I almost forgot.' I was about to say, 'I'll keep an eye on your boys for you,' and then thought better of it. 'I hope it all goes well,' I said.

'Don't worry. It will' – she lit up for a moment, seemed more normal – 'because it has to.'

Things with Reza weren't really changed. He was remorseful – he apologized to me the next day before school started – and besides, he didn't see the complicated ironies of the day before. He wasn't going to tell me what had actually happened, whether because he didn't want to be a tattletale or because he didn't want to repeat an insult to his mother; but he felt his punishment had befit his crime. It was all finished and forgotten, for him, at least – which was a relief.

⚊⚊

Sirena did only a half-decent job of cleaning up the studio before she went away. She put all the kids' detritus – cups, napkins – in a garbage bag, and she swept the floor for crumbs. She rearranged her Wonderland, replanting the flowers and folding away the river of cloth; but she left all the kids' unpainted masks higgledy-piggledy at my end of the room, and she let the papier-mâché glue harden in a bucket, which I then had to throw away. The studio was accumulating a lot of strange emotions, for me. It wasn't so easy to be there.

I tried to tidy up some more, in anticipation of her return. I arranged things neatly but visibly, the way a cleaning lady might arrange your bureau. Once this was done, Sirena's end of the L looked oddly forlorn, abortive, like a woman half dressed, and I had to turn my back on it. All that week I went only in the evenings, pretending to work, but really hoping to hear footsteps in the corridor, the secret knock.

He was busy, I knew. But surely also he wasn't able to see me because of the force of his emotion. It was possible, I knew, that he didn't want to deal with me; but I didn't want to believe that. Better for us both to be noble, to suffer in withdrawal. I certainly wouldn't telephone him. It continued to amaze me how the touch of skin on skin had altered things: curled in the crook of his arm, my head upon his breast, I'd sensed his heart beating and for a moment hadn't been sure whether it was mine. My fingertips could still trace the distinct coarseness of the hairs on his chest, the softness of those along his forearm. My cheeks and chin had stung, the morning after, from the evening bristle of his. And his body, his hands, his tongue: if I closed my eyes, they were still on me, in me, with me. I was always remembering him, a physical memory, like an imprint in the earth. There is, I came to realize, what the mind wants and what the body wants. The mind can excite the body, but its desires can also be false; whereas the body, the animal, wants what it wants.

13

The next weekend I was going with my father to see Aunt
Baby. I hadn't seen her since Christmas, and I'd rashly
promised that we'd spend the night on Saturday, in order to go
to mass with her on Sunday morning. On Friday night, I stayed
at the studio almost until midnight – not working on my rooms
at all, reading the newspaper online and drinking red wine out
of a teacup – but still there was no word from Skandar. On
Saturday morning, after a run around the reservoir that failed to
clear my head, I went to pick up my father, and some peonies
(my mother's favorite flower) and a Bundt cake (for most of my
life, my mother baked cakes for Aunt Baby; but I went to the
Coolidge Corner bakery she'd found when they moved to
Brookline and she could no longer cook), and we headed north
to Cape Ann.

'Did you speak to Matthew this week?' my father asked, looking out the windshield at I-95, and not at me.

'No. Should I have?'

'Tweety's birthday.'

'I forgot.' I always forgot. Sometimes I thought I forgot on purpose. She never remembered my birthday, either. 'Is every-body okay?'

'I guess so,' he said. And then nothing, for a few minutes, silence and the swish of passing cars, and then, 'But I think something's wrong.'

'How do you mean?'

'Something's wrong. I don't know exactly what. I didn't like to ask.'

'Why do you think so?'

'Because. Because when I asked to speak to Tweety, to wish her happy birthday, he said she was out.'

'Is that weird? People go out.'

'But then later, I said when will she be home, so I could call again' – he's very diligent, my father; he was, after all, in insur-ance all his life – 'and he said, in a very strange way, that he didn't know. That it was probably easier for her to call me.'

'What's weird about that, then?'

'There was something peculiar in his voice. It was . . . gravelly.'

'I don't know what that implies.'

'Rough. His voice was rough, like he was upset.' As far as I could tell – I was driving – my father hadn't once turned his head to look at me, but he did so now, and he looked wary, his eyes narrow, and he said, 'Besides, has Tweety ever called you?'

'Me? Of course not. Don't be ridiculous. Not in more than twenty years.'

'That's my point. She's never called me, either. Even when your mother was dying, she never called.'

'No, I remember.' I'd complained of it: 'What kind of family is this?' I'd asked.

'So either he's too upset to know what he's saying; or he's lying on purpose; or she's gone through some radical change . . . I can't make a story of it where there isn't something wrong between them.'

This wasn't like my father. It was more like me. 'So what sorts of stories have you got?'

'She's left him.'

'Of course!' I almost said, 'You wish!'

'Or she's sick.'

'Sick?'

'Any kind is possible – physical, mental, you know.'

'Okay.'

'. . . or the baby's sick.'

'The baby's not sick, Dad. And she's not really a baby anymore.'

'Or they've had a big fight and she's run off.'

'Wow. You've got a whole soap opera going for them. That's wild.'

'Or they could be worried about money—'

I started to laugh. 'Dad, this is whacked. You're talking insanity here.'

'Am I?'

'You've got too much time on your hands. If you're worried something's wrong, call Matthew and ask him. He'll probably laugh at you, but he *is* your son, and he'll only laugh at you in a nice way. You'll feel much better.'

'You're probably right.' My father cleared his throat and recrossed his ever-veinier hands and looked back to the front again, out the windshield. I could tell from how still he was that this had been bothering him a lot, and that now he was relieved; and of course, later, when he spoke to Matthew and found that Tweety had cracked a tooth that day on an olive pit and had rushed off to the dentist, he would be able frankly to laugh.

During the afternoon in Rockport – a strangely prolonged lunch involving lobster, that infernally overrated food; followed by a tortoise's stroll along the uneven breakwater to watch the fishermen and the furious, swooping gulls and a couple of intrepid surfers in satanic glistening wetsuits as they tackled the briny surf, a surf upon which an unsettling gray scum foamed, toxically; while Aunt Baby limped and leaned, in her powdery malodor, upon my arm; and my father, in his businessman's solitude and navy cotton cable sweater, ambled glumly behind us – I thought repeatedly about this unlikely conversation in the car, and about my advice to him. It was obvious; if you wanted transparency, you had to find the courage to be honest. This was in itself no guarantee that others would be honest with you; but what choice did you have?

I should have spoken to Sirena about my feelings months before, but I'd been afraid of possibility, and also of its limitations. It had been easier to live in my dream, and now it was impossible to speak to her. I must, I resolved, reach as best I could for what was real; which meant I had to telephone Skandar, and ask him outright what exactly was going on.

Once I'd resolved to do this, I became impatient for it. I caught myself being snappish with Aunt Baby: I wished she'd walk faster, speak more quickly, be more interesting, that the day itself, which seemed – compared to my regular life, in itself hardly thrilling – mired in a failure to progress, would *just be over*. But it wasn't until after nine that night that, dishes finally done, the ancient, rust-trimmed machine humming, the oldies ensconced again in tales of their late lamented, I was able to step along the cul-de-sac far enough toward the main road to catch a signal on my cell phone, and to call the Shahid house.

Saturday night. I imagined the phone ringing in their living room, the globed chandelier low on its dimmer switch. I imagined Maria, twiddling at her piercings and scoffing popcorn in front of the TV, while down the hall Reza's sleeping breast rose and fell in the colorful parade of jazz musicians. I knew their lives so well. But no: after the third ring, he answered.

I could picture him rising up from the creaking armchair, reading glasses dangling from one hand, blinking – his white shirt crumpled, the sleeves rolled halfway up his darkly matted forearms.

'Skandar?'

'Yes?' I could tell he didn't know it was me.

'It's Nora. Nora Eldridge.'

'Of course!' A pause. His tone unreadable. 'How are you, my dear Nora?'

'You know,' I said, trying to sound jolly, light, 'it's been kind of a tough week.'

'Yes.' A statement.

'I kept thinking our paths would cross. The dinner party night – when was it? – I thought I might see you . . .'

'I'm sorry. I was delayed – held hostage, you might say, by my ambition. Always a foolish thing to succumb to. Sirena makes fun of me for it.'

'Are you doing okay?'

'In what sense?' He sounded careful, which annoyed me. Didn't he see that we were both on the same side?

'I just meant – it's a lot, right? Sirena's away, you're on your own with Reza—'

'Ah, yes. Thank you for asking. Maria's courses are over now, so she has all her time. It's been okay.'

'Great.' This wasn't the exchange I'd hoped for. But I reminded myself that I needed to be fearless, to be honest, so I wouldn't be making up fictions in my head. I wanted to know the truth. 'Have you found it hard at all – the other?'

'The other?'

'The night in the studio. Are you okay about it?'

'Ah, my dear. How could it be okay? What words are there? My dear Nora, as we said, there are times when – how did you put it?'

'When you break through the mirror, I think I said. Like *Through the Looking-Glass.*'

'Yes. And as we said, it's such a rare gift, but it's also . . . '

'Separate from life?'

'Yes. Yes, that's a true way to put it. Separate from life.'

'We both know that protecting Sirena and Reza is the most important thing—'

'Protecting them?' He sounded genuinely surprised. Possibly worried.

'All I mean is that they never need to know, right? We're agreed on that, right?'

'Yes. Absolutely agreed.'

'Does she suspect anything, do you think?'

'Suspect? I don't think so, my dear. It's something separate, it was the heart's expression, a true moment. But it's not a story, sadly, because it can't be.'

'I just mean—'

'We shared something precious, and nothing will undo that. As we're agreed about what this means, it doesn't concern Sirena in the slightest. And you know, I don't think Sirena has any concerns, right now, except a very pressing worry about whether she can finish her installation in time and in a way she can be proud of. I think that right now, she's only thinking about that.'

Later, I wondered whether what he was telling me in that moment was that for some time she hadn't been paying him any more attention than she'd been paying me; that he'd been put out, or worse, by her neglect, and that he'd sought diversion, or temporary consolation, with me. Maybe he didn't even know that this was what he was saying.

I took a deep breath. 'Can I ask you something? About her installation?'

'What's that?'

'Skandar, what do you think it's *saying*?'

'Saying?' It sounded as though he was smoking a cigarette.

'What do you think she thinks it *means*?'

Skandar was definitely smoking a cigarette. He took a moment to reply. I shivered in the dark on the tarmac near the main road: it might be May, but the night breeze off the sea was cold. 'Why do you ask such a question? This isn't a question you'd ask about your own work ... It's meaningless. Each person can – and will – give their own answer – that's what she wants, and surely you also?'

'But think about it: it's a collection of signs, right? And they might combine in different ways to create several different interpretations, right? But they wouldn't be infinite, would they? I mean, there's a limit to what's plausible, a meaningful interpretation, don't you think?'

'Nora, I don't know what—'

'Let me put it another way. Are there interpretations that are plain wrong?'

'That Sirena would think were wrong?'

'Not even. No. I mean that are just plain objectively wrong – untrue, incorrect, false.'

'I haven't really thought about it, but if you ask me for an answer straight off, I'll say yes. With a set of facts, as in historical facts, there are obviously incorrect interpretations. So, with art – a different sort of assemblage of signs, and of course signs are not facts, although they may refer to facts – there might be more leeway, but there would certainly be a point at which a reading or interpretation would be not merely inept, or extreme, but simply wrong. Yes. I'm going to say yes. Why do you ask this question?'

I could tell from the tone of his voice that he was liking me better after I asked this than he had before. He wasn't humoring me; he was reminded, by it, of the conversations on our long night-time walks, and was distracted from the possibility that I was needy, someone who could prove troublesome to his loving and stable marriage in ways he hadn't foreseen.

'No reason,' I said. 'I just wondered. Sorry, Skandar, I've got to go now. My dad needs me for something.' Which might have been true. But in fact, after I hung up – and turned off – my cell phone, I loitered in the condo driveway for another ten minutes, feeling the sadness of what had been revealed to me.

You shouldn't ask a question if you don't want to know the answer. That's what it means to have the courage to be honest. I hadn't asked outright whether I meant anything to him, or what I meant, but he'd made it clear. The true sight of me might have been a passing pleasure, or even, as he said, a precious moment, the heart's expression – but it changed nothing in his life.

I stood with my arms crossed against the Rockport wind, trying to accept the loss of my newest and most necessary fantasy. I'd realized too late that Skandar was my Black Monk, my Chekhovian familiar. Even more than Sirena, Skandar was the one who could convince me of my substance, of my genius, of the significance of my thoughts and efforts. If you took away my Black Monk, what was I? If nobody at all could or would read in me the signs of worthiness – of artistic worth – then how could I be said to possess them? How could I convince myself, against the whole world's determination? It wasn't that I'd felt he had to choose me *over* her – you wouldn't ask that someone abandon his family – but I'd thought – I'd hoped – to find his choice harder to make. I'd hoped to get the sense that there was even a choice at all.

When you're the Woman Upstairs, nobody thinks of you *first*. Nobody calls you before anyone else, or sends you the first postcard. Once your mother dies, nobody loves you *best of all*. It's a small thing, you might think; and maybe it depends upon your temperament; maybe for some people it's a small thing. But for me, in that cul-de-sac outside Aunt Baby's, with my father and aunt done dissecting death and shuffling off to bed behind the crimson farmhouse door, preparing for morning mass as blameless as lambs and as lifeless as the slaughtered – I felt forsaken by hope. I felt I'd been seen, and seen clearly, and discarded, dropped back into the undiscriminated pile like a shell upon the shore. This wasn't about sex, desire, or not only, you must understand this – I never fully let him inside me in that way, not as everyone would assume; but what we did together and our union, if I can use that word, was nonetheless absolute; even more so, perhaps, because our limits were real, and created by real love for other people, and we kept true to that too; and the touch of his skin on mine – so much uncovered skin, that thinnest of pulsating sheaths between our souls: ours was a touching replete with all meaning. Or I'd thought so. It had *meant,* for me. There are other ways of reading the signs: 'We didn't even sleep together' would be one.

When I went inside, they'd turned off the downstairs lights. They must have thought I'd already gone to bed. I fumbled my way up to the second guest room – a closet, almost, with its monastic single bed, where the bedside lamp must have been all of twenty-five watts and there was no question of reading. I lay on top of the coverlet, fully dressed, listening first to my father and then to Aunt Baby snoring, their disharmonious, disconsolate wheezings, carried through the gimcrack condo walls as

though we all slept together, one and the other of them labor-
ing with each baleful inhalation toward his ever-nearing end,
and I, stock-still, eyes open, waiting for dawn, seized in an
unmasterable panic at the loss of my so-beloved, apparently
unreal life.

PART THREE

1

Sirena never came back to Cambridge.

No, that's not true: she came back for seventy-two hours, a week later, to pack up her part of the studio. The weird thing is that I have trouble remembering that time, and when I *think* about her, I always think that she didn't come back. Perhaps because she was so distracted, almost like a mad person. She'd been visited by the realization that her installation would properly exist only in the right place – what she said to me is 'Nora, it's like we've just been pretending. Like I've been playing at making my piece. And now there's almost no time, it's almost the show, which is like saying it's almost time to die, and I have to find a way to be ready. Not to be ready is not a possibility. So bang, the playing in Cambridge must stop, and the real life in Paris must begin again. Bang, like this, *now.*'

She was taking Reza home with her, and there was no point suggesting that this wasn't a good idea. If you could have seen her, an almost incandescent little body, furious with energy, with the passion for her project: the heart would be done on time, but only because she'd screamed so loudly at the man from the factory, and promised to pay him double – or nothing, if he didn't deliver. The giant canvas photographs would be ready six days early, but she was still calling the lab every day to be sure they didn't forget her, forget those girls and women in their enormous, glorious nakedness.

She had men with dollies and packing stuffs and wooden crates for her aspirin flowers and her Astroturf, for the shards of broken mirror and the giant Alice-blue heavenly canopy that I'd sewn for her. None of these things alone seemed to merit the special art-world moving men, who must have cost a fortune, not even the technical things – those video cameras, set up to film our third graders – it was all packed away with her bossily overseeing them, and by the time they were nailing shut the wooden crates it really did seem a more significant assemblage – or perhaps I should say a more significant disassemblage – than I could have anticipated.

Yes, I saw her, and I tried to help – I lugged two bulging garbage bags of Reza's outgrown clothes to the Goodwill shop at Davis Square, wondering whether some eight-year-old American boy would find himself transformed by the French sandals and Bermuda shorts of the previous fall – but any sense of our intimacy, of our close friendship of a year, was perforce put aside in favor of urgent practicalities. The closeness of our friendship was made, I suppose, into a thing of deeds instead of words, and I should perhaps have been flattered to be left to sweep and clean her end of the studio, flattered to be asked to pick up her dry cleaning and drop off her personal boxes at the UPS Store for mailing ... I should have been flattered to be given her half-full bottles of aged balsamic vinegar and French mustard, the remnants of her cotton balls and hair conditioner: that she chose me as their recipient was as much an intimacy, in its way, as had been entrusting her son to my babysitting expertise; and was similarly faintly demeaning, although I can't quite explain why.

So, yes, I did see her, and in fact saw quite a bit of her, and would have to agree that even in her frenzy to skip town – taking with her my beloved boy, who seemed cheerfully oblivious to the fact that I'd be left behind and was focused chiefly upon the retrieval of his old life, his old friends, his bedroom, even his skateboard – she managed to be affectionate, even apologetic. She said more than once that she'd miss me, and that I'd been an 'indispensable' friend. She even gave me her navy blue honeycomb scarf, my favorite, but one of hers, too. It was a gift of love, because she'd miss it.

But my memory is that she didn't come back because it was never again as it had been; and the more painful because I hadn't expected things to unravel so fast. I should have known that life is like that, because my mother's death was like that, and I'd been through it. For so long we knew my mother would eventually die from her illness, and we forestalled believing it, successfully, often, but strangely, the more successfully the nearer it got, because we'd become so intent upon surviving, and so equipped to survive, each new crisis. And until the last fortnight we always thought there'd be more time; and in truth even in the last forty-eight hours we thought it would go on, maybe a week, and so were taken aback – literally caught short of breath, that surprised – when suddenly she breathed her last.

So too with Sirena's departure; I'd known from the first that it would come; and then not that long before, I'd had the nasty shock of realizing it would come far sooner than I'd anticipated. But who could have expected it without warning, in quite this way?

Then, too, when we dismantled what there was, in the studio, of Wonderland, I was suddenly powerfully aware that it was only a half-built thing – not quite still an imaginary thing, but not fully a thing in the world, either. I'd lived so close to it in my head, her vision had been, to me, so fully realized, that I'd thought for a long time that the installation was closer to completion, there in the studio, than in actuality ever it was.

It's ridiculous, isn't it? All those hours spent with each of them, each separately, and such enormous reserves of passion in each case, and what could be more real than that? And it's not as though, like my mother, they were dying, not as though a great furnace was to pulverize them into a heap of dust no more real than a memory or a thought. They would continue to breathe and move and laugh and talk and think and create – just on a different spot on the planet; and not even on so very remote a spot. But it was a spot remote to me, and because I knew that the three of them would continue to be together and that their lives would have a solidity and continuity far greater than did mine, although I'd still be in the same place and my life would be, superficially, the less altered one – in that way, it was as if I were dying, rather than they. I was the one who had to give them up, and in so doing, give up the world.

I didn't go with Sirena and Reza to the airport when they left on a Wednesday evening in the second half of May, when there was still a month of school ahead at Appleton. I knew they were going and I made sure I had something to do: I went to see the film *The Interpreter* at the cinema at six o'clock, and let myself be thoroughly absorbed in the intrigues of Nicole Kidman and Sean Penn at the UN while their flight was taking off from Logan. I was inordinately moved to find a text from Sirena on my phone when I came out of the film into the summer gloaming: 'Miss u already,' it said. 'R sends special xx. Come 2 Paris!' She'd written from the airport. I hadn't allowed myself to imagine it, and to see her message – there it was again: Hope.

2

I did see Skandar before he, too, returned to Paris a fortnight later. He called me one evening, at a funny sort of time, around nine at night, and asked if I'd like to meet for a coffee. We met at the Algiers café in Harvard Square, the oldest people there, surrounded by undergrads in their callow exuberance. He looked tired, his eyes behind his glasses blurry, dark rimmed. I wanted simply to touch his cheek, as he sat across the table. I wouldn't have called it lust, or desire, particularly; not sexual, is what I mean, or perhaps not *proprietorial.*

These words, these words are so imprecise, so inadequate: when I speak of love, or desire, or even of longing, the freight of these words is for each of us so particular. If I could explain once and for all about my three Shahid loves: the sexual element was undeniably there, with both Sirena and Skandar. But it wasn't the point. It wasn't the core of what I experienced. It was longing – 'longing' is a better word than 'desire': it carries its quality of reaching but not attaining, of yearning, of a physical pull that is intense and yet melancholy, always already a little sorrowful, self-knowing, in some wise passionate and in some measure resigned. Desire suggests a burning, fervid, unreflective, something that wants, above all, satisfaction. And what you have to see about my Shahids is that always, at any moment – even when I briefly allowed myself to believe otherwise; even, in that one, precious instance, when I held one of them in my arms – I always knew that my desire *could not* be satisfied, that it would never be satisfied; but that I was still close enough to hold on, intermittently, to the fantasy of its satisfaction, and that *this,* this was enough to keep it, for so very long, alive.

So the fact is that I *longed* to touch his face – to have that contact, to feel his skin against my fingertips – but I also fully understood and accepted that it was not, in that visit, in the cards. (Although, how not to wish that I were different? What would the undergraduates have seen, if I'd dared to do it? What would they have cared, of two dull old people huddled in a corner? And what might have unfolded, and how might it have altered fate's course, if I'd had the temerity simply to stretch my hand out across the table, to press it gently to his sweet, slightly pouchy cheek?)

Skandar had with him a plastic shopping bag that he placed awkwardly on the table between his Turkish coffee and my urinously bright mint tea.

'I'm having to finish the packing alone,' he said, with his most apologetic look. 'I'm not very good at it. At first I think we must simply keep everything, but when I realize how much trouble it is to pack things, to send them, then I say we must throw everything away. It's much better Sirena's job, this kind of thing.' I could tell that he'd never before been left behind in this way.

'So then I thought of you,' he went on, 'who've been such a friend to us all. I thought perhaps you might like to have one or two things that it doesn't make sense for us to take back.' He pushed the bag across the table toward me, almost knocking my tea. I reached to take it. 'Don't worry,' he said. 'No need to look at it here. Because whatever you don't want to keep, you can just get rid of it.'

I laughed.

'No, no – I'm not saying this is a bag full of garbage; quite the opposite. But these are things that no matter what, I won't take home.'

We didn't stay long in the Algiers – he was flying to DC early for meetings, and still had a lot to take care of – and in the brief time we spent together the only thing he said to acknowledge what had happened between us was this: 'Live, my dear Nora. Satisfy your hunger. There's food all around you, you know.'

'What kind of food, I'd like to know?'

'Ah' – he smiled – 'you must taste all things, actually to know if you like them.'

And what good is that, I wanted to ask, if the most delicious fruit is forbidden?

When we parted on the sidewalk, he put his arms around me in a close embrace – I was enfolded – and he held me to him several good beats longer than form required. It was the sort of hug in which no passerby would have seen anything upon which to comment, and yet which I knew – or could claim to know – meant more than it appeared to. It was to be my sustenance for a long time to come. He was shy and averted his eyes, afterward, and he shuffled off down the pavement in the direction of his house. From behind, he looked small and his gait seemed an old man's, a short man's, and I was briefly, in a new way, touched by him yet again.

～

As for the bag, which would play so intently upon my imagination in the months – what am I talking about? In the *years*! – that followed: What was in the bag? I wish I were properly able

to tell you. I opened it and glanced in at its contents under the
light of a storefront at the corner of Brattle and Church streets.
I could see that it contained a copy of his most recent book in
English – a gift which, I imagined, he'd inscribed to me; and
while I was anxious to know what he'd written, I didn't think I
could pull out the book there on the street. There was a rolled-
up picture of Reza's – I could tell straight away that it was his
snow scene: we'd done them in art class back in January, and his
had been particularly inventive. There were, mysteriously, three
pairs of kitchen scissors in the bottom of the bag, the plastic-
handled kind you buy at the supermarket; and there was
something small, wrapped in tissue. In this, my impatience was
too great: I tore at the paper, which had been clumsily but thoroughly taped, and shredded it until I uncovered a heavy silver
chain with, hanging from it, an elaborate silver cross, inlaid with
turquoise and what looked, in the semi-dark, like a blood-red
stone. It was heavy in my hand, and rather elegant, a bit tar-
nished but still bright. What did it mean? Whose was it?

I let it slip back into the bottom of the bag. I wanted to think
he had chosen it with me in mind. More likely it was an end-of-
year gift from Reza, selected in haste by Sirena from a pile of
possibles, and forgotten in the rush of departure. The simplest
and least flattering explanation was always the right one, I'd
learned over the years.

But in fact, I'd never know for sure. In my efficient fore-
thoughtfulness, when called out into the night, I'd brought the
geography sheets about Samantha and Jordan's road trip through
state capitals, of which I needed twenty-two – no, now only
twenty-one – copies in the morning. So I popped over to the all-
night Kinko's next to the post office on Mt. Auburn. There was
a paper jam on about the third copy, and I had to track down
the bloated attendant, who blinked in the fluorescent light and
burrowed into the machine with his pale, fat fingers. All this

hoopla over a few photocopies – I'd thought to have been sim-
plifying my life, because the copier at school was always either
in use or out of order – and I got home to my apartment to realize that I'd left Skandar's plastic bag on the table next to
Self-Serve Copier Number Seven. I tried to call them, but
nobody answered. I contemplated going back, but it was after
eleven and my courage failed me.

In the morning I hurried over to Kinko's before school, but
the bleary girl who'd replaced the boy had no idea about a plastic bag. She showed me a lost-and-found box containing several
sets of keys, an umbrella, two mismatched winter gloves, and a
BlackBerry with a green dragon sticker on its back: this was the
only place where lost things might be found. Eric would be back
on at ten p.m., if I wanted to come in then and ask him personally; but unfortunately there was nothing further she could
do for me.

And so it went, and was gone: I'll never know the provenance
or purpose of the necklace, nor will I know what, if anything,
was written inside Skandar's book. I was, that way, free to imagine many different possibilities.

I never told them about losing the bag, and if they thought it
strange that I didn't thank them for their gifts, they didn't say so.
But the final imaginary nature of those few objects would matter
quite a bit, I think, in my peculiar ability to keep alive for so
long the intensity of my connection to them all.

3

The next time I saw Sirena was in New York, almost two years later, when her Wonderland installation was part of the inaugural exhibition at the new feminist wing of the Brooklyn Museum. She'd been represented in America by Anna Z for almost all that time, and the two had become very close friends – Anna Z was younger, and Sirena was her up-and-coming star. When I saw them standing together inside the door of Anna's gallery on West Thirteenth Street, there was something about their physical relation to one another that reminded me of how it had been between us, and I suffered a great wave of jealousy.

Sirena, although the smaller of the two, seemed to emanate intensity, light almost, and Anna bent toward her, like a plant toward the sun. There was no awkwardness when I approached – a familiar embrace from Sirena, who then held me at arm's length and said, 'Nora, darling, let me look at you!' Nobody would have known, perhaps least of all she herself, what she'd meant to me, what I'd lost, and now saw again from a sad and solitary distance.

We were meeting for drinks, Sirena and I, but not dinner: she was a Parisian artist in New York for a big opening, and her evenings were claimed by more important people than myself. But that afternoon, Sirena had the grace to introduce me to her gallerist as a dear artist friend from Boston. This meant that Anna Z, slightly praying mantis–like, looked at me as though I were potentially someone important. But then she wanted to know where I 'showed' – a Fun House term if ever there was one – and I could feel my cheeks redden as I muttered some vague guff about how family difficulties had forced me to put things on hold for a while. After that, Anna turned back toward her sun, and aside from a couple of faintly curious, faintly pitying glances, was done with me.

And with Sirena? Two years had passed. Two years in which we'd exchanged perhaps ten e-mails, but in which I'd thought about her – and about Skandar and Reza too – every single day. It used to be that when people said, 'Not a day goes by that I don't think of X or Y,' I considered it embarrassing and quaint hyperbole; but thanks to the Shahids, I now understood. In my thoughts, I'd even set aside times of day for them, and places, where I permitted myself the indulgence. For example, the wholesale fantasies – some old, some new – were permissible in bed after lights-out. There were still, distantly, dreams of an artist's life in Vermont or Tuscany; but more often, somewhat basely, I pictured myself in Paris – in a glittering restaurant with Skandar, our knees touching under the tablecloth as we discussed the differences between the French intellectuals and the Americans, or a post-Iraq world. Or I imagined grandly showing Sirena my artwork in a fashionable Spartan gallery that had courted me, while craven young girls in black looked on, awed, from the sidelines. I knew even as I had them that these dreams were impure – after all, the whole point of the Shahids, for me, had been to escape a world of pretending, to be seen for who I really was – but I couldn't help it: their natures, you could say,

had corrupted me. My need for their approval, and my understanding of what approval meant to them – this had changed the
shape of my self, even, let alone of my dreams.

At that time, two years after they left, I was ashamed still to
be at Appleton; ashamed because I believed that they'd write me
more often, that they'd pay me more mind, that they would love
me more intently, if I were more impressive in the world; which
made me – how pathetic we are – wish it were so.

You see, in addition to my bedtime imaginings, I permitted
myself to indulge my quiet obsession when the e-mail brought
me news of them. I had put both Sirena and Skandar on
Google Alerts; and you'd be amazed – I was – at how often the
ether tapped my shoulder with a new development in one life
or another. In this way, when I sat with Sirena in the dark bar
near Anna's gallery, I knew already about Skandar's promotion
at the university, and about the important lecture series he'd
given in the fall of 2006 at Oxford. I knew the lectures were to
be published as a book in late '07, and I even knew what the
cover of the book would look like; just as I knew that Skandar
had recently updated his author photo and now looked to the
world less blurry and more like himself. I'd heard him on the
BBC online, talking about the Israeli bombings in Lebanon,
which had made me think about him with great tenderness
for days afterward; and I'd seen him on YouTube discussing in-
comprehensibly in French the current politics of Algeria,
looking especially dapper in a crisp white shirt. I knew about
the enthusiastic reviews that Wonderland had received in Paris,
and then in Berlin, where the installation had been mounted
at the Hamburger Bahnhof as part of a show on the spiritual
in art. I knew collectors were leaping to acquire the videos she'd
made of people visiting the installation, and that the Saatchi
guy had bought one and in so doing made her valuable. She'd
filmed a naked man coming through; and a gaggle of French

schoolchildren, like our Appleton class that long-ago afternoon; and inevitably a girl dressed up as Alice herself. Now these videos, or rather, selections and compilations of them, got shown alongside the installation itself, so that everyone who visited knew that they were themselves being filmed; and someone had written a big essay in *Artforum* about this, about the viewer and the voyeur in Sirena Shahid's work. And because she'd made this gag her gag, she'd unwittingly led people to behave in extraordinary ways, sometimes, while they were visiting Wonderland: there'd been the couple that simulated fucking in public, and the university student who came through the installation in a furry white bunny suit, with enormous ears ... Of course, Sirena didn't show videos of these spontaneous interventions, but bemused critics wrote about them and asked probing questions about the line between art and exploitation, whether this was collaborative art or mere comedy, and whether there was a willful or incidental degradation in these cases, in the approach of art to reality television.

That said, nobody denied that Sirena made thoughtful and beautiful and emotionally affecting art – they all said so. In the space of two short years, she had successfully rendered herself controversial in certain ways, and this controversy had made her famous, certainly in Europe, but even in the North American art world, so that her inclusion in the Brooklyn Museum's inaugural feminist exhibition in the spring of 2007 seemed, ex post facto, by no means a favor or a risk taken by the curators but was, rather, artistically utterly de rigueur. That famous art historian–cum–curator could now assert that she would no more have left Sirena out of her show than she would have cut off her fingers or included a man.

All this I knew from my Google Alerts; but all this I feigned not to know. And it was interesting – always, she was interesting, even when she caused me pain – to hear how she spoke of herself, and of her boys, and of our by then long-gone time together.

'Isn't it funny,' she said, stroking with an inky finger the beads of condensation on her glass of white wine, 'that year was such an unhappy one, for me. Remember poor Reza? And Skandar away so much – and that *weather*. Do you remember, Nora? I've never had a harder time.' (Except, she said 'time-e'.)

'I guess I didn't realize it was that bad,' I said. What else could I say?

'Realize it was that bad? But that's the extraordinary thing. It can't have been so bad, or it was bad for a purpose – because the Wonderland I made—' She paused, and with a gentle tilt of her head, she added, 'That I made with your amazing help, and could not have made alone – that Wonderland has been an enormous change in my life. I sometimes forget, because it hasn't been always easy – I'm not supposed to say this, because then you're ungrateful for success, but to you, my Nora' – the hand upon my arm – 'I can tell the truth. So these past two years, they've been tough. All the travel, Reza doesn't like it; nor Skandar. He's not a showy person, but that's because he's the center of attention; and when the attention is not for him, he's not such a sunny character. He can be unhappy, and difficult, and behave badly. Also, his mother has been very sick, last year – she's better now, but cancer, does the worry ever go away afterward? – so, yes, it's all been much too busy, and not so easy' – all this time I was really looking at her, waiting for her to recognize me, waiting to see her properly in her eyes; but they were either downcast or darting about, and didn't focus on my face – 'but it's as if the time in Cambridge, yes, such a hard time for us all – is in a separate box, now it's put away, it doesn't have a place in my every day. Even though it's where things began to change, because it's where I met you, my friend, and made the beginnings of my Wonderland.'

'But you remember it?' As I asked, I had so clearly before me the winter light from the windows into the studio, the paint-spattered faucet at the sink, the chipped cups and the poufs and the grimy, bruise-colored rug under the coffee table. I could see their town house, feel the flimsiness of its painted plywood front door, the door handle slipping in its socket, see the stains on the beige broadloom going up the stairs inside the entrance, and smell the faintly institutional biscuity smell that the house retained even after they'd illicitly smoked many cigarettes in it. No, I could remember all of it: the waxiness of the paper bags from the cake shop; the light on her hair in the subterranean booth that afternoon at Amodeo's; the sound Skandar's dress shoes made behind me in the packed snow, when he walked me home in wintertime between the drifts, and the freeze in my throat when I gulped the air. The small, muscled roundness of Reza's upper arms when he undressed for bed, and the straw-berry birthmark on his left biceps, his rib cage naked and frail as a bird's breast; and the tidy silvery streak that emerged, over time, from the red welt near his eye – I could see that plastic sur-geon, too, with her unexpected high heels and her square hands and her fairy-tale deftness with the needle and thread ... any moment of it all, all of it, I could have handed over, translucent, shining bead upon shining bead, had Sirena but wanted to hold them – which, it seemed, she did not especially, as she said, 'Oh, I can remember if I try – I'm not that old yet! But it's all fuzzy, and in my memory, dark. Even though I know it can't be. Surely Boston isn't always dark?'

'No,' I said. 'That's your imagination. It's quite a bright city, actually.'

Many things had been all in my imagination, surely I knew that; but then there was what had been decidedly, entirely *real*, all the moments and details so vivid, still alive to me – and for Sirena, like so much flotsam, long jettisoned into the broad ocean of her past. As that Air France flight had risen into the night air, two years before, so Boston had fallen away beneath her.

'I can barely remember making the installation at all,' she said. 'I do remember you sewing together all the blue dresses, though.'

'There were a lot of them.'

'D'you know something funny,' she said. 'You remember that postcard you sent, the illustration from the early edition of *Alice in Wonderland,* the one where she is so big and her neck is so long?'

'Of course.' I'd sent it almost at once after they left, my first dispatch, never answered, to their mythical Paris address, timed to arrive for the opening of her exhibition.

'Well, it's still on our refrigerator,' she said, bemused. 'Right there, for the longest time. I don't know who saved it – I don't think it was me. Reza, maybe?'

I smiled. Reza.

'Yes, so there you are with us, all the time,' she said. 'Sometimes I'm taking out the orange juice, or the yogurt, and I see Alice there, so startled, with her long neck, and I think of you.' Sirena was finally looking at me, then, in the nasty bar, as she rifled blindly for a credit card in her overstuffed wallet, and her smile was real – the old smile, the old face, that I'd so loved.

It was in this affectionate spirit that I visited the Brooklyn Museum the next morning, soon after opening time, by myself. I was the only visitor walking through Wonderland in the quiet, and I was surprised by the coziness imparted by the canopy of Alice dresses, three wide swathes of blues draped overhead, rippling slightly in the air-conditioning breeze. The lighting fell upon the aspirin flowers so that their colors glowed as they bobbed, gently, above the electric-green grass; and the mirror shards glittered and glimmered, unignorable, unsettling, but not overwhelming. I hadn't forgotten the nudes, but my memory had changed their features, or else I saw them differently now – the girl's splayed toe, the dark-nippled heft of a slightly drooped breast, the delicate flaring of a freckled nostril, the rib that protruded at an un-ribly angle, witness to almost a century of life – and they were enormous, bigger than I was, where I'd seen them small upon a computer screen. They, like everything else, rippled slightly, as if they were breathing, as if the room were breathing around us.

And then the famous cast plastic heart, upon its pedestal, lurid, halved, its protruding ventricles like the blowing tubes of an airplane life jacket, its innards dark, wet-looking, although they were dry; and then the automatic intermittent pump of it, a slight hiss from its core, Sirena's precious rosewater mist rising to fill the air – the soul, it was meant to be, I think – consuming the room in scent, smelling of flowers and an instant later of death, in the way that rosewater does. And Sana, then, finally, twirling, gigantic, above it all. There was a pair of small black benches in this central space, and I sat on the left-hand one and watched – forgetting that I was myself being filmed, though of course, like everyone else, I was.

I must have stayed at least half an hour there, in the rosewater air among the glowing flowers. Wonderland, eat me, drink me; yes, yes, yes. I was still in love with this, with her, with them, and how could I help it if being inside her head felt to me so familiar, as if it were the inside of my own mind, as if I'd built this Wonderland myself, as if this life, all of this, were for me, too. I felt, in that half hour, so *full*, like an overflowing vessel, its trembling meniscus arced toward the sky. I felt – for months, I'd felt this every second, and then for two years had been denied that feeling – I felt as though in any given instant, anything might happen, all wonder and possibility, the antithesis of a Lucy Jordan moment. I felt brilliantly alive. And I thought, somehow, still, that she – that they – had given that to me. I couldn't be angry, not wholly angry, at someone or something that could fill me with such joy in life. You're bound to love such a gift, and its giver.

I grant that this wasn't much to go on, but it would sustain me, if you can believe it, for two more fallow years, years in which I still held on to the idea of her, of them, to the hope that they had offered me.

Think of that: two more years. More than four years in total, about fifteen hundred days, and every single day they were with me, somehow. Out of some sense of obligation, some sense that I should move on, I went on dates with several men – an anxious divorcé with three kids, ground down by bitterness and care; a fifty-year-old who seemed so clearly gay that surely only he didn't know it; a Buddhist with long thin fingers who spoke terribly softly and made me want to shout and pummel his contained and withholding chest – and yet every time I sat in a restaurant in that way, I'd hear Skandar's laugh, or see his apologetic smile, and remember – my Book of the Wonders of the World – how much more there was out there, beyond the limits of Cambridge, Massachusetts, and I'd want to turn and flee my mediocrity.

Having vacated the Somerville studio long before the lease was up, unable to bear its ghosts, I tried intermittently to work on my dioramas, without success, and ultimately without hope. They sat forlorn under a dust sheet in my second bedroom, my former so-called studio, lumpen as corpses, from which, if I had to enter the room, I averted my eyes. One thousand five hundred days, some surely alarming proportion of the time left to me on this planet, I dedicated in my heart to the Shahids. You could say it wasn't their fault; you could say it was nothing but my own madness; but that wouldn't be quite true.

I sent e-mails, every so often, to Sirena, mostly, or even to Reza —I asked if he'd studied life cycles yet, when our sixth graders, under a new science teacher, dissected eggs in various stages of development and shouted in the hallways in their awe at life. Once I even found an excuse to write to Skandar, with a link about a Kennedy School conference I'd read about, and he politely sent back a couple of lines saying they were all well, and asking if I was ever coming to Paris . . . but for the most part, I heard nothing from them.

I became aware, in the early fall of 2008, that Skandar had been in Cambridge without contacting me: when I turned on the local television late one Saturday night, he was there in his rumpled jacket, part of a panel discussion about race relations in America – meaning, in this instance, Arab relations – and he spoke eloquently about how the possible election of Obama might change the tenor of society. The program had been filmed five days before it aired; I was sure he would already have decamped. Was I hurt? Yes; but not offended. Think of what was between us, and of what separated us. Better to be close only in our hearts. Besides, these whirlwind business trips that important people make – they don't have time to look up old friends even if they want to. I knew that.

The Woman Upstairs is like that. We keep it together. You don't make a mess and you don't make mistakes and you don't call people weeping at four in the morning. You don't reveal secrets it would be unseemly for you to have. You turn forty and you laugh about it, and make jokes about needing martinis and how forty is the new thirty, and you don't say aloud and nobody else says aloud what all of you are thinking, which is 'Well, I guess she's never going to have kids now!' and then, still less admissibly, 'Is that because she didn't think she wanted them, or because she didn't get around to it (silly fool, a failure of time management) or is it, poor lamb, because of some physical impediment (pitiable case)? Why is she single, anyhow? It's not as if her career has been so spectacular – she's only a schoolteacher, and among schoolteachers she's not even Shauna McPhee.'

All these things the Woman Upstairs knows are being said, and she hates knowing, and is infuriated to know, and she valiantly hides both her knowledge and her fury, and everyone remembers her fortieth, held in the bar of the Charles Hotel, no expense spared, as the best party they've been to in a long while, a party the way they used to be before spouses and children, and you've got to hand it to her, Nora Eldridge really does make you feel that forty is the new thirty – yes, well. All of this you know, and you bury deep, like dead men, but they're there, the skeletons are there, and you're always with them.

You'd never tell the story of your friendship with the Shahids for a whole host of reasons – you have your dignity, after all – but among them, you wouldn't want to seem the unsavory sort of person who might acknowledge, simply in the telling, that people like the Shahids were more compelling, somehow higher on your personal totem pole, than the person to whom you were talking about them. The Woman Upstairs, whose face to the world is endlessly compassionate, would never have such a thing as a personal totem pole. The Woman Upstairs does not aspire in such self-serving ways. She must not appear to have an ugly heart. Who could love an ugly, lonely heart?

Skandar, Sirena, Reza – each of them was, in his or her way, my Black Monk. I had a veritable monastery inside me! Each one, in my impassioned interior conversations, granted me some aspect of my most dearly held, most fiercely hidden, heart's desires: life, art, motherhood, love and the great seductive promise that I *wasn't nothing,* that I could be seen for my unvarnished self and that this hidden self, this precious girl without a mask, unseen for decades, could – that she must, indeed – leave a trace upon the world. If this were so, then I could be an artist, and then it would be allowed. Who would allow it? They would. How would they allow it? I was waiting for a sign.

Traces, signs, I hoped for some evidence of what I might have meant – of the fact that I meant at all. Finally, a few short months ago, I got it. Finally, all the elucidation at once, the confirmation of what I meant to them. Yes, you hovered so very long in Doubt, embracing Doubt, teasing yourself with it; and then suddenly, at last you knew.

4

This is what's most surprising about life, really: the most enormous things – sometimes fatal things – occur in the flicker of an eye, the tremor of my mother's hand. Sometimes you don't even grasp an event's importance for a long time because you can't believe something momentous could possibly appear so nondescript.

Aunt Baby died, mercifully and suddenly, between Thanksgiving and Christmas last year. Never plagued by ill health, which had been her great, spinsterly anxiety, she lived long enough to see the new president inaugurated and then some, and to hope, in her piety, that God had a handle on the economy. In her careful frugality, she didn't die penniless, and although her estate was divided among six of us – Matthew, me, and those distant cousins in the photos – there was still, after the depressed sale of her Rockport condo and after taxes, a tidy sum of more than a hundred thousand dollars apiece. Matthew and Tweety said the inheritance was for the brat's college fund – the sensible couple, making the sensible choice. My father got no money, but was made the earthly custodian of two large and unlovely Victorian paintings of cows in the fields, ornately framed, and a silver tea set.

The condo was sold in April, and as soon as I received my aunt's legacy, I made a radical choice: I decided to take a year's leave from Appleton. Money in the bank, middle age on the way – I'd turned forty-two already by then, and was looking at forty-three. I was getting arthritis in my left knee, which made running harder, and I'd started to dye my hair just to look normal. I needed glasses for the print on the aspirin bottle. All in the space of a couple of years. Death knocking. The sniper on the roof. I'd almost renounced bearing a child of my own, but this didn't mean I didn't *want* children. I'd renounced, I thought, once and for all, the fantasy of being an artist of any renown, but I would still have said I hoped to make art; and I suppose I thought that time, or rather a lack of it, was my impediment.

I'd also been teaching at Appleton for ten years, an entire decade, and even Shauna McPhee was moving on (although not, in her case, willingly: the parental revolution against her, which had never subsided, had finally moved the functionaries at City Hall, who had, in turn, moved *her*). So my official reason was that after long service, I needed a short break, to recharge the batteries, rediscover the world; and the perceived reason was surely that I needed to weather some small midlife crisis – oh, Nora, she's worked hard, sweet woman, so patient with the kids, and she's had to contend with a lot, you know? And the official real reason was that I needed time and space properly to give my art a try, because I hadn't been able to manage it, these past few years, on top of the demands of school and my aging father; and the secret real reason was that I was miserable, because even all these years later, every night when I lay down to bed, I still clung to the shreds of my Shahids – so little to keep me going, a few perfunctory e-mails and that one sighting, each memory worn threadbare from overuse – and in clinging, I still hoped for the richer and more fulfilling and more wondrously open and aware existence that so briefly had seemed possible. Well beyond forty now, I wanted genuinely to give myself the chance at that life, although I didn't know, really, what it might entail.

I signed up for a sculpture class at Mass Art, starting in September, and for a pottery class in a studio off Monsignor O'Brien Highway, because I thought perhaps I needed to explore new media. I ordered an expensive digital camera off the Internet, so I could explore photography on my own. I was the teacher planning a curriculum for a single pupil: myself. I ordered books from the library – Emmet Gowin, Sally Mann, shocking, wonderful, intimate photographs – aware as I did so that I had no family to photograph, aside from my father, or Matthew and Tweety and the kid, who didn't count.

The most dramatic thing I did was to book a summer trip to Europe. Why not? I didn't ask my dad if he'd like to go with me. I jokingly suggested to Didi that she might come along – without Esther and Lili, it went without saying – and she laughed. 'How're you going to meet any guys if you've got me in tow? I'm like the opposite of a beard: fake lesbian lover as potential mate deterrent!'

'It's not about meeting anybody. What a ridiculous idea.'

'Well, it ought to be,' she said. 'It's about time.'

'About time for what?'

'You're in your prime! Like Miss Jean Brodie. Remember her? It doesn't last forever, so don't waste it.'

'Waste it?'

'Nora Adora, do I have to get blunt with you? When was the last time you even had a fling?'

I shrugged.

'I'm not trying to push domesticity down your throat. I'm not saying what I've got is for everyone. Not what you want – totally cool. But you've got to want *something*.'

'What if I don't?'

'If you *say* you don't, then you're either lying to yourself or you're lying to me. Because I know you for a wanting sort of person.'

'How about a Buddhist conversion? Like you've wished upon me all these years?'

'Buddhist bullshit. A Labrador puppy is more of a Buddhist . . . Nora, promise me it's not still the same old?'

'What are you talking about?'

'Buddhist, no, obsessive, yes. I know you too well, and I know you hoard things under your rock to nibble away at when you're alone. So I'm asking, no bullshit, is it same old, same old?'

I loved her for asking. She was making the gesture of a true friend, and in life you don't get many. But I laughed with an insouciance I hadn't known I could fake, and I said, 'You are one crazy lady. I don't have any idea what you're talking about.'

The whole summer trip to Europe – almost three weeks of it – was really organized around Paris. Around being in Paris when they were going to be there. Obviously I wasn't planning to spend three weeks in Paris – it was only five days. But they were headed off to Italy in the first instance, to Sirena's family, and then, after a brief stop back at home, on to Beirut for a spell. Reza got out of school at the end of June and they were leaving at once; so I made sure to time my visit to the City of Light to coincide with them.

I hadn't been there since my management consultant days, an extravagant, dreamlike distant time when I'd stayed at the Royal Monceau and ordered room service, a breakfast I still remembered for its glinting heavy pewter pots and its stiff white cloth, the table rolled silently across the carpet and set up facing the window, as if it were my own private restaurant. This would be a more modest experience: I'd booked a single room in a three-star near St. Michel, named (one hoped eponymously) the Plaisant Hotel, the twenty-first-century revamp of a Jean Rhys hotel, I could tell from the website, with narrow corridors and creaking floors and faulty plumbing, and the gleam of sage-colored paint on walls that had once been wrapped in smoke-infused crimson damask wallpaper.

Was my trip memorable and extraordinary? Need you ask? I can rave about the vastness of the spaces on the road to Oban, or the sun-filled mist hovering above the earth in the early morning at Grasmere. I can describe my sweet hotel in Bloomsbury with, in my room, the smallest bathroom – and surely the most minute sink – known to man. I can bore you with photographs of Big Ben or the Bay of Naples, and feed you on tidbits about Nelson and Emma in love, or about Anne Boleyn in the Tower. I purchased souvenirs unthinkingly to show my third-grade class, only to remember I would not have, this year, a third-grade class. I chatted with a family from Milwaukee at the next table while I ate Welsh rarebit at Fortnum & Mason, and I bought four hopelessly impractical gilt-rimmed champagne glasses in Portobello Market, that I then had to lug around Europe in a specially wrapped box with a handle, as though they were eggshells, or a bomb.

Early on, in the B&B in Grasmere, lying in bed looking with one eye closed at the sprigged wallpaper and the pale blue sink in the corner of the room, I thought to myself that I could lie there all day and no one would mind. I could fib and say I'd seen Wordsworth's house, without seeing a single thing, without doing more than buying a postcard from the gift shop – but probably I wouldn't need to lie, because who would ask me? What finally got me moving was not my own desires – I had none, except to get to Paris – but rather the thought that I might miss my cooked English breakfast, prepared by Mrs Crocker with her lacy apron and her appraising eye; and that should I not get out of the house relatively promptly, that same Mrs Crocker would appear at my door in a different apron, the housekeeping apron, with a dustpan and brush and a bucket full of solvents, and would chase me, sourly, from the room. My motivation, even in anticipated shame, lay always in others. You can take the woman out of upstairs, but you can't take the upstairs out of her.

Naples was marginally better, because I could muster some genuine will for the sites, and because the crumbling, garbage-filled city itself frightened me, and fear is a strong emotion and one I've had much truck with in my life. When I came out of an empty museum on the hill and had to walk alone across the empty park surrounding it, I had to ask myself whether my palpitations and breathlessness were caused by genuine risk to my life, or whether I was merely indulging a habit in the hope that my fear would keep me safe. Safe! When you're over forty, nowhere is safe. An airplane is suddenly the safest place in the world. Death and his zealous minions – dread, despair, disease – can find you anywhere at all, and the armor plate of youth will no longer protect you. Sirena had Skandar, and Skandar, Sirena; as my mother, I now understood, had had my father, humble protector though he might be; and he had her. Matthew had Tweety; Didi had Esther; Aunt Baby, of course, would have had her Lord – because although not strictly a Bride of Christ, she'd lived with Him most of her life. And I, charging across the empty park in the late afternoon with my fists clenched, had only myself.

Who is he who walks always beside you? No-fucking-body, thank you very much. I walk alone.

My Plaisant Hotel proved indeed wonderfully pleasant, tucked in a short cul-de-sac on the less fashionable side of St. Michel, facing a walled garden. Stucco-fronted, its facade was embellished by riotous purple and blue and red window boxes, and looked almost English from the outside. My room faced the street, with those wonderful old doors (that egg-shaped handle that moves a long metal bar up into its socket: a mechanism simultaneously antique and of a futuristic simplicity) that open almost onto the void, or rather, onto a void from which you are protected by the most delicate of wrought-iron balconies. When I entered my room and put down my bags and opened the windows wide, I reverberated with the joy of being in Paris. My hotel had no room service, I overlooked a view of parked cars and scrubby yard rather than the Eiffel Tower or the Arc de Triomphe, but it didn't matter: the particular pitch of the police sirens was to me exotic; as were the burning rubber smell in the subway and the tawny gold of the monuments' stone in the sunlight. All the clichés of a city are new to any individual visitor and hence not clichés; just as love, in spite of the paltry means we have to express it, is, each time experienced, completely new: it can be pyrotechnic in its intensity or slow and tender but overwhelming, like a glacier passing over a landscape; or evanescent but glorious like the field of fireflies on Martha's Vineyard in my youth – whatever it is, each time it is familiar and new at once, an overturning.

And Paris, well: the young North African man at the hotel reception smiled at me in a conspiratorial way; the waiter in the tourist café in St. Michel where I stopped for a drink that first afternoon – an expensive beer, but a great view of Notre Dame – asked me why a beautiful young woman like myself was traveling alone. Bathetic bullshit, but winning – a different set of rules, a different Fun House, and one more palatable maybe just for being unknown. But it made me wonder again how much of what I loved about the Shahids was their foreignness, and their impermanence – whether I'd all this time longed for them simply because I couldn't have them. After so much time, they were all figment now.

The difference is that they live and breathe. My mother no longer does, nor Aunt Baby, even; and there is no place on this earth that they can be found. Whereas on the evening of my second day in Paris, as agreed by e-mail and confirmed by telephone (did I feel a twitch, a frisson, at the sound of her voice? Or did I hear a different voice, now, in my head, and ultimately prefer it?), I took a taxi over to their fashionably seedy neighborhood behind the Bastille.

I'd spent a lot of time imagining their place, and inevitably the reality did not correspond. The building was on the wrong side of the street. Its entrance hall was smaller than I'd expected. But then the elevator, old-style, with the accordion grille, was exactly as I'd pictured, and consequently too small for me to brave. I walked up four flights, and then there they were – no, there was Sirena, in the doorway, her crow's-feet more pronounced, her shoulders more four-square, and although it took me a few minutes to put my finger on the change, her hair all black now – enough, she'd thought, of the aging experiment; and she looked, ironically, older for it. Maybe she just looked older, plain and simple. *We're at that age,* as they say and I now say also. Years older than I am, she's perilously close to fifty. She said all the right things, as did I, and we hugged, and I waited for my heart to open. But as she led me into their apartment, the thought that came unbidden was: Here is someone that I used to love. Or even: Here is someone who resembles, to a large degree but imperfectly, someone that I used to love. I didn't want to feel, of all things, wistful and melancholic: I had a case against these people, who had packed up my soul along with their blankets and books, and had kept it without caring for it all these years.

A case against these three Black Monks who had prophesied for me – all but promised – a future which had not begun to come to pass; and who, with their promises in hand, had abandoned me as if it were a mere lark – I had a case—

But who could have a case against that laugh? Or against Skandar's long-lost smile, as if he'd been dropped by parachute into his own living room and didn't quite know where he was … He, too, seemed genuinely pleased to see me – how long had it been? – and after we embraced, he held me by the wrist for a moment, almost unthinkingly – as if, I thought, Sirena were not in the room and as if, oddly, I were a child. Then Reza came out of his room, somewhere in the back of the apartment: in this big-footed and gawky manlet, his features oddly proportioned in the way of boys almost pubescent – a pimple, yes, perhaps even two, upon his chin – I strained to see my perfect child. His eyebrows were now frankly heavy, his voice croaking; but his eyelashes, and his eyes: yes, there he was entirely recognizable. Not in manner, though: you'd think he'd never known me, or else that it was he who'd kissed my bare breasts among the aspirin flowers – he was that bashful, that awkward, glancing up like a coy maiden, shuffling and rustling his enormous hands and feet, adult puppet pieces on his boy's body. His curls were longish, in fashion: I noticed this. I knew he'd be the boy the girls dreamed of. I'd known that from the moment I first saw him. He showed such palpable relief when his mother told him to go do his homework, that we'd catch up at dinner, that I had to let him go happily. As his door shut, Sirena rolled her eyes – in that moment, more typically motherly than I'd ever seen her. She said, 'Homework? What do you think, it's a nonsense. At this age, it's all Facebook, all the time. From video games to Facebook – for boys, this is the socialization process.' She snickered. 'I'm thinking of how to make an artwork really to say something about this. But it's difficult ... Nora, my friend, a cocktail? A wine? What would you like?'

And she was off – we were off – and it was familiar, but it was also different. Just as Reza had trained her into motherhood, day after day, over years, so, too, she'd been trained, since last we'd spent time together, to think of herself as an artist of importance in the world; and it was obvious, somewhat wearingly, even when she was supposedly being lighthearted about her work.

A scientist acquaintance once explained to me that to attain nuclear fusion – which would apparently solve the global energy crisis – you have to replicate exactly the conditions of the birth of a star. This is obviously very hard, and very rare, and very fleeting. And I realized, in the Shahids' living room, that I'd fallen in love not only with a particular configuration of people, but with that particular configuration in a particular moment in their lives and in mine. It wouldn't have mattered if I were myself Peter Pan, ever unaltered: the minute Wendy starts to change, the idyll is over. Each of them was different, even though they were much the same. Their configuration was different. You couldn't replicate what had been.

That didn't make it worthless. We were friends. I still envied them their family; and I felt my blood swell with tenderness at certain gestures, certain expressions, tics that carried me back. But I left – with the promise that Sirena and I would have lunch, or at least breakfast, on Thursday (I was returning to Boston on Friday) – thinking I'd been wrong to imagine there'd been a breach of trust, flushed with the warmth of their charm and at least a bottle of wine, touched by the supper Sirena had prepared—

('Oh,' I said, 'you remembered! How sweet!'

'Remembered?'

'The first time you had me over in Cambridge? This is the stew you prepared.'

'Imagine! I'd completely forgotten. I'm afraid it's just a sign of how limited is the . . .'

'Repertoire,' said Skandar, winking at me; and I couldn't tell whether the wink said that he, too, remembered that evening; or whether it just agreed that together we would tease his wife.)

—touched by the details Reza recalled from his long ago Cambridge classroom – painting – the twins – times tables. I looked, at the dinner table, for the trace of the scar by his eye: when he leaned into the light, I thought I could glimpse the faintest of white lines, though I couldn't be wholly sure. I still loved them, if differently. I felt full of forgiveness, and sanity. But not hope. As I fell into my pleasant low bed in my pleasant room in my pleasant hotel, I was conscious in my semiconsciousness of feeling the opposite of hope – which would be despair. I was clear, right before slumber took me off, that this was why I'd chosen a light, bright, post–Jean Rhys, anti–Emily Dickinson, never Virginia Woolf hotel: because everything about its pleasantness insisted, inarguably, No Suicides Here.

I had all this anger. Years of it, decades of it, my very body full of it, bloody with it. And I'd lumbered across the Atlantic to lay it all down upon a doorstep. Almost like blackmail: love me absolutely, or take this shit from me. I had the mother lode. Yes, the term is apt. It was to be assuaged or offloaded. And yet, while I left their home feeling welcomed, even loved, it was a different, smaller sort of love than I'd wanted – not so much a glacier or a fireworks display as a light shawl against an evening breeze. Recognizably love, but useless in a gale.

5

There's so much to see and do in Paris. So much that it's a wonder I saw it. A wonder that I saw that I could see it. But for so long I'd trained myself to read and find the references to Sirena and Skandar, that it would have been a shock of another kind had I missed it. I had a lot of time, really, in Paris: five whole days. I arrived on Monday, was leaving on Friday. We'd had dinner on Tuesday. I was to call Sirena on Wednesday night or Thursday morning. On Wednesday, I got up and descended the stairs to the breakfast room – a sweet atrium, with pots of flowers in the corners and an electric fountain against the wall, a naked cherub with an overturned ewer, trickling water into a shell-shaped bowl – spectacular, cheerful kitsch – with my *Pariscope* in hand. It listed everything – films, gay nightclubs, poetry readings, gallery shows.

Ignoring my zealous spread of baguette crumbs over cloth, clothes and newsprint, I flipped through beyond the museum listings to the private galleries. Here was a city, like New York and unlike Boston, where a private dealer might have an exhibit of Picasso lithographs. Or where you could see Robert Polidori's enormous Chernobyl photos, up for sale at over 20,000 euros

apiece. It was half as a lark that I looked for Sirena's name – she
didn't have any major installations at present, she'd told me over
supper: her next was a commission for a group show at the
Serpentine Gallery in London the following spring, on the
theme of rebirth and renewal. But there she was, a listing at a
gallery in the 7th, a show open only for a few more days. A show
titled *After the Fall: The Wonderland Tapes*. Here, without the
installation itself, would be the videos she'd made at, or in, the
installation, to get people to respond to the responses to her
work.

It seemed a favor to her to go to see them – the videos, as far
as I was concerned, were the least interesting part of her art;
although I knew important critics disagreed with me – and I was
aware that if I hated them, I might just lie and pretend I didn't
know about them. Credit to her modesty, I thought, that Sirena
hadn't told me about the show; or perhaps credit to her now
arrogant grandeur: perhaps she thought the videos were too tri-
fling to bother with? Either way, I'd go out of my own curiosity,
pure or impure, and would see what I thought. If it felt like
spying on her life – how little it was, compared to all the Google
Alerts I'd assiduously studied, all the details I'd hoarded and
treasured as if she'd told me of them herself, as if we were in the
kind of regular contact that close friends ought to be.

I decided to do the Louvre that morning, and then the Musée
d'Orsay, and then to make my way back on foot through the
Quartier Latin toward my hotel. It was neither forced nor peculiar to pass in front of the Galerie Werther – I could almost
chance upon it, with that itinerary in mind. Certainly she
couldn't accuse me of having gone out of my way.

The day was hot, and the museums thronged, the visits gruel-
ing. The only respite came in the wing of the Louvre that houses
Napoléon's apartments, full of brocaded textiles and gilded furniture, rooms of china and silverware of no interest to anyone

(including me) and, as a consequence, all but empty. I made the mistake of having lunch late, near the Musée d'Orsay on an abandoned street, in a hushed restaurant astronomically priced, where in shock I ordered only a starter, a tiny puff pastry with a tablespoon of creamed chicken inside and a watercress garnish; which perhaps was insufficient sustenance for the full-on Grand Central–like mill of the second museum. Somehow, I felt I had to see as much as possible – who knew when I might return to Paris? – and so I forced myself into the crowded narrow corridors and craned my neck to peer at paintings, blocked by the audio-guide set, a mass that drifted slow and imperturbable as oxen through the galleries.

It was all a bit much. When I came out, I should have stopped in a pastry shop for an éclair, or at least a restorative coffee. But I was daunted by the Frenchness of it all, couldn't face waffling to the server in atrocious French, or lapsing, to their triumphant disdain, into my American English. I was shaky on my pins, walking the streets, finding the distances farther than I'd anticipated. All of this I explain – why? In order to excuse, or temper, what I then felt, which would have been dramatic regardless, but was surely intensified by my vulnerability just then.

Galerie Werther was on a trendy street parallel to the Seine, a few blocks in from the river but below the Boulevard Saint Germain. The sidewalks were lively in the late afternoon, though not anything like the museums; yet the gallery was very quiet, empty but for an etiolated young man in a black shirt and black jeans, who gave me only a nod as I came in. The room had lower ceilings than I would have imagined, and was smaller. But it was spare, and white, and it had a blue poured concrete floor, and seemed every bit the sort of gallery one would expect for a star.

There were six video screens – framed and back-lit, flat screen, very chic – hanging on the walls. I was looking, in part, for my Appleton darlings, for my lost paradisiac year. The videos didn't seem to have any particular narrative order, or any particular shape or duration. One seemed to be stills, cobbled together; another, in which four random patrons of the crowded exhibit started twirling in front of Sana's video, was clearly scripted, and reminded me of an ad for cell phones, filmed at Heathrow, that I'd seen on YouTube. For each of the screens there were headphones on a stick, and you could listen to one of three soundtracks – each incongruous, sometimes funny. I was thinking, almost begrudgingly, 'She's good. She's very good at this – whatever this is.'

I saw my video last. It was on the back of a column in the middle of the gallery, so at first you didn't even know it was there. From afar, it looked grainier, less professional than the others, more like a 1980s tape, with that slightly titillating quality of spontaneity, of the unexpected find. I could see, too, as I approached, that it was one of only two videos marked with a red dot, which meant – as I knew from the gallery sheet I'd picked up at the door – that the edition was fully sold out. There were five copies of each video for sale; and of this one, no more.

As I got closer, I realized that what I saw was not the same Wonderland as in the other videos. In addition to being a grainier image, the setting itself was partial, unfinished, differently lit. It was indeed a Wonderland I knew: our Somerville studio. My heart lifted. I thought I'd see Reza, as he'd been, running boisterously among the aspirin flowers. Maybe it hadn't been entirely ruined, after all, by my shrieking intervention? I thought I'd see Chastity and Ebullience wrapping themselves in swaths of Alice-blue cloth, tripping and falling on top of each other, or even Noah, picking the flowers, picking his fight with

Reza – and then I was close enough to see what the video actually showed. And then, you see, I couldn't help it: I lost my breath. I couldn't breathe. My vision closed in like a tunnel, and then I couldn't see anything at all.

The young assistant had to manhandle me, which was for us both a grave humiliation. He didn't even bother speaking French – clearly my clothes, or my shape, my general New England sensibleness, screamed 'USA' – and he kept saying, 'Are you okay, madame? You are okay, madame. Are you okay?' He pulled his own chair out from behind the desk and had me sit in it. He gave me water. He suggested that I put my head between my knees. He proved more practical on all fronts than his aspect might have suggested, but I could also tell that he was annoyed by me, that I seemed to him like some stray off the streets, come in to foul his pristine temple to Sirena's art. Heaven forbid that her temple should be fouled!

And yet this was what the video showed, for all the world to see: the fouling of Wonderland, by none other than myself. The fact that I was essentially supine in the images, and half undressed, and pretending (not that the viewer would know this) to be Edie Sedgwick, the fact that the etiolated youth could never have guessed that the zealous masturbator in the Wonderland video was the sensible Merrell-wearing Woman Upstairs who'd stolen his chair and spoiled his calm, didn't make the facts less true.

Somehow, I had been filmed in that most private moment. Somehow, I had been seen; and could then be displayed, an object, like one of the artists in my own dioramas. I could be sacrificed. In the upper grades at school, you teach the kids ethics: you ask them, would they push a button that would kill an anonymous person in China, if they'd get a million dollars. Would they push the button if it made them famous. If nobody knew they'd pushed the button. If it meant the whole world would acclaim you as an artist. If it showed the world some genuine truth about what it was like to be a sad, lonely fucker. Would you?

Yes, it was true, if I thought about it, the cameras had already been set up, by then, for the kids – we'd set them up weeks ahead of time. I'd helped her do it. But how did she film me? She hadn't been in the studio that day at all – had she? I couldn't remember for sure. There must have been a motion-sensitive setting. She must have set the cameras to tape anytime anyone set foot in her Wonderland. Maybe she was taping herself? Maybe it wasn't the plan to trap me, like a fish in a net; or maybe it was. Maybe she'd hoped she'd catch me there somehow – but she could never have anticipated such prize footage, such a perfect humiliation. When had she seen it? Had *he* seen it, too? And if he had, then suddenly his visit to the studio, his supposed seduction, became something completely different. It became something *between them,* something that had nothing to do with me. Something for which I was the unwitting scapegoat. She'd cared little enough to use the tape – to *sell* the tape – or else she'd been angry enough. But not angry enough to confront me; not angry enough (if she had known about Skandar and me) to think it merited discussion. I had been so discountable that she could do this to me, and claim to have remained my friend. What a year it had been: I'd been useful in so many ways.

There is what is imaginary and there is what is real. What is imaginary – how she taped me, why she taped me, whether she taped Skandar and me, when she decided to use the tape – these are things you cannot reach. Even if I asked her, I would never know the truth. What is imaginary – our friendships, my loves,

these people, my inventions – is untouchable, if not inviolate.
And then, there is reality: there is what happens, what you know,
or think you know, with certainty. But maybe these two are
ultimately one; maybe you can't protect the one from the other.
There's that room inside your mind where you are most freely
and unconcernedly yourself, and then there are the many layers
of masquerade by which you protect that skinless core; but there
she was, my most unguarded self (a fantasy self!), famous at last,
visible but invisible, hanging on a wall in Paris and five times
sold.

And this, needless to say, by the woman – and not to forget,
her husband – whom, among all mortals, I had chosen and
drawn close to and loved, yes, wholeheartedly loved, and forgiven a myriad of shortcomings. But not this one. Never this
one. I knew that even then, perched on the chair in the gallery
sipping my cloudy glass of tepid, overchlorinated water and
insisting to the youth that I did not need a taxi, or a doctor, that
I would be on my feet and on my way in a matter of minutes –
I knew in the middle of all this that I would never, ever, ever for-
give her this. That she had – again, no: that they both had,
because he must have known, at some point, he had *known,* and
done nothing; or worse, had come to me only because he'd
known – but this, surely, was not thinkable – not thinkable,
that – they had ruthlessly destroyed everything, betrayed everything.

You don't need suicides where there is murder.

I didn't call them. I couldn't even imagine calling them. I didn't
call Didi, either, although I might have, because I didn't want to
get into it. How could I begin to explain what it meant, to see
myself laid bare on Sirena's gallery wall, the great rippling

outrage of what it meant – about each of us, about myself perhaps most of all, about the lies I'd persistently told myself these
many years. And all certain things suddenly wildly uncertain.
And what about art, and being an artist: Is this, then, what it
took to be something, to become someone? Was this what was
meant by 'sacrificing everything' for your art? Or at least, everyone?

Here's the good part: I carried all this anger, full to the brim
with it, and now it's allowable. Now it's justified. I've learned
from my mistakes. I've been liberated by my failings: I've been
a fool, but now I'm a wise fool. I've been crushed by the universe; I've frittered the gold of my affection on worthless
baubles; I've been treated like dirt. You don't want to know how
angry I am. Nobody wants to know about that. I am furious at
both of them – at the lie of their friendship, their false promises of the world and of art and of love – but just as mad at
myself, at my stupid dreams, my misplaced trust, my worthless
longing.

But to be furious, murderously furious, is to be *alive*. No
longer young, no longer pretty, no longer loved, or sweet, or lov-
able, unmasked, writhing on the ground for all to see in my utter
ingloriousness, there's no telling what I might do. I could film my
anger and sell it, I could do some unmasking of my own, beat the
fuckers at their own game, and on the way I could become the
best-known fucking artist in America, out of sheer spite. You
never know. I'm angry enough to set fire to a house just by looking at it. It can't be contained, stored away with the recycling. I'm
done staying quietly upstairs. My anger is not a little person's, a
sweet girl's, a dutiful daughter's. My anger is prodigious. My
anger is a colossus. I'm angry enough to understand why Emily

Dickinson shut out the world altogether, why Alice Neel betrayed her children, even though she loved them mightily. I'm angry enough to see why you walk into the water with rocks in your pockets, even though that's not the kind of angry I am. Virginia Woolf, in her rage, stopped being afraid of death; but I'm angry enough, at last, to stop being afraid of life, and angry enough – finally, God willing, with my mother's anger also on my shoulders, a great boil of rage like the sun's fire in me – before I die to fucking well *live*.

Just watch me.

ACKNOWLEDGMENTS

The writing of this book would not have been possible without the generous support of the Humanities Center at Harvard, where it was begun, and of the Wissenschaftskolleg zu Berlin, where it was completed. I am particularly grateful for the kindnesses of Professor Homi Bhabha and of Professors Joachim Nettelbeck and Luca Giuliani. My thanks also to Stephen Greenblatt and Ramie Targoff, for pointing me toward Berlin; to Diala Ezzedine and Hashim Sarkis, for sharing their knowledge, and Beirut, with me; to Beatrice Gruendler, for our discussions about Arabic literary history; and to all my fellow Fellows at the Kolleg, for inspiring conversations.

My thanks also, always, to my literary agents, Georges and Anne Borchardt; to my British agent, Felicity Rubinstein; to my British editor and dear friend Ursula Doyle at Virago; and to my U.S. editor Robin Desser at Knopf.

In what have been challenging years, the precious faith and friendship of a few have been invaluable. My particular thanks to Elizabeth Messud, Susanna Kaysen and John Daniels, Melissa Franklin, Sheila Gallagher, Shefali Malhoutra, Mark Gevisser, Ira Sachs, Mary Bing and Doug Ellis, Fiona Sinclair,

Julie Livingston and, it goes without saying, to my indefatiga-
ble optimist, James Wood, and our two beloved children, Livia
and Lucian.

My especial and ineffable gratitude to my father, François
Michel Messud (1931–2010), who taught me the importance of
laughter, and of rage, and who had no tolerance for the Fun
House; and to my mother, Margaret Riches Messud
(1933–2012), who lived lightly upon this earth, whose letters
taught me how to write and whose eyes taught me how to see.

PERMISSIONS ACKNOWLEDGMENT

Grateful acknowledgment is made to Hal Leonard Corporation for permission to reprint 'My Happy Ending,' words and music by Avril Lavigne and Butch Walker. Copyright © 2004 by Almo Music Corp., Avril Lavigne Publishing Ltd., EMI Blackwood Music Inc. and Sonotrock Music. All rights for Avril Lavigne Publishing Ltd. controlled and administered by Almo Music Corp. All rights for Sonotrock Music controlled and administered by EMI Blackwood Music Inc. All rights reserved. Reprinted by permission of Hal Leonard Corporation.

virago

To buy any of our books and to find out more
about Virago Press and Virago Modern Classics,
our authors and titles, as well as events and
book club forum, visit our websites

www.virago.co.uk
www.littlebrown.co.uk

and follow us on Twitter

@ViragoBooks

To order any Virago titles p & p free in the UK,
please contact our mail order supplier on:

+ 44 (0)1832 737525

Customers not based in the UK should contact
the same number for appropriate postage
and packing costs.